Infamous Madame's Will

Nina Curttright

Infamous Madame's *Will*

PALMETTO
PUBLISHING
Charleston, SC
www.PalmettoPublishing.com

Paperback: 979-8-8229-3540-2
eBook: 979-8-8229-3541-9

Dedication

My mother suffered a debilitating stroke in the spring of 1956. I was five years old. Despite her prognosis, she regained her speech, learned to walk with a brace, and to write with her nondominated hand. Our shared dresser had a shoebox filled with pill bottles I dare not touch.

When I was eight years old we moved into an historic 1868 octagon mansion. It sounds grand yet the house was a shell of its former self. My mother rented a shabby first-floor tenement flat and, like our immigrant and pensioner neighbors, we existed day to day. Our apartment walls were half-inch plywood with gaps at the ceiling. Nothing was soundproof and the other tenants provided a wealth of material for my stories. Mom and I shared a rollup bed that served as my writing space and my invalid mother was my willing reader. I cherished her praise!

The paralysis caused my mother's limp half-smile and her hazel eyes no longer sparkled. Mama never spoke about her life before I came along. I know now it was a tale of betrayal and tenacity. She endured and stayed with me as long as she could but when I was thirteen her heart gave up the struggle.

I was heartbroken and rebellious without my mother's rudder. Adrift with a bent compass I let the currents sweep me in and out of many a precarious situation. Late one night I took a shortcut down a perilous alleyway when an intuitive spark turned me around and

Grace literally saved my life. Today when I remember to pay attention I feel the presence of my guardian angel watching over me.

Whatever happened to my storyteller self? Her writings grew dark and melancholy, a miserable reflection of my hurt psyche. In my twenties I broke my pencil and burned the lot of it. For forty years I wandered aimlessly (that's a fact, not a metaphor) until a profound awakening saved me. Subtle clarity and peace opened my eyes, I took a deep breath and my storyteller awakened from her slumber.

With thanks to my angel, I dedicate this book and its nom de plume to my mother, Nina Curttright. Until we meet again mama, this is my promise fulfilled.

Contents

Preface

I wrote the Infamous Madame's Will to free myself from a long-ignored promise. To my surprise the Will practically wrote itself.

Writers do not create in a vacuum. Instead we sponge from a collective universal mind while adding a pinch of personal soul to the words. We accept the credit but the words pour through us—not from us.

Two preservationists, the late Bill Spiedel and the Seattle Museum of History and Industry did posterity a favor. The candor of their saved stories and photos reveals a saga still relevant today. The past begs us to never forget where we came from. Though not always pretty, it proves beyond a doubt that we are all truly related.

My writer hero, Samuel Clemens, took his creative persona from a nautical term. The boatsmen called out Mark Twain when a river was at safe depth. Twain warned, "You can't depend on your eyes when your imagination's out of focus." I agree with Cousin Sam. We either listen to our Intuitive self or we chance running aground.

The Infamous Madame's Will is a fanciful reminder of humanity's chequered past. Our ancestors unchecked egos set a wayward course with pure grit and ingenuity saving them from themselves. When society's upbraid slammed a door, a kindness unlocked it. Digging into our dodgy legacy is a lesson and an invitation to do better.

In Clare Scott's hymn she sang, "Open my eyes, that I may see glimpses of Truth thou hast for me; place in my hand the wonderous key that shall unclasp and set me free." What if Cousin Clare was right? Perhaps a keen Intuition is the angelic key that unlocks heaven's gate within.

My infamous heroine invites you to the reading of her last will and testament. The real Lou Graham was a 19th century madame of an infamous pleasure parlor. Judge not, dear reader, lest ye misjudge! In her time Miss Lou was a powerful force and in this imagined tale no gender, caste nor ghost can be discounted.

A disclaimer: This tale is peppered with bits of actual history. No, not the boring kind and only enough to aid in the telling. Victorian speech swung from genteel to loutish to vulgar and little has changed. A whitewashing cannot mask our misdeeds and bias. If not for a jarring slap of truth we will always swim in the shallows afraid to go deeper. For the good of Creation, let us dive in and own from whence we came.

References to real persons and events further the tale and are not intended as absolute truths. Likewise the character language and manners reflect the times. Prejudice was freely practiced in all walks of life and climbing the ladder meant keeping a foot firmly on the fellow below you. Lavish wealth was revered and girthy words like fatcat, portly or rotund were compliments to a man's status. Good or bad is always in the eye of the beholder so let's ignore the history books to see our forefathers and ourselves from a less viewed angle.

Prologue

Chance Hollow Co-op Quarterly News, June 1904

Our Sons Abandon Their Heritage
Leaving a Farm to Go Farrow!

Editor's Note: The new Century yields an alarming trend as farm boys leave us for a citified life. Our pups desert us and for what? Fancy britches? Factories? Our heritage is as old as the soil yet gentrification now diktats our demise. Prodigal sons listen up! All that glistens is not gold. Why must you abandon our treasure trove for a wanton cause?

Letter to the Editor: I say humbug to your myopic rant! You linger in bygone days. How does leaving a dusty field with its rusted plow make me a gadabout? Change is inevitable sir; I beg you to come along or step aside. Respect gives and it takes, so please honor my choice and let me be. Sincerely, Jackson Hamby

□ □ □

"Oh, dear me! Jackson why must you write to the paper? Your papa works with those folks so you mustn't insult them. You know the pastor says the Holy Ghost spurns an ungrateful rascal."

"Really mama? The pastor's a duffer with a pulpit full of dusty sermons. I don't believe in spirits, nor will I keep to Old-time superstitions. I am a modern man."

There's nothing new in the generations butting heads. However, the Co-op editor got one thing right: a wayward boy will soon learn his lesson.

Jackson Hamby escapes westward where he meets an Irish lass named Ellie Flannery. Ellie introduces him to her lingering ghostly madame, if only Jack dare see her. The girl's tales of life in Lou Graham's brothel are intriguing. Was the notorious madame a brazen sinner or a patron saint? Dead or alive, aren't we all restless spirits? Do ghosts actually exist or are they imagined? Is there a secret portal to a veiled existence or is it just a whimsical perception?

Ellie says life is a puzzle with a piece gone missing and Jack knows her stories are clues to a mystery. He senses the clock is ticking and his life somehow hangs in the balance. Can he solve the puzzle in time? Jackson Hamby has a ghost of a chance, if he sees beyond banality to what truly matters.

CHAPTER 1

Go West Young Man

Did it really happen? I must write it down before my memory fades. Truth or fiction, I'll let you decide. So how does an Indiana farm boy end up in a notorious madame's saloon with a Chinaman, an Irish murderess and her lawyer lover? No, this is not a punch line. I miraculously leapt from humdrum nest to living my dream and if a fella as thick as me can figure it out, I reckon anyone can.

It all began in rural Indiana in the summer of 1894. I say being born in a farmhouse does not make me a farmer. Agriculture is admirable for some, but tilling the earth is not my inheritance. My father disagrees. He says its blasphemy to question our lineage. My dad, granddad, and great granddad tilled this plot with its ancestral graveyard resting in the back forty. Our farm? Ha! Do we own the soil or does the land own us? No matter, I shall toss aside my manure-caked boots and escape this bucolic leach field forever.

What keeps me going amidst this dreary existence? I dream of leaving Chance Hollow though it puts me at odds with my father. He wants a farmhand while I hide in the hayloft reading my penny novelettes and newsprint. Their imagery takes me beyond the hollow to exotic places far, far away. I long to live a gentrified life remote from the toils my father endures! Alas, my elaborate escape is often hijacked by my dad's booming voice.

"Jackson ya knucklehead! Stop readín those infernal stories and get to milkín. The cow's bustín a gut and she ain't gonna squeeze herself. Why do you fret so for what lies beyond our fences? Ain't nothín better out there than what you was born to."

Daddy thinks my aspirations are contrary to our way of life so I hide in the loft to read and dream. My favorite stories are of a place called Seattle, a port ferrying miners to the Alaska gold rush. While stuck in purgatory I read of a promised land free of shucking corn and mucking out barns. Oh to breathe the salty ocean air and watch waves billow in the seaward winds! Our acres of corn pale in contrast to Seattle's bustling port and boundless waters. The proclaimed Queen City doth beckon me, so why do I linger in Chance Hollow? I just can't seem to find my way.

Ten years pass and we've entered a new century. I've married my childhood sweetheart Anne Campbell and we live in town with Annie's parents. Her father makes a fair living as the only veterinary in the county. We don't have a medical doctor so Doc Campbell sometimes mends a human patient. It was Doc who saved a younger me from a deadly fever.

Living with my in-laws allowed me to attend college and my new degree is our ticket out of the hollow. Life with the Campbells is tolerable, except when my parochial in-law offers advice. Without an invitation he gushes his wisdom like a clogged gutter and splatters me with his 'if I was you.'

The Campbell home is lovely, but our personal space is tight. Three years ago today Anne gave me a daughter. However, we won't add another child anytime soon. Mother Campbell's bedroom is next door to ours and her proximity dampens my wife's romantic inclinations. Did I mention our babe sleeps with us? We conjured Belle Elizabeth on our honeymoon and moved into Campbell manor soon after. We have no room for a toddler crib so our precious lump sleeps between us blissfully unaware of our pain.

Obviously, I haven't' left Chance Hollow. I've dreamt and dreamt with my feet firmly rooted in this tiny way back. However, I am now a graduated certified public accountant. Accounting is no gold rush but it allows me to search for work outside of this hollow.

This Saturday heralds two special occasions; Anne is in the kitchen preparing a backyard feast for friends and family. Most of the village will soon be here so Anne, the mothers, and our sisters are preparing the food whilst I sit in the parlor scouring the Chicago Tribune.

The 20th century has arrived. Have I lost the chance to move to the Queen City on the bay? But wait! According to this article: Seattle is a bustling metropolis at the edge of our civilized nation. Determined pioneers tamed the natives and shrank the wilderness to make way for an exciting new town.

Yes! My prospects still abound but am I too naïve for the journey? Will I quit if the article proclaims a great peril? What if it said: 'Beware Seattle's well-mannered veil. Its so-called civility hides a feral persona not yet housebroken. The unsettled 1890's do linger and a dodgy legacy lurks in back-alleys and saloons.

Balderdash! I don't care if the wicked dwell in bawdy places. I'm on an honorable quest from which I cannot stray.

My dad says I'm full of it. He claims, "Your fancy title is doublespeak for pushín papers. A man's work is sweat and grime. Boy your angst is a paper cut."

You see I lose nothing by leaving Chance Hollow. Why not uproot my young family from this stagnant bog? A new century welcomes this thinking man. It beckons me and I intend to answer. I must move with the times and reinvent myself beyond this hamlet!

Today was supposed to celebrate my graduation from Valparaiso Lutheran College. Doc Campbell and I are the only graduated men in the hollow but no one cares. Why am I so miffed? Because I sit second chair to Belle's birthday bash. She's the only granddaughter amidst a slew of boy cousins and my stupid brothers tease me for not having a son.

What irks me is a lack of respect for my sacrifice. What did it take to earn my degree? Early Monday mornings I rode horseback to Gary City in all sorts of weather. There was no money for a boarding house so I shared a livery stall with my horse. Did I splurge a nickel on a meal? No, Anne filled my backpack with hardtack and apples. Come Wednesday night I rode home without ever stopping for a pint. My drudgery was study and shoveling cornmeal at the coop to support us. I endured it all and for what? A pampered little girl steals my thunder! Am I on the pity pot? Yes! I must find work and escape family as soon as possible.

Aha! Here it is, the answer to my prayers. Wanted: full-time accountant and notary public, CPA a plus. Opportunity abounds in the crown city of the Great Northwest! Apply to the Auditor's Office, King County, Seattle WA.

Hurrah! Seattle still beckons! Back in 1896, the papers gushed of gold rush news and the Queen City was the port to the Klondike. Newspapers chronicled it as the 'gateway to the goldfields' with pictographs of sailing ships, majestic mountains, and totem pole villages. I often sat at the kitchen table reading to mama. "Listen to the caption under this picture! It says, 'Mercantile provisions overflow onto the walkways. Fights erupt as prospectors and sellers haggle over prices.' Mama how exciting! Can you smell the sea air and hear the salty talk?"

"It's interesting honey but we're farmer folk. Why must you dream so far away? I say the devil you know is better than the one you don't."

"The only demon haunting me is monotony. I use his pitchfork to muck out the barn."

"Young man you best keep that to yourself and don't let daddy hear your blasphemy."

My mother echoes dad's words. I'm ornery maybe but it's not blasphemy. To quote my old man, "Jackson you're an uppity cuss."

It irritates my father that I call out his annoying ways; like when he votes to re-elect our mayor. Dad says the man's an imbecile but he still votes for him. Why? Because the dolt married my Aunt Lucy. Weary of his grumblings I say, "You know pops, only a dead fish goes with the flow. Try swimming upstream for once." When I grew too old for a spanking my dad exiled me to the barn though it was more a reprieve than a punishment.

Dad hated my daydreaming and told folks, "Jackson's a book-smart dimwit." I did not help my cause. While other fellas played baseball and dated girls, I courted invisibility. My dad worried about me ever coming of age and often spouted his version of Corinthians at me: "Fifteen years old and still a dreamer. Boy don't go testin the

Gospel! You best lay down your childish ways and act like you got a lick a sense!"

Mama cautioned, "Young man you hold your tongue. Disagreeing with your father only fuels his fires."

Pops and I do agree on one fact: no Hamby man ever kept an opinion to himself. It's just not in our nature.

My father no longer languishes over me cause I'm a responsible father who does his duty. What worries me these days is becoming my dad, nose hair and all; the nightmare keeps me up at night. This hollow was once a wilderness conquered by brave risktakers and the present-day residents hardly resemble their ancestors. A century of inbreeding has reduced them to mindless dullards. Will the curse of complacency trap me here as well? No siree bob! Not Jackson Filmore Hamby, CPA. The Tribune is my Almighty sign that Seattle still beckons. A persistent yen still sings from within me and I'll find my adventure even if it mystifies my family.

"Jackson honey wake up! Our guests are here. Mind your manners and come greet them."

"What? Oh the party, coming mama." It's time to play the polite host. At least I have an interesting tidbit to share. I head to the back porch and ring the dinner bell. The chatting crowd stops and turns to face me. My people no doubt expect a witticism about little Belle's milestone.

"Ladies and gentlemen please gather round. I have unexpected and exciting news!"

The womenfolk look at my wife. Did my words sound like a baby announcement? Sorry ladies, there's no bun in the oven; the bakers haven't had a night alone in weeks. What is my news? Behold! I expect to leave this Podunk village in my dust.

"Folks I've found an exciting job prospect. Please pray for me as I apply for the position of auditor's clerk in (I pause for dramatic effect) Seattle Washington!"

Befuddled looks and bug eyes greet me. It's downright lonely until my father says, "Jackson war in blazes is Saddle Warshenton? It ain't near Chance Haller!"

No, his speech is not impaired; a thick Midwest drawl is the inelegant culprit. My uncle Hubert is our postman and geography expert. Besting his older brother is my uncle's hobby so Bert shouts, "Bennie the boy wants to move to Sea-ah-till. Don't you know it's out west midway twixt San Fran and Aylaska?"

No doubt the entire hollow heard my uncle. Muffled snickering erupts into loud guffaws and a cousin says, "Ha! Jackson jokes but his folks ain't laughin."

Not amused is an understatement. The grandparents circle round my baby; each one glaring at me with parental distain. Was my announcement ill-timed? I didn't consult my wife prior to sharing. What is Anne's reaction? Cheeks flushed, her left eye twitches and she rubs her temple as if soothing a sudden pain. Anne purses her lips and scowls at me. Oh lord, I know that look; her glare is every husband's nightmare.

Therein goes the rest of my day. I am besieged by parental sermons, and our brothers stupid jokes. What kind of taunts you ask?

What did the accountant-cowboy say to his pencil? Draw partner! Ha-ha-ha, clam up Jackson and pray the clueless sheep leave you be.

The herd finally wanders away to graze at the food tables but the joke's on them. There is only one person who can dissuade me. I shall save my defense for the girl who truly matters.

Later that night I sit with Anne in the refuge of our tiny room. There are no surprises in my litany of pent-up desires; Annie understands me better than anyone.

"You know dear, I never forgot Seattle and kismet has sent me a wonderful opportunity. Imagine interning with a powerful man in a vibrant city. Our prospects are limitless and I could end up as city auditor or even mayor!"

"Jackson I've heard it all before but your resolve is new. Go ahead and apply with one condition; do not discuss this with anyone else. Our folks are set in their ways, so be considerate. You mustn't rustle feathers without knowing the outcome."

My girl handles family better than me and has more sense than any man I know. What does Anne really think? Mrs. Hamby swears neutrality nevertheless I know my wife. Seattle is not Anne's dream; It is her worst nightmare.

Two long weeks pass while I work in Uncle Bert's general store. I bartered free groceries to balance his ledgers and insist on minding the postal alcove. It allows me to catch my telegram before the family sees it. I keep my promise to Anne and await the news with my trap shut.

My uncle is a townie by necessity. Bert and dad shared big plans for the farm until a thrasher savagely maimed my uncle who survived with a crippled leg, no left thumb, and a dead dream. Old man Boehner owned the mercantile back then and gave Uncle Bert a new vision. Mama says those two were as close as family. Mr. Boehner was a widower with no kin so my uncle inherited the store.

Manning the telegraph was clever until Nature did me in. I stand counting knotholes on the outhouse wall while Fate delivers my telegram to my aunt Sadie. Sadie's a sweetheart but she's family and she'll blab to mama who will tell Mother Campbell. Good golly how the furies will howl! I must find Anne before Sadie spills the beans. She hands me the message without saying a word and that's fine by me. I have no desire to discuss it. What will my family think if I get the job? No doubt a choir of harpies will beg Anne to reel me in.

I help Sadie with her shawl, hold the door for her and she gives me a polite nod before heading up the hill to the farm. I grab my coat and sprint towards the Campbell house. Darn it! Anne and her mother are in the kitchen baking bread. I'll not make a fool of myself again. Take a breath Jackson and mind your words. "Hello mother Campbell, your bread smells wonderful. Sweetheart might I have a word?" The question is rhetorical as I nudge Anne from the counter, up the back stairs to our room and secure the door.

"Jackson Hamby what is wrong with you? The dough's not risen and there's nothing to smell. What are you up to?"

I wave the telegram. "Seattle answered my inquiry and I want us both to open it."

"Well don't stand there waving it like a flag."

It says, 'Dear Mr. Hamby: Please accept the position of auditor clerk. Confirm as soon as possible so my staff can help find your lodging. Sincere congratulations, Samuel C. Barr, Auditor, City of Seattle.'

Eureka and hallelujah! I grab Anne and twirl her about until we collapse out of breath onto the bed. My euphoria fades into panic and I plead, "Honey, they want an answer right away. Please, we must go!"

Why do I fear her rejection? A young Annie made house calls with her dad and stayed with me while I lingered with Rheumatic fever. She could've played with friends but chose to comfort a frightened little boy. I had temporarily lost my sight and Annie read to me. Our shared vision was perfect through her eyes. It still is.

My wife smiles at me and quotes from her wedding vows, "Wherever this man goes I shall follow." I love her now more than ever.

The next two weeks are bittersweet; is there a bigger ask than choosing between spouse and family? Anne sorts our belongings while the pleading choir sings, "Let your dad have a look at Jackson. He'll cure what ails him." For better or worse Anne stands by her daft husband. My wife and mama see a saner me and they are arm-in-arm against the herd. Mama says, "Jackson is not barmy. He dreams beyond the hollow." Anne chose me over many suitors. When questioned she says, "Be it piglets, puppies, or a sickly boy, I love the runt of the litter." Bless her heart cause I'm the luckiest runt alive.

A devoted Lutheran, my father sees with a saint's eye. Dad calls me peculiar but he admires my spunk. None of my siblings dare talk back and I am his lone uppity cuss. Dad says I stood tall against youth's devil urges. Sorry sir I wasn't being prudent. Rheumatic fever drained the vigor from me like a leaky spicket and a pair of thick spectacles still frame my face. Me virtuous? No sir, I was blinded to temptation. Impish playmates deserted me and adventure books were my friends save one exception: Little Anne was by my side.

It is all ancient history now. The new century heralds a fresh start and this dreamer has a pent-up BLEVE of plans ready to blow!

CHAPTER 2

The Getaway

My planning has failed me. Sheer tenacity takes over against the setbacks testing my nerve. Why are we still here? How do I escape the hollow? Did my office find us suitable lodging? I know nothing! A twister took down a mile of telegraph poles and we're cut off from the world. I can't wire Seattle or the rail station and must trek to Gary for freight transport and train tickets.

What else stalls us? Why must my last will and testament have a male executor? Anne manages us just fine and doesn't need anyone bossing her. And what if tragedy takes us both? Who gets little Belle? Be it grandmas or godparents, who wins custody and who gets hurt?

Do the Hamby and Campbell men help us? Ha! They bask in my irritability. Through it all Anne keeps the high watch and the angel deserves my apology.

"Sweetheart I'm sorry for what's left behind. Shipping freight is expensive and the train agent says it's best we start anew. Our future forces a giveaway but I swear we'll profit from this move. I'll find my way and you'll have a grand manor!"

"Jackson I've never doubted you and I'll sacrifice most everything except my porcelain plates. My great grandma brought them from England and they're coming with me."

"Yes dear, of course."

Anne is a wonder as she fits our necessities into two suitcases, a steamer trunk and one hutch. Letting go of my books was difficult. I gave them to our one-room school and built extra shelves for the collection. Am I coldhearted to love books more than people? I feel as if I've deserted loyal chums. Those books were my friends when needed most; I hope other children discover their timeless worth.

Finally! Moving day is here and I cannot curb my joy! I've endured years of limbo for this moment. We sit on the front porch waiting on the freight wagon from Gary city. Belle sits on my bouncing knee while Anne listens to our womenfolk spout last-minute travel advice. That's rich! These girls never travelled outside the hollow except to compete for a ribbon at the state fair. They packed a box of pies and cakes while we've pack up our life to move cross country. I focus on Belle and ignore their cackling. My clansmen, of course, are absent. Necessity or reproachful solidarity keeps them away. This hollow reminds me of the Gerstäcker's tale; a village asleep only to come alive for one day every hundred years.

Hurrah! I see a team of Clydesdales at the crest of the hill. It's the Himmler freight wagon headed our way. Mr. Himmler is the brother of our local pastor. You can always trust the German Lutheran to be spot on time.

His youngest son manages the horses and jumps from the rig as soon as it stops. The elder Himmler descends one boot at a time until he touches solid ground. He wastes no time barking orders at his son and I as we struggle to fit my belongings into one wooden crate. Anne double-wrapped her plates in newspaper and I pray they make it to Seattle without a crack. Mr. Himmler and son will transport our crate to their freight office in Gary city where more Himmler sons will muscle our belongings to a Chicago freight yard. We won't see the crate again until Seattle.

The Himmler van fades from view and a mob of well-wishers magically appear. Our mothers organized a farewell party. Did I say party? This goodbye resembles a mournful wake with a backyard overflowing with potluck food, tears, and unsolicited advice. The women are serving sweet cider and that's a pity. I'm left stone sober to face a gaggle of assailing patched overalls. Again and again the men snap at me with a tiresome counsel, "Jackass get this foolishness out of your system and bring the girls home safe. You should be pushing papers at the coop."

I beg to differ. The coop is the nickname for our Co-op mill where generations have surrendered the fruits of their labor. Now my peers feed the mill save one exception; I cannot return with my tail between my legs. If I fail I'll never hear the end of it. Damn this one-horse town!

I have good reason to skip the party. A long journey awaits and I need a fitful sleep. However, tearful grandmas cling to little Belle and our guests beg a last word or a hug. The line of huggers and jawers finally subsides so I grab Belle and sprint for our room.

Anne awakens me at dawn. A fog lingers in the valley as men head for the fields while I eat a quick breakfast before the intercity Omnibus arrives. My mother spent the night and the grandmas take turns holding their precious baby girl.

The Omnibus is finally here. I load our bags and Anne puts Belle in her seat. We take our leave amid tearful hugs and a dozen promises to write.

The bus slowly ascends the hill allowing me one last look back. Mama stands on the porch waving a hanky; her smile contradicts the tears streaming down her face. I will miss my mother most of all. Putting a hand to heart, I blow her a kiss. "I love you dearest, I always will."

The Omni makes a monthly run from rural areas into Gary city. The four-hour trip on the weathered roads has several stops before reaching the dock on Lake Michigan's shore. My horse and I traveled to Gary in two hours but the slow clomp of the Omni Clydesdales gives me time to review my boyhood memories. Familiar cornfields line the road and I relive working in the dusty fields. As we round the bend, I see my father waiting on a fence rail.

Dad shouts at me one last time, "Jackson you go to church and write mother once a week, ya hear me?" He slides off the rail and walks into the rows of tall corn.

"Yes sir I'll do my best. Goodbye dad." I doubt my father heard me. Why would he start listening now? I add, "Brethren go watch your corn grow! This Hamby follows his dreams. When we meet again I'll be a visitor on holiday. God bless and good riddance."

Annie whispers in my ear, "Reel it in honey. The tether's broken with no need to keep a grudge."

Belle Elizabeth crawls into my lap singing, 'Froggie went a court'n, he did go. 'I smile at my babe and chime in, 'Froggie went a court'n, his true love for to see, Froggie bid Miss Mousey, will you marry me. '

It is now early afternoon; a water taxi ferried us from Gary to Chicago and a hackney cab is taking us from the dock to the rail station.

Belle laughs at the flour-sack adorning the rearend of our cabby's horse. I tell her, "There are so many horses in the city; if not for the diapers the streets would fill with dung!"

This bustling metropolis dwarfs our Indiana village. Our whole county is smaller than a sprawling Chicago with its modern architecture towering an amazing sixteen stories above us. However, it's not all wonder. Stoic faces scurry by without so much as a nod. A wide-eyed Belle begs to be carried and her daddy cringes at the peevish swarm. Buck up man! You must be brave for the women.

The Wells Street station is an immense echoing cathedral with no sense of sanctuary. It segregates us into boxes as if we're veggies bound for the market. Situated next to us is a five-foot mahogany wall meant to separate us from our betters. Behind the wall are plush leather chairs and café tables with uniform waiters bussing food to wealthy patrons.

My family sits in the coach section on a low-back oak pew. A solitary twist-turn gumball machine stands nearby with a tattered note on its knob. The message reads: 'Ate my penny!' My pouting seems childish as I look to the far corner of the cathedral. Away from view is a windowless room with weathered pine benches. A sign over the door reads, 'Immigrants and Coloreds Wait Here.' At least my seat's in the open air.

Chance Hollow is an isolated hamlet with years of common ancestry; we tolerate each other and the few travelers we see. Our village accepts an odd duck as long as he works hard and keeps his word. I am proof of that. The hollow has no social awareness save one tenet: the Golden Rule. Dad says the only way to get respect is to give it. I try to keep his example.

I walk to the loading dock where a rail worker helps me tag my trunk for the journey. "Keep the stub sir. You'll claim your steamer at the end of the line."

I offer two cents for his time. "Thank you for the help. I apologize for the paltry sum, it's what I can offer."

The uniform tips his cap. "No worries sir, I take any tip but a foreigner's coin. Their money's useless to me."

I weave my way back through the crowded station. A giant timetable says we'll board on time. What a blessing to have this day unfold as planned. The girls sit across the massive hall but my view's blocked by a mass of steamy humanity. An endless chatter vibrates the air and the giant structure echoes like a vast cave. I feel so small here. A solitary soul loses the Sacred so I pray aloud, "Lord shield my family amid this turbulence that we may know Your peace." No one hears me as the chaos absorbs my voice but God surely did. Dad says a prayer finds its way in tranquility or madness.

I arrive back at the commuter hold and settle in for the wait. What can I do to entertain my girls? Perhaps I'll read the pamphlet that came with our tickets. The words are old news to Anne who heard them last night and the night before. My wife smiles at me while she plays with Belle. It is her 'I married an idiot' grin.

The pamphlet says: Welcome aboard the North Coast Limited railway! Your train is a special excursion bound for Yellowstone Park and beyond. Our new steam locomotive pulls eight cars at a speed of 20 miles per hour! Passenger service includes a luxury class sleeper, a first-class scenic lounge, a dining car, a Pullman sleeper, and a third-class transport. An added flatbed observatory offers amazing outdoor scenes. Your Pullman coach has cushioned berths on either side of a wide aisle and every berth converts to a two-bunk curtained sleeper for a peaceful night's rest.

Anne, Belle, and I are in berth 8, with two seats facing each other. Belle rides on a lap for free. We are situated in the rear of the car across from the porter's berth.

The pamphlet continues: Your porter folds down the sleep rack above your seat. A berth sleeps two but a small child nestles in nicely. The train's gentle motion gives both child and parent a restful slumber. A flush toilet and adjoining wash station are situated at the front of your car. (Rules require we lock the toilet room when in station.) Convenient vestibule doors at both ends of your coach open to the observation or the dining car. The porter will arrange dining seating for you. Roadhouse cafes and quaint trackside stands offer a local flair along the way.

We can't afford a dining car or roadhouse café so Anne packed our food and I have two dollars for treats. The ticket agent said our travel time is fifty hours not including service stops or delays. The wilderness route is prone to delays so we expect a five-day trip. Our provisions will suffice with minimal delays.

I finish our pamphlet and look around for something else to do. A first-class passenger discarded his leaflet near our pew. Let's see how our wealthy betters fair. I snatch his litter from the floor.

It says: The North Coast Railway thanks you for your patronage and your comfort is our foremost concern. Our luxury cars contain four suites with convertible couch-beds and day tables. Each car is equipped with a porcelain flush toilet and bath chamber. Vestibule doors connect to a first-class lounge with games, smokes and appetizers provided. You may purchase spirits at the bar and the dining car offers you its gold star menu. After a delicious meal walk forward through the coach car to the observation deck. It provides a stupendous open-air view of the vast prairies and starlit skies. Your steward shields your belongings from ordinary fares while you're away. Our staff aims to serve you at any hour.

Well la-di-dah! My porter sleeps across the aisle from this ordinary fare. I'll someday treat Anne to an opulent voyage but we're on a budget and the amenities provided suit us.

I hear the third-class immigrant and negro travelers are less fortunate. Rumors say their car is a reclaimed 1860's troop transport with fixed slats for windows. Several pine slabs stretch across the width of the car with one lengthwise walkway dividing them and baggage is stored in overhead racks or under a bench. A fitful rest is a luxury for those dozing on or under the benches and folks navigate sideways along the narrow aisle. It must be difficult to not trip enroute to the toilet.

I hear the boxcar has an antiquated squat toilet inside a tin-lined alcove. An eight-inch floor hole and gravity feeds the waste onto the tracks. A sign on the wall tells a man to squat and pee cause a moving train makes it impossible to aim. I hope the man can read. The privy provides a tattered Roebucks catalog for wiping, a handrail for balance, and an ill-fitting curtain for privacy. With no running water a rider must bring a canteen with him. The brakeman decides when the crapper's ripe for a hosing and I'm told a U.S. coin tweaks his judgment. Thanks be! My family's flush enough to afford a modern commode!

There's no live-in porter and the first-class, commuter and dining car is off limits as well. A coal tender and the mail car separate the boxcar from the engine's smoke and ash but its cinders fly through the open slats.

Third class travel is a no-frills ride but it's cheaper than my fare. Late season discounts helped but our berth cost a hefty $145 or double my monthly earnings. I spent all our savings and borrowed the rest from my mother's stash. My father doesn't know about mama's money jar in the root cellar. The jar and my loan are our secret. Mama's saving for a new sewing machine. Her apparatus skips every third stitch but Dad says it ain't broke enough yet. Ornery miser! He's lucky mama thinks the same of him. I'll soon make enough to help mama with her necessities.

Annie pokes me out of my daydream. "Look honey a porter's rounding up the first-class fares."

"Finally! Let's get our things and go to our platform." I lift Belle in one arm and the heavier suitcase in the other. Anne grabs the lighter case and our food bag. The bag is a canvas horse feeder gifted by Uncle Bert. We can't afford a horse so the bag will stow Anne's small garden tools. For now it holds bread, preserves, jerky, and apples. Anne also packed a canteen, tin camp plates and cups. Station vendors along the way will offer penny coffee, tea, and fresh milk.

The first-class travelers board unfettered while porters stow their bags. No one helps us. We are one of five couples with children packing our coach; a lone porter checks our tickets at the door.

What the heck? We're joined to the boxcar without the observation car to separate us. All manner of foreigners speaking several languages mingle outside their ride. The brakeman checks tickets while a man helps his pregnant wife and toddler up the steps. He glances my way and I shrug as if to say, whatever were we thinking? The alien smiles at me and disappears inside. We are kindred souls shepherding our families toward a better life, or so we're told. Does a missing flatcar portend other broken promises?

The stationmaster shouts all aboard and blows two short blasts from his whistle. Porters aside each car snap to attention, salute in unison, grab their footstools and hop inside. The stationmaster signals the engineer and our engine jerks forward with its cars in tow. The slow-motion exit reminds me of our escape from the hollow. Nevertheless, our adventure begins!

CHAPTER 3

Pamphlet Shamplet

The light fades as our North Coast Limited passes by several aromatic stockyards. Hungry children watch their mothers assemble picnic suppers as we head westward into shadowy forests with waterways lit by a colossal wolf moon.

Exhaustion settles in and the day's eager tenor fades into quiet dialog. Our savvy porter lowers the sleeper racks as women bustle children to and frow the toilet. Men light up their smokes and share a casual word across the aisle. The porter's berth is empty so I tap the seat of the man at my back. He turns around and nods.

"Good evening sir, I'm Jackson Hamby. This modern train is a wonder, don't you think?"

"Yup, the industrial age pushes us forward."

That's it; his wife and son return from the toilet and I get no introduction. I guess neighborly is different outside the hollow.

The immigrant boxcar is crowded and cold. Cramped strangers sit shoulder to shoulder or vie for a space on the floor under the benches. The kindred man who met my gaze is amongst the crowd. Rail noise makes talking with his Sicilian elder a shouting match so he hollers, "Already I am exhausted. A hundred Hail Mary's cannot comfort my worry. Gesù Cristo! The night chill seeps through the slats with its cinder and smoke. It is unpleasant and this car sways like a crazed mule! My poor pregnant wife suffers and I fear a horrible accident awaits us."

The older gent spits into a can he holds in his hand. "Settle down boy. Our conditions are merciless but worry won't help us. This train is no different from any other. It provides little comfort yet is mostly safe."

"I pray you are correct but what is that awful smell? We are minutes from Chicago and already the air is putrid. Do you think it's the toilet?"

"The piss-hole ripens soon enough. No, I think the smell comes from that Polack eating a tin of fish. It doesn't matter; wretched or not, our fate is sealed. Remember boy, 'Cui cerca, trova; cui sècuta, vinci! Vincerò!' You best pray for patience young man. Our sacrifice is for a better life."

"Yes of course." The young father bends his right arm to cradle his sleeping son. His pregnant wife cuddles on the bench with her head resting on his left thigh. He tucks his sweater between the wall and his already stiff neck. The rocking motion annoys him but fatigue wins out and his elder's words echo a mantra for his sleepy mind. 'He who seeks, finds, who perseveres, wins!'

Our coach offers its own dilemma. I am trapped in a rack above my girls and the closed curtain is claustrophobic. Stale air and snoring sounds fill the already clickety-clacking car. A berth window opens after midnight and offers relief until the chill creeps in. A passenger shouts from behind his curtain, "Shut the darn window ya clown!" and a defiant voice dares, "Come on over and make me you sod!"

That did it! Sleepy children fuss and our porter jumps up to keep the skirmish from getting ugly. Civility prevails with apologies all round and our porter closes the window. Alas, the snores and farty smells return.

Ugh! This rack is far too short for me. I fear I'll kick my neighbor's head yet I can't sleep nose to nose with a stranger. Tomorrow I'll try laying foot-to-foot. Our coach groans as I drowse with my eyelids at half-mast. Deep curves defy the promise of a gentle ride and I grab the guardrail for fear of tumbling to the floor!

The train rolls into the Minneapolis station at daybreak where a stationmaster announces a maintenance layover of exactly seventy-five minutes, no less and no more. Wealthy riders follow the breakfast aroma to a nearby eatery while my family settles for a sweet roll from a platform vendor.

Anne eyes Belle's sticky fingers. "Belle and I need a restroom sink for a proper cleanup. Are you coming?"

"I'll stroll about the grounds, perhaps a walk on terra firma will ease my grogginess."

The brakeman opens the boxcar door. A hoard of immigrants pours onto the platform and a familiar face approaches me. "Ciao Bello signore. Beautiful sunrise, yes?"

I reach into my vest pocket for my smoke tin. The alma mater crested amenity is meant to impress. "Good morning to you sir. Cigarillo?"

"No, I cannot. The train engine's smoke is more than I need. Please you go ahead."

It sounds awful so I commiserate. "When I was a boy I nicked a cigar from our mercantile. My dad made me pay for the cigar and smoke it to its nubs. Puking my guts out cured me of all curiosity and I haven't smoked since."

Turns out my kindred friend is Italian. Spouting my compulsory Latin is no match for his mastery of English so I chuck my strategy of one-upmanship. Mama says sincerity makes the best of friends so I try a humbler tone. "My name is Jackson Hamby. I'm taking my family from Indiana to Seattle. You are?"

"Nuncio Giordano from Trapani Sicily. My family is enroute to Tillamook Oregon."

"Why travel so far? Do you have relatives in Oregon?"

"Si, my wife's brother raises goats and cows. He sells the cheese to a city market. The famine dirt of my homeland is no good. I will work on a farm again while my children play in the lush fields of grass. A bless-ed life awaits us in Tillamook."

Just my luck, the man's a contented farmer who misses his muck. I stay clear of his tending. "You have a good future ahead of you. I work in a city as a certified accountant. How are your travels fairing?"

"I am all right. My wife is with child and not feeling so good. The boxcar is crowded and the air is foul. Last night I sat up with my boy and wife using me as a pillow."

"Oh my I hope your journey improves."

He sounds deflated and my mother would pinch me if I flaunted my betters. A tootling whistle signals us to take our seats. I like Nuncio and look forward to chatting with him again.

I take my seat and Annie says, "I see you made a friend from the freight car. It's awful how the railroad treats them."

"His name is Nuncio; he hails from Sicily enroute to Oregon with his wife and little boy. The wife is pregnant, poor dear. Their conditions are inhumane and I feel for them." I lower my voice to a whisper, "Nuncio is kind and well-mannered. I wish his family had the seats behind us. I'll introduce you first chance we get."

CHAPTER 4

The Wild West?

The women quickly transform our roving hotel into a household in absentia. Their impressive domesticity stows the bedding with no help from the porter. Shawls adorn the seatbacks and one clever gal (my wife) adjusts the windows to minimize the dust. The children play in seats closest to the toilet; it is a logical tactic and diaper pins run berth curtains across the car to segregate us men from the hen's knitting circle. My seat is in the back of the male sanctuary. Other men play cards with their pipe smoke floating out the open windows. The gals banned foul smelling cigars and that's fine by me. I've no quarrel with women ruling the roost as it reminds me of home.

There is one irritation; did I mention my aversion to crowds? My mother says company is a gift. Sorry mama most folks are a damnable nuisance. Sitting across from our unassuming porter was peaceful until an ensemble of bored travelers formed this morning. They invade my sanctuary forcing snacks and idle conversation upon me like "isn't train travel marvelous!" and "how'd ya sleep? or "my wife's a dandy baker. Do try one of her cookies."

Arg! My asylum is ruined as the snoops leer through our aft door into the dining car. A spy stands next to my seat awaiting his turn and sneaks a peak at my journal. That does it! I retaliate against the voyeur by drawing an ogling caricature on the page. Ha! The snoop sees himself and growls. Serves him right!

Anne hears the commotion and shoots me a look. It's the one that freezes naughty babes and makes a husband cringe. Why must I behave when others do not? I put down my journal and look out the window. Oh to be on a solitary walk in the footsteps of Lewis and Clark! This is going to be a long journey.

Our second full day on the rails affords more tedium with a change of scenery. The lush Midwest forests and lakes give way to rolling prairies and the monotonous landscape offers only an occasional ranch or tiny settlement. Full-service railway stations morph into weathered outposts where boredom, heat, and a latched toilet force us from our coaches. These barebone waystations charge extortionate prices for a dubious fare. There's always a gamey stew with hardtack biscuits and coffee fresh as a wilted daisy leaving an earthy grit in your mouth. Atop a crate sits a jar of pickled something or a keg of homebrew and the cost of a pint is too pricey for me. These company outposts are the true train-robbers so I keep to our feedbag.

Traveling twenty miles an hour seems fast at first but the endless prairie reduces our pace to a snail's crawl. Rolling sage litters the rails and clogs our wheelsets forcing the crew to stop and remove the clinging menace. Majestic bison are long gone having been replaced by herds of mindless cattle. The beefers are unimpressed with our engineer's whistle and stand their ground until a nudge from the cowcatcher moves them off the tracks.

Belle and I pass the time counting prairie dogs popping out of their holes. With so many critters the game's monotony is akin to singing ♪ninety-nine bottles of beer on the wall.♪ Ah fudge, the song is stuck in my head.

I need some civilization to distract me from whining children. Their spats irk me and Anne chides, "Jackson you're worse than a child. Please find a way to ease your cabin fever."

My wife's observation only adds to my irritability so I ask our porter, "Sam what happened to the observation car? I could sorely use a change of scenery."

"It's a comin sir, we'll add the car at Bismarck. Sorry for the long haul. It's a big country ain't it."

"Like it goes on forever."

There is a bit of good news; the roaming snoops disbanded! The dining car peep show ended this morning when Sam shut the dining curtain. Seems our gawkers gave a fatcat indigestion. Our car is apathetic save one grump. He huffs, "Porter I insist you pin our forward door curtain shut. We can't have a filthy migrant ogling our womenfolk."

He has replaced his own spying ways with a baseless accusation and Sam says, "Sir their boxcar don't got winders. They cain't see us."

The man stands toe to toe with our porter. "Are you deaf? I pay your wages so you best mind me. Shut the damn curtain!"

Ah jeez! Sam needs a backup against the idiot defender of propriety. "That whiner needs a slap of manners. I'm gonna go stand with Sam."

My wife grabs my wrist. "Jackson Hamby you stay put. Your feisty mood's more a lack of sleep than honorable indignation. Sam can handle an ornery cuss without you. Here eat an apple."

"Woman I can't be pacified like a mule. The bully's more a jackass than me!"

"Uh huh. I'm begging you please take a nap."

Sam does manage without me. He closes the curtain and offers the man a lollipop meant for the kiddies. "Ha! Look at that Annie. Sam gave a sucker to the sucker! I bet the fool missed the porter's jab."

"Jackson please! Let me read in peace. Climb up top with your daughter and don't you dare wake her."

"Yes dear." I obey but I can't fall asleep. Anne's right as usual. I'm desperate for a pastime until an awakened little girl comes to my rescue. My babe brags to her chums, "Daddy tells magical stories. He makes fairies, cowboys and scary ghosts come alive! Come hear my daddy's tales."

I cannot refuse her flattery. Mr. Hamby is a hero to babes and wearied mothers alike. The time passes quicker for all of us until Anne rescues my fading voice. "How about a cup of honey tea with supper?"

"Thanks dear, the tea sounds good but I've no appetite for bag food. I'll take a cup and retire to my rack."

My bunk orbit is closing in on me. How do I manage my claustrophobia? I concede to a loss of privacy and open my curtain partway.

CHAPTER 5

So Sad and Pointless

ay three begins at another shabby service stop with a rooster bragging outside my window. Last night was a fitful sleep; no snoring or train noise bothered my dreams of the Seattle port scene. Sweet sleep makes for a glorious morning despite the bland surroundings until three toots of the engineer's whistle interrupts my revelry and I stare out the window as our coach pulls away from the platform.

What's this? Something is amiss! An immigrant runs from behind the outpost yelling "Fermo, Fermo!" A wide-brimmed hat worn by the Sicilian farmers obscures his face. Good heavens! Is Nuncio running after us? The figure is close to our car now, too close for safety. Our porter leans out an open window shouting, "You there back off! Git away!" Someone pulls the emergency cord and the brakes squeal in protest as the Italian attempts to grab our stairway handrail. Oh no! He's gone without a trace.

The train's brakes strain for a good distance before they quiet. Sam yells "yawl stay put" as he joins the crewmen running down the track. I open my window and lean out as far as I dare. The crew huddles ten yards back of the train around a motionless heap of a man. The brakeman turns and walks towards us, passes under my window without a word, slides the boxcar door open and hauls himself up inside. A woman screams and a couple of men poke their heads out of the boxcar door. The brakeman reappears cradling a sobbing woman in his arms. He shoves a looky-loo aside, jumps to the ground and helps the woman out of the car. She leans on the trainman as they slowly walk towards the crumpled mass. The woman's eyes are vacant now, her wailing reduced to a whimper. She must be in shock. I can clearly see her frame as they pass underneath my window. She is not with child and Nuncio Giordano isn't the dead heap. Darn it Jackson! The woman agonizes and I dare feel relief instead of pity. Shame on me.

Minutes pass as the woman kneels beside her man. Our porter sits with her while the train crew rummages through a nearby woodpile. Sam stands, says something to another porter and both men walk towards us. The other porter boards the elite coach and Sam joins us with the saddest of news.

"Sorry for the delay folks. An Italian fella was in the outhouse when he heard our whistle. The fool, God rest his soul, tried to hop a moving train and the wheels sucked him under. There was nothin' we could do for him but it was merciful quick." A woman gasps and covers her child's ears. "Sorry for the detailed account ma'am. Truth is we're miles from anywhere and the widow begs to be near the grave. She took my counsel to wait for the next big settlement. This is a tragedy but it happens. You must show caution around our unforgiv'n machines. The railroad company will prorate the widow's ticket but it ain't much so the crew's collecting an offering to help the family settle. Please give anythin' you can." The porter takes off his cap, adds his share and walks down the aisle. Sam reaches us and Anne eyes a meager handful of coins in the cap. Our family is poor compared to most in this car yet Anne digs deep into her coin purse to add five dimes and a fifty-cent piece. Sam smiles at her generosity and walks away. I whisper, "I admire your charity but we're not moneyed people. Let others give their fair share." Anne puts her index finger to my lips. "No one did and the family needs our help. We lose nothing by being charitable. Generosity always repays itself."

"Of course I know that." Why am I so annoyed with her? Anne Hamby has always been my sextant correcting my course when worry pulls me astray.

The horrible accident creates an unfortunate delay and we're forced to sit in our stifling coach while the train crew builds a makeshift coffin. Open windows and doors do not ease the heat yet we dare not leave. Workmen finally load the corpse into the mail car, the engine fires up and we chug through the Dakota landscape as fast as we can.

Two hours later the train pulls up next to the Bismarck platform where a rattled Nuncio joins me. "It is an unlucky omen my friend. The toilet smell permeates everything and the lazy brakeman does nothing. My kinsman said he was going to the outhouse for privacy and to clean the lingering smell of piss from his shoes."

"Oh Nuncio I'm so sorry. As a lad my chore was to haul chamber pots to the outhouse. A nasty backyard goose as big as me often gave chase. I hated it when he drew blood or I spilled pee on my shoes. The sweet aroma of that fowl roasting in the oven was my best Christmas gift ever! No doubt the dead man regrets his decision; a smelly toilet isn't worth dying over."

"Si, so sad and pointless. The eldest boy is twelve years old and vows to support his family; such innocent bravado! With no kin in America the widow will save money to return to Sicily."

"She has my prayers but Bismarck's a small farming settlement. Her boy might work in a grain elevator or in the railyard and she can take in mending but necessities can rob a piggy bank. It's not easy to escape a small town. Maybe a rancher needs a wife. Remarrying gives her security and it provides him with free fieldhands."

Our trainmen offload the makeshift casket from the mailcar onto the platform. Sam tips his hat to the widow and offers a small pouch of money while other crewmen hurry passengers onto the train. My window frames the stricken family next to their lost provider. A stunned widow and her three balling babes stand beside the fallen patriarch while he rests in a casket hastily put together from scrap. It's shorter than a regular coffin. With no room to stretch out I imagine the decease cradles his dismembered legs under his chin. The vision makes me smile and I am immediately ashamed. Jackson Hamby you are such a child! Surely an undertaker will offer a fit casket if the widow can pay.

The fatherless brood waves goodbye to their boxcar brethren. They're home now miles away from their intended destination. Where will they sleep tonight and thereafter? God only knows. A foolish man chased a moving train and lost control of his family's destiny.

The train whistle blows, our car jerks forward and we speed away as fast as the engine can chug. The crew rushes through our service stops trying to make up for lost time. Sam the porter explains, "An entitled gent wired our owners complain'n about his ruined trip and demands a full refund. The man can't harangue Fate so he fleeces the railroad. I don't git his angst; he's got a rich life and two good legs. He's no right to commandeer a widow's grief."

Yes, the whiner usurped the tragedy. He bemoans lost time as if it were a real thing when he should be reflecting on his many blessings. How self-absorbed can a man be?

Our spirits rebound with access to a new pastime; the observation car joined us in Bismarck. The flatbed has pine benches and siderails with signs warning us not to sit on the railing. Given recent events I'm inclined to obey.

A new social experiment unfolds before me. Propriety held us to our assigned coaches but proximity offers paupers and the elite a chance to mingle or at least make eye contact. Yet the outdoor experience is not without its challenges as roving dust devils interrupt our mingling. The swirling winds make us run for our cars like the prairie dogs we see diving for their holes. Once the dust settles we pop out one by one until another tiny twister forces us inside. The silly game is nature's way of disrupting the monotony.

After supper the night skies create a placid backdrop. The moonless sky isn't dark at all. Instead it sparkles with an infinite number of stars and comets streak across the vast sky causing the crowd to gasp with every flash of light! I wish to grab a falling star as if it were a firefly and capture it forever in a mason jar.

Nuncio's family joins us followed by more incomers and with them comes a flute, a mandolin, and a harmonica. The band's impromptu serenade sparks dancing amongst the crowd. Nuncio puts my toddler on his shoes and twirls a laughing Belle round and round. "See Jackson how your Bella dances! I love my boy but I pray Sophia has a bambina. How fun to have my own dancing angel!" Belle misses her doting grandparents and no doubt relishes the attention.

Sam and his banjo join us to play a well-known camp song though his lyrics differ from mine. He sings, 'The life of a voyager that of a sojourner. Travels round and round but not from town-to-town. Paddles the lake and stream, follows an ancient dream. Peace on the Milky Way blue sky or cloudy day. Winds rustle through the trees, God's voice on every breeze. I've but one home from which I'll never roam. Place of true happiness, my soul in God's c-a-r-e-s-s.'

Folks join in with surprising harmony but I'm more pensive. Aided by the celestial canopy, I ponder the past few days. Oh to spend this night alone under the soothing stars! Alas, a fussing Belle interrupts my muse. My wife sighs, "Our girl's done. I'll take her to bed."

Anne endures much from her silly husband yet blessed me with this little beauty. Putting Belle to bed is the least I can do. "No dear, you stay with our friends. I'll put her in bed. You linger a bit longer and enjoy the night."

Anne smiles and squeezes my hand. I swoop our girl into my arms and wander back inside. An exhausted Belle is asleep before I finish her story. Her innocent smile reminds me of my youth and I whisper, "Long ago your pawpaw fell asleep to grammy's lullabies. She sang, 'Hush-a-bye, don't you cry, go to sleep sweet baby. When you wake you shall have a pretty little horsey.' Daddy loves you so much, more than I can say. I can't promise you a pony but we'll see majestic mountains, vast waters, and totem pole villages. Let's both dream of Seattle and bless our journey."

My evening ritual quiets me as I speak my gratitude and bless those in need. "Lord hold close a grieving widow and the meekest amongst us. Do forgive my judgements and help me let go a fearful bully and a miser who values his ledgers over kindness. As for my own faults help me put them to rest with this day. Bless my sleeping angel and her mama for putting up with Your humble servant. Amen."

CHAPTER 6

Say What?

Our fourth day puts us in Livingston Montana, the excursion stop for Yellowstone National Park. Buckboard wagons with drivers clad in cowboy chaps sit beside the platform ready to take folks to their lodging.

Our coach is almost empty and I say, "Annie see all the vacant seats! So many folks left and the loud snorer is gone. Look around! I have my choice of lower bunks!"

"Yes and I'll not bump my head on your rack or endure a lengthy wait for the toilet."

The train engine fires up and we head ever westward with brief service stops across Montana and Idaho to pick up and drop off miners. What a relief to have all this space. Testing each empty berth for the least lumpy sleeper makes me think of poor Nuncio. Only two incomers left the boxcar at Yellowstone. They snagged work in the lodge's kitchen and stable. "Sam a moment please. Might my boxcar friends ride with us?"

"So sorry Mr. Hamby but railroad policy forbids it."

"And what if my friend had money or a title? Would the railroad make allowances for him?"

"Yup, status always pays the way. Pity he's got nothin to bargain with."

The scenery changes for the better as volcanic stone-carved foothills rise up from the prairie floor. A greener landscape returns with long needled pine trees and haystacks framing my view. We cross over into Washington State with only a sliver of light on the horizon. Our first stop is Spokane City and Nuncio's family stands on the platform. I leave my seat to bid them a proper farewell.

Nuncio smiles when he sees me and puts down his weathered carpetbag. "This is goodbye my friend. Our next train goes to Oregon City where my family awaits. We are almost home."

He is excited yet genuinely sad to leave me behind. Nuncio's a rarity on this train, a real gentleman. My friend hands me a scrap of paper with a post box address and I stuff the paper into my vest pocket.

"Thank you Nuncio, I'll write as soon as I get settled." Why do I give him false hope. Our distance is more than miles, we shared a train ride and nothing more. What's to write about once we're settled? Nuncio's goat cheese and my boring office gibberish?

"Take care Jackson, may God be with you."

"And also with you."

Nuncio's posture leaves me wondering. Did he sense my fib? His boarding whistle beckons, Nuncio lets go my hand and the family waves as they walk away. I wave and turn in the opposite direction.

Moneyed folks wander over to a Harvey Roadhouse while I follow the smokey aroma of bacon sizzling on a vendor's grill. Sandwiches wrapped in yesterday's news do tempt me. I can't remember my last decent meal but my wallet's nearly empty. I order a milk for Belle and return to my seat.

The train jerks forward, Anne hands me the remnants of our food bag and I force a thank you. My resourceful girl makes do and

I mustn't share my bad mood with her. I suck on a piece of jerky and stare out the window as our train clickety-clacks along endless miles of farmland. We chug westward away from Spokane and the rising sun.

It's late afternoon when the train pulls into Wenatchee station where an agitated stationmaster gestures for our porters to join him on the platform. Sam tells us to stay put and walks over to the worried agent.

I stand on the coach steps for what seems like an eternity until the huddle breaks and Sam returns. "We gots trouble up ahead causín a delay. An avalanche outside of Icicle Flats covered the rails with boulders and a fix-it crew's enroute. Sir you stay put, a delay's unreliable and we could leave in an hour or be here for days."

"Be serious Sam. We'll keep to the schedule, won't we?"

Sam gives a toothy grin and shakes his head. "Mr. Hamby, you be an educated man. You cain't believe a worried stationmaster with a crystal ball. His timetable is nothín but wishful thinkín." The brakeman walks near us carrying his brush and bucket. Sam raises his voice so the man can hear. "Yes sir, da bosses hate it when we lose a rider specially when a fool's laziness kills one. Ain't that right Herman?" The brakeman mutters an unkind cuss, spits on the ground, and keeps on walking. Sam whispers, "An incomer died cause Herman ignored a filthy toilet. He'll forfeit this trip's pay but he shoulda got sacked. Nobody asks me so I do my job and mind my own business. Well, the lounge porter needs help filling his potty barrels. Mr. Hamby you stay put ya hear?"

I'll stay close but I can't sit in the stuffy coach. Across the railyard is a buckboard wagon with its swayback mule tied to a telegraph pole. The mule stretches his lead to snag a bite of sweetgrass while a leathered old woman serves food from back of her wagon. This is not the usual vendor stand; folks milling about the wagon look like locals and railmen.

The cookpot aroma draws me closer; I've not smelt anything so exotic or tempting while our food bag waifs of bruised apples and aging bread. I must see what's being offered. My girls join me and I say to Anne, "We've watched our budget and deserve a real meal."

"Do you want to try the Harvey House?"

"No, it's much too expensive. The sign on that wagon says three tacos for a dime."

"What's a taco?"

"Damned if I know but it smells tempting."

The three of us walk up to the wagon and the old woman smiles, "Buoy knows tar they seine your. Poo aye dough a you dare low."

Say what? Her words make no sense and I glance to Anne who whispers, "Go ahead and ask your question."

I can't understand the old woman but I give it a go. "Do you speak American?"

"No a blow in glees, sin ore. Um moment poor favor." The woman turns to a shadow playing beside the wagon. "Me guile ben a key."

I turn to leave when a small boy runs up and tugs on my coat. "Hey mister my granny speaks only Española and her native Téwa. I am Miguel and I will order for you."

Anne smiles at the boy. "Hello Miguel. What a bright young man you are. We'd like to try your granny's food but we don't know what to order."

"Do you like beans, corn, and pig?"

"Yes we do."

"A quarter gets you a full plate and a drink. Mi abuela wraps the carnitas in her corn tortillas. She is the best cook in all of Wenatchee!"

His pint-sized bravado enchants my Annie. "Excellent! Serve up two plates please."

Miguel turns to his elder. "Nana, dose plate toes pear lose grin goes e sir vases poor favor."

It's gibberish to me but the granny understands and serves the food. Our tiny waiter balances the plates and cups enroute to a picnic table under a nearby tree.

"Is this okay señora?"

My wife sniffs her cup. "Miguel honey, is this beer?"

"Sí."

"Do you have a drink without alcohol?"

"Of course, un momento por favor." Miguel returns the rejected brew to his granny who takes a sip before stirring the rest into her pot. The old woman raps something in newsprint and hands it to Miguel, she pours a new drink, whacks the top of her grandson's head with her spoon and Miguel returns with a cup and the wrapped gift.

"Here you are señora, this is nana's sarsaparilla. The fry bread is for the little one, no charge. La salsa molé is very spicy today so you be careful, yes?"

Miguel stands next to me with an expectant smile. Anne pokes me. "I think our waiter wants a gratuity."

"Certainly, his service is impeccable." I smile and give Miguel five pennies. "Two coins for you and three for your granny. Please thank her for her kindness."

The smiling boy pockets his coins and heads back to the wagon. Miguel's right about the pepper sauce; it does break a sweat. I finish my part and all of Belle's leftovers. Tacos are my new favorite food.

"Anne you must learn to make this meal, especially the fried bread. Let's wrap up the rest for breakfast."

I give Miguel and his grandma a salute and we head back to the train where Sam helps Anne up the steps. He offers me a shiny foil-wrapped cigar from his coat pocket and whispers, "It's pinched from the first-class humidor so don't tell nobody where you got it. How'd you like Maria's food? Good eats eh?"

I give the pricy stinker an obligatory sniff and put it in my tin. It will make a fine gift. "Thanks Sam, Maria's food has a kick but it's tasty. I love the fluffy bread!"

"Yup the frybread's Maria's specialty. It's a decent dessert and the ole girl knows it. She don't share the recipe with nobody. Maria migrated here from the Mex-Hopi territory to pick fruit. The ole girl cain't climb a ladder no more so she feeds a lucky fella. Claims she cain't speak English though I speck she can. Maria once told me her native words is prettier than mine." Sam chuckles, "I says to her Miz Maria, everythin's prettier than me."

"So you speak her languages?"

"I speak a little Spanish but it don't matter; Maria's always got a grandbaby talkin for her. I do admire your gumption sir. Not many passengers eat her food."

Anne smiles at our porter. "Sam you must call us Anne and Jackson. Honestly, we're not daring as much as thrifty. Lucky for us Maria is a marvelous cook."

The chatty porter smiles back. He doesn't share a nicked cigar or an earnest talk with other fares. We Hamby's aren't big tippers but we're nicer than most. "Yup you did good Miss Anne." Our porter sighs. "My oh my, I'm done in. Wrestling heavy water barrels gits harder by the day. The wife wants me to retire on her porch swing.

Do I look like a swinger to you? Nope, I cain't see livín on a pension just yet so I'll finagle another trip or two. Tomorrow we go over the mountain and into Seattle. I reckon y'all are happy about that! You're almost home."

I guess I should be happy but I'm worried. Will I feel at home? Has my office found us a place to live? Was my family right about me? Oh stop your fretting Jackson. You got this far and there's no turning back. Your wallet's almost empty and it's a long sorry walk back to Chance Hollow.

CHAPTER 7

Home at Last?

$\mathcal{A}$ lower rack and near empty car made for a pleasant sleep. The dawn signals day five of travel as a stationmaster stands on a deserted platform calling all aboard. The porters do not snap to attention or offer precision salutes. They yawn, snatch up their stepstools, hop aboard and disappear inside the cars. Washington state is a long way from civilization's pomposity.

The engineer swapped the flatbed for a second engine. Sam says we'll need the extra oomph to trek up the Cascade Mountains. Our train flies through miles of orchards spewing smoke and ash over the river valley. We slow down at Icicle Flats where boulders the size of parlor chairs lay aside the tracks. Weary workers sit atop the rocks toasting us with flasks meant to vanquish the morning chill. We open our windows and sing thank yous for their labor. West of Icicle Flats is a rapid creek colored green with glacial runoff fed by dozens of tiny waterfalls jutting from the cliffsides.

Our path shrivels as we ascend along a mountain ledge. The eagle's view of the canyon is beautiful but not for the faint of heart. All of a sudden the peaks and harrowing valley disappear and we plunge into absolute darkness. The eleven-mile tunnel dwarfs the dank limestone caverns back home. Our only light is Sam's lantern casting eerie shadows onto the rock outside our cabin window. A wide-eyed Belle clings to my vest as clanking wheelsets reverberate underneath.

My pocket watch ticks away a half-hour before the daylight and an icy sleet greet us. Both sides of the track are cloaked in a thick green virgin forest.

A church bell signals midday when our train pulls into its sleepy town. The lumber hamlet bills itself as 'Skykomish at Heaven's Gate.' That's what a sign over the stationhouse claims and being cloaked in clouds makes it believable. The train engineer stands at the snack shack sorting through a jar of pickled eggs. His is a curious profession and I wonder what kind of man steers a massive snaking train. I walk up beside him and fill my coffee tin. "Good day sir, may I ask how you navigate through the maze of peaks and valleys?"

His smile reveals a sizeable pair of buckteeth. "Hell's bells sonny, you cain't steer a wildebeestie! The brakeman and me feeds her belly like madmen on the incline and I grips the brake for all I'm worth on the downslide. Rail and gravity owns the rest." The engineer pops two whole eggs into his mouth and his cheeks bulge making him look like a chubby chipmunk. The man tips his cap, waddles back to his beast, tugs a chain and the steam whistle squeals.

We leave Heaven's Gate headed down the mountain in an icy drizzle that makes the engineer brake for all he's worth. Our ride is as terrifying and delightful as a coaster at the state fair. It must be awful for the boxcar folks who hold on for dear life.

The rain stops when we enter the westward foothills. Logged forests give a peekaboo glimpse of Puget Sound and the rural stops build anticipation of our arrival.

Three hours later passengers cheer as our train enters the King Street station. What a week! Sam crosses himself and grabs his necklace medallion. "Saints be praised, ole Christopher saved us again! The traveler's patron delivered us safe and sound. Well most of us anyways."

What a hoot to hear him praise a pendant! No modern man believes in ancestral superstitions. I keep my opinion to myself and grease Sam's palm with my last coin. Annie does me one better with a hug and Sam's wrinkled skin conceals a blush.

"Mr. Jackson and Miss Anne it's been a pleasure to serve you. All the best to you and little Belle."

We're in line to claim our steamer trunk and I say to the clerk, "Why does the room sway? Is it an earthquake?"

The clerk smiles. "No sir it's a case of rail legs playing with your equilibrium but you'll be normal by the morning."

Belle tugs at her mommy's skirt asking for the potty and my girls leave me wondering what to do. An office mate was supposed to meet us. Where can he be?

A few minutes later my question's answered when a man bursts through the front door shouting, "Has anybody seen Jackson Hamby?"

I call out with a sigh of relief, "Over here sir!"

The poor fellow's gulping for air. "Phewy! I'm Floyd Snypes at your service. Hope you didn't wait long. The train ran late and I still missed my time. Sorry about that." Snypes pauses for another breath. "I had the freight yard deliver your crate to your place. Lucky for you the goods are intact. We figured you'd be tired so my Carrie's fixing supper."

How does he know my goods are intact? Did Snypes open my crate? Mind you there's a fine line between helping and snooping. Jeez Jackson! Miss Carrie probably needed our dishes to feed us.

Snypes seems harmless enough and he's offering a homecooked meal. "I'm grateful for your help Mr. Snypes."

"Just Floyd will do. Carrie's my wife for better or worse. I borrowed a wagon from the city yard. What say we load up and get you home?"

"Wonderful! I look forward to a good meal and a bed."

My girls join Floyd and I as we finish loading the trunk. I help Anne up top next to Floyd while Belle and I sit on the trunk with the buckboard at our backs.

Floyd takes us north along a craggy dock spur. Belle's delighted as the cart bounces on the gravel road but I fear a rut might bust an axle. Floyd seems adept at dodging disaster so I relax and enjoy the view. Before me is a déjà vu look at the Olympic mountains, anchored sailing ships and a marina full of fishing boats. This is the postcard scene I coveted in mama's kitchen so long ago.

The bruising ride is mercifully short. Floyd turns the horses uphill onto a dirt road lined with identical row houses with a stunning water view. However the locale is rustic and definitely not Seattle proper.

Floyd says, "This is tiny Belltown. A pioneer named William Nathaniel Bell settled here until his hubris undid him. The tribes warned Bell not to squat on ancient burial lands but ole Willie ignored them. His hexed family endured Indian raids, house fires, and the consumption but most folks believe the Bells' were besieged by spiteful spirits. Mr. Bell lived to be seventy with little memory of past events. I suppose dementia's a blessing for some. That was over sixty years ago and a Belltown rental is still dirt cheap. Jackson do you believe in spirits?"

"Absolutely not."

"In case you change your mind, my wife's priest does a house cleansing and our place's peaceful except for Carrie barking at me."

Floyd stops in front of a tiny cabin. This is nothing like the Campbell house but Anne thinks it's cute and heads along a stone walkway in search of a backyard garden space. A picket fence separates our property from the next and I swear I can touch the neighbor's window.

Oh my! The backyard's a muddy mess with a new pumphouse and not much else. There's room enough for a garden though it'll take a lot of work. A delivery alley runs along the back of the properties.

Creaking wooden steps lead us under the house. Low ceiling beams cause me to stoop as I adjust my eyes to survey the dank cellar. One corner has a coal chute feeding into an apple crate. A labyrinth of spider webs connects the clammy stone walls and an earthen floor reeks of a musty pong.

Annie squeezes my hand. "No worries dear, it needs a good cleaning, a stone floor, and canning shelves. Perhaps a cider keg for you."

I frown, "And an exorcism to evict the spooks."

Annie looks down at a wide-eyed little Belle. "Not funny Jackson."

We move the tour back out front where steep steps go up to a covered porch big enough for two chairs or a swing. However, the roominess ends at the entry.

The front door opens into a living room the size of my in-law's reading parlor. There is no foyer or proper closet. Inside the door is a five-point antler rack hanging just inside the door; I assume it's for coats.

A sizable wood stove sits against the far wall of the room. It's large enough to heat the space and our dinner's bubbling on its burners. The relic uses wood so why the coal box in the cellar?

Two high back chairs and a pipe stand sits near the stove. Behind the sitting area is a dining table and behind the table is a lane where Miss Carrie bustles between the icebox, prepping counter, and a hand-pump sink. Do I dare call it a kitchen or is it a galley?

Not wanting to bother his wife, Floyd guides us into the short hallway. The hall goes by a linen closet enroute to two doors on opposite sides of the hall. Our bedroom holds a full-sized double bed, an armoire, and a petite potbelly stove in the corner. Belle's room is smaller with bunkbeds, a dresser, and a potbelly stove. The cellar coal must be for the bedrooms.

We circle back to Miss Carrie for an introduction. Our hostess looks to be a tad older than Anne. My wife smiles, "Missus Snypes, your kindness is a blessing."

"Please call me Carrie. You've had a long journey and it's the least we can do. The dinner's almost ready."

"How can I help?"

"No you go relax. Floyd will set the table. You two make yourselves at home."

I grab my wife's hand. "Let's explore the back porch." Floyd said the outhouse was in piss-poor condition. The landlord replaced it with a newfangled inhouse septic flush but there's no toilet room in the house. I walk outside and turn left through a curtained doorway. The space holds a water trough, a washboard and a water barrel connected to a roof drain. The trough is big enough to wash clothes or a body. There's a hook outside the room with a clothesline that runs the length of the porch. I imagine it also stretches across the yard to the shed. Rain or shine we can dry clothes in the sea breeze.

The other side of the porch has a tiny room with a Dutch door. I open the door and Eureka! There sits my throne. Thank God I won't need a chamber pot! I say to Anne, "Well the toilet's almost indoors. Its plank walls aren't chinked and I must seal the holes to keep out the wind."

My wife sits on the backstep waving for me to join her. I sit down and put my arm around her waist. "Sorry babe, this isn't your parent's comfortable house."

"Be patient Jackson. My folks started out just like us and we'll make this a home. It's furnished and the landlord put in a new well and a septic tank. That's a plus. Pity he didn't finish with a grass lawn. I'll make a garden plot and start a patch of grass for Belle. You'll fix up my canning room and lay a stone path for deliveries. I'll not have mud tracked into my house."

"Yes dear, right after I fix the toilet seat. It's a relic from the outhouse and I'll need a plainer to smooth out the splinters. The wood's too rough for Belle's little tush."

"I doubt her comfort is your only concern. You can order a porcelain seat at the mercantile."

"Good idea, I'll buy it with my first paycheck. For now I'll need a plainer."

Miss Carrie calls out, "Soups on. Come and get it."

I squeeze Anne. "Saved by the dinner bell! Let's go enjoy a delicious homecooked meal."

We sit with our hands folded for Grace but Floyd misses the cue. He reaches for the stew pot and Miss Carrie jabs his thumb with her fork. Floyd winces and gives her a woeful stare. Ha! I didn't expect supper and a show. Anne kicks me under the table to stifle my smirk.

I mustn't complain to Miss Carrie but her supper lacks a proper seasoning. To be fair it's better than aging apples and stale bread. Anne and Carrie are planning a trip to the market while Floyd talks of work. His insights are mostly gossip. "Andy's a good fellow but Mr. Barr's assistant is a pain. Ole Nesbitt is a pufferfish and bossier than the boss man himself. Carrie and I live up the road so I'll walk you to work in the morning. Be ready by six o'clock sharp."

I nod and try not to yawn. Floyd is clueless but Miss Carrie takes notice. She clears the plates and orders Floyd to the sink. They wash our dishes and Carrie ushers Floyd out the front door. He waves and repeats, "Six o'clock sharp!"

"They're an odd pair don't you think? I bet there's a fun story about those two."

"Let's talk in the morning. It's time for bed."

The homecoming was nice but I relish our time alone. I tuck a sleepy Belle into her bed and crawl into mine. The train inertia still plays with my senses as a tremor sways the bed. It's an illusion and I focus on the whimsical sound of our porch chimes. This is a welcome change from the clattering train.

I am thousands of miles from Indiana yet a stranger in my own house. It must be the exhaustion troubling me. Why all the trepidation? This is what you wanted, to be alone with your bride beside you. I turn towards Anne with my best come-hither look. Alas, my wife is already asleep. It's probably for the best; vertigo and exhaustion surely ruin a lovemaking.

I'm halfway into the Lord's Prayer when a tiny hand touches my sleeve. "Daddy my room has spooks."

"Belle Elizabeth there's no such thing."

"But you said the cellar's full of them and now they're in my room!"

"Honey daddy was joking. The stove heat's probably casting shadows onto your wall. Come here baby." I put Belle between Anne and me just like bedtime in the hollow. It's a comfort really. "Go to sleep precious. Tomorrow we're gonna sleep in our own beds."

CHAPTER 8

Welcome to Seattle

Dawdling stars fill the predawn sky. My wobbliness is gone but a worry lingers. What's it like to work in a big city office? Anne prepares our breakfast as I shave in the sink. I'm not good with a straight razor and her proximity makes me nervous. Perhaps a mirror and a basin on the back porch would be safer.

We finish our coffee and Anne says, "Floyd's running late."

"It's his way I guess but what can I do? I don't know the way to work."

Belle and I help mommy clean the galley until Floyd calls from the road. "Hey Jackson get a wiggle on. We're way late so let's be quick about it."

I rush out the door and down the porch steps. Whoa! A slippery third step sends me flying with both feet in the air and I grab the rail to stop my fall.

"Ooey! Come on man! Stop playing around. We can't be tardy on your first day."

"I'll tackle that slimey moss after work. I can't have my girls tumbling down the stairs."

We race off conversing as best we can and I say, "What is that musty smell? It wasn't here yesterday. Is it fish guts from the cannery dump?"

"Nope. The seagulls and rats pick the pile clean. It must be the minus tide. The fog pushes chimney smoke to the ground and it mingles with the kelp odor. A high tide takes the smell away. I'm used to it so I don't notice. This here's the trolley stop. It climbs Profanity hill on the hour. The ride's pricey and truth is, we can walk it quicker than a horse. If you don't mind we'll hoof it and save a penny."

"Folks in Indiana would call this a massif slope. I guess I'll add whittling a cane to my chore list."

Here I am in a real office and frankly it disappoints. Floyd's desk is buried in papers, a busy clerk named Andy sits next to Floyd and the persnickety Mr. Nesbitt guards the boss's door. I reckon that sums it up. Ha! Sums it up! Anne never laughs at my accounting humor but it's funny all the same.

The paper stacks are a towering bore and the office safe holds no mystery. A man of considerable girth lumbers out of his private office. My mates snap to parade rest and say good morning sir. Our benefactor nods to each man as he makes his way to me.

Samuel Clayton Barr extends his hand. "Welcome aboard Mr. Hamby. I trust Snypes helped you and the wife settle in."

Ole Nesbitt breaks our handshake and hands Mr. Barr his briefcase. "Sir you're late and the council's waiting."

I doubt Mr. Barr heard my genial (albeit rehearsed) reply. His doorkeeper pushed me aside and led our boss into the hallway.

Floyd whispers, "Don't be offended. That's typical for Nesbitt. Mr. Barr does the politics and we do the work. Take heed Jackson, a trip to his chamber is no social call and it's best to stay clear of Mr. Barr. You're low man on the totem pole so your desk guards the door. Just greet a customer, find out what he wants, and direct him to one of us. Try to be friendly even if you get an ornery cuss. I left a few simple permits and estate plans in your basket. Give it a go and I'll answer your questions."

I have a question; what was I thinking moving to this odd locale?

Carrie Snypes knocks at the front door. Anne's helping Belle get dressed and calls from the bedroom, "Come on in Carrie. There's coffee on the stove."

"It's a lovely day Anne with not one cloud's in the big blue sky. We best be quick to the market; our take is freshest in the morn and gone if we dawdle."

"Of course. I'll get Belle's coat and we'll be off."

"My mama's house is on the way. We can drop the sweetie off there." Carrie's voice takes on a wistful sadness. "Mama loves babies."

"Belle is one of several grandbabies though she's the only girl. I imagine your mother pesters you and Floyd to start a family."

"Mama's waiting on a miracle. I got pregnant last year but it didn't take. Doc says the clap caused my miscarry. My Floyd's got a weakness for dock whores and his rabbiting around done broke my babymaker. Sure he's sorry but he don't stop. A week after the funeral he poked his wick into another dirty candle! The prickers can eat spoils and sleep in the nursery until doomsday for all I care! Mama figured Floyd right off but I didn't listen. She says Floyd's a warped piece of wood and now all I hear is her sassy 'I told ya so.' Being a good Catholic I'm stuck with Floyd until death frees me. The bugger hasn't been in church since the wedding and my priest says it's my duty to drag him to the confessional. I tried but the wicked debaucher won't repent. He says

God made him this way so he don't need a priest's pardon. I swear it's gonna be him or me!"

"Oh dear girl! So many women endure a still birth. I've been spared though I've sat with those in mourning. It is a trying time." Anne doesn't know what to say about Floyd. Seattle is not Chance Hollow.

I spend my first day orienting myself with liquor permits and estate papers. Perusing a will is interesting but it's no grand task. Ten hours later I'm headed back down Profanity hill. A warm sun dried my mossy steps but I'm not fooled. I'll scrape the murderous green fur after supper. This place needs work yet it's all mine. There's no father kibitzing my every move and an absent landlord sends his solicitor to collect the rent.

The trip to the market consumed most of Anne's day. Belle's helping unpack our belongings and Anne wants to start supper; her look begs me to take Belle away. "Let's go Bellie. You and papaw can walk to the water."

Elliot Bay is everything I imagined with an energy that amazes the senses. The papers described a heaven on earth without capturing its sounds and smells. Belle and I sit on a log watching the rhythm of waves march ashore and I'm delighted to see Belle as infatuated as her daddy.

Meanwhile our mistress prepares her first supper. It's a bittersweet moment without family to impress. Belle and I return as Anne takes the main course from the stove. "Hey, you two take off your shoes. I won't have sand in my house."

I stand corrected. This is not my domain; it belongs to Mrs. Hamby. Anne relates Carrie's saga while she plates our food. I stick my finger into the berry dessert bound for the stovetop. "Floyd's a catch all right. It's good to hear Carrie's cookery was by design but she might've rested his penance for our sakes."

I didn't eat much on the train so I'm ravenous. Anne's a better cook than Carrie Snypes. Her pan-fried salmon, corn fritters, and green beans with bits of bacon are a delight and the Marionberry cobbler is a sweet treat.

Anne puts Belle to bed while I tackle the mossy step. I'm done first so I set a pot of tea and a second helping of dessert on the table. This moment is my dream come true.

It's midway through my second workday and I'm already bored. I make a mental note to impress my boss so he'll expand my humdrum duties.

Our building on prestigious First Hill is surrounded by mansions with a breathtaking view of Elliott Bay. Superior men do not sweat and the early pundits built this majestic castle for an easy commute from their homes. They did not consider their unfortunate underlings. Without a buggy or trolley it was and is an exhausting climb. Circumstances are different now. I'm told the snooty matrons dislike us and the new trolley makes it easy for the bosses to keep their offices downtown.

Floyd and I sit on the entrance steps eating our lunch. He sums it up, "Yup this place is as useless as tits on a bull. We hate the hill and a hoity missus thinks we're stinkweed in her garden. Ahh, but a copper begs a shift up here. The Chapel District is dangerous work while a First Hill patrol shoos away peddlers or helps a sloshed dandy find his way. A hilltop gent tips the copper for a courtesy sleepover in our tiny jail. It beats listening to his preachy wife!"

The banter's interesting but what about the upcoming changes? "Do you know about the move? Nesbitt says the courthouse is closing and we're headed down the hill."

"Ole fussbudget's right though the fire's barely lit. It takes a county levy to move us and Mr. Barr's mired in the politics of the vote."

"Well I'm all for it! The view goes away but so does a slippery climb!"

I take in the vista and sea breeze while I can. The cooler temps and low humidity are a relief from the muggy Midwest. It's a joy to behold and I'm reveling in the moment until a pair of walkers distracts me. The girl is a true beauty with an infectious laugh and her companion is an elder Oriental man who wears a fine tailored suit, a bowler hat and a braided ponytail hanging down his back. Where does he hail from?

Seattle challenges my Midwestern upbringing but it's not that different. Seems there's an unspoken apple-pie orderliness everywhere I go. Even homely Chance Hollow had a colored livery man. His youngest child and I played chess in the church basement while our parents prayed upstairs. That was it; he mustn't hang with me in the schoolyard. Apple-pie orderly has its limits. Proper Seattle twinges at the sight of Indians, negroes, and incomers. The unsaid rule keeps everyone in their place.

So why is this man uptown with a white woman? Her beauty makes a dead man rise up and take notice. The man's lucky to be with her but what does she see in him? A look at his expensive suit says it all.

Floyd was born here and barely notices the pair. My mate gives them a nod and tosses a bit of Carrie's stale lunch to the seagulls. "Just a fancy wagtail and her boy out for a stroll. This ain't your Indiana homeland."

"A prostitute, really? I've never seen one before! Who is she?"

"Mr. Hamby I've some experience in the matter so let me school you. Sometimes pretty ain't worth the risk and you best stay clear of that one. The girl will empty your pockets and she's a danger to boot. Most all agree she killed Caleb Ambary and got away with it. Her name's Ellie and she worked for Lou Graham. Sweet Lou covered up the mess and kept the girl from the gallows." Floyd tosses more of Carrie's spite to the shrilling birds.

"Lou Graham is the name on the estate file you gave me. What kind of man was he?"

"My apologies. Nasty Nesbitt gave me the file to get my goat. I've a weakness for street girls so the jokes on me. By the by, Lou Graham was the queen madame of White Chapel and I was happy to work the case until Carrie caught me red-peckered. Miss Holy Britches skipped Mass to sneak after me. Now she's sewn my fly shut and I can't catch a break cause her pope forbids divorce. What does a priest know about marriage anywho? Diddlysquat that's what! Carrie says I'm going to hell and she bought herself a black dress for my wake. I think she's poisoning me. Can you smell arsenic in my sandwich? Does that beggar seagull look sick to you? My daddy says a man with wicked urges must clean his own musket and I'm polishing mine like a madman. The Graham file was a temptation so I gave it to you."

Floyd does paint a colorful metaphor. "I can manage the file but why is the will reading on First Hill? Isn't the White Chapel district down by the docks?"

"Lardy Jackson you gots lots to learn. Lou Graham was no ordinary madame. She was richer than rich. Take the file and welcome to Seattle!"

Floyd stands and walks up the courthouse steps. What kind of gift has he bestowed? I rush upstairs to dissect the will but it's sealed and the attached business papers show no hint of nefarious trade. Whatever favor I've gained must wait until tomorrow. With its grand intrigue—the Queen City continues to amaze!

CHAPTER 9

A Murderess You Say

I couldn't sleep wondering what today might bring. Here I am on the steps of a prodigious First hill mansion wondering what's behind its front door. With the Graham reputation, I doubt it'll be a somber affair.

Perhaps this bizarre doorknocker foretells the event. A playful ten-inch silver mermaid stands on her tail atop a wave. She has a voluptuous torso and braids of copper hair hang over her breasts like a discreet veil. The seamaid's amethyst eyes beg me to touch her so I grip the erotic creature and giggle. Jackson Hamby you are such a child. I regain my composure and give the knocker three whacks.

Can a will reading rival the bawdiest of vaudeville shows or might it unravel the mystery of Caleb Ambary's death? Is this Ellie girl a real murderess? Am I a clueless actor being tossed onto an immersive stage? Good heavens Jackson you've got a fertile imagination!

A disinterested servant answers the door, checks my credentials, and guides me to a lavish parlor just off the grand foyer. "Are you aware of the time? You're way early. Be respectful and take a seat; I can't have you wandering about."

I was so excited I didn't pay attention to the clock. "No worries sir. I am a gentleman..." The surly servant turns and walks away before I finish talking.

A large portrait looms over the parlor fireplace. Who might the beauty be? The black crape adorning the picture frame is a dead giveaway. Lou Graham looks down at me, her blue eyes glistening as if she heard my pun. It's spooky; she seems to follow my every move. Don't be silly. It's only the glint of humidity on the canvas.

A blazing fire warms the space yet I'm chilled to the bone. I move to the far corner of the room. What again? The elegant chair next to me compels me to sit. Am I being haunted? I opt to stand and play along. "Hello Madame. Tell me, are the chair's jewels precious or fake?"

"They're real all right. Tis an original Louis XIV Les os de mouton with gold-leaf inlay."

Did the spook just reply? That is ridiculous! Ghosts aren't real so I spin about to confront my imagination. There it is again, the laughter from yesterday noon. No ghost glides from the hallway into the parlor. This vision is a live mankiller.

"Sorry to disappoint, I'm not Miss Lou. Is it me or does her chair look lonely. No one dared sit there save our mistress and the expectant vultures still avoid her seat. You'd think out of respect but it's really a fear of haunting."

The enchantress smiles and settles into the chair like an heir apparent. This girl doesn't fear spirits or the living. Is she mocking me or merely confirming my caution.

"We held a séance last night and Lou sat here just like a thousand nights before. She laughed and toasted us with a glass of her finest brandy." The girl makes a toasting motion, lets her hand fall onto the chair and stares at the portrait above the fireplace. "How can someone so vibrant leave me all alone? I'm very annoyed with you dearest."

She turns to me. "Doc says it was a hazard of the profession. Such poppycock! 'Twas a cruel twist on a hornswoggle of a life." Her focus mimics the portrait's intensity. "You seem familiar, have we met?"

"No, I'm n-new and m-moved here for w-work. I was on the c-court steps when you s-strolled by. I'm j-j-Jackson Hamby."

She sits silently as if waiting on me. What caused a return to my youthful stutter? I stumble again, "I'm here to n-notarize the w-will reading." How embarrassing! I quit my stammer years ago yet I've lost control again. "You c-called her m-mistress and not madame?" That was judgmental and unkind. Have I offended the girl?

"A stranger might wonder if I'm a whore, a servant, or family. Tis debatable for sure without checking the facts."

What a relief! The girl is unaffected by my awkward act and her manners mimic the door knocker's playfulness. She stands and takes my hand. Such a strong grip! Most women shake like a limp fish.

"Tis a pleasure to meet you Jack. May I call you Jack? Jackson's a bit formal, don't ya think? My given name is Ellis but do call me Ellie. Seems Miss Lou's pleased you came so let's sit and chat, shall we? This house is duller than dull but I've a tale as savory a sipper as Lou's brandy. It'll take away the chill of this mausoleum."

I want to shout: 'Yes! I hang on to your every word! Some folks say you're a murderess. Is it true or a metaphor for your killer smile? Beautiful! Your eyes are liquid pools of green and hazel stardust and the cadence of your lilting accent enchants this bumbling clod. Tell me your story dear charming Ellie and fill my day with your laughter!' Of course, I say no such thing. I've better etiquette and mama would sorely pinch me. With manners in tow I offer, "Miss Ellie I am delighted to have your company."

Ellie smiles, "C'mon Jack Hamby and have a sit."

She keeps my hand and leads me to the settee in the bay window. Ellie releases me and sits down with one arm resting on the back rim of the couch. Her free hand wiggles a come-hither finger at me.

Is she flirting? I am a dunce when it comes to divining women yet I doubt she's dangerous. I see coy and seductive but not a killer. I can't believe Floyd's foreboding portrayal so I'll forego caution and learn for myself. Ellie's allure is a mystery and I'm somehow connected to it though I can't fathom why. Yes I must sit and listen if only to hear her lilting Gaelic voice.

CHAPTER 10

Patron Saint or Sinner?

*A*nne Hamby shoulders a pickaxe borrowed from Carrie Snypes, little Belle wraps her hand around mommy's thumb and they march down the back porch steps. Belle sits on a patchwork quilt away from danger as Anne rolls up her sleeves. "Honey the seasons are different here. A planting can't wait on daddy and we don't need him really. I grew up tending the family gardens and we've got the Campbell spirit with us. We can do this!"

Belle jumps as the first swing bounces back at mommy. The blade barely broke the glacial-till forcing Anne to tighten her grip. This is not Indiana's black soil. She raises the axe higher, swings and inches deeper into the clay. The axe stops with a thud, Anne grabs an unearthed stone and tosses it in Belle's direction.

"It's okay babe, sweat will win the day."

Belle sorts her stones into three piles. Mommy wants the cellar floor to be a cushion of small bits topped by larger flat pieces. The third pile of larger stones is for daddy to bury as a well-drained footpath. With the rainy season coming, a raised path will keep the mud outdoors and there'll be no dirt tracked into mommy's house.

"It's a relief to work the soil again. We mustn't stray from nature's touch. Our Ojibway friends say we're a mix of stardust and earth and I feel my best when I'm tending a garden." Anne wipes her brow and takes another swing. "I admit leaving family was difficult. It's sad to be so far away but we couldn't stay. Don't tattle on me girl; this is our little secret. I chose your dad with eyes wide open and I know the man better than he knows himself. He's a decent soul; a dreamer with potential and I believe in him. Still a practical woman ferrets her choices. This is what grandma told me: Easygoing and kindness endures long after pretty and charming fades. Carrie Snype bless her heart chose sweet talk over merit. Your dad grabs a fragrant rose, thorns, and all. The man can't read a room to save his soul but his gentleness made him my obvious choice. I will always be his respite." Anne smiles at Belle sorting her stones. "You are so much like your father. I doubt you heard a word I said."

Anne raises the pick high in the air and lets gravity break more soil. Mrs. Hamby is making a home.

Back at Graham manor: Ellie and Jack sit in the bay window unaware of the arriving guests. Ellie speaks in a mesmerizing Irish lilt. "I know I'll soon be well-heeled. I loyally served the houses of Lou Graham but not out of obligation. I love her in the truest sense of the word. The rumors about our mistress are half-baked at best. Detractors think she's a common prostitute but I swear there's nothing common about her. No street girl lifts an entire town out of bankruptcy and Lou Graham did just that! Can you solve a riddle Jack Hamby? How can an infamous sinner also be a patron saint? Miss Lou saved many a soul including me and this is our side of the story."

I joined Lou's House when I was but ten years old. No she didn't groom me to entertain. Our mistress was a fine judge of character and she knew I couldn't be a consort.

Lou said, "Ellie you've no patience for pandering. We are all blessed with unique gifts and the parlor is not yours."

Thanks to Lou I became a writer. She saw through the street slime to cultivate my potential. Sweet Lou had a talent for discerning substance over bravado.

Ellie breaks from her story. "Jack have you wandered about this grand monstrosity?"

"No, the butler was clear…"

Ellie butts in. "No worries, you can see it another time. I hate this mausoleum. Yes it served its purpose. However, grand living is nothing but a stage prop that wows until you get close enough to see it's all for show. Miss Lou played the game but her passions ran deeper than material looks. Let's get back to my story, shall we?"

Miss Lou practiced the art of being and she expected no less from her staff. Expanding our world came as natural as breath to Lou. Our mistress filled her library with the classics, hired tutors and insisted her work-family speak two languages. Skid-roaders barely learned their letters while I studied German, grammar, history, finance, and music. Miss Lou painted this life with a broad canvas; an open mind and insight were her brushes.

I do a fair impression of the ole girl. She'd say, "An education unlocks us. Grammar, history, and arithmetic are necessities for this life. However those endeavors won't help us realize the true bodhi. Satisfaction evades us without a deep-seated reflection. The Oceti Sakowin people say Mitakuye Oyasin; it means All My Relations. We are all woven into one cosmic fabric and tearing at the majestic weave dooms a man to be a pittance of his intended self."

Our poetic mistress honored the great fabric though she kept two peeves. Lou loathed bad grammar and cruel behavior. She said, "A dummkopf is a waste of time but the wicked must never be ignored. A cretin always digs his own grave and we must be there to hand him a shovel!"

Ellie again breaks from her tale. "Jack it's important you understand us as humans and not 'those people.' Did I give a clear sense of our mistress?"

"Is that a rhetorical question Miss Ellie?"

"Oh very feisty sir, I'm told I do ramble. 'Twas a gift from me dad, the prince of talkers. I'll keep to my story."

Ellie drifts in time speaking as if her madame lingers nearby. My mistress was born into aristocracy yet she's no arrogant priss. Life's a game of cards to Lou and she's always all-in. The gal lives in present tense so stay awake to engage her. Those who cross Lou Graham reap an unsparing but just consequence.

Lou cultivates her beliefs by reading free thinkers like Henry Thoreau and Ralph Emerson. She despises a pedantic windbag like the arrogant Edward Clark. He claims educating a woman explodes her feeble brain and shrinks the womb. Lou says, "Clark is a cowed grub who picks a fight to feed his own ego. He's afraid of losing his status quo so he pigeonholes us as weaklings. The righteous think I'm Beelzebub's concubine. Such humbug! I need no exorcism. A worn Psalms sits atop my nightstand and its inspiration feeds my prayers."

Lou understands a truer grace than most. She says, "Thoreau didn't tout a righteous vengeance or claim a fallen angel tempts us. Free expression isn't a curse, it is a gift! Like a baby bird we must flap our wings and choosing the nest over soaring is a waste of feathers! It's no accident that every holy book has a flowery respite. The Creator is our root and we are entwined as Its fruit. We triumph with nature as our kin and fail when we abuse it. Yes, reverence for all is our true calling and a true pulpiteer preaches our affinity. So beware a snide gospeler who preys on the fearful. To paraphrase Voltaire: We mustn't preach absurdity or condone atrocities against others lest our arrogance and contempt destroy us all."

Lou doesn't believe in titles or naming things after ourselves. She says its folly to seek perpetuity and we're better off living in the moment. Yes, she's wealthy but it's her company folks treasure; Lou always makes a castaway feel worthy. 'Twas Providence that left me on her doorstep and I know I'm the better for it.

Lou calls us kindred spirits. She and I are immigrants born of clueless fathers. My family's port of call was Belfast some eight years after Lou left Europe. Lou was but sixteen-years-old when she boarded a steamer in Bremen Germany. I often pester her about the past but she won't share. "Ellie let it be, Bavaria was just a birthplace. I'm here now with no need to look backward."

"I can't help it Miss Lou. Secrets hide in a nutshell and I must crack the nut for its prize."

Lou Graham was a tough nut to crack and what I know of her before Seattle is a patchwork of gossipers' tales.

CHAPTER 11

Bon Voyage!

Rumor says Lou was born Dorothea Emilé Oben in Hamburg town. She's named after her Omá and the family calls her Emilé to avoid confusion.

Her Bavarian father lost his title under Prussian rule but he has royal Austrian ties and the family lives an opulent life. Herr Oben travels for business and the tiny heiress rarely sees him. When home her stoic father is a strict patriarch and it's the wife who showers her babes with love. Her mutti's hugs were like burying a head into two fluffy pillows.

Little Emilé is sent to boarding school at age six. She misses her mum and blames Herr Oben for her exile thus Emilé the misfit is born. Her repertoire of mutinous pranks grows with the years as does her reprimands and expulsions. The stodgy Herr Oben pushes back. "A father knows what's best for his child. Emilé will learn her place and ready herself to be another man's challenge."

On her fourteenth birthday the rebel girl receives a note from her father's secretary. It's a summons to a gala celebrating Emmy's betrothal to her brother's college mate. Herr Oben and the boy's dad struck the deal. Her papa says, "The children are strangers but a proper engagement will acquaint them. It is my duty and delight to see this daughter married off."

Emilé stands her ground. "Papa I must decline your dealmaking. I don't want a husband or a bumptious meddler bidding for me."

Herr Oben responds, "Daughter your foul mood is irrelevant. Our parents' pact served both mother and me and our bond grew secure with time." Herr Oben orders his daughter home for a gala arranged by her fiancé's dad.

"So be it papa. It will be a night you'll not forget!"

The train runs late making the portly man on the platform ring his hands. Meister Heinrich is Herr Oben's secretary. Heinrich has dealt with the girl before and knows his worry is justified.

"A German train running late is unacceptable. Where is the Express? Is the sassy child even aboard? There's no telling what the spoiled brat might do."

Twenty minutes later the train limps into the station. A drunken Emilé stumbles from her coach and the furious conductor says to Heinrich, "Take the demon away! She pulled the emergency cord three times and our schedule is ruined! If it weren't for her father's influence she'd be walking home!"

Emilé ignores the porter's rant. "Heinie so good to see you. Have a swig to toast my nuptials."

Heinrich snatches the empty bottle from her hand and tosses it aside. "Miss Emilé your father will blame me for your drunken tardiness. Are you trying to get me sacked?"

Emilé pokes at the man's stomach. "You've gained a belly since last Christmas. No doubt a second helping of cook's food. Still trying to get into her panties?"

Emilé is the only one smiling. Heinrich lifts the girl into the carriage and orders the driver to whip the horses.

Adalard is Emilé's brother. The young man waits on the mansion steps tapping his pocket watch. "For Christ's sake where are they? What is Emilé up to?"

A half-hour later the carriage enters the mansion's circle drive, stops at her brother's feet and Adalard helps Heinrich with his sister.

"Emmy you're late and your breath reeks of alcohol. Father will be furious!"

"Oh get a spine Adie. You care too much what papa thinks. Let's enjoy this lavish fraud, shall we? Do show me to my Romeo!"

Emilé takes her brother's arm, they enter the ballroom and Adalard walks his sister over to his chum. "Bertrand Müeller may I present my sister Emilé."

Emmy smiles, "Oh Adie why so formal with family. Bertie you seem a bit bashful. Relax darling and think of the hefty dowry my papa pays you to be rid of me."

Bertrand blushes as he extends an arm to his pretty fiancé. The girl ignores him, turns away and wanders off amongst the crowd. Her goal is to flirt with all the men.

The dinner chime rings with no Emilé in sight. An irritated Herr Oben barks at Adalard and Bertrand. "Where is Emilé? You were supposed to keep the girl in tow. Search the grounds and get a hand on her."

The boys find Emilé and their classmate swimming in the garden pond. The pair's clothes and an empty flask lay abandoned on the dock. Bertrand squeaks, "Miss Emilé this is not proper. Whatever were you thinking?"

"Oh liebchen don't be a prude. You'll soon have your own dalliances just like our papas."

The betrayal circulates throughout the mansion and a furious Herr Müeller rages, "My wife requires sedation and my son cannot marry a sullied girl. Herr Oben I demand you nullify the agreement and compensate me for this lavish disaster!"

A calmer Herr Oben speaks to the gathering. "My sincere apologies for the girl's conduct. My wife is upstairs tending to our troubled Emilé. Of course the engagement is done and I will reimburse the Müeller family, my apologies to young Bertrand as well. Friends it seems wasteful to ignore Herr Müeller's lavish efforts; please stay and enjoy the festivities. Adalard will assume my hosting duties while I attend to family matters."

Herr Oben's humble act disappears behind closed doors. The failed betrothal is the last straw and this papa is done taming his shrew. Frau Oben tries to heal the rift but her man declares the insolent Emilé persona non-grata and banishes her to a nearby town. With her mum's frequent visits and a monthly stipend delivered by Heinrich, Emilé takes the exile in stride. However recurring stories of her vulgar exploits continue to embarrass Herr Oben.

Heinrich makes a final visit on her sixteenth birthday saying, "Fräulein your father's gift is your emancipation. Herr Oben no longer finances your mischief. The quittance is lavish and comes with a caveat; you must leave Bavaria. Perhaps Paris is a better fit for your coquetries. Here is your funding. Might I suggest a hasty departure benefits all."

Emilé fights back tears; she won't give the pompous Heinrich the satisfaction. "Indeed Heinie, tell papa I accept his terms and request my mutti visit me one last time. I must have her adieu before I go."

Heinrich bows and Emilé forces a smile. She snatches the leather satchel and closes the door.

"The bastard wants me gone. Then fare-thee-well papa, I shall sail away leaving all of Europe in my wake!"

And so Emilé Oben sacks her legacy for a life abroad. Her mum writes often but her letters stop after two years' time. Adalard sends a letter with the awful news: 'Our dear mother has passed away from influenza. Her last words were a prayer for you. Father says you needn't come home.'

"Finally, something papa and I agree upon. Farewell mutti, I will never forget you."

There's more sad news for the Oben clan. A year later Lou reads a news article detailing a Franco-Prussian skirmish at Bapaume France. Prussian oberleutnants Oben and Müeller are listed as casualties. The French author heaped praise on the sniper hidden in a belltower. 'The two Boche boys never heard the patriot rifle's deadly crack.' Adie and Bert were buried in the church graveyard where they fell and fifty comrades joined them before their side won the day.

Adalard was the sole Oben namesake and heir. Tattlers say Herr Oben mourned his son with drink while others whispered of a pregnant servant and hasty marriage. When twin girls were born, Herr Oben sank into deep despair and died of syphlic paralysis a year later. Folks say it was a result of his pandering. The twins remained a rumor until they arrived here to ruin our séance. They're camped upstairs waiting on their inheritance. Did Lou include her half-sisters in the will? We shall see. Lou always said, "A life inherited never satisfies as much as a dream pursued."

Ellie stops her tale and looks out the window at the boats on the bay. "Just like a ship in the fog, Lou was with us for a time and (poof!) she's gone lost in the mist." Ellie sighs and returns to her tale.

A young Emilé sails first-class on a new pristine steamer and New York greets the first voyage of ship and passenger with a brass band and fireworks. Lou disembarks, hails a taxi for a swank hotel and dines at the Delmonico. Tis there the pretty fräulein introduces herself as Lou Graham. Alas her little Emilé went overboard at sea.

Herr Oben didn't leave Lou a dime but she inherited his smarts. Her first parlor serves New York's elite, Lou's business acumen grows her portfolio and that's only the beginning. Miss Lou takes her fortune out west on a bold and risqué adventure. Tis a pity her father never valued the girl's wit. The obstinate coot was too busy trying to break her spirit.

Ellie stands and walks to a table adorned with crystal decanters, pours two glasses and returns to the cozy sofa. "Lou and I met in the fall of 1885 but that's a story for another time. This sherry was a gift from a railroad tycoon the city bosses courted. Seattle didn't win the contract but Miss Lou gets a case of imported spirits every December 24th." Ellie hands me a glass and sits back down. "Back to my tale, shall we?"

CHAPTER 12

Chasing Prosperity

A decade after Lou's voyage the Flannery's departed Ireland on the very same steamship. My dad was chasing prosperity and our migration is a pauper's tale.

The rough north seas made the sail anything but grand. My family shared a steerage cabin with a family of five as desperate as us. The crowded deck offered fresh air but the aging rust bucket still reeked of seasickness and there was a burial at sea almost every day. For two months we bobbed on the waves in an ageing rust bucket powered by my mother's Hail Mary's.

Ellie sinks back into her tale: Our ship of fools arrives in New York with no fanfare or transport to greet us. My family hoofs it using a tattered map mailed to us by my uncle Festus. He didn't meet us at the dock cause his map was the last we heard of him. Folks assume he's dead but there's no proof of it.

Mum and I take turns holding her babe and dad carries the carpetbag. It's an endless walk to an Irish Labor Hall on the lower east side and we trudge through several immigrant ghettos before the Hall comes into view. Tis there a man hands dad a voucher for a hostel we passed two city blocks back.

Turns out our prosperity is a grimy sixth-floor studio flat and lucky for us we've no trunk to haul up the stairs. Our room has a foldup bed for my parents, baby Mike sleeps in the dresser's bottom drawer and I lay on the floor nestled in dad's overcoat. The room has a window with a knotted fire-escape rope, a tiny table with one chair, a camp lamp, and no heat. A communal toilet sits out back of our tenement next to two firepits. House rules say No Cooking and No Food indoors cause a fire danger and the rats.

Our one sure meal comes from the nuns of Sweet Charity who run a kitchen at the Irish parish. The nuns serve porridge and a piece of soda bread twice a day and if ya go to Communion the priest hands out another bite. When a nun looks away I snatch an extra slice from the basket. My thieving beats listening to a boring Mass.

Dad tries hard but there's no steady work and the old guard makes it tough on an incomer. New York overflows with haughty folks who forgot where their ancestors came from. NINA (no Irish need apply) signs are everywhere and gossipers label us as lazy duffers, crooks, drunkards, and anarchists. Pop says, "Us Irish are the last off the boat so I gets the shaft. Only a low paying, disgusting or breakneck job comes me way."

If not for big city livín and the nuns feeding us, it's like we never left the famine. It's a miserable time until a railroad recruiter comes to the labor hall, jumps on dad's sad tale, and hires him as a gandy dancer. I say the man's an eejit cause dad's got two left feet and no rhythm. Silly me, dad's new gig isn't a jig at all.

Dad says the West abounds with prosperity but we're not there yet. He's working a Great Northern Railway fix-it train with other laborers repairing weathered track. The climate along our route changes from a sweat to a blizzard in the blink of an eye. Lodging is brutal as we huddle together in a drafty boxcar full of other misfits. The car's mostly dry and a closed door keeps the wild critters at bay.

Pops spends his days mending the rails while mama and I work the camp kitchen. Except for a whore wagon visiting from a nearby town, mama and I are the only girls in camp. Daddy harps at the boys to keep a distance and the choir answers, "Yeah bub we know, lookey no pokey."

Mum's vigilant about herself and me. She says, "Ellie you watch your step. The wolf around here is two-legged so you stay close, ya hear?

My mother's no shrinking violet; Missus Flannery keeps a filet knife woven into her skirt to clean whatever we can catch. Mama and I gut crappie, rabbit, and squirrel with her sharp blade. Tis a game to see who's the quicker.

Mama always keeps an eye out and a hand near her knife. One day mama's bent over the fire stirring a pot of stew when a bloke decides to ignore dad's warning. The goof grabs mum's arse and makes a pumping motion against her skirt. He and his mates are laughing but it doesn't last. Mama tosses the ladle, grabs her knife, and pricks his family jewels. Now I'm giggling while the looky-loos wince and grab their crotches. One crying bloke goes for help and me pop's comes runnín.

Dad's fixín for a fight but our wrangler steps between him and the whimpering dancer yelling, "Charlie O'Brien that was a damn fool stunt. I can't have bad blood in my camp. You best collect your things and move on." Dancing Charlie's severance pay is a quarter, a blanket, and a sack of beans. Dad retells Mum's story with himself as the hero but the boys know the score. You best keep clear of Missus Flannery or she'll cut up your tallywags for her criadilla stew!

Our wrangler says cash-on-hand tempts a robber so he keeps a wage ledger and we buy necessities from the storage boxcar. He deducts our purchases from our pay tally and Mama doesn't trust him.

"The fool twitches when he talks. I can do arithmetic and the dim-wick's cookín the books!" Did I mention dad can't read nor write? He does a good day's work and mama keeps an eye on our paltry savings. Tis her dream of a better life for us.

Rail workers own little except the clothes on our backs. We bathe when camped near a stream and look like a bunch of ragged strays. Tis an invisible shackle what binds us to this life. The railway discourages us from leaving camp for town. Stationmasters claim we're shiftless and the townies greet us with the slap of propriety. A visit seems a waste of energy and dangerous to boot.

I heard tell of a rail worker who pocketed a piece of candy and the sheriff beat a confession outta him for stealing the mayor's prize turkey. They hung the poor bugger before a hunter came forward to set the record straight. His hound caught a bird with a bejeweled collar and the silly thing died of fright. Did they hang the dog? No sir, he was just doing his job and a good retriever is a treasure.

There's but one laborer lower than an Irishman and that's an Oriental johnny. A white man can quit and trade his tally for supplies but a johnny's bound to an indentured contract. A johnny on the run keeps a watchful eye cause a bounty hunter gets his fee dead or alive and a dead johnny's no hassle at all.

Pop's luck is with us as usual. We're camped outside a town called WallaWalla when unholy sorrow strikes. Tis there we bury mama and little Mike. There's no doctor in camp but it wouldn't matter. A vicious fever kills all but a third of us. It takes the frail ones first and mum serves as camp nurse before she gets sick. Mum lingers longer than most, until the fever wins out and she reluctantly lets us go. Her last breath is "take care of papa chuisle mo chroí." Pulse of my heart is the Gaelic goodbye that still haunts me. Mum meant it as a sweet comfort but her parting words cut me deep. A flood of tears can't wash away the pain and I've inherited more than I can handle, an inconsolable drunkard.

Dad curses his luck and drinks a month's liquor ration in a week. So pitiful is he, I twice catch him bartering our food for a johnny's mash hooch. The wrangler's an Irishman whose sympathetic until dad costs him a deadline. I know he has to fire us but dad's hopping mad. "Good riddance to ya a-hole! Only a no-good kinsman sacks a widower and his baby girl. Ya got no soul brudder! Get yaself buggered sideways and upside down! Don't ya fret baby girl, our pot of gold's around the bend. Just ya wait and see."

So we're off on another leprechaun hunt. This time we hitch a ride with a wagon train bound for the Port of Seattle and it's got me longin for the rails. My pain is a mix of tailgate splinters and a broken heart. I cannot hold back the tears as dad pries a splinter from me bum.

"Buck up baby girl. Hold still darn it! Think about our new digs in that boomtown Seattle. They say even a mick like me gets top dollar on the docks. A port's a sure bounty for a widower and his baby girl. Tis our ticket to prosperity!"

"Jesus crackers man, open your eyes. Do I look like a baby? No sir I do not and I'm darn tired of your promises! Your friggin dreams killed my mama. Remember how she charged me with your care and not vice versa? I might be a midget but I'm smarter than you!"

Dad's face goes crimson and he wallops me upside the head. "Watch yer mouth girlie! Ya don't know squat, this life's more stinkweed than roses. You so smart why can't ya see that for yaself? Modder's gone and we're here so chin up and shut your pie-hole. I can't abide your backtalk and blubbering so don't make me take off ma belt!"

What a miserable bastard! I know he loved mama as much as me. Why can't we share the grief?

It's late and I'm lying in the wagon next to a crate of sleepy chickens. Dad and the driver shared a moonshine pint for supper and they're snoring away in their blankets below me. A bright star hangs in the sky above and I reckon it's mum watching over me.

"Mama please help us; see the shiner your husband gave me. Keeping dad ain't easy when he beats his misery into me. I'm lucky to be cast in your likeness. See my skirt mama? I sewed in your sheath and I keep me hand near the blade. Mama I miss you. I miss your lullabies. Will you sing with me once more? ♪O'er the mountain, over the sea, back where my heart longs to be. Oh let the light that shines on me, shine on the ones I love.♪

Shine down on me mum. Be my angel and keep watch o'er me always."

CHAPTER 13

Prosperity My Patootie

Surprise, surprise! Seattle is not the promise land and Pop's prediction is more gullyfluff than fact. I swore to keep dad's house but our lodging's a rented room midway twix Chinatown and Skid Road. To be kind it's better than a rail car or a tenement slum. Ella Mae Peavey runs the rental and her husband Henry owns the saloon next door. Tis a good fit for us; dad's got a watering hole nearby, the Peaveys like me and I keep our wallet.

We rent a third-floor attic with two bunks and a portal window looking out onto the bay. I like the view and fresh sea breeze but the portal's a magnet for curious birds and bats. Nonetheless the vista's better than the street with its weird smells and goings-on after dark.

Our loft has a rickety ladder, a deadbolt, and a cramped ceiling that keeps me dad bent over. Tis amusing when he forgets and bruises his noggin, especially when he's been beatin on me. Dad works a ten-hour day, six days a week. I don't see much of him and that's okay. I got me own life to live.

The floor below us has rooms filled with bunks and no doors. The racks are bolted to the wall and Ella Mae charges a man a nickel a night. Henry salvaged my window and the racks from a scuttled ship that ran aground.

Henry's saloon has all twenty-six nautical flags hanging from the rafters and the theme makes a beached sailor feel right at home. There's also a dart board centered on a salvaged helmsman's wheel though it's near impossible to get a max score. The wheel still spins and Henry swears its haunted. Truth is, Henry hung it and he's no handyman.

Behind the saloon sits a three-stall outhouse shared with our boarding house. Henry Peavey built it himself and claims it's a self-cleaning wonder. He says a hightide washes away the dung without him having to clean it. However a sign above the privy door says 'User Beware the Tides' cause a rowdy wave tosses a deposit right back at ya. An ebb tide fairs no better when the exposed muck lets go a shitty smell. Henry says the odor's rotting kelp but his wife says, "Da bastard's full of crap." Tis hard to say if Ella Mae speaks of the toilet or her man.

Ella charges a nickel for meals but the parish feeds us for free. Henry spots me a breakfast when I sweep out the saloon and that saves me a hike to the church. He'd feed me a lunch if I'd clean the saloon spittoons. Ha! I will never-ever touch a raunchy spit bucket.

Locals know our street as Skid Road cause the logging settlers greased wooden slats with animal fat to skid their timber downhill into the bay. Now the skid's a brick road between the infamous White Chapel district and proper Seattle. Ella May says, "Fancy uptowners own their beds while folks in the Chapel is lucky to rent from me."

Yes, our district is a waystation for itinerants sleeping it off in flophouses and brothels. This raucous wasteland has buildings sitting atop wooden stilts dug deep into liquefied mudflats and boardwalks along the roads keep folks from sinking into the muck. Otherwise a drunk or a careless walker might drown in the quicksand. Am I overstating? No, deceptive sinkholes overwhelmed a friend of mine. Hightide makes a sinkhole a decent swim for us guttersnipes but a tide demands caution and the tiny lad disappeared before our eyes. The newspapers spewed outrage and that got the politicians involved; city hall installed life buoys on random posts while howling soapbox complainers demanded the cops round up neglected kiddies. I laid low until the ruckus died down and, of course, nothing really changed.

Yes a good day in the Chapel is hard to fathom. You might say the good times are the luck of the Irish. Ha! I'm pullín your leg. Any fool knows the Irish hereabouts got no luck. Tis common to step over a dispirited kinsman passed out on the boardwalk. Our hardship is what it is and a Chapel snipe knows nothing better.

Me? I'm an optimist just like me mum. This little Alice explores her dingy Wonderland without a care or a misery and my routine's comfortable until my tenth birthday. On that day Providence strikes me aga!

It's Saturday and I'm out after candlelight without me dad. The smelly fart hasn't been home; he got paid and he's probably on a bender. I'm pissed cause he kept the rent money and he broke a solemn pinky swear. Tis my birthday and I was supposed to get a real bakery cake. Is nothing sacred to that man? I'm standing in the parish supper line when two snoopy penguins spot me. "Dear me sister, the dockhand's babe is alone again; poor little beggar."

"Yes the girl belongs in an orphanage. Our Savior cannot protect a lamb on these streets after dark."

"Hey sisters I ain't deaf. Not even a nun can call me a beggar!" I toss my viddles to the floor and bolt for the door. "This little lamb has family and by golly I'll knock on every brothel door 'til I find him!"

Across the street from the church is the three-story Graham House. Everyone in White Chapel knows of Lou Graham. She's a legend dubbed Sweet Lou by her clientele and her reputation irritates me dad to no end. I can still hear his Irish tenor in my head. "The uppity whore's a thief! Only a chump pays more than two bits for a nip and a tug. I ain't wastín a nickel in that place."

An uptown kiddie can't catch dad's drift but any snipe will. Naïveté is a luxury to a street urchin. Where might me dad go on a bender? No doubt he's shacked up in some sleazy joint off a dock alley. Standing next to this lit palace makes me wonder what's inside. Rumor says it's full of secrets no one dare reveal. Am I scared? Heck no! I got street smarts and me own secret: this little lamb's got a guardian angel called mama.

Men linger out front causing me to go to the back door. A man stands at the stove with his back to me so I knock and he turns about. Good golly it's a Chinaman! The clap's more popular in Seattle than his kind. What are the odds of seeing one up close outside of Rickshaw Alley?

I often stand at Chinatown's red gate adorned with its bright-colored lanterns. A giant dragon sits atop the gate guarding the entrance; his big eyes bob and his toothy grin always make me smile. The exotic smells of incense and roasted meats waft from inside the gate; the strange chatter and the music are downright alluring. Pops says, "No baby girl, only missionaries go inside the devil's liar. I catch you there and you'll pay!" Yeah yeah, there's ways around me dad's penalties.

The Chinaman's voice draws me back to the porch. "Yes girl what can I do for you?"

His words make me giggle; I never heard a johnny speak proper English before. This little fellow's uppity for his kind. "Uh, I'm after me pops. You got any dock rats sleeping it off in there?"

"Young lady we serve gentlemen here. What is your father's name?"

Wow! This prim pigtail is hilarious. He speaks as good as an uptowner so I mimic his proper tone, "The gent's name is Thomas Hugh Flannery."

"One minute please."

The Chinaman closes the door and disappears through a curtain of sparkling beads. The kitchen smells so good it makes me tummy ache and I sit down on the top step to wait.

CHAPTER 14

From Rags to Riches

A chilly breeze makes every minute feel like hours. If I sit here much longer me arse is gonna freeze so I stand to leave. At that moment Fate opens the kitchen door with an aura surrounding a vision of royal loveliness. Should I curtsy before the grand dame? Wait, her majesty speaks!

"Hello Miss Flannery. My name is Lou Graham and I own the House. How may we help you?"

Her tone's casual yet this is a regal lady. Sweet Lou is tiny like a picture I saw of England's Queen Victoria and, if it weren't for those fancy heels, she'd be but an inch taller than the Chinaman. Miss Lou's blue eyes twinkle, her hair's done up with feathers and her jewelry's pricey. Her bustled satin gown and corseted waist accent her curvy frame. Sweet Lou looks like a manikin from an uptown dress shop. She's the epitome of elegance with a sultry Bavarian accent and full figure. What is that sound? Her majesty doth disrupt my awestruck stupor.

"Missy you're shivering in the night air. Don't just stand there gawking."

Her warm smile and bejeweled hand beckon me to sit at the kitchen table. I ignore instinct and step inside but my hand's resting on my knife.

"You are very thin dear. There's no substance to you and the wind must chill you to the bone. Are you hungry? Mr. Chin please feed our waif."

The Chinaman must be a mind reader cause my supper's already plated and it smells so good if I don't eat I'll surely faint. I forget Grace and snatch a fork from the servant's hand. Shoveling food hand to mouth I bark at the johnny. "Hey boy, housabout a coffee with sugar, lots a sugar!" The room turns as cold as the outdoors. Did I forget my manners spouting orders in a stranger's house? "Sorry bout bossing your houseboy ma'am. I shoulda asked you first." The uppity servant stiffens and rolls his eyes while his mistress gives me a stern look. "Why the fuss lady? I said I was sorry."

Sweet Lou melts the ice with a sigh. "Mr. Chin is not a boy. He is your elder and my house manager. Mister Chin, perhaps a cup of hot cocoa for our guest?"

"Golly, I meant no disrespect. I ain't familiar with fancy titles and this fella's an oddity to me."

"I understand, apology accepted. My doorman says he worked on the docks with your papa. You two are alone in this world and it's difficult to raise a child in this district."

Yeah we're stuck with each other, what of it? Tis a chore keeping me dad and not vice versa. Lou's bouncer no doubt heard the crap my old man spins. Be you crippled, deaf, blind, or crazy, my dad chats you up. He starts with losing mum and his precious boy and ends with raking the bosses. Tom Flannery's always the hero of his tale taking care of his (ugh!) baby girl. Tis poppycock! I give Miss Lou a polite nod and keep eating. This stew is for sure the best I ever ate. Whatever his title the little chink can cook.

Miss Lou interrupts my thinking. "It isn't safe for a young girl to roam these streets after dark."

"Yeah I hear that blarney a lot (slurp) but I manage just fine." Tis strange to hear her repeat the nun's caution. I doubt they share a cup of tea, their services being opposite sides of a coin. Why are the adults so feckín afraid for me? I carry myself tough and a grownup ought a give me my due.

Lou finishes her thought. "We've an empty bed in the maid's room over there." The madame points to a curtain in the corner. "You stay the night and we'll find your papa in the morning."

Her tone's more parental than inviting but I remember my manners. "No disrespect Miz Graham but dad and me got a room."

"Dad and I have a room. It is important to speak with distinction. You are Irish, yes?"

Miss Lou's tenor is matter of fact but she's struck a nerve. I can be touchy about me roots. "Saints preserve us! Sure I'm a Celt, what of it? Folks like you keep my dad from getting a decent wage." I lean into my Irish lilt, "Does me Irish offend ya lass? I respect me elders but I got limits! Ya know we're all foreigners here so why must a Kraut toffer jab at me?" Damn and bless it, my mouth's gone off again! What was I thinking? I've caboshed all hope of getting a tasty dessert.

What's this? Sweet Lou claps her hands and hoots the best laugh ever. Her laughter's mighty infectious and I can't help but join in. We're soon a pair of gigglemugs chasín a breath, but the Chinaman stands silent; he's as sober as a teetotalist.

Miz Lou calms down and gives my shoulder a squeeze. "Young lady I like your spunk and your Irish is charming. A Yank finds our accents irresistible but my concern is your grammar. To own our destinies, emigrant women need mind our words. We shan't let a man dismiss us as brainless twits especially if blessed with a charismatic intelligence. Please think about a delicious Mr. Chin breakfast." Lou gives me a playful wink. "Help clean the kitchen after the morning rush and I'll pay you fifty cents."

I don't get a chance to respond. A raucous noise from above signals a man's fallen down the stairs and the parlor guests sing out with laughter. I want to go see it!

"Oh my, what a hullabaloo! I must return to my guests. Mr. Chin please take care of our little friend." Miss Lou points at my bare feet and grimaces, "Do wash those before getting into one of my beds." A twirl of her dress sends the madame towards the laughter.

I look to Mr. Chin for comment but the chef is mute. He hands me a dish of cobbler and snatches back his hand. His caution prompts my best impish grin and the proper man walks away. He no doubt wonders why his mistress took me in and he's not alone.

Good heaven this dessert's tasty! Every bite makes the walk home less appealing. Mr. Chin returns with a folded nightshirt and disappears again. I reckon the shirt is his cause there's no girly frills, missing buttons or mending marks and the weave is as soft as a baby blanket. I bet a Graham bed is just as cozy. Mr. Chin reappears with a towel and washbasin, sets the tub at my feet, fills it with hot water and a bar of perfumed soap bobs to the top. Mr. Grumps points to my feet and returns to his chores.

My only pair of real shoes are giveaways from the nuns and I keep them under my bed for special occasions cause they're too tight for everyday wear. Most snipes go barefoot until the first freeze and come winter; I wear a pair of dad's hand-me-downs. Pops knows a wily undertaker who buries his charges without their footwear. A viewing doesn't show a corpse's feet and my dad buys his boots at the mortuary. I get his old ones but dad's boots are way too big so I lift two pairs of woolies from the mercantile. Yes stealing's a sin but frostbite is way worse. Given the recent cold spell, boot season ain't far off.

Ahh! The temperature of the soapy water is perfect and the soak's heaven for my calluses. Tis a swell birthday for sure and there's nothing back home but a mealy mattress. What might a Mr. Chin breakfast be? I am curious. So what if dad comes back to an empty nest. Like I care! He can keep his darn bakery cake. Pops makes twenty cents an hour and he don't cook. Nobody with a lick of sense passes on a decent breakfast and a half-dollar. My empty pockets tip the scale. Why not bed down in the House of Lou Graham. The meddlesome can think what they want.

I finish washing my feet and retire to the back room. Yes my knife's under the pillow, what of it? Tis my ritual at Ella Mae's boarding house as well. A mudflatter trusts no one and I can still hear mama's voice. "Ellie girl remember this: two pints of Guinness can turn a saint into a gobshite!"

"Ah mama, why did you leave me with such a useless duffer? Your windbag hubby can't defend against the rowdy fellas stayín below us. A rickety ladder, a deadbolt and your blade are my protection!"

Miss Lou and a tasty supper remind me of life with mum. It's been a stretch since I felt cared for and Holy Chance just landed me on the steps of a kind lady. Go on with those thinkín she's a sinner. Judge lest ye be judged, ain't that right? The nosey dogmats shame Miz Lou cause she won't kowtow to their meddling.

I know it's true; I get pigeonholed by the heartless all the time. I've been spit on, called a misfit, a gypsy, a mick, a gabber, a sass, a beggar, and a slew of words I won't repeat. So what if Fate put me here in this so-called den of iniquity. I say hip-hip hurrah for Lou Graham and her band of bohemians!

CHAPTER 15

Watch Your Step

I awaken mid-morn to laughter coming from the kitchen. Shoot! Did I miss breakfast? A peek through the curtain reveals a mix-breed squaw and a Frenchy dressed in fancy silk robes. They sit at the table with coffee and a plate of fresh-baked jelly rolls. My sweet tooth twinges with anticipation; I do love an ooey-gooey jelly roll!

The girls are talking about last night's antics and the Indian girl called Kettie says, "The gent wasn't satisfied with my hospitality. This one's nasty as a polecat and slaps me hard across the face. Can you see the mark?" She touches her bruised cheek. "That's when I yell for Mr. Earl. Our hero grabs the boy, bounces him down the stairs and tosses him into the street! Yes I did throw the spoiled brat's trousers out the window. I hope his fancy britches hit a puddle!"

The Québecoise says, "What a commotion! Did you hear the applause from zee parlor? I say the boy got his due. His papa was playing cards. Such a furieux! Zee father yanked on his son's ear shouting, "Damnation! Your college stole my money and taught you nothing! If you want to inherit my business you best apologize to Sweet Lou. Put your pants on, get on home and don't let mother catch you sozzled!"

Kettie laughs at her friend's impression. The boy's departure must be the fracas I heard last night. I open the curtain and step forward.

"Oh hallo. I am Cherié. Would you like a beignet? Monsieur Chin infuses them with his own raspberry puree. Exquise! You are the Flannery girl, yes?"

I snatch a fancy donut, take a bite, and pocket a second helping. "Hmm, really good eats around here. Thanks for sharing. Yes I be Ellie Flannery. Miz Lou says she can find me dad."

Kettie says, "Our Lou is well connected; no scoundrel can hide from her. Wherever your father's hold up, she'll roust him."

"Me dad ain't far away. He means well but a misery consumes him; I reckon a sorry man gets corned up now and again. Tis hard for dad not to lose his way." My words belched outta nowhere. Why do I defend the drunkard? Oh lordy, here comes another burst! "Our situation's temporary. Pops says we're headed for the Idaho hills where a fortune in shiny silver lays a waitin' for the takin'." How pathetic am I repeating dad's rhymes? Why do I mimic the bastard?

"I'm sorry sweetie I meant no offense. My daddy drifted in search of furs. Some men wander but you can trust Miss Lou to find anyone."

The saving angel appears with a menacing blue-black giant in her tow. The goliath's muscles ripple as he ducks through the doorway. A wink from their madame excuses the two women. "Let's have a talk, shall we?" Miss Lou motions for the colored man and I to sit. "This gentleman is Mr. Earl Hazard. He worked the docks with your papa."

Earl smiles a big ole grin. "How do Sweet Pea. Your daddy was sure a talker."

The giant has the deep bass voice of a church soloist. Big Earl's more than his daunting looks but why did he say dad *was* a talker?

"I do okay Mr. Hazard. Thank you for asking. Yessir my dad's somethin all right. Ya know you're kinda scary until you open your mouth."

Earl chuckles and Lou says, "I told you this one's a pip; she does speak her mind." "What shall we call you dear? Miss Flannery seems a bit formal."

"My christened name is Ellis Megan but most folks call me Ellie."

"Charmed I'm sure. Please call me Miss Lou. I sent our Mr. Hazard out at daybreak to look for your papa. I assume you know the story of the Great Fire and how it affected our sidewalks?"

"Uh-oh! Is my dad okay?"

Ellie stops her story and gives Jack a quizzical look. "What do you know about the Great Fire?"

"Never heard of it, I've only been here a few days."

"Well you must grasp its significance. My dad's tale makes no sense unless you know how a consuming blaze changed this town. The story's bizarre but I swear it's true."

Seattle grew up around Hank Yesler's lumbermill. Back then buildings and sidewalks were all wood. The seasoned kindling and a windy day are why the Great Fire of '89 burned with such a fury.

Tis a typical day for merchants with kerosene tins and mining explosives spilling out-of-doors onto the walkways. Seattle is a tinderbox waiting for a spark when a carpenter's apprentice bumps a cauldron of boiling glue and (poof!) the floor's ablaze. The carpenter rights the bubbling pot but the lit floorboards chase both men out into the street.

Our fire-corps fares no better cause every man's a green volunteer and the captain's at a convention in San Fran though his know-how couldn't save us. The water comes from wooden pipes running downhill from the lake and the fire sucks up those pipes like they was tasty ramen noodles! With no water in the hoses the boys grab buckets and run for the bay. Sadly a minus tide makes the beach a muddy pit and the stand-in captain bellows through his bull horn, "The flames are right behind ya fellas! You best run into the muck and swim for it!"

It's then a well-meaning gent says, "Why not dynamite the buildings ahead of the blaze? A firebreak will slow down the inferno." Alas the do-gooder forgot one crucial factor: a westerly sea breeze. Helpless spectators watch from the hilltops as hot embers spew mayhem beyond the firebreak. Only a handful of scorched building survived the blaze and the hot embers forbid a walkabout until the next day.

At dawn our city bosses survey the devastated ruins. Seattle lost its port and all supporting commerce with the first Graham palace amongst the casualties. Tis a wonder no one died. A quick rebuild demands a massive cleanup but the council finds a positive twist to the disaster. Why not control the tidal flooding? The council votes to bury the mucky flats with tons of rock and dirt. Fill comes off of Denny hill by the wagonload creating a mammoth seawall and the result is amazing! The hill is half its original size and the mudflats are gone. With the heavy lifting done our council declares victory and walks away.

However, there's one wee problem. The old sidewalks are six feet below the new streets making the buildings first floor entrances useless. Outraged proprietors demand the city fix the problem but the bosses spent all the money. The stubborn stalemate continues for years with storekeepers building footbridges to access the second floor. Snaking beneath the gangplanks are trenches with ladders down to the abandoned sidewalks and basements. Questionable road waste washes onto folks using the lower paths until the Alaska Gold Rush lavish profits allow a monumental fix.

Thick glass bricks provide a see-through canopy over the maze of tunnels as folks walk on the translucent bricks with daylight streaming down-under. Torches light a basement bazaar of iniquitous dens and the cellar society calls itself the Underground.

The Underground today is still a mecca of forbidden trade and there's always talk of condemning it. Topside merchants say there's a rat-festered plague below. Tis a convenient tale. The rats roam topside and no one's getting sick. I've been underground and I'm still kicking.

The rub is the Underground's a nefarious market with no rules or fatcat bosses. The tunnel trade robs profits from the surface merchants and an innocent rat gets the blame.

CHAPTER 16

Pinched!

Ellie returns from her tale. "Jack do you understand my dad's dilemma?"

"I'm so sorry. This doesn't end well does it."

An awkward silence is Lou's tell. Her sad eyes speak volumes and it seems like an eternity passes before Lou finds her voice. "Ellie dear, Mr. Hazard found your papa. The police blotter says he reeked of alcohol. Your dad with his cakebox fell from a dock street onto an abandoned sidewalk. The fall knocked him out and he drowned in a puddle of water. Do you understand? Dear girl your father's..."

Miss Lou's voice fades away. Before me stands a misty vision of mum and dad holding hands.

The madame's voice returns, "A police blotter listed your papa as a John Doe. Earl found him at the morgue and claimed the remains. May I see to a proper burial? I am so sorry for your loss."

Loss? Pa-Leese! Dad was born lost. I'm told a drunkard lands on his luck. Ah but don't you see the irony? The Irishman had no luck! Who else but me dad drowns in a puddle of water? Am I sad? Heck no! I'm furious!

"Ya needn't be sad Miz Lou. Good riddance and dash the bastard all to hell! There a tis mama, I'll not excuse your man again. Look at what he's done! His damn schemes killed all of you. And what of your baby girl now daddy? What excuses will ya give the devil? How about the truth for once. Saphead! You've left me broke and homeless. Damn you, damn ya all to hell!"

I'm out of words and my pent-up rant fizzles into a blubbering. A quake ripples through me as I shudder to think what lies ahead. I am a penniless orphan with nowhere to go. Waterworks spew out of me like a busted levee while unruly hiccups almost bounce me off the chair. I look up at the two strangers seated across from me. The gentle giant has tears in his eyes. Lou says nothing as she reaches out and cloaks me in her arms. Her rocking motion wraps me in a calm cuddle and I sense mum smiling down on us. Mama in my misery you sent a fallen angel to hug me but what's next for your little chuisle mo chroí?

Ellie sets her gaze on Jack. "Of course Miss Lou gave me a home but now my savior's got fanciful places to go. Her time here was a whistle stop and she can't miss the outbound train. Sad to say Lou's time with us is almost gone. Sorry lad, that's all I have for now. You must come again soon; my story's only just begun."

Ellie looks up at the portrait, goes lost in meditation and even I sense a presence. Is it Miss Lou's ghost? No the energy's masculine and nervous. Folks cease their chatter and an awkward silence seizes the room.

Before me are two fidgeting figures standing in front of Ellie. They sport identical woolen uniforms, chin-length sideburns, and handlebar mustaches. The twin constables appear fraternal as if born of like mind yet different mothers. Their distinction is height and hair; a long-legged, orange-haired gent stands idle while his squat, dark-haired brother snaps to attention.

"Miss Ellis Flannery we've come fer ya."

My beautiful companion awakens and smiles. "Archie Whipple as I live and breathe. Why so formal lad? And Danny Blaycock look at you! When did you join the force? Yer cousin's kinda full of hisself ain't he."

Orange-haired Danny smiles and brushes a finger across his shiny badge. Archie's cheeks flush as he whines, "Ah Ellie this ain't funny. You're in big trouble." He regains his official composure. "Miss Flannery I have a warrant for your arrest."

The room gasps yet not one person utters a word; they won't miss what's to come. Officer Danny gives Archie an impatient jab. "Jeez Arch get to it. Ellie honey we came to fetch ya. The warrant says Murder in the First Degree."

The parlor guests burst into chatter as Ellie gives her police friends a disarming smile and stands to adjust her shawl. A Chinaman enters the room and approaches his charge. This must be the unwonted Mr. Chin. The chef says, "Ellie whatever is going on here?"

"Well it seems I'm nicked and in need of a lawyer."

"Not funny young lady. Constables why are you here? This is not the agreed upon protocol; our attorney manages all disputes."

"Mr. Chin the boys aren't here on House business, I am a wanted woman."

"That's ridiculous. Who dares accuse you?"

"There's only one death I'm blamed for; I reckon it's Caleb Ambary clambering from the grave."

Everyone looks to the twin coppers; their uniform head-bobbing affirms Ellie's suspicion and the chatter resumes.

Ellie sighs, "That ratbag refuses to give up the ghost. I regret ever knowing the Ambary clan. Boys shall we ride or walk down the hill to the pokey?"

The two men flank Ellie; each one offers their prisoner an arm. Archie says, "Honey the Tomb ain't fit for an elegant skirt! We're told to book ya up here in the tiny jail."

"How considerate and nearby! Jack Hamby, you look a bit pale. Are you feeling faint? I hope you'll come visit me tomorrow."

I too stand up. "I-I'm fine. I'll see you tomorrow."

The policemen whisk Ellie out the door with Mr. Chin assuring her that it's all a mistake. He stops to address the gathering. "As Miss Lou's executor I am postponing the reading until this absurdity is re-solved. I apologize for the bother." Mr. Chin does an about face and walks out in search of the House lawyer followed by others racing off to spread the news. I am alone with only the portrait of a beauty for company.

"Miss Graham I doubt your girl killed anyone. What's the story here?" The portraits piercing eyes stare back at me. "Jeez Louise, why do I quiz a painted likeness?"

What happens next I swear on my mother's bible. The madame smiles at me and closes one eyelid. Lou Graham just winked at me!

CHAPTER 17

Strictly Business

I can't wait on a tardy Floyd Snypes or the trolley so I race up Profanity Hill eager to share yesterday's news. However Mr. Barr's in no mood for gossip and bellows from behind his door, "Who's minding my store? This isn't a social club you know!" The baritone explosion scatters the men and I'm left alone to process permits.

I watch the clock tick away the hours until it strikes twelve. The building has a grand front staircase but I'm after a more discreet route. There's a fire escape window with a rod-iron ladder on the backside of the building. What's this? The window's been nailed shut. Why do that? The notice says: 'Closed by Order of the Police. In case of fire break the window.' I give the sash a frustrated thwack and walk down the well-used stairs.

Inside the station is a uniform sitting at the desk and a solid metal door hangs on the wall behind him. The officer motions for me to come closer.

"Afternoon constable. I'm here to see Miss Ellie. Please say Jackson, no, say Jack Hamby's calling." Calling? I sound like a pimpled boy courting his date.

"Hold your tongue sonny. I be the watch sergeant with three chevrons on me arm. A constable's got no stripes, a corporal's got two, and a sergeant earns these three bad boys."

"Sorry sir I meant no offense; I don't know anything about police rank and file. May I please see Ellie?"

The sergeant frowns, stands and keys the formidable door. A wave of his hand motions me to follow and we walk in silence down the narrow hallway. To my right is a damp stone wall that smells like my musty cellar and two small cells line the hallway to my left. Each one has a tiny window high up on its back wall.

The lockup's empty save a third cell at the very end. This is no ordinary slammer; it's been transformed into an elegant bedroom with ruffled curtains concealing the bars to create the illusion of privacy. The sergeant taps the bars, keys the lock and says, "Ellie girl Jack Hamby's here."

"Just a minute boys."

Now we wait; I look at the floor to avoid the sergeant's stare. Please hurry girl and open the door before the scary man pounces.

Ellie finally appears. "Jack Hamby how kind of you to visit." The sergeant elbows me inside, shuts the door and clicks the lock. It's an eerie feeling yet Ellie seems unfazed by her confinement.

This larger cell is known as the drunkard tank where a gaggle of men sleep it off before facing their angry wives. The dungeon's been magically recast into an elegant suite with a fresh coat of pastel blue covering the scrubbed walls and a curtain hides its barred window. The cell's metal racks and mattress rolls are stacked in an adjoining cell and in their stead sits an ornate canopy bed; no doubt taken from Ellie's chamber. Soft linens adorn the overstuffed mattress and atop the bed is a puffy comforter with five plush pillows leaning against the cell bars.

A porcelain basin sits atop an antique vanity and next to it sits a tiny potbelly stove with its smoke pipe diverted out the window. The cell isn't chilled or musty as a whistling pot of herbal tea sits on the stove next to a seashell filled with glowing sweetgrass.

Nearest the cell door is a tiny desk with a vase of fresh lilacs; its cubbies filled with a book, cards, a cribbage board, an ink well, and a journal. Beside the desk is a liquor cart and a compact spinet piano with a music folder at the ready. Underneath it all is a plush Oriental rug.

The room is elegant and warm except for the odd piece under the window. Why did they haul Lou Graham's parlor chair over here? Hung above the chair is a portrait of a young Ellie and Miss Lou with a calligraphy signature that reads 'Always with you.'

My eyes go back to Ellie who leans against the bedpost watching me. "Wow I love what you've done with the place! It's like a fancy hotel room." I know it sounds corny but I so want to console the poor girl.

"Ha! Call it what you want Jack Hamby. I'm jailed all the same and my own lawyer refuses me bail. He says I'm safer in here than outside. Mr. Chin threw a conniption when he saw me shivering in a tiny cell and ordered the boys to refurbish this one with a few things from the mansion."

A few things? It's furnished better than my home.

"Mr. Chin caters to the coppers and they love it! Last night he delivered a buffet with a kegger for their evening cards. These guys hope I never leave." Ellie points to the cart. "Your boss and my lawyer visited last night and drank up all my whiskey. They didn't touch the tea, hard cider, or brandy so wet your whistle and have a sit."

I point toward the ceiling. "I'd love to stay but I'll get into trouble."

"Nonsense, Samuel Barr's an uncle. Tis a moniker Lou gave her business pals when I was small and they're stuck with it. Uncle Sam won't mind you keepín me company. The cooler has sandwiches and there's raspberry scones in the basket next to Lou's chair. Help yourself."

Ellie motions me towards the antique. No way am I sitting there!

Ellie yells up front, "Hello fellas, I'm running a bit low on spirits. Someone run down to Lou's place and grab a bottle of the good scotch. Thanks so much."

The sergeant left his metal door ajar, no doubt keeping an eye on me. He swings it wide open and calls back, "Yes princess. Anything else fer ya?"

"Well a bag of saltwater taffy would be nice."

"Corporal we're running a damn hotel now; go fetch our smartass guest her booze and candy." The sarge slams the metal door.

Ellie turns back to me. "The police chief doubled the watch and Sergeant Pete isn't happy with the changes. Makes ya wonder if I'm a prisoner or in protective custody. I'm more bored than scared cause my lawyer nixed most visitors, especially reporters. An invading hack's gonna find himself in a downtown cell courtín a ruffian. Come on Jack have a sit and spill some gossip."

I glance at the ghost chair. Yes I admit the antique spooks me. "Ellie it's best you don't see the newspapers. Every story reads like a sleezy novelette. How can anyone suspect you of such a thing?"

Ellie smiles and squeezes my hand. She is so pretty; dead men surely rise up to greet her killer smile. However, I'm very much alive and must honor my wedding vows. I'll be a friend and nothing more. Ellie's eyes flash and her head nods. Can the girl read my thoughts?

"Jack Hamby you are the sweetest man ever. You know little of me yet rise to my defense. Yes a newsy boss does take liberties to sell his papers; tis blarney though an amusing read. I'll soon tell my side but I'd like to get to know you better. Please sit." Ellie points to the creepy chair.

I pour a glass of tea and peruse the scones. Of course I'm stalling; how shall I approach a possessed throne? I guess I'll take a page from my mother's playbook. Mama bless her heart begs permission from her ethereal friends. It works for her so here goes. "Pardon me dear spirit may I sit upon your velveteen seat?"

Ellie laughs, "Oh sweetie, the chair won't bite. Only a wicked bum need fear its ire and I see no venom in you."

I take in a breath, sit and my exhale signals all is well. Ellie winks. "See no harm done; so where was I yesterday? Oh yes, I quit my tale just before the cops grabbed me."

CHAPTER 18

Tis a Quandary

I was about to bury me dad. Tossing pops in a White Chapel grave seemed a cruel penance even for him. A high tide sets a coffin adrift in the liquid ooze. Tis sad to think of him floating in muck with a crab nibbling at his big schnoz.

Lou says he belongs next to mama. She offers to pay and I cannot refuse her kindness. Three days later Lou, me, Mr. Chin, and Big Earl are on a train headed for WallaWalla. Dad's on ice in the mail car alongside a proper coffin for mama and Mikie. Mr. Chin reserved a four-suite car for the living with a private lounge full of books, games, and treats! The ride's great fun but I feel sorry for dad. Only four mourners will sit for his funeral.

Why do I feel anything for the buggar? Mama never got Last Rights or a proper Mass. We put her in a splintered coffin with Mikie cradled in her arms. There was no money for a marker so dad widdled a small wooden cross with our name on it. I reckon the cross is termite dust by now but we'll find the grave under the cherry tree my daddy planted. Mum loved cherry blossoms.

Lou says my family deserves a proper plot and wires ahead to a stonemason. She leaves their epitaph to me and I say it's fitting to use me mum's words. Mama always said "Let Saint Peter be our judge. The only earthly farewell we deserves is free at last." I know what wore my daddy out and the mason did himself proud. The tombstone reads: Dear Mum, Mikie and Dad: Welcome to Prosperity, Free at Last.

A well-dressed dandy stands on the parish steps beside an impatient priest. To my surprise Lou gives the stranger an affectionate hug and takes his arm. The priest rushes us to our seats before I can get a proper introduction.

Lou bought me a black dress, matching patent leather shoes, a hat, and a veil. The veil makes me nose itch so I rub it with my sleeve. Mr. Chin thinks I'm weepy and hands me his kerchief. I am not crying! The smelly incense makes my nose run and the Mass is giving me a headache. I only speak Piggy Latin and my fidgeting isn't sorrow, it's boredom. Yeah! The priest ran out of holies and motions to the dandy.

"Miss Ellie I am so sorry for your loss. My name is Hannibal Conover and I own the dock where your father worked. I knew Tom Flannery to be a decent man who did an honest day's work. Your dad spun a tale with the best of them." Mr. Conover smiles at me and sits back down. Tis all the gentry could muster.

Did he call my pops decent? The gent must be thinkín of another Irishman. Miss Lou must've asked him to say a nice word but calling pops decent is a stretch. Dad was dad, a man with dreams and no wherewithal. He fed us hand to mouth, was never there for me and I despised his drunken meanness. There may be a time when I relent and forgive the dullard but this is not that day. I cannot pardon a hapless dreamer. I do appreciate the gent's eulogy; it was kind and mercifully short.

The priest sets us free and I make a point to shake Hannibal Conover's hand. "Thanks for sugarcoating my pop's faults. He lost hisself when mama died. Good for him that she got him back. My temper got the best of me and I regret condemning the fool to hell. I swear I didn't mean it. A hot head is all dad left me. May he rest in peace with mama and little Mike."

"You're welcome Ellie. You are very clever and you remind me of Lou. Did you know she and I are business partners? I think the world of our Bavarian maverick."

The dandy rides home with us and we play Texas Hold'em to pass the time. Uncle Hannibal is a certified gentleman who lets me win without being obvious. How do I know? He was a riverboat gambler able to pull any card from a deck without being caught. However this gent's no cheater. Hannibal learned the trick to spot a swindler and he won big on the boats until his babies came. Boat-life cramps a growing family so Hannibal quit and moved out west. Mr. Conover is a standup fella but he's no exception. To the man my uncles are all decent blokes.

Ellie stops her story, her hazel-green eyes flaring. Heaven's mercy! What a temper.

"C'mon Jack Hamby I see your smirk! You needn't judge us. We're no eviler than the next guy. Beingness has a depth best seen from all sides and only an evangelist or a one-eyed crow sees life from just one angle.

Can you solve a riddle? Why can't a sanctimonious gospeler own a mirror? Cause he'd peck at his reflection just like a parakeet. The witless peckers seek heaven not by merit but by judging others. Lou says Saint Pete and the devil flip a coin for a gospeler and the loser gets the snoot!

Human nature befuddles me; why does a smart man sit through a spiteful sermon? There's no redemption in a petrified prayer and listening to the bigot's ramblings is a true hell! The pious fart just like the rest of us and know nothing for sure. I'll not trust my salvation to a prophet's quackery. My guide is pure Intuition."

I am a startled opossum waiting for Ellie's next move. Could she harm me in a fit of rage? Is there a knife hidden in her skirt? The papers say the blade that killed Caleb Ambary was snatched from the coroner's lockup. Gossipers claim Earl Hazard stole it for Ellie but they offer no proof.

The girl softens her gaze. "Sweetie I'm sorry. I do go on just like me dad. Tis a blessing and a curse. Mr. Chin says we're all a work in progress and must let go what does not serve us."

"Yes I often battle my fears and worry; there's a whole hive of should-a buzzing in my head."

Ellie pats my hand and returns to her tale.

Our House is no den of vipers. It's bona fide business with the chamber of commerce meeting in our dining room more than its own office. City bosses tempt investors with our hospitality and a success pays dividends for us all.

No uptown venue offers more than Lou. We're the Northwest's finest hotel and burlesque package but Lou's influence goes beyond hospitality. She is a savvy business partner. A bank demands collateral for a noble idea yet raises its rates with the tide. During the Panic of 1893 the banks stopped lending money when needed most so Lou opened her vault to keep our friends afloat. Folks can deny it but truth is truth. Miss Lou saved a bankrupt Seattle.

Ritzy wives despised the lender but they took her money all the same. The dames outta send thank-you notes instead of bad-mouthing us! Why do they hate Miss Lou so? Tis a righteous wrath born of jealousy. It stings a wife to know her man prefers his time with us. Those matrons keep a stuffy manor full of do's and don'ts while Sweet Lou offers comfort sans the sass. As sure as fish on Friday, astute men make more money here than they spend.

Lou's place is more than a drink and a tickle; we're a respite from the storm. An exhausted man claims his spoiled wife ignores the din of business. Tis a quandary to blend ethics with profit when greed churns the muck. A man must tread between plenty and cutthroat excess. Who might keep this man from losing his soul? Not the wife, it's Lou who listens and understands. Ah shucks I'm off topic again.

Dad left me nothing. The street pimps and nuns came after me with little disparity in their bidding. I'm no wagtail but an orphanage, jeez Louise! Adoptions favor a cute babe or a strong lad and an older girl ends up a parsonage servant until she's old enough to be married off to a faithful tither or given a nun's coif. With no say in the matter I'm a runaway for sure.

Miss Lou and I talk it over and settle on an amicable pact. Lou gives a judge friend a mug of tokens for my legal guardianship. And me? This emancipated girl gets a chance to own her destiny!

Lou says, "Ellie I'll see to your refinement and your uncles will chip in. However, living under this roof means you obey my rules. I promise you a stellar portfolio when you finish college. Shake my hand and it's done."

"Wow! I accept your offer and swear on mama's bible to obey. Thank you Miz Lou, no guttersnipe ever had so perfect a life!"

"Ellie Flannery you are not a guttersnipe! No one is. The moniker disgusts me and we've talked about choosing a better phrase. The voice is a keen sword that dubs a knight or cuts him to the quick. Insulting others or yourself stabs at a worthy soul so watch your speech young lady and count your blessings. This is no grammar lesson; it is a choice for dignity and self-worth."

"Yes ma'am, I'm blessed for sure but what about a sweet treat?"

"Oh my girl I see a bumpy road ahead. Mr. Chin and I will guide you but the path is yours. And yes, you'll have treats along the way."

Miss Lou says educating a castaway is a boon for all humanity and my learning is her greatest challenge. Bless our house family for supporting my recitals cause I do torture a tuned piano. My tutor says a lack of patience hinders my talent and it's Lou's firm resolve that keeps me plunking along.

What is my employment? I tell my chums I'm a lady-in-waiting for my royal sovereign. Tis a puffy lie; I tend the girls' wardrobes and help Mr. Chin in the kitchen. My real challenge is steaming all the fancy dresses.

Lou doesn't work the parlor cause the parlor and inn are fronts for her dealmaking. We work late hours and I awaken Lou mid-morning with sweet rolls and coffee for her majesty and an occasional tryst de jour.

Miss Lou saved me from a hellish serfdom yet it is her company I treasure. Living with Lou Graham is both work and an adventure. 'Twas Holy intuition that left me on her doorstep. It's more than I bargained for and her lessons in the art of living make it all worthwhile.

I admit I am a handful. An absent peasant let me run amuck while Lou prefers a metered nurturing. She expects much, praises often and loathes a lack of good sense. Lou has a clearer vision for me than I do. Uncle Hannibal says we came from the same casting and it's my goal to live up to the compliment.

Miss Lou and I have a secret. I dare not speak about my courier duties although there's nothing nefarious to tell. Lou doesn't trust a saloon runner and for good reason. She says "A parcel boy has no loyalty. He turns thief or snitch for an extra nickel. Ellie is my trusted agent."

Yes indeedy! The jealous and jilted spread malicious lies about our House but the truth is tame. Miss Lou is an entrepreneur and my loyalty keeps both rivals and meddlers at bay. I deliver Miss Lou's dispatches away from prying eyes, the uncles provide for me with generous tips and Lou stipends my treats.

Miss Lou mail-ordered a shiny Yale bicycle all the way from Toledo Ohio for my deliveries. I race about leaving a gaggle of jealous snipes in my dust and they don't know the half of it. Miss Lou swore me to secrecy. "Ellie, the humble never boast of riches. Bragging repels a good friend and attracts a scheming hangers-on."

CHAPTER 19

Keswitched

W here was my story going? Oh yes! Miss Lou owns two houses in Seattle. You saw the First Hill mansion up amongst the rich and spoiled. The other house sits on the edge of the dock district. Tis a three-story brick palace across from Our Lady of Good Help church. The clients joke they can sin away the night and seek absolution in a sunrise confessional.

The Graham House has an impenetrable Pennington bank vault buried underneath in the ghostly Underground. Access to the crypt-like saferoom is a ladder in our liquor closet. Our main floor holds an upscale bar, a dining room, a parlor, and a dancehall. The dancehall has a small stage for shows and it's where I perform my muddled recitals. Our kitchen flaunts Mr. Chin's gourmet talents. His cookery staff provides meals, hors d'oeuvres and room service from dawn until midnight. However only Mr. Chin cooks for Miss Lou.

The second floor is guest suites with an elegant toilet and a steam room at the end of the hall. Flush toilets came with the rebuild after the Great Fire. Indoor plumbing is the rage yet most folks keep an outhouse for the help. Lou poo-poos the idea, "What utter nonsense! I'll not waste a nickel on a segregated crapper."

Our guest suites rival the best stays in San Francisco. Every room has an imported Balinese desk, a chaise lounge, a coal heater, washbasin, an armoire, and a copper spittoon. The alcove has a four-post bed with matching comforter and curtains. Suites and our consorts are rentable by the hour or the night.

The third floor is an employee sanctuary with private rooms, a shared parlor to relax, a soaker tub and toilet rooms at the end of the hall. Our floor is sorority-like without the silly ceremony. Lou says an educated staff is good company and good business. Clients prefer refinement and a polishing is a must for upward mobility. Lou allows dating if there's no friction amongst us. However it's a terminable offense to bring a paying client up to the third floor.

Pearl Munchhausen knew how to play the game. She was born a lowly miner's daughter. At twelve-years-old Pearl inherited her dad and five siblings after the mama died in childbirth. A cave-in took her pa two years later. The mum's best friend kept the orphans but it was a struggle. Pearl left to find work and sent money whenever she could.

Pearl's only assets are a pretty frame and a head for numbers yet it's enough to work as a market fishmonger. However the fishes aren't the only thing that smells. Her boss holds Pearl's pay unless she works after hours. Am I being too coy? The man's a horny bastard eager to cop a feel. Pearl gets fed up and puts a tiny jellyfish down his pants. She chooses the perilous streets in hopes the money and smell are better than peddling fish.

A client thinks Pearl deserves a better situation and tells Miss Lou about the good-natured chippie. Our mistress is always looking for good help. She invites Pearl to lunch and the meeting ends with Miss Lou's trademark handshake. Lou loves a quick-witted decision and often says, "Intuition is God-speaking and listening is a skill worth honing."

Sweet Pearl thrives with us cause the money's good and our house is safer than the streets. Pimps make a wagtail a slave and it's a terrible choice for a chippie. Does she get pummeled by a mean john or be a pimp's cow. Yes landing with us is a Godsend for Pearl.

Then along comes Jacob Daley. Jake the engineer runs the Black Diamond mine for Artemis Keswick. He rarely followed a shipment to port until he met Pearl and now he sees to every transport with confections in hand. Pearl watches her figure so I get a fair share of the sweets. The pair's goofiness betrays their secret and the paying client pretense ends with Jake staying upstairs with us.

The affair's no problem until Jake confronts a patron and takes a chair to the face before Earl can intervene. Mr. Hazard snatches the dazed boy by the belt and carries him like a suitcase into Lou's office. "Earl please put Mr. Daley in a seat and fetch a pot of tea. Oh my! And a steak for the poor boy's face."

"I'm so sorry Lou. I know not to meddle and I'll pay for damages but the bastard's trouble. I had to protect my girl." Earl suppresses a laugh and leaves the room.

"Really darling?" Lou grabs a hand mirror from her desk drawer. "Take a good look at your protection. I think I'll keep my bouncer."

Mr. Chin arrives with tea and the cold raw meat. Lou smiles and he exits the room. Our manager never injects himself into Lou's affairs.

"Jake you must get off the fence. When are you going to marry my girl?"

"Ha! Sweet Lou's taken up matchmaking."

"No sir, I'm an anxious proprietor who cherishes her assets and your hard head cracked my pricey import!"

Jake winces and adjusts the steak against his swollen face. He does propose to Pearl but there's no time for a proper engagement. Jake's behind his time and he's overdue at the mine.

Monday business is slow and mostly reserved for staff schooling. Tis a perfect time for a wedding with a red velvet cake and no tutors for me! Mr. Chin decks out our First Hill mansion garden and a lavish reception entertains guests long after the newlyweds depart. A company train took them to Black Diamond in the foothills of the Cascades.

Mr. Keswick is not impressed with tardiness and he docks his man a day's pay. However his displeasure is nothing compared to the wife's reckoning. Muriel Keswick thinks herself the pillar of her community. Dutybound by the Almighty Word, she persists in chastising Pearl's sinful past. That is until a profound vision changes her mind. Missus Keswick tells her guild how Saint Paul himself leapt from Corinthians into her dreams. "Ladies heed my vision! His holiness left it to me to absolve the sinner. I shall purify the wayward lamb and welcome home her reborn soul. Amen and Amen!"

'Twas a convenient dream. Not an angel but a husband spoke up for Pearl Daley. Mr. Keswick intervened after Jake begged his help. The boss oversees his mine from an office window while Jake runs the show and Keswick can ill afford a sullen engineer.

Yet nothing happens in her town without Muriel's say so. She gathers folks on the shores of Jones Lake and the choir screeches, 'Glory, glory, down to the Sacred waves' as Muriel dunks Pearl into the freezing glacial waters. It is a splendid baptism!

Pearl sees the soggy affair from a different angle. "Jake that loon tried to drown me and Miz Keswick's lucky I didn't pull her under!

I will yield for your sake but I got limits. The dame best keep her distance and pray I don't slap the smug from her lips!"

"Honey we've bigger fish to fry. Your siblings arrive next week. Let's make a loving home for family and let Mrs. Keswick be. Please do this for your weary husband."

"I'll do my best for you and family but not that biddy."

As I said, Mr. Keswick needs his engineer and pays a handsome wage to keep him. The salary includes a lakefront farmhouse, two acres of good soil for crops, a poultry shed, a fishing dock and a farmhand. Pearl's grateful yet she sees life through a miner's eye. Her family is blessed but others are not. Why do the snooty Keswick's treat folks so poorly?

Jake says, "Keswick Coal is this town. What the boss says goes and folks make do with the facts."

Jake's right. Keswick manor sits on a hill overlooking the village and the town owes its living to the mine. The post office, telegraph, and the rail spur are company run and miners shop on credit at the mercantile where Miz Keswick discounts a churchgoer. Single men share a bunkhouse and eat in the company mess while a family gets a three-room cabin with a fireplace for heating and cooking. Communal outhouses, laundry, and bathing shacks are adequate though impossible to keep clean cause a fine coat of coal dust settles onto everything.

Yes all are beholden to the Keswick mine including a daft digger who tends a quitter's grave. Ole Digger's name is his profession and he keeps the town's two cemeteries. The in-town graveyard remembers its baptized residents with fresh flowers and tombstone epitaphs. Two miles out of town are graves with numbered markers for the black-spit victims and the unforgiven; may they rest in peace and not haunt the living!

The Keswick family estate rises above the dust and daily grind. Mr. Keswick is a proud British Tory three times removed. God save the queen! He curses the bloody rebellion, flies the Union Jack on his flagpole and dreams of one day visiting the English kin he's never met.

The Anglican cross is the only steeple allowed in Black Diamond. Keswick is the deacon but Muriel oversees the church including renting a roving pastor for weddings and funerals. On Sundays Mr. Keswick stands in the pulpit reading Muriel's chosen scriptures and the family sits up front in their Gothic pew; it's a replica of an ancestral seat in Cumbia England. Townies sit behind them on milled planks and the bathed miners stand in the rear of the church. The Keswick's refer to the miners as pitmen. Bathed or not, a pitman's skin is as black as the prevailing dust.

Muriel enforces a strict blue law on Sunday making the town and the mine shut down for church services. Keeping on Muriel's good side requires a baptism and a church tithe. The church patrons use a King James bible and an Anglican hymnal. The collection plate pays for clergy visits and the town doctor. Churchgoers endure a three-hour service to feast on a ham-n-fixings supper supplied by Mrs. Keswick. She insists leftovers go to an infirmed believer or to her pig troughs. "The wicked do not deserve our charity. Heathens must repent or go without."

Yes Black Diamond is a one religion town and a poor man's survival depends on Muriel's saving baptism. Her victims get a free bible and a bookmark sewn by Muriel's guild. Most miners can't read and attend church for one of two reasons: they're faithful or in need of a decent meal. The splendid church supper breaks the monotony of soda bread, beans, and varmint stew.

Mr. Keswick is the town mayor and his wife runs the ladies guild. Elections are a formality since no one dares challenge a Keswick for office. The church is used for town functions but there's no schoolroom. Pearl sees the need and petitions Muriel to start a school. The school will, of course, include coalminers and their children.

A nanny tutors a tiny Keswick while older siblings attend an elite boarding school in Seattle. Muriel wrinkles her nose at Pearl's suggestion. "Tsk-tsk Missus Daley! Status dictates the need for instruction so why educate a pitman's litter? Tutelage adds nothing to the life our Lord gave them and my Artemis says it creates a foul discontent amongst the pitmen."

Pearl clenches a fist behind her back. "Ma'am might a Christian mentor like yourself see the charity in this?"

"Young lady I know when I'm being shined. For charity's sake ha! You're new to your station so I'll allow you this folly. Go ahead and seek the funding. You'll see I'm right."

Pearl hears the smug in Muriel's voice yet offers a demure smile. She thinks to herself, 'Her ladyship doubts a miner's spawn can manage a school. Well Miz Uppity, you shall see! I'll get the supplies and teach for free.' Pearl comes to us and we pass the hat to cover the startup. She can't wait to wave her cash in Muriel's face.

Forgetting all humility Pearl brags to her ladies guild about Lou's contribution and Miz Keswick throws a hissy fit. "Missus Daley whatever were you thinking. No good comes from Satan's coin and my husband cannot allow this travesty in our midst."

Lou loses it when she gets the return money order. I never saw our mistress so mad. "How dare that witch deny innocent babes an education! And for what? To spite me? The beast begs a comeuppance."

A calmer Lou assembles her First Hill lady friends in the very parlor where you and I met. She hopes they'll help with Pearl's school idea.

Grace Conover speaks up, "Hannibal and I socialize with his clients. I like most everyone but the Keswick's are a peculiar pair. Hannibal and I visited Black Diamond for a social meet and greet. The scenery was stunning but Mrs. Keswick was obsessed with snooty teas and odd foods. Our supper was steamed eel served with curried venison and plain boiled potatoes. Her brunch was a runny-egg black pudding with blood sausages. The entire weekend was unsavory and contrived and I gave Hannibal an earful on the train ride home. I'll not keep company with that odd duck ever again but we must help Pearl…from a distance."

"Gracie I fear Lady Keswitch won't take a dime from me." Lou alters the Keswick surname to fit Muriel's spiteful disposition.

"Yes dear we must fudge the truth so I'll add your sum to my quilting circle's donation. Artemis needs the Conover barges. He'll play along and I'll add a note praising Muriel for starting a school. May God bless her selflessness and all that! No doubt her acceptance will be long and pompous. Lou you must be a silent partner. Is that agreeable to you? What are your plans for Muriel Keswick? Please sit on your vendetta so Pearl can have her school."

"I admire your cunning dear. No I'm not done with Lady Keswitch, but I'll bide my time for the school's sake." That is how a backwater spit gave every wanting soul an education.

Lou loves her mentoring but she's practical as well. Clients prefer a young face and our mistress helps older employees with marriage contracts while our tutors foster bookkeepers, paralegals, teachers, shop owners, and even a doula. Lou knows she must freshen her parlor. A consort's tenure ends at age nineteen but Miss Lou helps the girls invest. She gives a decent severance and provides a loan for a clever idea. Lou's reward is our sincere loyalty.

Miss Lou's retirement plans included a grand hacienda in the Napa vineyards. According to Lou, "We are alive when we become our dreams and there's no profit in killing time."

Ellie stops her story, looks at the happy picture on the wall and a single tear escapes down her cheek. "Ah Jack, Lou never saw her vineyard. Tis a sucker punch to a grand lady and I feel cheated for what could've been."

"I'm so sorry for your loss. We can't escape life's sorrows and I fear the best remedy is time passed. Your mistress lived life to the fullest and you do embody her persona. In disparaging times I find comfort in a fond memory and a grateful blessing. A sweet beatitude does raise me up."

Ellie squeezes my hand. "Ah Jackie, tis good advice but you sound like a sappy nun."

CHAPTER 20

And So He Plays His Part

Tap...tap...tap. The jailer raps his keyring on the bars. Ellie's eyes glisten with tears. "Lou wished for a vineyard without pouncing and her wistfulness withered on the vine. Tis best we chase a fervent dream."

"Miss Lou was a character; I'm sorry I missed her."

"Oh she's not quite gone. A mystery's afoot though I can't quite grasp it. I wish you sensed her presence the way I do. There's an unspoken bond twix the three of us. She's with us Jack, and you must look beyond your nose."

Tap...tap...tap. It is the jailer's keys again. Ellie snaps, "What is so all-fired important?"

"Don't git feisty with me girl lest I feed your supper to my horse. The folk's upstairs is looking for yer friend."

"Are they now, how do they expect Jack to work and keep me company?" The sarge lets go a growl and puffs his way down the hall.

"He doesn't appreciate your sarcasm. You know the man's just doing his job."

"No worries, ole Pete is bless-ed forgetful. He can't keep a grudge from one minute to the next."

"I'm not sure how my office found me. I didn't say where I was headed."

"Precious there's no such thing as a secret. The entire building knows you're with me. Go on with ya and head upstairs. Tell your

125

boss its cash only tonight; I'll not accept his promissory note. May I see you tomorrow?"

"Tomorrow for sure."

Office mates greet me with silent stares and that's fine by me. My travels are none of their business.

Mr. Barr's assistant squints and motions me over to his desk. "The boss deems a word if it's convenient, Mas-tar Hamby."

Nesbitt's a sarcastic minion! I'd like to return fire but I mustn't. I turn towards Mr. Barr's door, take a breath and rap twice. A deep baritone voice answers from within. "Come." I enter the forbidden sanctuary prepared for my benefactor's wrath. Barr speaks from behind his splayed newspaper, "Have a seat boy."

Our team respects the boss's station. Samuel Clayton Barr is an elected official and a consummate politician. He does what's necessary within proper limits, charming yet ruthless if crossed. Floyd says Mr. Barr doesn't socialize with the help except at Christmastime and a summons to his inner chamber is no social call.

I sit in front of an enormous Myrtle wood desk, on the payroll a week and already in trouble. My anxiety builds as Barr keeps reading his paper. Am I on the chopping block? How will I support my family without this job? In front of me are the paper deck-lines shouting a repetitive take on the Ambary tragedy. Mr. Barr folds his paper and stares at me. Is he enjoying this? Does my employer relish torture? What passes for humane in these parts?

"Sorry for my tardiness sir. It won't happen again."

"No it will not. Relax son, you're not being sacked. Tardiness won't do but that's not why you're here. This is about Ellie."

"Ellie Flannery?"

"Yes of course! Don't toy with me boy. How many girls named Ellie do we have in common?"

Why is the boss so irritated? I wasn't trying to spark a match.

Mr. Barr takes a breath and continues. "Lou and I were friends and I've known Ellie since she was tiny. That girl was and is a handful. Not that the sprite welcomes it but Lou charged us uncles with her care. We swore an oath and kept it until the Ambary brat ambushed us. None of us saw that dimwit coming!"

There's a fire in Mr. Barr's eyes. Who dares cross this man and why is he confiding to his help? If this visit is about Ellie, whatever does he expect of me?

"I'll do whatever I can sir."

Mr. Barr taps the newspaper. "I'll take care of this rubbish. Nesbitt says you're handling the Graham file. Ellie's taken a liking to you so spend as much time with her as she wants. I'll let folks know you're there on my orders so stop sneaking around, it gives the wrong impression. Your job is to keep Ellie company during this ridiculous ordeal. You can talk to her or play cards but don't embarrass me! Do you understand?"

Indeed I do! Mr. Barr says to play hooky with a beauty and I can hardly contain myself. "You can depend on me sir. I'll do my humble best."

Barr picks up his newspaper and mumbles, "Never met an Ambary worth his salt. The house is a nest of coldblooded rattlers." I stand, turn for the door and Mr. Barr says, "Jack wait."

My boss called me by my first name. Is the familiarity a compliment or a worry? I stop shy of the door. "Yes sir?"

"James Ambary is a dangerous man so be discreet and watch your back. We uncles honor loyalty but we can't protect an idiot." Sam Barr's tone is foreboding if not downright scary.

"Roger that sir, I'm no fool and you can trust me. Mr. Barr sir, Ellie has a message for you."

"What does she want?"

"She won't accept a promissory note so bring cash to the game tonight."

Barr smiles, "That's my girl. Lou raised her right."

Sam Barr and I have one thing in common; we like his so-called niece. I walk to my desk pondering his pledge of allegiance. Just how many uncles are there and are they all benevolent? More important, do they see me as a person or cannon fodder for their cause?

At end of day I march home with a clear intent. Anne must know about my visits with Ellie. I can't let idle gossip upset her.

I share my thoughts on Ellie and her specter during our supper; my wife doesn't react and digests my story with her meal. However, she stops me when she notices Belle hanging on my every word. Thanks to me our girl relishes any mention of a ghost. My tale can wait until we're alone. I change topics and hold the details for later.

We put Belle in her room and ready ourselves for bed. Anne asks, "Honestly dear do I have anything to fear from the charming Miss Flannery?"

"Darling I have two true loves: my wife and baby. Yes Ellie's fetching but I'm hopelessly devoted to you. I have no explanation for the instant friendship except to say Ellie's tales resonate in my gut. Kismet fueled our coming to Seattle and I doubt our meeting was a chance encounter. Ellie's ghost-mistress reminds me of the ethereal guides my mother fancies." Annie gives me a puckish grin; I'm pouring my heart out and my wife mocks me! "Please don't ridicule me. I'm as serious as a heart attack."

"Oh save your ticker and don't pout. I believe you, truly I do. As for your intuition, how can I stand between a man and his gut? All I ask is you share everything about Miss Flannery and her ghost friend."

"Done. I absolutely adore you! How did I land such a perfect wife?"

Sweet Anne pulls me onto the bed. "You did nothing sir. Most days you tax my patience. I must be a simpleton or a saint to put up with you."

My wife is neither one; she is a temptress. Her touch awakens me and I surrender to her charms. Jackson Hamby is one lucky cuss!

CHAPTER 21

A Charmed Life

The next day I sign in as Sam Barr's liaison and tell Ellie about my conversations with Mr. Barr and Anne. Well not everything; omitting the embarrassing details is tricky but less humbling for me. Dad says a man never admits to mushy feelings. I often ignore my father's outdated notions but this one serves the moment. Ellie no doubt senses the gaps in my story yet her beguiling smile hides all suspicion.

"Your Anne sounds delightful. Let's all go to my favorite restaurant in Chinatown. I'm sure little Belle will love it!" Ellie's eyes flash with delight until a glance at the cell door subdues her. "You say my uncles have my back? Well then I need better kinfolk. Sam's as poor a relative as he is a cribbage player." Ellie looks to the ceiling and points towards my office. "Sam Barr you're a muggins for letting Jimmy steal the point. You best get it together on the next crib or we're all in trouble!"

"Ellie be of good cheer; your uncle's confident and I know your freedom is at hand."

"My dear sweet naïve lamb you best wise up before the jackals get ya. Let's forego the Ambary mess for now. Where was I in my tale? Oh yes, 'twas life in our manor house."

Ellie nods for me to sit in the chair. Why do I concede to its spooky presence? Well answer me this: can anyone truly prove or disprove a ghost? I whisper, "Dear madame I'm disinclined to believe in you yet an open mind overrules me. My mother says a polite nod cajoles a spirit and blesses the mortal."

Ellie's grinning at my one-sided discourse. So be it if my lunacy amuses her. I'm here to please and I want to hear the next chapter of her story.

Our mistress demands her First Hill monstrosity rival the most lavish houses and Lou gives Mr. Chin carte blanche to uphold her image. The little guy never disappoints so the palace is an elegant setting to wine and dine a moneyed prospect. Lou and the bosses court visiting moguls or politicians with stylish buffets and, of course, beautiful escorts. A man who fancies an after-supper aperitif can trolley down the hill to our other house.

However the mansion's highbrow elegance doesn't impress this lass. It gives me the willies with its ancient breakables casting weird shadows everywhere. And the silly rules, good golly a kid can hardly breathe! For instance, Mr. Chin has a no shoes rule and makes us wear wool slippers to keep the place clean. Except for our guests the shoes come off at the door.

It surprises folks that Miss Lou knits our woolies. What's wrong with their thinkers? Is it so strange for a madame to knit? Lou says the repetition clears her mind. She chants 'set up one, fear goes out, loop back two, goodbye doubt, stitch away worry, and the joy comes out!' She tries teaching me but we quit to save her sanity.

I often misplace a slipper and blame it on the house fairies. Lou says there's no such thing but Mr. Chin's a believer. Tis fun to mess with the both of em. Cuss it! I'm off my story again.

Wily spirits aside, the mansion's a yawn compared to our dock street house. Lou disagrees saying, "A mudflat rouse is where the shrilling seagulls fight for garbage scraps. My uptown garden is full of gentle songbirds and it's where I must retreat from the hustling crowd."

Her garden is full of songbirds, butterflies, and hummingbirds. Its lush greenery supports a hobby Mr. Chin calls homeopathy and his concoctions cured my childhood maladies. This girl kept her health while my mates fell ill with fevers and cough. At the first signs of the syphilis Mr. Chin treats Lou with herbal potions. However the dire prognosis forces Lou to add a medicinal tonic. Mr. Chin says Lou's better off with his remedies and he's right. The mercury tincture causes Lou to lose clumps of her beautiful hair. Bless Granny Chin who makes a wig from the fallen locks. With no cure in sight we all shared Lou's worry. Ah but I digress. Lou always says my mind's a winding road with no shortcuts.

Our grand monstrosity is also where Lou hosts teas for distinguished ladies. The upper crust is a royal pain in the arse so Lou invites a few chatty ex-employees who married upscale and one true blueblood. As I said, Gracie is a gem and the Conover's are a special kind of gentry.

Grace's ancestral bible came with family on the first pilgrim's crossing. The two sweethearts grew up in Boston with servants as did their parents but a young Hannibal fancied adventure over heritage. He was supposed to be a lawyer like his dad but he dreamt of life on a Mississippi paddleboat. At seventeen years Hannibal skedaddled telling Gracie he'd send for her when she came of age. Months passed without a word and the girl was a melancholy mess. Her mother told her, "Hannibal Conover is a troubled boy. Do move on and stop your pining."

"You're wrong mother. Han will send for me; you just wait and see!" Sure enough Hannibal's letter arrived on Gracie's sixteenth birthday. She responded with a telegram that read: 'Dearest Han: my train departs on the 18th. The Number 6 arrives in St. Louis on the 25th. All my love, Grace.'

The star-crossed lovers married in Hannibal Missouri on the deck of a riverboat. Tis kinda funny that Hannibal got hitched in Hannibal but the Bostonians aren't laughing. The children's elopement slaps of disrespect and his dad loathes young Hannibal's chosen profession. The prominent Beacon Hill lawyer has a cardsharp son and his gambling is a disgrace worthy of disinheritance.

What is Hannibal's response to the threat? "Do what you want with your money sir. I have no use for unearned wealth."

Hannibal's defiance is a pisser and Gracie's letters return unopened until a chance meeting changes everything. A family friend visiting New Orleans happens upon Grace and her baby girl at a ferry terminal. They chat until a paddleboat's whistle beckons and the friend returns home to share his news.

"Grace and her toddler are well and in good spirits. She says Hannibal does very well on the boats and her attire backs her up. Gracie misses you all and sends her love."

A chance encounter is the first news of a grandbaby and the elated grandmas forego paternal consent to send gifts. However Grace's thank-you notes return unopened and the unending manly feud stabs at Grace's heart. Of course, Hannibal blames his dad but Gracie says there's a mule's likeness between this father and son.

The young Conover's continue roaming up and down Ole Miss until Grace blesses Hannibal with a baby boy. One little babe on a ferryboat is a handful but two rambunctious children is chaos so Hannibal packs up his family and settles down as far away from Boston as possible.

The family moves to Seattle where Hannibal secures Lou's backing for his biggest gamble and the tug and barge company soon dominates traffic up and down the coast. When it's all said and done, Hannibal just wanted to steer his own course and repaid his wife's loyalty with a handmade fortune. Gracie loves her new life though she misses family asking, "Han, will our babies ever know our parents?" The grandmas take a similar stand and the menfolk are forced to make peace.

Yes indeed, the Conover's are genuine folk. They look beyond the obvious to what's truly important.

Ellie breaks her trance to focus on me. "Ahh Jack, 'twas an amazing sight! Over a thousand folks attended Lou's viewing with a line of devoted mourners, kerchiefs in hand, meandering out our door and around the block. Curious gawkers joined the wake and a flock of spiteful vultures circled the casket. The righteous biddies wanted proof of Lou's demise. Our feisty mistress was full of surprises yet cheating death was not in the cards. The prudish guild cawed, "Aha, the queen of Hades goes home to her devil husband!" The spiteful do-gooders couldn't tell an angel's wing from a turkey's butt feather!"

Ellie slips back into her story. Those virtuous biddies are relentless. Their priggery often invades our district with chants of "Magdalene was a fallen woman. Follow us too be saved!" The callous killjoys thrust their missionary position on us and it's a bloody waste of time! In the Chapel district heaven's a daily meal and a safe place to sleep. When livín day to day a street girl has no use of a flowery afterlife.

The righteous jury is on a mission to enlighten us with their insufferable hymns. We'd laugh at the chants of doom if it weren't for the awful racket! A working girl sleeps in the morning and the unwanted street sacraments are a pisser!

The fervent cranks close ranks to storm our place but Mr. Earl blocks the doorway while the girls lean out of our windows booing the intrusion; their shouts of 'hooray for iniquity' counter the insults from below.

Lou also addresses the fanatics. "Lord bless us ladies, my girls deserve their beauty sleep and your peevish invite awakens us all! Alas, your rigid Glory train serves a bitter tea. We sinners prefer a comfy coach with laughter and bubbling wine." Lou gives a queenlike wave and disappears behind her curtain.

Lardy! If hoots could kill we'd all be goners! Preferring action over words, I pour gin into a condom and slingshot it into the crowd. Hurrah! I hit a drum and the balloon bursts. I fill another and another until the condom box is almost empty and their dresses are soaked in sinful booze. How exciting to watch the whimpered retreat!

Shoot! Mr. Chin's at the door; my fun is over and I'm in big trouble. Turns out Goodyear condoms and Tanqueray gin are pricey ammo. My tacky barrage was uncalled-for, or so I'm told, and I'll forfeit a week's allowance to pay for lost inventory. I hate those women!

Might an uncle intervene on our behalf? A sympathetic patron will surely stop his meddling wife, if only Lou would ask. She won't.

"Petition assistance, whatever for? Peaceful assembly is a granted freedom and I enjoy irritating pomposity. Being a thorn in a charlatan's crown is its own reward."

CHAPTER 22

Our Mister Chin

The calm voice amongst us is Mr. Li Po Chin. The keeper of our houses is a meticulous but kind taskmaster who considers his situation a blessing. Anyone who knows the man respects his ways. He's well-mannered, easygoing and his quietude embodies the best of a proud heritage.

Mr. Chin is a descendant of the first Li Po. His ancestral beginnings tells of the Suyab poet who loved plum wine and paddled the Yellow River. Alas the ancient Li Po drank too much, stood up in his canoe and drowned himself. It's said the quixotic poet was reaching skyward for his love, a moon goddess called Chang'e the Immortal.

Name-passing is a Chinese tradition but our modern Li Po is neither a drunkard nor a zealous romantic. Our chef manages booze for business and his poetry is a delicious meal.

I admit our first meeting was awkward. Mr. Chin says, "Proximity educates a willing mind and a change of heart opens many a door." Yes he sounds like a fortune cookie but he means well. I was an ill-mannered brat until proximity to our gentleman changed me. 'Twas impossible to live with myself without making an amends.

"Mr. Chin please forgive this uncouth lass. I fear a biased upbringing poisoned my senses."

"Apology accepted child; however I forgave you long ago. Blame is an empty pout and begrudging curses us both. Why not impugn your thinking and let go the past? Life is a quest to master the moment, is it not? Consider this: The sunrise forgives and invites us to do better."

The wise cookie's words defy his social status and I did learn my lesson: My contempt hurt me more than my rival. But wait! What my elder said next really spun my compass!

"Ellie life is in the eye of the beholder. A petulant mutt chasing its tail ends up dazed and dissatisfied. However a master chases nothing. He quiets himself, listens within and a melody emerges. 'Rest in me. Hear my refrain, be humble and let your heart sing my reticence'. And so it is, the enlightened cannot be bound, led astray, or offended."

The Chapel district is a noisy cluster and practicing silence is like playing the piano; the world spins without me as I let go the mind's chatter, ignore my ego, and find my inner rhythm. Tis then I hear my soul singing in the stillness.

My ever-patient mentor takes me beyond the clatter and gives me a copy of the Dao Te Ching. Mr. Chin follows the Dao. He says it's a natural fit for me but I got me doubts. Tis a subtle read and subtlety is as foreign as Mr. Chin. I want to please him so I attack hell-bent on capturing the Dao's flag! Alas every verse is an impenetrable foe.

"Mr. Chin I'm drowning here! My shallow mind can't fathom a deeper meaning and I'm not worthy of its teaching. Tis a waste of time! Why must I flounder with no hope of reward?"

My mentor places a calming hand on top my head. "Child take a breath. You belittle yourself and drown in your drama. Tackling the Dao muddles its wisdom. You must replace an ambush with a humble surrender, quiet your mind and engage your heart. Follow your breath and exhale deeply; sit in peace and let the ancient Truth find you. Only then will the Dao speak to you." He's right of course. Bless his fortune cookie heart.

Lou trusts Mr. Chin with her goodbye and puts him in charge of the funeral. I want no part in her finale and abhor the incessant planning. The thought of losing Lou chokes me up but the always reliable Mr. Chin ensures every detail is the theater she wants.

Lou says, "Return from my grave with a New Orleans style processional and a brass band playing a jubilant rendition of Awake My Soul, to Joyful Lays."

'Awake My Soul' is from Miss Lou's Lutheran hymnal. I remember but one verse: ♪ Though mighty hosts of cruel foes, where earth and hell my way oppose, He safely leads my soul along, His loving kindness, Oh how strong! ♪

Yes, a sacred song keeps the faithful on an eternal path and Lou's at peace with her mortal end. Her body gives up as Lou predicted. The Queen of Seattle collapses in a train's lounge headed for home. Mr. Chin interns her remains on Capitol Hill in the Lake View cemetery. No seawater laps at Lou's bones; the cemetery sits high atop a bluff overlooking the Puget waters where the wealthy recline in splendor. Mr. Chin can't abide his friend hobnobbing with Bigbugs so he purchases side-by-side plots in the commoner section and tasks me to ensure they'll someday rest together. Tis a whites only cemetery but that won't stop me. Mama always said, "There's no haughty betters in heaven and only a puffy dryshite dares to claim otherwise." As long as Mr. Chin is in the casket any name on the tombstone will do.

Ellie's gone lost in her mourning. I interrupt the mood and draw her back to me. "Ellie dear, how did Mr. Chin and Miss Lou meet?"

"Ah Jack thanks for the lifeline. Sometimes my grief does pull me under. Mr. Chin came to San Francisco as an indentured servant. Lou was visiting friends who invited her to a French bistro owned by Li Po's master. The meal was delicious and Lou insisted she meet the chef. Unaware of his undoing, the pompous owner obliged his wealthy customer. Lou tells it better than me so I'll use her voice."

Ellie slips into a perfect Bavarian accent: The owner is a frettchen with a faux French libretto. I hear the ferret's distinct twang booming from the kitchen. He says, "What's a matters wit ya! Moves it. Some fancy broad wants ta meets yous." The door swings open with the puffed-up twit parading steps ahead of his bowed servant. He's a wretched ingrate who steals the credit while a real culinary genius walks in his tow! I cannot haggle cost when free expression is at stake so I buy the contract outright and take the chef with me. The next day my friends complain to the Board of Health; seems a giant rat has run of the café. I say the phony made his choice and it was justice served. To quote Milton's Paradise Lost, "The mind is its own place, in itself makes a heaven of hell, a hell of heaven."

Our madame brings her find back home and gathers the staff in the parlor. She holds up the indentured contract for all to see. "Friends I won't keep this filthy paper a minute longer. It reeks of interest paid with no hope of freedom."

Lou tosses the contract into the blazing fire and the room explodes with applause save one exception. A stunned Mr. Chin puts a hand to his heart and sighs, "Mistress you are most kind."

Lou says, "Dear ones join with me now; we shan't condone a yoke placed upon another. Ralph Emerson says a master shackling his slave chains two souls. Let us break the bonds of complicity and free ourselves of its cruel stench. I paid extra for a meal worth every penny. It is our good fortune to taste his talents. Ladies and gentlemen I give you our new chef, Mr. Li Po Chin. Please raise your glasses to his free expression!" Mr. Chin blossoms beyond culinary skills to manage both our houses. More important, he is Lou Graham's most trusted ally.

Learning my trade from Mr. Chin has its difficulties. Can you imagine this feisty child mastering manners, table settings and dress mending? Yet by my eleventh birthday I held a tray of food one-handed and packed a trunk sans one wrinkle. I admit these are menial chores but Mr. Chin was quick to remind me of their value. "Ellie listen to yourself ramble on. Your thoughts spin like a carousel. It makes me dizzy. Please focus on the task at hand."

Ironing dresses for Lou and the girls is tedious labor. My ironing board is in the maid's room near the kitchen and I must reheat my iron and keep a steamy kettle nearby. Mr. Chin walks into the room with yet another bundle so I explode from inside out, "Mr. Chin I can't take anymore! My arm's gonna fall off!"

"Little one why are you so melodramatic? Can you not see the unseen value in a menial task? Why do you prefer money over a rich lesson? Sweat and grit yields more than a penny."

"I get your gist sir but I'm not all-in. A penny buys a bag of sweets but you see my sweat and make me bathe."

My mentor tosses the dresses onto the bed. "Then enjoy your pity-party and dance in your misery."

Misery indeed, where did I stash my peppermint puffs?

What I truly fancy is our walks through the streets of Chinatown. Mr. Chin's daily sojourn freshens our pantry and I beg to go with him.

All that talk of perilous Orientals is a convenient bashing cause a labor fight has Seattle spooked. Migrants work for less than a Union Joe and organizers don't like foreigners taking their wages. It starts with the posting of a vile cartoon of a slant-eyed thief picking a pocket. Then there's the vulgar graffiti threatening anyone but union boys touching the freight. Don't forget the leaflets of mandarin-collared tigers stealing children into slavery, wary pulpits warning their flock of invading Oriental voodoo and newspapers spinning the opium crisis as a foreign takeover: 'Beware of the Chink Gangs Poisoning Our Youth!' Yee-haw! A union man is one of us, not them. True patriots must rise up and crush the wicked yellow hoard! Only a violent purge restores our natural order and preserves America for Americans. Your country needs you!

Tis a bunch of rotten smelly hooey. Lou says, "The greedy play with fire and they know it. They sound a bogus alarm but it's an ageless ploy. Incessant drums ignite a primal urge best left alone. Fearful dupes repeat the lies as gospel and spit on those who debunk the twisted claims!"

Of course the awful scheme succeeds. No Chinaman, woman or child is safe on the streets as riotous mobs beat their kind into the marshes. Union lads spite the devil and win back the docks, hurrah! Tis unholy hogwash!

The crusade's a whitewashed swindle and Lou refuses to back the rapacious swine. "Boys do not defile my house with your power grabbing filth. Shame on you shatting your smelly hatred everywhere. Your oinking mafia drowns out reason, shams common sense, and attacks our civil liberties. And for what? The only threat here is your incessant grunting. Why must you ignore history? Rabblerousing for a false idol trumps the fool and it never ends well. Repent your ugly ways or leave my house. Go on get out! I won't entertain charlatans or their dummkopfs."

Truth be told Chinatown is not a ruinous scene. It's an amazing place with the aroma of street carts permeating the senses! Roasted skewers dipped in chili paste awaken a sweat and tasty bean-curd candies rival a Chapel merchant's chews! Did I mention the humble alchemist healing ailments with ancient herbal recipes? This culture is a wonder to behold, though I admit the chatter baffles me. German is my second tongue outta respect for Lou. Well mostly. Mr. Chin hoped I'd learn Mandarin but its crazy cadence intimidates me.

Ellie stops her tale and gives me a stern look. "Jack Hamby you best listen up! 'Twas easy to judge with a blind eye to myself. Yes Chinatown has its troubles but no more than anywhere else. Exploring its newness fed my curiosity and seeing for myself confirmed my suspicions. Chinatown is not the devil's lair and I will never accept what I'm told without a firsthand look."

Ellie smears her finger on my thick glasses. "Mister beware the warped view of a hand-me-down assumption. A corrective lens cannot correct a fearful distortion and small-minded vision."

CHAPTER 23

What in the Sam Hill?

Ellie's warning is a puzzle but I've no time to ask a question. As if on cue the dayshift sergeant raps on the cell door. "Ellie ya got another visitor. It be James Ambary and I'm guessín you want me to send him packín."

"No sir, please bring him here. Let's see what the bumble's up to."

Sergeant Pete walks back to his desk muttering, "The girl's got more spunk than sense. Her lawyer ain't gonna like this."

Ellie smiles at his comment and turns her attention to me. "Jack there'll be more stories tomorrow. It's time for you to go."

"Is this the Ambary who jailed you? The man has some nerve coming here. Do you know what he wants? Shouldn't I stay close?"

"Oh I've a good idea about Jimmy and your chivalry's touching but unnecessary. I'm safer in this cell than on the streets."

Two pairs of footsteps approach, a key turns the lock and the door opens. The guard steps aside revealing a lanky fair-haired man. Mama would call him sissified handsome. The guard stiffens and stares at the gent. "Mr. Ambary ya git your pistol back when ya leave. Keep it civil now. I'm down the hall and in no mood for trouble. Ya hear me?"

The dandy waves a dismissive hand. "Thank you constable, you can run along now."

"Sonny I earned these stripes. It's Sergeant O'Grady to the likes of you." The jailer glares at Ambary before stepping away.

Jimmy eyes me. His grin fades but he's quick to recover. Ambary takes in the plush décor and whistles. "Ooey! I see you moved right in. Mind you a real prison won't be this accommodating."

"Mind your manners darlín. You're on thin ice with me and I won't waste a precious minute on your baoise. You're being rude to Mr. Hamby from the Auditor's office. He's servicing Lou's will for my uncle Sam."

Ambary eyes me as if I magically reappeared, looks me over and quickly loses interest. Poof! I am invisible again. "Ellie does Sam Barr know his help makes house calls?"

The rude bastard thinks me a deaf lackey. I dislike him more by the minute if that's possible. Ellie senses my transfixed tension. In a mocking Irish tone she says, "Ah Jimmy you're a bodach just like yer feckín brother. Any gombeen knows I can't visit Sam's office." Ellie speaks to Ambary yet smiles at me; her eyes are asking me to go.

I have no choice but to trust her instincts. "By your leave Miss Ellie. I am but a call away."

I sidestep the weasel and our eyes lock. James Ambary stares into my thick lens as if to challenge me. He thinks me a lesser man but Jimmy's wrong. Given a fair fight I'd gladly clean his clock! Ambary's foot kicks the door causing the bars to literally hit my butt on the way out. That did it! I must stay put. Sorry mama, I know prying's rude but this tactless ass is my friend's nemesis. I move three steps away from the cell and lean against the far wall. It's not my finest hour yet the shadows and curtain conceal my meddling.

Ambary wastes no time and moves on; he ignores Ellies odious stare and pours himself a drink. "By all means ya mooch, help yourself to my liquor. Lou warned me not to play with vermin and silly me ignored her. It took long enough to show your face. Tell me darlin, what makes an Ambary such a presuming arse?"

"Well, my mother said not to bed street trash yet here we are. I've lost a dear brother and you're in jail." Ambary drinks the entire shot glass and pours another.

"Jeez Jimmy! Look around will ya. Do I look humbled? You lied that night on the ship and you're a liar now. Don't you dare pretend to grieve Caleb; you despised each other. The only bond you shared was thievery and chasín garters. Your pout's nothing more than an expedient sham."

Jimmy's posture stiffens, he downs his drink and slams the glass onto the tray. The noise startles him and Jimmy rethinks his temper. "Ahh, you're a delight as always. It's like old times without the heavy petting. Pity I can't stay to socialize. Unlike you I've places to go."

That did it! Ellie steps toe-to-toe with Ambary. "Then state your business and be gone. What do you want?"

"Only what's owed me. Miss Lou stole my map."

"I knew it! Jimmy boy you gotta give up the fantasy; you never owned the map in the first place. Not that it matters but I told you it was a fake. Your loony mum was out to hang me and Lou angled the phony as bait." Ellie looks to Lou's portrait and raises her voice to the heavens. "Lou the noddy's back again. How can I deal with him?"

The guard door bangs against the cellblock wall and the sergeant moans, "Damn it! I'm a comín fer ya and I ain't happy about it."

Ellie shakes her head. "We're fine dad, don't trouble yourself."

"Well you best keep it down, I ain't playín no games."

The Sarge eyes me leaning against the wall. He already thinks me an idiot so I shrug my shoulders and grin. Pete shakes his head, leaves the door open and mutters, "This ain't no jail. It's a friggin looney bin."

I return to the conversation inside the cell. Ambary says, "Come on Ellie stop talking to the ethers. Mother and Lou are cold dead. It's just us now so drop the vazey act. Lou put my map in her will and I have a legal transfer for your signature. It's a fair trade; I get what's mine and you're free to go. Now stop wasting my time."

I can't believe my ears! Despite his station James Ambary is no gentleman. What species of crassness speaks that way to a lady? If mama heard me utter those words I'd be sleeping with the pigs. She'd say, "I'll pardon a cuss when a finger's pinched. However a constant swearing is lazy and mudslinging is an ungodly sin! Jackson go sleep in the barn and take the dictionary with you; the pig can read you a few new words. Only a mannered boy sups at my table." Ambary deserves a fortnight shivering in a pigsty. Whatever did Ellie see in him. I sneak closer to better hear the conversation.

Ambary reaches into his pocket and retrieves the pact.

"Nice language Jimbo. Your fancy university surely taught a better phrase. Oh but you filched exams instead of giving it an honest try. How much did your hijinks cost your mama? Perhaps a new library or a science building."

Ellie's delivery makes me think she's up to something. What sort of risky game is the girl playing? I wish the curtain offered more than a peekaboo view.

Ambary clinches a fist, his eyes narrow and his neck veins pop. "Street filth like you taught me to cuss. At least I went to a real university and not a girlie academy. Tell me dear, what does a puss do with a writing degree? Fashion or perhaps church reporting? Maybe a food critic? Working a scullery certainly qualifies you."

Ellie smiles and stands her ground. Tis fun to rile the bastard but her demeanor has a grander purpose. What does Jimmy know about the will? "You dare barter my freedom? That's a good one. Lou and Mike did the will in secrecy and I doubt you're on speaking terms with either one."

"I don't need the shyster or your ghost. A living Lou spoke to me years ago. I remember it like it was yesterday. Lou said, "James you behave or lose the map forever. It's mine for now and willed to Ellie thereafter." Yes the map's in the will and you'll bargain with me or rot in jail." He takes the fountain pen from its ink well. "Stop being a mulish snit and sign over the map." Ellie slaps the pen from Jimmy's hand causing it to splatter ink onto his suit. "Dammit! This is my best waistcoat. Ornery tramp! You best behave or I'll see you swing from the rafters!"

"James Ambary you are an incurable putz. Listen up and hear me good. I'm content to stay here or stand before the noose. You'll get nothing from me save grief so stay the course and join Caleb in hell. You know I mean every word."

Yikes! Ellie's delivery gives me the chills. I hope she's bluffing and not plotting another killing. Who are these people? Why do I care and why did Ellie befriend the likes of me? Am I bait in some nefarious game? Chance Hollow's boring but it's civil. Common decency seems optional here. Are my dreams delusional? Am I just another lunatic in this bedlam? The dank walls are closing in on me. With no fresh air to breathe I rush past the sergeant and out the front door. My sole desire is to hug my innocent girls.

I pause to catch a breath and my quandary catches up to me. What do I tell Anne? Dad says no man whimpers before his bride. If I can't go home where do I go? I turn away from Belltown to wander the uptown streets. There must be a saving solution up here somewhere.

CHAPTER 24

What Choice Have I?

An hour later I stand lost at the end of a dead-end road. In front of me is a tranquil park where two elder gents are playing horseshoes. I stand exhausted under a majestic Madrona and lay down to watch a sky full of puffy clouds float by.

Each passing puff morphs into this shape or that. It could be a scene from my childhood with a sickly boy laying under a tree asking God to intervene. My youthful prayer still rings true. "Dear Lord, I beg a moment of your time. Please fix me and give me the strength to carry on."

Clouds shapeshift above me and the only sound I hear is the clink of horseshoes dead on target.

"Lord you've seen how I manage alone. Why do You leave me to my own devices? What can I say to Anne that doesn't paint me a fool?" The heavens remain mute. I feel abandoned with just my own voice for comfort. "C'mon Jackson find your own way! Perhaps I say nothing and wait on the dust to settle. That's it! Don't overthink the situation; let a meal and a fitful sleep offer a solution."

I hear one old codger grumble and see his friend nod. The two men stop playing and stare at me. Did I speak my thoughts aloud? Are they mocking me? I stand up mortified by my ineptness and leave to retrace my steps back home.

As if sensing my sadness sweet Belle greets me with a squeezing hug. The pleasant aroma of supper drifts from the stove but my head is throbbing and there's an uneasy feeling in my stomach. Great! I must add guilt to my discontent. I walk down the hallway groaning, "Sorry dearest a migraine sends me to my bed." Mind you I'm not trying to avoid my wife. It's as if a mule kicked me in my head. No not so! I'm the jackass who inflicts this pain upon himself.

Sleep eludes me all the way to dawn's light. Tossing and turning only fuels my melancholy and the morning is no pardon. The smell of breakfast all but gags me. I can't offer a fit excuse and so I make a hasty retreat. My stunned girls watch from the window as I stumble down the steps towards the trolley.

This startup does not bode well. A soggy fog hugs the ground, my umbrella's hanging on its antler tine and the trolley left me to walk up the hill in the chill. Can this day get any worse? Of course it can. A seagull hovers above me looking for handouts. "Go away beggar. I've nothing for you." Ah but he has a gift for me. With a vengeful shrill the bird shats a perfect plop of stink upon my shoulder.

"Damn flying rat! Filthy avenger!" I pick up a rock but the gull's gone lost in the fog. "Cuss it all! What else can go wrong?"

It's then I hear my mother's caution. "Hush up boy, tempting fate isn't the answer. You best watch your speech. When you ask what misery awaits Fate obliges you tenfold!"

"Yes ma'am, thank goodness a cow can't fly. Imagine a fresh poopie splatting on my noggin! Please tell me, what's the unseen benefit to this madness?"

Silence. Mama's memory's gone mute so I trudge up the steep hill lost in my misery.

What else can go wrong? The answer is an envelope placed on my desk. The note reads: 'Shame on you Jack Hamby, spying is beneath you. No doubt you ran off with the wrong idea. Please don't abandon me. I'm no siren luring you to your doom and I swear an untold truth acquits me. Let's try again tomorrow. Take a breather and come see me in the afternoon. Your friend Ellie.'

The desk sergeant probably snitched or was it my clumsy exit? This hayseed is no match for Ellie and I'm in over my head. My family's right about me, I am daft! Jeez! A dozen thoughts clamor in my head until an unsettling belch alerts me. Oh God I'm going to puke! I choke back a second warning and run for the toilet.

Turns out my hasty retreat was for not. I haven't eaten and it's all dry heaves. Several minutes pass before I return to a wary huddle of workers who fear a contagion and insist I go home.

My downhill descent is a metaphor for time travel and I am a child again. My mother tucks me into bed and feeds me a bowl of chicken broth to sooth my sour stomach. It is a sweet memory but it's no reprieve. An indifferent wife greets me as I sulk past her and collapse onto the bed.

Make no mistake, Anne is not my mother. "Jackson Hamby I just put fresh linens on the bed! Put your filthy boots on the floor and your dramatic pout isn't welcome here. Are you going to tell me what's going on." I am once again a frightened opossum. "Nothing to say buster? Well then take Belle to the beach. Go on, get up and carry your sorry self away from me."

I help little Belle negotiate the steep steps as my wife, broom in hand, shoos my behind. Belle and I head down the road with Anne calling after us, "Never let a soup boil over. Keep a low flame or the bottom scalds. Don't scrape it lest you liberate a burnt fond; the ruination floats to the top and spoils the best of intentions." Good grief! My life's in chaos and Anne quotes from her What Every Bride Should Know cookbook. Why is the girl so useless when needed most? I scoop Belle onto my shoulders and walk towards the beach.

It takes no time at all for my mood to change. Nature and my innocent babe provide the calm I crave. Belle and I have a bond forged the first time I held her and an outing with my Bellybutton renews her Papaw. It's a simple yet powerful miracle. Belle cares nothing about adult troubles. She giggles at a tiny crab sparring with her twig and delights in my mediocre skipping of stones across the calm surf. Her only faceoff is a game of tag with the incoming tide.

Anne's cooking advice makes perfect sense now. Life does not marinate on my watch. My meddling ego stirs the pot ruining a good intent. Dad says a prayer's answered even before it's prayed. I believe he's right and take my little girl's hand. "Come on sweet cheeks, I must talk to mommy."

Anne greets us with a sweetened milk for Belle and a cup of broth for me. Her intuition is both annoying and a comfort. My wife and I sit in the living room after Belle goes down for her nap. Humble tears fill my eyes as Anne listens to my ramble. She squeezes my hand. "Darling you look exhausted. We haven't spent much time together of late. How about the three of us bake a batch of molasses cookies before supper."

"That sounds wonderful. I'm so sorry for letting my troubles on the hill consume me."

Sharing time with my lovelies puts me at ease and the aroma of baked spices soothes my weariness. We enjoy a fine supper, put little Belle to bed and I fall asleep in the arms of my best friend.

CHAPTER 25

Na Zdravje!

My colleagues greet me with skepticism. I tell them "Relax fellas it was just an upset stomach and not a plague. I'm feeling much better today." I offer each man a cookie from my basket and keep the remaining sweets as a peace offering to Ellie.

No doubt she entertained an uncle into the late hours so I wait for the noon bell before heading downstairs to my second amends. Ellie greets me as if nothing's happened. "Yum! Is that sweet molasses and ginger I smell?"

"Annie, Belle, and I baked cookies. Well, Anne baked and her helpers made a floury mess."

"Please thank her for me. So about Jimmy, I should a warned you about him but I wanted you to see a better me before I talked about the tragedy. It all seems out of context without a glimpse at my childhood."

"Your instincts are good and you mustn't apologize. Savoring a rambling oral history is time well spent. I am an impatient and nosey bumpkin. Sometimes I wonder why the good Lord made me a father."

"Mum always said God grants a life and a parent bears the rest. As dads go your tiny Belle got a gem. There's plenty worse out there mishandling their duty."

"Ellie you endured a life I can't begin to understand. While you suffered real-life abuse this sickly boy laid in bed reading tall tales.

The newspaper paints you as ruthless but I don't see you that way. Help me understand your journey, tell me your story and I'll listen sans a judge's robes." It is my most eloquent soliloquy to date. We're both teary-eyed and I hold her hand for comfort. Did recent events catch up to Ellie? I am here to help anyway I can.

"Ahh Jack that was lovely but you needn't worry. Tis a sucker's bet to hold onto the past. Mr. Fortune Cookie says a sweeter today requires I let go of a sour yesterday. Do you remember the tale of the one-eyed crow? It warns us that the same tired view wears a body out so I read this life in chapters like a book. I turn the page and let go of yesterday."

Ellie removes the tea towel from the molasses cookies. "Let's dunk these beauties in a glass of scotch. Dad and I dunked a cookie in his drink and I never lost the taste for it."

"Miss Flannery you are a remarkable spirit. I marvel at your grasp of wonderment." Ellie gives my arm a playful jab, grabs the scotch and pours us a glass. I dunk my cookie into the booze. "Cheers dear girl!"

Ellie splashes her cookie. "Na zdravje Jack Hamby!"

"What kind of salute is that?"

"Naz-drav-gee is a Slovene toast to your good health."

"Well then Na zdravje Ellie Flannery!"

"Lou always said fine scotch is a sipping man's tea. Tis palatable without eatín your guts out. Now a drink like Slivovka; that one's pure trouble. I tried it once on a dare. The Slavic turpentine kicks like a mule and causes a man to forget his troubles, his name, and all common sense! Mr. Earl once told me how Slivovka did in me dad." Armed with a fortified cookie Ellie again slips back in time.

Earl Hazard wasn't always our houseman. Miss Lou spotted him laboring on Uncle Hannibal's dock. "Good heavens Hannibal, look at the size of that man. He'd make a formidable bouncer for my House."

"Earl's one of my best men but he's free to make his own way so poach him if you can. If Earl goes with you it's my loss."

"A perfect deal done and done!"

Lou feeds the colossal man a Li Po special and hires Mr. Hazard as her doorman. He's a gem all right and soon travels with us as Lou's personal guard. Our madame covets good-natured employees and always calls us by our proper name. No matter our homeland or color Miss Lou respects us and makes us feel worthy.

Gossipers say Earl captained a Caribbean pirate ship. Tis blarney! A carnival barker told the tale to sell tickets. Truth is Earl's more American than the rest of our house. Born in Colorado he wandered about and ended up here.

Lou respects a person's roots and their journey. No she's not wearing rose-colored glasses. Like us, our mistress knows the slap of a foul bias. Lou says, "A birth lot is not the sum of us and the runes foretell nothing. We assume a father's wealth or poverty as our fervent choice. Others may deny us and it's their loss. A man's true worth emerges when he sees himself as worthy." Miz Graham never tried to yoke us to her life. She maintained this life was ours to make.

The Emancipation freed Earl's parents and they chose the Colorado territory over their plantation roots. Earl was born a miner's son a way up in the mountains.

One day a traveling carney set up his boxing ring in a corral outside a livery where Earl worked. He watched as the big lad unloaded hay bales from a wagon. Earl was fourteen years old yet he tossed a bale like a fluffy down pillow.

The hawker assumed Earl's a grown man and calls out, "Hey boy come on over here. Want to go three rounds with my boxer? I'll give you two bucks win, lose, or draw." The promoter doesn't see a contender but he knows tossing a negro into the ring ups the ante a coin or two. Two dollars is a week's pay for Earl and he jumps on the offer. "Yessir I'll give it a go."

The afternoon exhibit features a seasoned champ with a bent flat nose. He's a large white Kentuckian called the Blue Ridge Mountaineer. Seasoned is double-speak for too old to box the main event but make no mistake, ole Blue can handle a novice. An early bout is the primer to excite the town for an evening event. The night fights are the real moneymakers.

Turns out Earl is a natural bare-fisted talent. He gets his footing in the first round and decks Ole Blue a minute into the second. It takes smelling salts and a splash of water to revive the veteran. Problem is every men assembled put a penny on the mountaineer and shouts of swindle rumble through the crowd. The wily promoter reads the upset as potential but he's got a vengeful swarm to placate. "Boys I'm as surprised as yawl! Housabout I refund the purse and mosey on outta here. No hard feelíns."

With a tar and feathering averted the barker seeks his real prize. The carney pulls Earl into the barn and whispers, "Here's your two eagles and an extra quarter for an amazín punchout! You gotta minute to discuss your future? Boy that was a remarkable show of fisticuffs but did ya hear the fellas bellyaching? More than once I heard ya called uppity and in need of a lesson. Sonny you ain't safe here no more. Might ya consider traveling with me? With my smarts and those fists we'll be rich in no time!"

Earl understands his situation all too well. He weighs his options and opts to leave his family in peace. The promoter brands Earl the 'Fiery Tortuga Pirate' and hawks his prize throughout the territories. Granted Earl isn't Haitian born. He couldn't sail the length of a pond let alone plunder the Caribbean Seas. "Why the silly name sir? I ain't none of those things."

"Relax boy and embrace the theatrics. With a costume and your looks you're a pirate all right and the name sells tickets. I say you're a champion bareknuckle fighter so act the part. We're gonna put butts in the seats and coin in our pockets!" He hands Earl a glitzy championship belt but it's a fake; negroes can't fight in a sanctioned event. The barker says, "It's every boy's dream to fight a real pirate and these suckers believe what's in front of them. Every blowhard from here to Timbuktu is gonna beg to step in the ring."

The barker's right. Many a fool boasts, "Put a nickel on me fellas and I'll pummel the savage beast. Arg!" Eager crowds pony up and the carney fleeces them all.

"Listen up Earl. Give it two rounds to excite the crowd. Stagger now and again like their man landed a punch and I'll up the ante before the third round. They'll think me stupid and add to the pot. It's then you bid the braggart goodnight."

The winning strategy spreads Earl's pugilistic lore far and wide. His notoriety vaults the Tortuga Pirate into the coveted evening bout and puts them a step closer to what the promoter calls the Big Show. The barker says, "Larger towns like Seattle are the key to a real purse. A showing there is our ticket back east to the lucrative negro boxing circuit."

Earl sees it from a different angle. He's weary of the fight game and longs for an honest living. The Tortuga Pirate weighs anchor in Seattle. Turns out Mr. Hazard is a natural longshoreman and Uncle Hannibal snatches him up.

One day Earl goes to church to pray with his people and stays for a potluck. It's there a pretty lass serves him a glass of punch. Earl recalls, "The girl had a sweet smile that knocked me out. It was then and there I knew Miss Emma was the one for me." Earl takes to marriage and working the docks but no life is perfect. It's friggin impossible to retire his reputation and Earl's accosted by a slew of blowhard challengers.

A lighter load on his body and peace of mind makes Lou's offer a no-brainer. However, it's her nature that seals the deal. Earl will do most anything for Miss Lou. He says, "the little lady is a hoot and smart to boot!"

CHAPTER 26

Death and Taxes

Earl often accompanies my deliveries and I tell the jealous saloon runners, "y'all leave me alone cause Big Earl's my sworn protector. You mess with me and you're gonna dance with my giant." Mr. Hazard shuns monikers like big or giant. I respect the man so I tootle his prowess out of earshot.

Where was I going with this? Yes our Earl tells a good story. It was two years after pop's demise when he spilled the beans on how it all came undone.

Sweetpea I claimed your daddy's remains from the coroner. Miss Lou sent me looking and I headed straight for the docks where two Moravian brothers worked the pallet crane. They laughed at my mention of Tom Flannery.

The older one says, "We saw the Irishman. He came to work yesterday with a cake all boxed up. Said it was fresh baked for his baby girl and to keep our mitts off it or we'd deal with him. He's like a bird who's always puffing out his feathers."

His brother adds, "Yes Tommy's a talker! It was payday and Tom says he bought the cake to celebrate his baby girl's birthday. That's when we got into it over the Slivovka."

"Slivovka what's that?"

"It's our country's drink and us Polacks love its sweet nectar. Toss bitter plums and sugar mash into an aged oak barrel, let it sit a year and voilà! It turns into one-hundred and fifty proof brandy!"

"My brother's right. Our papa sent us a bottle for the holidays and we showed it to the Irishman. The doofus said it smelled like a sissy fruit punch."

"We didn't take no offense cause the mick's ignorant of our ways. Our men drink the liquor in half shots. It's too strong for the gals so they add sugar and boil it into a tea."

"I'm confused fellas. You weren't mad at Tom but there was a fight?"

"No fists Earl; it was a friendly wager. Tommy grabs the jug and says he can down it. I say no don't waste it! My brother dared Tom to drink three shots and I warned he might go blind for days."

"I'm guessín Flannery took the bet."

"Oh yes the Irishman said it was a piece of cake and wagered half the girl's gift."

"Tommy downs the first and second shots but chokes on the third. That's when we split the pastry and he staggers off mumbling "no wee girlie needs a whole bless-ed cake.""

The elder brother frowns. "Our half was a stale brick. Tommy talks big but he's honest. I'm guessín the baker stiffed him."

"Thanks for your time boys." I follow your dad's route and stop to talk with folks along the way. An Underground shopkeeper re-members Tommy or what was left of him.

"I climbed down the ladder to open up my shop and there it was face-down in a puddle of water. I check him for life and soon regret it. What a sight with its bloody noggin and cloudy bug-eyes staring

back at me! I let go the shoulder and climbs back up top to flag a
copper. The meat wagon takes its sweet time so I cleans up as best
I could. Business is slow and I don't need no ghost helpín me so I
sprinkled some cornmeal to shoo away a haunting."

I bid the shopkeep good day and left for the morgue. The coroner didn't have a Flannery but he had a John Doe covered in cake
bits. I'm so sorry Sweet Pea; it was your pops all right. Being a payday I checked his pockets but they was empty. I reckon somebody
snatched his wallet.

Your daddy took it bad when your mama died. He lost his way
with booze and a slippery slope sent him to Glory.

Ellie breaks from her story voice. "Mr. Chin says plum liquor and a
vision killed his namesake. History repeats for a reason and we best
take heed; fermented plums of any nation are a wicked libation. My
advice to all is simple: take a polite sip but not one drop more." Ellie
crosses herself and sighs. "Let's talk of happier times, shall we? Did
I tell you how the Chin family migrated here? No? Our chef paid a
ransom for his kin's passage. Mr. Chin's younger brother worked the
railyard while his wife and mother were real seamstresses in a Chinatown laundry. Why do I say real seamstress? Tis a convenient tale of
how the wagtails kept Seattle in stitches!"

Ellie slips back into her tale: it's the 1880's when a Bigbug pays no
taxes and a poor schmuck picks up the tab. There's a wagtail for every
43rd man in town but a crazy ordinance makes prostitution a crime.
The bosses didn't think it through cause a criminal pays no taxes. It's a
fiscal disaster for the town so our civic geniuses invent a tax tailormade

for profit. The bosses anoint a hundred new seamstresses who keep the johns buttoned up, and the city coffers teeming!

Lou pays a hotel tax with no seamy stigma attached. Our room and concierge services are costly compared to wagtail prices. A wag barters at market value and when the fleet's in port she ups the ante. However a thrifty sailor can always haggle the cost of altering his jib. Lou knows a wag's life is hard and she gives to a local doctor and a free kitchen to help out. It's all routine until the Great Fire levels Seattle.

A new building code replaces wood with costly stone and the wags can't afford to rebuild. Their forced to dally in alleyways or burnt-out shanties until a lengthy cold snap makes the girls rethink their situation and they threaten to move south. Seattle can ill afford a loss of revenue so our council stifles the uprising with a code variance. Dozens of permitted shacks pop-up and the blinkered constables ignore a taxpaying seamstress. Life is good yet not all is bliss.

Fancy-pants patrons complain of waking up in the bog with achy noggins and empty pockets. The newspaper sniffs a moneymaker and crucifies the bosses for their lackluster policing. The council responds with bans on trapdoors in the crib shacks and flowerpots on second-story ledges but the wayward scamps are undeterred. They keep on fleecing a rich john until February of 1891 when a flummoxed city hall calls for a wagtail roundup. The police Valentine's Day raid hits every Chapel corner and a witless recruit sets off fireworks worthy of the 4th of July!

CHAPTER 27

Trial and Tribulation

An unsuspecting Lou steps outside her palace for a bit of fresh air. The city replaced its dull whale oil flagons with bright kerosene wicks and an always curious Lou wants a look-see. That's when the newbie uniform cuffs her. Our lawyer awakens a judge friend who bails her out but it's too late to squash the news. A reporter reads the police blog and his morning editorial decries 'Notorious Madame Nailed! Seattle Awaits a Trial of the Century!' The scandalous read causes subscriptions to skyrocket and a daily rehashing of the story consumes all of Seattle.

Lou is neither irritated nor worried. She loves good theater and jokes about her arrest. "The boy knew nothing of me. I stood on a street corner for heaven's sake! He was very apologetic and I gave him a token for a drink."

Our madame seizes the moment to shop for a flowing satin costume with a large-plumed hat and her jeweler offers a rare diamond and green-garnet necklace heralded in royal circles across Europe. Pious folks consider its snakelike look sinful and of course, Lou loves it! Lou owns a fancy Landau C-Spring carriage for her business. She often sends out a pretty new hire in the veiled cab as a tease for her parlor. The trial demands an envious look so the livery boys gussy up the horses and polish the brass. Lou says Earl needs a fancy coachman's uniform but he's not happy with Granny Chin's fittings. Our madame pacifies Earl with a silver coin in his pocket and we're set for a grand showing.

The 21st of February is a lovely Northwest Day. The sun is out, snowy Olympic peaks rise above a choppy Puget Sound and there's a beret shaped cloud sitting atop Mount Tahoma. It feels like a festive Marti Gras!

Our courthouse survived the Great Fire though its north face is scarred with blistered paint and black soot. The wooden relic sits two blocks away from our place and onlookers pack the streets. Sweet Lou stands on our steps basking in their cheers while Earl clears a path to her buggy. Alas a small troop of onlookers boo, carry signs and chant, "Miscreant repent" and "The wages of sin await Lou!" Our mistress laughs and blows kisses to the hecklers. She does love a corny pun.

Lou's trial is a done deal cause the bosses oiled the wheels of justice at our bar and friends stand at the courthouse awaiting their random jury selection. The courtroom's already overflowing so I opt to sit in the gallery. I toss a peanut over the rail but it's too crowded below to hit the floor.

The relic creaks from the strain forcing the bailiff to clear the aisles. After the delay the judge's gavel quiets the circus and the attorneys agree on seven fair-minded men. The famous orator J.T. Roland represents Miss Lou. Roland is a renowned prosecutor and a contender on the Reform ticket for superior court judge; most everyone thinks he's a shoo in. J.T. has a thunderous voice and his rotund stature intimidates any foe. Litigators sparring with J.T. are either brave or touched in the head.

Our second-chair defender is an upstart named Samuel Piles. Sam aspires to someday be a U.S. senator and jumps across the aisle to defend Lou. We have the best lawyers so who's prosecuting? A scrawny welp fidgets in the accuser's chair but nobody near me recalls his name.

The spectators mount a second assault and the bailiff bars the door. We're pinched together like a can of sardines as opening remarks get underway. Mr. Rowland eyes the crowd's discomfort and foregoes his remarks. The pimpled prosecutor does likewise calling the arresting officer to the stand. The flustered uniform steps into the witness box and the bailiff asks, "You gonna be truthful so help you God?"

"I reckon so."

The prosecutor stands. "Constable what transpired on Valentine's night?"

"I did what I was told, found the defendant on a street corner after dark and arrested her as instructed by the watch sergeant's briefing."

"No more questions your honor." The prosecutor sits down with his hands folded on the table.

Mr. Roland stands to take his turn. "For the record young man do you shave?"

"I-I do sir, every other Saturday in my bath."

"Good for you, yours is a grave duty for one so young. Thank you for your service."

The prosecutor raises a hand. "Your honor the defense needn't hint the obvious. We'll stipulate to the recruit's lack of experience if it moves things along."

The judge nods. "J.T. enough with the meandering, get us on track."

Roland gives the sprite a sour look and turns back to the witness. "Constable did my client act unseemly. Perhaps you heard an illicit invite?"

The boy tugs at his woolen uniform collar. "No sir, she just stood there lookín up at the lamp."

Mr. Roland sticks a thumb in his vest pocket. "Did the defendant proposition you?"

The copper turns a scarlet hue. "Golly no! She smiled and bid me good evening."

"Was that all?"

"No sir, the lady was after a bit of fresh air."

"Have you seen her working the streets before?"

"No sir, it was my very first night on duty."

"Sonny, are you involved with my client?"

"What? You mean, gee-whiz, no!"

The crowd snickers and the lad again fidgets with his collar. J.T. gives him a reassuring wink. "Does Miss Graham have a history of said crime?"

"No sir, my superiors say she's got no record at all."

"So, you handcuffed a peaceable woman outside her own front door. Is that a correct summation?"

"I-I was only following orders."

Mr. Roland smiles at the jury and sits down. The judge eyes the prosecutor. "Sonny any redirect questions?"

Boy-lawyer looks to a man seated in the first row of spectators. The boss shakes his head and the prosecutor echoes, "No sir, we're done with this witness."

The uniform bolts from his seat like a lamb freed of a shearing. Next up are his superiors sent to bemoan peacekeeping in the district.

They chime "the ordered raid put a strain on our roster" and "we had no choice but to put a recruit on the streets" and "the idiot was on the wrong street corner!" The last captain adds, "Miss Graham is a peaceable business owner. The boy needn't have cuffed her." J.T. waves his cross-examination and motions for the prosecutor to proceed.

"Your honor our last witness is Mr. Phineas Dunbar."

Pinhead Dunbar is no stranger to our House. The man's a blowhard and a sleazy opportunist. J.T. laments, "Judge we all know Dunbar owns the attacking newspaper. His own editorials quote unnamed sources and defame my client without a hint of proof."

"Noted and overruled; the first amendment grants immunity to a free press. Let's see what Phinney spouts under oath and then you can have at him."

Seattle lawyers are our House regulars. I've not seen this tadpole jurist so I'm guessin' he's a sacrificial puppet. J.T. locks eyes with the boy while the bailiff swears in the witness. The baby barrister gulps, "Your honor I beg a moment for consultation" and steps to the spectator rail for a word with his boss.

The courtroom is a sweltering box causing the judge to unbutton his robes. From the balcony I can see his honor's britches got left in chambers. The judge sighs, "Young man it's miserable hot and I've no patience for sidebars."

Lawyer-boy turns around. "Sorry sir. Mr. Dunbar your paper criticized the city and called the accused a common whore in fancy cloth. Rather harsh don't you think?"

"Harsh? No indeedy, it's a paper's civic duty since Franklin's Press to call out a wrongdoing. Why..."

The prosecutor interrupts his own witness before Mr. Rowland can shout irrelevant; good for him for being a nose quicker than a seasoned lawyer. The kid says, "About your sources, did you vet the confessors as credible men?"

"Yes, yes of course. They are upstanding, God-fearing citizens led astray by that wicked woman. I merely withheld the names to shield them from their mortified wives. As I was saying, I often pester the police about that filthy district. Let me tell you…"

Mr. Rowland beats his adversary to the draw with his voice reverberating off the walls. "The defense objects! The witness answered the question; must he bore us with his insufferable crusade? His incessant whine suffocates us all!"

Hoots lambasting the witness erupt all round me and the judge bangs his gavel. "You boys upstairs settle down! There'll be no uprising in my court. J.T. it's too hot for your theatrics and Phineas, get off your darn soapbox. I'll not allow opinion over fact in my courtroom. The objection is sustained. Counselors move on!"

Lawyer-boy looks to his boss who clears his throat and nods. The prosecutor turns back to the judge. "No more questions your honor, the prosecution rests." The lad lets go an exalted sigh and takes his seat.

Phineas Dunbar jumps up, curls his fists and shouts, "I object! Stand up you coward and do your job. How dare you quit on me before I have my say!"

The judge glares into the witness box. "Phinney sit down! A witness can't object. This is my final warning; you behave or be held in contempt!"

The room is hotter than a livery kiln. Dunbar wipes his face with his snotinger and returns it to a pocket. He takes a seat and whispers to his honor, "Justice with a drink and a wink, eh Bartholomew?" The judge ignores him and waves at the defense counsel to proceed.

Sam Pile stands up, removes his jacket, and drapes it over his chairback. He thumbs his suspenders, walks to the jury box, and leans his backside against the rail. Both Sam and the jury eye the witness. "Hot enough for you Dunbar?"

"Damn straight."

"Let's review, shall we? You say the confessors came to you instead of the clergy. Your newsroom seems an odd confessional, but I digress. I understand you are trying to protect a man's reputation yet that's not your testimony. You feared the wife's temper. Nonetheless, spirited by Ben Franklin you went ahead and printed your tale. Dunbar your testimony has more holes in it than a No Hunting sign."

The judge raises his gavel to quiet the crowd but not before Dunbar shouts, "She runs a wicked brothel and the police do nothing! I did my civic duty. How dare you twist my words!"

Sam Pile smiles and says, "Move to strike; the witness response is malicious hearsay not in evidence."

"Motion granted. Phineas you're in contempt and you owe the court five dollars. Spout off again and my bailiff will jail you. Mr. Pile are you done?"

"Not quite your honor, I'd like to know how many papers his allegations sold."

The judge frowns. "Sam you know better than that. Ask the witness a proper question."

Our defender flashes a sheepish grin and changes his tone. "How often do you frequent the Graham House?"

"I attend proper luncheons and such. What of it?"

Folks around me erupt with laughter and the judge responds, "One more outburst and I'll toss the gallery!"

Sam seizes the moment. "What of it indeed, you never mentioned a proper meeting in your writings."

"A good newsman like myself doesn't bore his readers."

"Yes of course. And that explains why your steamy account sounds like you're the one in bed. In fact, your words read like a veiled mea culpa and I must ask; are you the bragging cock who's afraid of his hen?"

Phineas Xavier Dunbar grabs his hankie and wipes the sweat from his schnozzle. He must protect his good name and the witness box is no confessional. Phinney glares at his attacker. "You dare to call me a wagmonger! You're a mendacious son of a…!"

A precious child in the loft shouts, "Fess up Pinhead!" and everyone laughs save Phineas and Miss Lou. 'Twas a costly outburst but worth the few seconds of fame.

Sam doesn't back down. "How many papers did your seditious unbosoming sell?" Hooting hecklers and the judge's gavel bury the prosecutor's objection. Sam smiles and returns to his seat. "I withdraw the question your honor. The defense rests."

Only closing arguments stand between us and a cool breeze. The lawyer-boy rehashes district troubles while lauding a valiant police effort and our steamy room lends a collective yawn.

J.T. Roland ambles to the jury box, leans on the rail and commences jawing. "Boys it's obvious what happened. The recruit and his superiors gave it a go, but the raid was doomed from the start. A dubious and self-serving press forced the city to act beyond its means. One look at my client tells us all we need to know. Lou Graham is no common street wag. You must find in her favor."

No sir, there's nothing common about Sweet Lou. It takes one vote to free her and no one waits on the judge's dismissal. A hoard of sweaty souls burst out the door into the refreshing chill. I head for our kitchen to help with the buffet and our exonerated mistress soon stands at our door offering the faithful a drink token. Boy lawyer and the gangly police recruit enjoy a backslapping on the way to the bar.

The newspaper gives it one last go: ranting against inept governing and calling for political blood. Who must pay for the mishandled raid? After much hoopla, the smelly blame lands on the mayor's desk. Relentless editorials demand a recall but his honor has other plans. Our mayor's done with politics and summons a gathering to offer his resignation. "Boys my nerves are shot cause a you. My doctor says I've got neurasthenia and must retire to my cabin. I'm gonna fish in peace without you jackals critiquing my flies. I declare the only good use of a newspaper is gutting a catch. You hacks be warned, trespass on my land and you'll get a tuchus full of buckshot. You're a gaggle of smelly dingleberries and you'll no longer cling to my behind. Be sure to quote me on that!"

The newspaper spins his farewell rant as its victory but there's no profit in old news and the Snoops look elsewhere. Wall Street warns of fiscal instability, but no one heeds the financial pages. The Farmer's Almanac predictions are more useful for the spring thaw. Besides, the pundits say we're immune to a finance ruckus. One fatcat lauds, "Our mecca nets fish, harvests clam, logs the forest and mines. We're not beholden to the New York Stock Exchange. Our good times go back as far as memory serves and we've no reason to perspire."

The blowhard's dead wrong and the Panic of 1893 drains the nation's fortunes. Our bosses play the victim card. They pout 'We were robbed' and 'The Wall Street suits are crooks' or 'It's the Fed's fault! Hang the politicians!' The whiners splat the blame on others and it's so predictably lame.

No one's immune to the suffering. The far-reaching Panic crushes our economy and, of course, the common fella suffers most. A proud laborer once earning twenty dollars a week now begs for a day's work.

Our Miz Lou's solvency never wavers. She pads her fortune buying up pieces of our flailing town. Lou takes a hit, but it's a flesh wound and her generosity fortifies our friends. With Sweet Lou as a silent partner a dandy survives the Panic and his workers don't starve. The history books never say it, nonetheless, a madame kept the Queen city afloat!

CHAPTER 28

Mike Quinn, Esquire

We hear footsteps approaching and Ellie pauses her story. The quick rhythm isn't the sergeant's lumbering plunk and slide step. Who made it beyond the vigilant guard? A look at Ellie fussing with her hair consoles me as a deep baritone voice calls from behind the curtain "Ellie honey, are you decent?"

Ellie beams. "I plead the fifth sweetie. Come on in and see for yourself!"

The door unlocks for a handsome man with jail keys in hand. This is the Graham House lawyer who handles the estate and Ellie's defense. Michael Quinn has the same goofy grin on his face. "You're in fine spirits girl. Oh hello Mr. Hamby; nice to see you again."

I stand to accept the lawyer's firm grip. Mr. Quinn was at my office a day before the will reading. The man has a formidable yet relaxed presence. His charismatic ways offer substance and his good manners are the antithesis of James Ambary. Reputation and my instincts say Mr. Quinn is a trustworthy gentleman.

Ellie coos, "Is this a jailbreak? Did you overpower the guard to spring me?"

"No Miss Flannery. I am a court officer and you are my prisoner. Seriously babe you gotta cut Pete some slack. His gout's acting up and it hurts to limp down here on your whims." Mike turns to me.

"I'm glad to see you Mr. Hamby. I'd like to meet this afternoon if you have the time. I've been talking to Sam Barr and..."

Ellie interrupts. "You're both here now so why go upstairs? Are you keeping secrets? It isn't polite you know."

"Missy, not all my practice evolves around you. I've a sizable workload that's none of your concern."

Ellie fakes a pout and goes to the table for a glass of tea.

"Mr. Hamby can you spare the time?"

"Of course, I am at your service."

"Excellent. Now if you don't mind, I need a private word with my client." Mike's smitten smile says I'm the odd man out.

"Certainly, until later sir. Ellie, I'll see you tomorrow then." Ellie nods yes without taking her eyes off Quinn.

The afternoon hours crawl by and I am stupefied. It's difficult to stay on task with my mind elsewhere. What does Quinn want? It must be the will. I forgot all about the Graham reading when Ellie was jailed.

My mates pack it in for the day and Quinn is a no show. Mr. Barr opens his door and barks, "Hamby stay put." Exiting coworkers stare as they leave and Floyd stops at my desk. "Jesus crackers Jackson, whadaudo now? I've been in that chamber three times in seven years and you're gonna have my record in a week." I shrug my shoulders and Floyd leaves me alone. With nothing to do I sit and ponder. I followed orders, whatever does Sam Barr want?

Several minutes pass before Barr waves me into his chamber. I step through the door to see Michael Quinn seated with his feet atop Barr's desk. My boss opens his private back door and turns to face me. "Have a seat Jack. Mike has an interesting plan that requires your help. Hear him out and let us know. I'm off to cajole a bag of money from Chicago. I'll be at Lou's place if you need me."

Quinn gives Mr. Barr a two-finger salute. "Put a drink on my tab and we'll keep you informed." Barr exits and Quinn turns to me. "Please sit-down Mr. Hamby. Might we be less formal? Ellie and Sam call you Jack. Do you prefer Jack over Jackson?"

"Ellie calls me Jack; Mr. Barr heard it from her and I'm warming to it. Do you go by Mike or Michael?"

"My friends call me Mike; I hope we can be friends. Tell me what you know about Caleb Ambary's death."

Wow! I know nothing about what's going on around here, save my wrong assumptions. Does Mike know about my eavesdropping? Why wouldn't he? Ellie claims there's no such thing as a secret. "It's hard not to overhear things. Ellie and Ambary dated awhile back, and he wants a map he says is in the will. Ellie talks of times before that awful night and hasn't got around to the alleged charges."

Mike smiles and moves his feet to the floor. "Thank you for saying alleged, most folks don't bother. I'll share the case details with you if you'll help me foil Jimmy's vendetta."

"Go on, I'm listening." At last! I'll hear a true account of the tragedy and Mike has my full attention.

"My version does come with a disclaimer. Only Ellie and Jim know what truly happened. Neither account tells all, nor do their stories match. Jimmy's unreliable and Ellie's protecting Lou's legacy. This is what I know happened.

A man calling himself Harman Hamadan sponsored an expedition to collect antiquities. The crew, including a younger me, foraged coastal villages for precious relics. I was a fresh-faced deckhand earning a buck and Hamadan swore we salvaged abandoned villages but that wasn't the case. The tribes said we looted their homes while they were away at their whaling camps. Both sides argued with righteous indignation and the tribes pressed charges. In the end, Hamadan paid off the tribes and it never went to court.

CHAPTER 29

The Fateful Voyage

Hamadan advertises the sojourn as a rite of passage for a few worthy young men and all the First Hill families beg him to include their sons, but one clan doesn't make the cut. Its humiliated matriarch, Gretchen Ambary, summons Mr. Hamadan saying, "You mustn't believe envious gossip meant to sully my late husband's name. My sons will toe the line and overlooking us is a misstep you'll soon regret. That sir, is a fact!"

Hamadan doesn't appreciate the threat, yet he can't afford a scandal. He orders the boys placed on the manifest and the flabbergasted skipper runs to the fleet owner saying, "Mr. Heigl sir, I can't let those two scalawags aboard. Tis a bad omen for us all."

"I hear you captain, but my hands are tied. The man paid me a handsome sum for our services, and I won't let two spoiled brats stand between me and a generous profit. If it helps you, I will join you on the journey."

Truth is, Fritz had already invited Lou and Ellie. Lou didn't trust an Ambary and she revoked Ellie's invitation when she heard Jimmy was aboard. An undeterred Ellie pestered Lou until she relented. It was a rare misstep for our mistress.

Ole man Ambary was an underhanded cheat and the boys are his blood. The facts were in evidence, but a smitten Ellie refused to listen and it didn't take long for Jimmy to show his cards.

We're two days underway and my mates sit topside bemoaning our labors and swearing like seasoned sailors when an uninvited Jimmy fakes a sweat and joins us. It's then he brags about bedding Ellie.

"My brother pays for his whores, so I razzed him saying I'd do one for free. Caleb wagered a fiver but tossed a virgin ringer into the ante. Sweet Lou's girl was the prize and I said no problem cause I got irresistible charms. I nailed her last night and it was easy money!"

I truly regret sitting there while the fellas played along. Tis a poor excuse to be a youngling just trying to fit in. Lord help me, I hate the Ambary's! Leonard Ambary cheated his workers and customers alike. My granddad was his idea man and the bastard patented Bop's inventions but it's not just the copyright feud. Ellie and I grew up together and I failed her when needed most. Why didn't I crack a rib, or break his bloody smeller when I had the chance? I shoulda pummeled the bastard and no confessional can absolve my guilt.

"Mike, I know how hard it is to fix a regret. I recant mine daily, but rarely do I get a chance at a do-over. How can I help you?"

"Be patient Jack, I'm getting there."

Two weeks later we're navigating a reef called the Graveyard of the Pacific. That's where a half-dozen ships lay wrecked along its shallow jagged edge. 'Twas then Caleb up and dies but the wicked reef, fog and an ebbing tide nixes us getting near a port. With no ice aboard, Caleb's body has to go overboard so the captain sails us into deeper water and we put Caleb to rest. When at sea a captain is judge and he presides over the inquiry. The night watchman witnessed the fight and I've a copy of his original deposition. Mike takes a manuscript from a folder and hands it to me.

The mate's account reads: "The two Ambary boys, the girl, and a guide is on the bow and I'm on the bridge above the foursome. It's a foggy night with no moon but a lantern lights their shadows. There's a breeze blowin at my backside mufflin their speech and the group seems to be socializin with Caleb holdin a pint. It seems harmless until Caleb gets angry and shakes a fist. I think he yells somethin about street trash and thievin heathens. (The captain asks when the sailor saw the gun.) Caleb pulls somethin from his pocket and that's when the girl steps between him and the scout. A shouting commences and the girl grabs a shiny thing from her skirt. Jim Ambary's leaning on a barrel to steady hisself. He lunges at the girl, slips on the wet deck, and knocks the lantern. I cain't see nothin but fog with the wick out and that's when the gun explodes. What a frightful noise! I bolts down the ladder to find Caleb on his back with a knife in his belly and a derringer in his hand. Jimmy's kneeling beside him and Caleb mumbles, "Get the map dumbass." Excuse my language ladies, it's what he said. Caleb gasps and takes on a stare. A bit of blood trickles out his mouth. He's gone all right, so I grabs both weapons and blows me whistle."

Tis a confusing mess for sure, Jim and Ellie's stories don't jive and Fritz Heigl swears he saw the scout lower a lifeboat. The boat's upside-down in the churning surf and I secure it with a rescue hook but there's no scout. The reef's perilously close so the captain ends the search.

The watchman's report and physical evidence are the only real clues until the gun and knife go missing. The watch brief is sketchy and with all the hard evidence missing, I can't say what truly happened.

Folks assume the map went overboard with the scout or maybe Miss Lou took it. Lou jumps on the rumors to keep Jimmy at bay.

Scuttlebutt says the scout's a killer, but Ellie denies it. A pair of First Hill gents testify how Caleb loved to brag about being the rightful heir to the Ambary fortune. They say Miz Gretchen spoiled Caleb and treated Jimmy like a lowly spare.

Jimmy calls the witnesses jealous ninnies. He claims he adored his brother; Caleb pulled his gun in self-defense and Ellie's plan was to murder them both.

He's a lying bag of sod. Ellie's prank was meant to embarrass the boys. Lou pays Hamadan's lawyer to defend Ellie and her counsel says male prowess and the gun favored Caleb. The defenseless girl gambit belittles Ellie but it plays to the crowd. The lawyer says, "Liquor instigated the chaos and Ellie's bruised neck proves Caleb's nature. Her harmless prank failed when the inebriated brute attacked. Fate saved the poor girl when Caleb slipped on the deck and skewered himself on her blade. It's unfortunate that the raging drunk died but that's on him."

The captains findings read: This is a sad ending to our historic voyage. I've heard three versions of the tragedy and each one casts doubt upon the other. Why did an innocent man jump ship? We can only guess. Did Ellie plan a murder? Jimmy says so, but he has a motive as well. I must make sense of the chaos.

Drunk or sober, Caleb Ambary was a nasty fellow. Both Ambary's stole from Mr. Hamadan and my leniency nearly caused a mutiny. I regret taking the two no-loads aboard and, Jimmy, I shan't coddle you now.

Miss Ellie, seeking vengeance never satisfies and I'm sure a hurt still lingers. Yes, your prank was flawed but I see no malicious intent. Being taken in by the Ambary clan is no crime, aye Mr. Hamadan?

I've heard good men testify to Jimmy's motive; his accusations are un-proven, and we know Caleb attacked. My watchman gives the unbi-ased account; two stupefied drunks, exasperated by liquor and foul moods, slipped on the wet deck. James crashed the lantern and Caleb most likely fell on the knife. Therefore, I find Caleb Ambary at fault for his own demise and reprimand a drunken James Ambary for his clumsiness. James, you'll continue to work the galley until we dock. As the presiding judge, I declare this matter closed and pray Davy Jones locker didn't snare Caleb or the tribesman."

Mike Quinn continues his tale: We all know the tragic play is but half-over. An unsuspecting Miz Gretchen stands on the dock and everyone hears her screams echo off the hills as Caleb's joyous home-coming dissolves into a pathetic wake. Missus Ambary resents losing her beloved son and goes full kilter after Ellie. She sandbags a circuit judge crying, "It was a biased inquest conveniently staged in open waters. A real court must charge the floozie. She murdered my boy!"

However, Gretchen isn't the only one holding court. Miss Lou invites Jim to lunch. He recants his story saying, "The chaos confused me. On reflection, I'm sure the Indian stuck my brother." A judge can't hang a dead man, so he dismisses the petition and Miz Gretchen lights into Jimmy. To his credit the defiant boy holds his ground.

Caleb's memorial is a fitting tribute. Mama Gretchen forsakes all reality, walks into the church on Caleb's arm, and introduces her risen son to the preacher. Tis but a fortnight before a smiling Jimmy commits his mum to an asylum.

The Old Testament says a leopard can't change his spots and Jim's the living proof of it. He squandered his wealth on drink, wagtails, and gambling; he's a footnote to the tale until his well runs dry. Tis then the eejit goes after the sunken treasure. Knowing Jimmy, I shoulda seen it coming.

CHAPTER 30

You Expect Me to What!

"Lou's left us and Jimmy's back with his lies. He revised the watchman's statement saying Lou paid the sailor to lie and he revived the drowned scout to testify for him. His cheating's typical but dredging up a dead man? That's original! Jimmy always coerces folks to do his bidding and he'll likely intimidate the jury as well. It's all bupkis and I've got a gumshoe debunking it.

Jack it pains me to see Ellie locked up. Jimmy isn't after justice, he pissed away his money and his lender notes are due. It's true the foursome argued over a treasure. Silly really, it's a sea tale and nothing more. Lou hinted she had the map and told Jimmy to play nice. Truth is, she never had it. 'Twas a gossiper's delight and Ambary fell for it. The map's long gone and the doofus can't tell fact from fiction."

"It seems simple enough Mike, why not unseal the will and let Ambary see for himself?"

"Ahh Jack, logic only works on a sane man. Ellie made a fake map to get her revenge. That fateful night, she told the boys it was all a hoax and Caleb lost it. Jimmy's bonkers and desperate. He refuses a fact and says we're conspiring against him. I shoulda punched the loon when I had the chance. You see, I'm as guilty as sin. I started this mess when I told Ellie about the bet."

I see the torment in his eyes, Mike can't let his part go.

"Jack, Lou was a master prankster and Ellie fancied herself a prodigy; the outlandish ruse was payback for the boys' cruelty. Ellie enlisted a guide who gladly took it on. I helped set up the prank and testified to it on Ellie's behalf. On the night Ellie flaunted her hoax, Caleb blew into a rage and attacked the scout. Ellie stepped in and her angel mama saved the day."

"What? Are you saying a ghost intervened?"

"Have you not noticed Ellie's uncanny gift? She says her mama saved her and I won't argue. I'm dealin with a livin lunatic who's comin after Ellie."

"I'm not sure how I can help."

"Ellie isn't safe until Jim's put away. You play your part and we can free her."

"What, me an actor? I'm not the least bit theatrical."

"I've heard the gossip. I want you to play Ellie's lover and offer Jimmy the map for a split of the fortune."

"You can't be serious. I'm no cheater and I can't embarrass or endanger my family."

"I have thrice the wit of a James Ambary. Try on your part and see how believable you are. I promise a safe haven for your family."

Mike's determination counters my every doubt and his enthusiasm is contagious. Can I really do this?

"I'll consider it, but I must consult my wife." Ha! Quinn doesn't know Anne. She'll never allow this.

"Please tell her there's a small part for her as well. However, this is our secret and Jimmy mustn't hear of it." Mike and I shake on it and I take my leave.

I walk down the hill practicing what to say to Anne. Every step takes me back in time; why must my doubts always stalk me? I traveled cross-country to escape my past so why pack my insecurity with my necessities?

My fearful-self answers, 'C'mon Jackson, this isn't us. Back-alley intrigue, we can't do it! We're certified pencil-pushers. What of the wimpy kid always left behind? That's us, that's the true Jackson Hamby.'

The panicked me has a point. I'm a pragmatist with no artistic talent and my doubts might get me killed. Oh crap! What if Anne agrees? No, no, no! This is ludicrous. Oh hell, my pounding head-ache is back.

I put a smile on my face and open the front door. Will Anne sense my trepidation? Of course, I dare not engage her query and say, "Bellybutton come to the beach with Papaw!" My dodge gets me out of the house, but the walk is fruitless. Neither the tide nor a brilliant sunset consoles me. Saddened by nature's disregard, I scoop up Belle and walk home.

My wife serves our meal and sits down opposite me. I can feel Anne's stare so I bless the food and clam up. I am a stone-faced Sphinx guarding its secret while the inevitable question plays in my head: will it be minutes or hours before I crumble and fess up?

A full moon shines above the Olympic peaks. How do I know? I'm on the front porch watching the white globe move across the sky. I beg the crisp air to clear my doubts, but my plea goes unnoticed. What can I do? I am a useless cog and must refuse Mike's plan. The skies begin to lighten and I hear Anne stirring. I must leave a note and run for it.

Why do I choose work over family? Because Jackson Hamby is a gutless cad.

CHAPTER 31

Same Old Jackson

The morning drags on while I sit perusing page after page of bureaucratic dogma. With my mind elsewhere, I can't say what I've read or stamped. Noontime nears and the clock's about to chime my doom. I do not relish this visit, yet Ellie expects me. How do I keep a secret from a girl who reads my mind? I have no idea.

A chatty Ellie greets me asking for news from the outside. Afraid of saying too much, I shrug and answer with brief nondescript phrases like "you know, the usual."

"Why so quiet Bucko? Bite your tongue?"

I'm not fooled by her ploy. The girl's fishing and I've no defense against her intuitive senses. "No, it's just w-work. There's a m-mound of p-paper on m-my desk." Why do I stutter like a schoolboy? Jesus man pull it together! "Ellie, I can s-sorely use a s-story. Perhaps a m-memory from the g-gold rush? The news s-sent back east was m-magical!"

"Can't spit out your troubles, eh Jack? Mark my words boy, keeping secrets won't save ya. You want my version of the Klondike Rush? Sorry those days were far from enchanting. Promoters sent out half-baked truths crowning us the only route to the gold. San Fran and Portland took issue with our poetic license, but we were smarter. We knew a shiny nugget was the seed of dreams and commerce was the real goldmine! Local boys like the Nordstroms went up north and came home with a modest strike. 'Twas creativity what turned a bit of gold into a fortune. Mercantile supplied a seeker and our House kept him happy. However, Lou's real moneymaker was cash advances to her business partners."

Interesting, yet not the fanciful tale I wanted. This day continues to disappoint. Why can't Ellie help me escape my dilemma? "Frankly your story lacks its usual pizazz. Was the news all a lie?"

"I'd say exaggerated more than faked. Seattle struck gold long before the Rush. The 1880's made this sleepy port a boomtown! That's when lumber and fishing took second place to mining and shipping. Why even President Harrison visited us. The Alaska Rush wasn't our startup; Seattle quakes with an earthy energy that beckons a risktaker. You want an account of the mayhem? Here a tis, the truth's a tale worth spinning!"

The Panic of '93 is a hard slap, and the Klondike rush is our ticket to prosperity. Our newsies propound it and gold fever floods us with forty-thousand wannabes hellbent on riches! Slum houses and fine hotels teem with miners with amenities matching a man's purse. Hostel floormats cost fifty cents a night while an elegant hotel suite demands six dollars. Poor Joe's settle on secondhand tools while fat-cats buy new Cooper and Levy gear. Some lads eat hardtack and share a steerage cabin while a rich man pays for a private suite and sups with the captain. Thousands of men sail on Fritz's Alaska fleet and fights erupt when a purser bungles a boarding pass.

Meanwhile the Chapel streets explode with nefarious goings-on and the naïve tourists are easy pickings. Saloon shysters sell fusty moonshine and keep a wag upstairs with a hollow pipe connecting her room to a bucket behind the bar. An armed guard makes sure the spent patron drops a coin down the pipe and a poor girl might do thirty tricks a day. Pregnancy and French Pox are epidemic, so the girls use a Coca berry douche. When the Coca proves addictive, the pimps switch to lye soap. The cops call it a twofer cause it reduces the overdose and abortion deaths. Sad to say the lye also makes a girl barren.

Our refined House is a haven amongst the pig swill. Hoity gents are allergic to scandal and Miss Lou respects their delicate condition. She stocks our closet with quinine douche and condoms from Charlie Goodyear's factory. The pimps rinse and reuse a lamb-gut shield, but our girls always toss a rubber. The tidiness draws looters and I sit upstairs with my slingshot at the ready. Am I afraid of a vengeful pimp? Nah, he'll take my painful aim over an Earl Hazard beatdown. Tis sad to see a tiny snipe rummaging for leftovers so I tell Mr. Chin and he leaves lunch sacks on the back porch. No kid need dig through our trash to survive.

My gold mine is the tips! How do I tell a generous dandy from a stingy desperado? A flush man wears a costly cologne while the stingy reek of exigent sweat.

Conover Tug and Barge hauls farm animals, salted lard and flour sacks up the coast to Dawson City. Scarcity makes local food prices soar like a Chinese rocket, but our guests pay top dollar and Mr. Chin is up to the challenge. Grimy district canteens with their mealy food and Ptomaine are no match for a Chin delicacy.

Seattle's Rush story was a mix of suckers, mean blokes and pirate thieves. 'Twas an adventure, for sure.

Ellie takes a breathier to freshen our tea. "Sorry bub, there's little romance in the truth of it. Tis why the papers exaggerated so."

Why can't a storyteller like Ellie find a fun fact? Was it all so weepy? "Please friend I beg you. What entertained Ellie Flannery back then?"

"Hmm. Where's the hoot? Oh, I know!"

Our Queen City's in chaos: with many a worker sailing for Alaska without giving notice. Bonuses help, but the labor pool is shallow pickings. The bosses say, "Hey bud, got a pulse? You're hired! Past misstep? No worries lest you're a thief or a mean drunk." Relatives are hired on the spot and Lou does her part recruiting decent blokes with free tokens.

Our mayor's visiting San Fran when the news breaks and he stays on to ship freight with his brother. A ferryman gauges profit by the ton and padding a ship's manifest means bigger profits. Still every captain has his limits. No skipper sails an overloaded ship in rough seas. One day our mayor overrules his captain, and a mutiny ensues. The skipper weighs anchor and his honor's left on the dock with a bunch of angry miners. The riotous men encircle the mayor and someone shouts, "Get a rope!" Imagine his surprise as the mayor dangles from a crane. They actually lynched him!

An alert copper saves him, but the mayor's throat and mind are forever scarred. The port authority demands the captain finish loading and a month later a squall sinks his ship at the Skagway dock. All are ashore save one mule and a crate of chickens. The critters drowned in the frozen surf.

As you might expect our lynched mayor returns home a bit cracked. He medicates himself with elixirs and wanders about wearing misbuttoned long johns. His honor screams at imagined chickens and a ghostly mule baying at his heels. "Yowzah boys! Are ya deaf? Get after those incessant cackling chicks! Shoot em all! See the son of a jack with a noose in his teeth? The darn donkey's gaining on me. Save me fellas, save me!"

Folks call back "you best button your fly mayor" and "where's yer britches." His honor loses his post to a man on a mule cart trading chicken eggs for votes. Kinda funny, yes? In these parts insanity is as common as dandelion wine and Seattle can't help but cradle a go-getter with a mad bent.

Ellie breaks from her tale. "Jack, have you seen the totem pole outside the trolley stop in Pioneer Square? Now that's a surefire tribute to blurry thinking!"

"You mean the weathered wooden sculpture dwarfed by the modern stone buildings?"

"The very one, tis proof that the eejits run the show."

CHAPTER 32

Totems, Bears & Secrets, Oh My!

The Gold Rush is waning, and the city needs a new moneymaker. Our councilmen say, "Improved train travel brings tourists to buy our souvenirs. Let's erect a trading post with a totem pole and trinkets. That's a surefire profit!"

Now a sane man pays a local to carve the pole, but not our boneheads. They want a seasoned totem with history and such. Did Seattle ever get its trading post? Heck no! The selfish fatcats reneged and erected the totem at the trolley stop outside their office windows. However, the quest for the pole is a story worth repeating.

Mimicking earlier expeditions our boys sailed up the north coast in search of the perfect totem. They swear the isle was deserted, but that's a lie. The gents eyed their prize with a spyglass and sent the crew ashore to cut it down. A federal grand jury later indicted the 'Committee of Fifteen' for invading a Tlingit village on Tongass Isle.

One sailor reported back. "Governors it's a camp of old folks. Seems unholy to take their possessions without compensation."

The indignant bosses rage, "You dare shame us? Our noble act saves an antiquity from nature's neglect. We shan't be maligned by an ignorant seadog!"

The crew downs the totem and loads it onto the ship. As for the decent sailor, he's left ashore to find his own way home. Our triumphant nobles return and erect the totem in Pioneer Square and hundreds of proud citizens attend the dedication.

Meanwhile, returning Tlingit fishermen discover the theft of their precious relic. Seems in 1790 their ancestors sculpted the totem with a raven topper to honor a woman called Chief of All Women. Native lore says a raven humbles witless humans and our pompous poachers did fit the bill. Had the boys read a map they'd a known the U.S. Land Office protects Tongass Isle and a federal grand jury later indicts our boys for vandalism and theft of a government asset. Our indignant commerce boys claim it's a grievous misunderstanding and vow to never stand trial.

At that very moment a sickly bear ransacks an Alaskan outhouse with an unlucky territorial magistrate inside. One old-timer laments, "Raiding grizzlies eat our trash and drop their smelly poop wherever they please. Ya cain't expect a critter with the runs to wait for his turn at the john!"

Who dares replace the mauled judge? Rumor says an eejit was caught diddling his boss's wife and was volunteered at gunpoint. The ship carrying the exiled judge makes a fortuitous stop in Seattle and our indicted boys seize their redemption with a lavish party honoring the new magistrate.

The boosted jurist toasts his hosts saying, "What a gracious affair! A frigid tundra cannot offer such fine amenities. I will always remember a kinder Seattle." The sloshed jurist never saw a reporter chronicling his antics and our social columns remain silent for a price. The next morning the hungover dupe sails north obliged to settle a 'regrettable spat.' Our commerce boys pay the Tlingit a hefty $250.00 and keep the totem.

Ellie ends her tale with a yawn. "Sorry bub that's the gospel as I recall it. 'Twas a flood of dreamers and tricksters and then it was gone. As for the riches, a smart egg struck gold without ever leaving her porch. I really must nap before tonight's cribbage. Sam upped the ante and I best be on my game." Ellie gives me a hug and I take my leave.

The walk down Profanity hill drains my resolve. Newspapers fed me tales of plucky sojourners, but it turns out the miners were as naïve as me. Dreamers have no business tackling desperadoes and I've got more bravado in me than bravery. It's time to talk with Annie.

Will Anne be supportive or incredulous? What will she think of me? Every footfall stomps on my fragile ego. How can I reconcile my doubts? As a child I read of brave men beating the elements, yet those stories omitted the mischiefs of a human foe. How does this hayseed hoodwink an expert fiend and who am I to sign onto Mike Quinn's folly? Ellie says disillusioned miners abandoned their claims and some disappeared without a trace. I wish I could disappear cause my head's gonna explode!

Thanks be, Anne is already in bed. Look at her sleeping so peacefully. With nothing to offer I bless my reprieve. How does a smart woman put up with the likes of me? Why did this angel marry a fraud like Jackson Filmore Hamby?

It's morning and a tension fills the air prickling the hairs on my arm. There's a storm brewing and her name is Anne Hamby. I'm shunned now but the quiet won't last. Annie wants a fight, so I best get out while I can. What a pitiful sight as I slog up Profanity hill with hunched shoulders and eyes fixed to the ground. Jackson Hamby is a wretched coward who doesn't deserve Ellie's friendship.

Thoughts of my desk with stacked papers cause me to linger in the drizzle. I stall on the courthouse steps mindlessly shaking the mist from my umbrella. Might Ellie offer a story or a wise tidbit to ease my angst. At least she's a respite from my wretched self. I close my umbrella and head up the steps to the precinct desk.

The sergeant shuffles his morning paper. "It's a bit early for checkers. I don't want Ellie tossing insults at me cause a you."

I give the man a pitiful pleading look and to my surprise he relents. We walk back to Ellie's cell where my gentle rap on the bars reverberates through the quiet. It is incredibly early, and I wonder if Ellie will answer.

An eternity passes before the sleepy girl opens the door. She blinks and yawns. "Jack Hamby this is unexpected. Is something wrong?"

"No dear, I'm sorry to bother you so early. Have you eaten breakfast?"

The sergeant lets go a blast of air causing his lips to flutter. My nod confirms. 'Yes, I'm an idiot.' The sergeant shakes his head and walks back towards his newspaper. Why does he bother locking Ellie's door?

"Ah-hum Jack, pay attention. No, I've not eaten breakfast and you're avoiding your duties."

The clever girl reads my situation, and her good nature is a relief. "I could use a respite. Perhaps you'll send a note upstairs?"

"Ha! Send a note to wrangle my uncle! That's a good one. Lucky for you he finished off a bottle playing cards last night. No doubt the ole boy's still in his bed."

Ellie tootles for the Sarge who growls, "What now?"

"Garçon please send a courier to Mr. Chin. Tis breakfast for two a bit early this morning. Do be quick about it; our poor lad's wasting away."

"You ain't funny missy." The policeman growls an unkind cuss and slams the metal door behind him.

Ellie smiles and pokes me in the chest. "Now see what you've done. I don't think ole Pete likes you."

I stand outside the curtain while Ellie primps for her day. Why all the fuss? Her beauty needs no paint or powder. Minutes pass before I'm allowed into her sanctuary and a lighthearted chat precludes our meal. Ellie has a way about her that makes a man grateful for her company.

The food arrives so we sit on the bed to devour it. Ellie unwraps the wool keepers from the chafing dish revealing herbed French toast stuffed with ham, a potato-jalapeno hash, and a chunky applesauce laced with bits of rhubarb. Lou was right about a Mr. Chin breakfast. Delicious!

Ellie and I have a comfortable routine predicated on her calming ways. No doubt she learned manners from her mistress. At the Graham House a worry hung on the hat rack while Miss Lou pampered its owner. It's no wonder the clientele loved to visit but I know my stay is tenuous at best. Ellie's candid views grant me a reprieve with no hope of a pardon.

Ellie draws me back from my thoughts. "Jackie boy there's no such thing as a secret. Tis a toxic ooze waitín to bust as stitch. This life's a mix of wonders and warts; a worrywart like yourself mustn't let a trouble fester."

She's right of course and there's no hiding my folly. The inevitable shows up at a most inconvenient time. My amnesty's like a morning mist; it vaporizes in the light to reveal my sorry side.

We finish our sumptuous feast and I opt to drink my tea in the ghost chair. I raise my cup to placate or, at least, amuse Miss Lou but a rude nudge greets my bum. It's as if a hot poker stabs at me. Is the ghost unhappy with me? Ouch! That's a definite yes. Shall I return to the bed? Another jab makes me jump. Thank you madame; point taken.

Ellie gives me a quizzical look and swaps places with me. She must think of me as a country clown yet smiles and cuddles herself into the chair's embrace. "Jackie please hand me a shawl and fill my teacup."

"It is my pleasure to serve my lady."

The night chill lingers so I add a chunk of coal to the fire. Ellie wraps her shawl around her shoulders and motions me to sit. It is time to begin her next chapter.

CHAPTER 33

Fritz & Mark Twain

$\mathcal{A}$lrighty then let's talk about Fritz Heigl. Lou's friend is a fellow expat who owns a bustling ferry fleet and he's a shrewd cookie. The Panic of '93 was a hiccup to Fritz who recouped his losses in the gold rush boon. Uncle Fritz and Lou are the best of friends and Lou says they bonded over Mr. Chin's sauerkraut. Tis a comfort to our Bavarian expats. I'm told its secret is apple vinegar aged in oak barrels with a pinch of caraway seed and crisp bacon added before serving. I'm not a veggie fan yet I love this kraut. Serve it with a wiener schnitzel and the dish sells out every time.

Miz Elsa attends her guild and choir meetings on Monday and Wednesday nights, so Fritz eats with us. After supper the Bavarians drink schnapps and Fritz smokes his pipe while they play cribbage. The card wars are a stalemate with Monday's loser a winner on Wednesday.

However, their bond is more than cards. Fritz loves to gamble on business startups and Miz Elsa whirls like a dervish when her husband risks a nickel. Fritz and Lou have a pact where Fritz tips bank tellers for leads on men turned down for a loan. The geezer corners a rejected man saying, "Go to Lou's Haus. Ve'll feed ya and maybe help with your schnapsidees!" A clever man leaves our place owning 70% of his shop with Fritz and Lou holding title to the rest.

Mike Quinn's dad, Donovan, had a plan. Grandpa Angus immigrated from Ireland in the 1840's and was a high-climber lumberjack for Leonard Ambary until he took a bad fall. Angus took up tool-making, but he never got credit for his talents. Baron Ambary stole Bops patents for himself.

A ten-year-old Donovan worked beside his dad, but it was no lark. Every able-bodied Quinn worked to support the family. The grandsons and I learned highclimbing from their Buppa. We climbed way up in the trees like monkeys with our slingshots at the ready. Many a surprised passerby felt a pinecone slung from our invisible perch; we scored a point for a hat and two points if we plunked an arse! Ahh, but I'm off me story again. As I said the Quinn family struggled to survive. Donovan was never a true sawyer and came to Lou with a startup idea. He said, "Me dad can fashion tools for the miners but we need our own smithy. We'll sell right off the fire and not gouge prices like Mr. Ambary." Mike's dad got his money, Fritz helped broaden the clientele, and Quinn Metalworks struck gold. The Quinn's believe in education and an honest day's work, so the boys worked and studied in the smithy. I dare say Fritz and Miz Lou enjoyed picking Leonard Ambary's pocket.

The duo are an interesting pair and folks assume they share a bed, but I've nothing juicy to tell. I swear it was all cards and business. Uncle Fritz is a faithful man who grumbles about the missus and heads home all the same. Lou says Fritz might stay home if Miz Elsa let him drink, smoke, and play cards in the house.

Friends needn't worry about gambling in Lou's House. The cops never raid us, and Earl bounces a sleazy cardsharp. We have two snooker tables, darts, and the dining room's setup for cards. Lou hosts a friendly poker game every other Tuesday. She's a consummate bluffer who often wins a pot from a well-known guest though the papers never tattle on visiting celebrities, tycoons, and politicians. On this night my personal hero, Sam Clemens came calling. Yes, I speak of *the* Samuel Clemens, otherwise known as Mark Twain.

Mr. Twain is in Seattle on a whistle-stop tour headed for Australia. He loves his role as orator for hire but isn't keen on this tour. The '93 Panic dug a hole and a flawed invention pushed Sam into the abyss. A cash broke Clemens laments, "My trip's a compulsory penance for my stupidity." His misery is our town's good fortune and a banner hangs atop the theater door proclaiming a sold-out performance. Lazy me procrastinated and can't beg a ticket.

Where was I going with this? Oh yes, Fritz and Sam waltz in our door singing a bawdy German ditty. They're sober as judges yet neither man carries the tune. Sam learned his German one summer while renting a villa near Fritz's relatives and Miz Elsa insists the Clemens stay with her. The gents are at our place for a drink and a cigar.

Sam spots a vacancy at the poker table and sits down. He says, "No-no, please play on without me. I'm inclined to watch." Sam looks on and sips his whisky neat. His writings boast of Mark Twain's love of drink but it's all for show. Mr. Clemens is no boozehound. Sam watches a couple of hands before temptation seizes him. Fritz warns him but Sam buys in and Lou empties his pockets. "Damnation Fritz! What just happened? I didn't even get a chance to finish my drink. This darn tour is supposed to resurrect my accounts and I can't afford to lose another!"

"Tsk-tsk ole man, I varned you about Lou Graham. Ve best head back to my place."

Clemens keeps his seat. "Herr Heigl please freshen my drink and leave the nagging to my wife; Olivia is far more resourceful at it than you. Fräulein Graham, may I ask where you acquired your talent?"

"Sam I don't stand on formality, please call me Lou. I learned poker on a steamer ship. It is a long crossing from Bremen to New York; I grew weary of the lady's lounge and wandered into the men's smoker. The purser tried to shoo me away, but I didn't budge. Talking my way into the game was easy. I said, 'Hello boys, what a treat to see such skill. May I sit and watch? It's warm in here and I'm parched. Who might buy me a sherry?' A gent offered his seat and it's mine for the rest of the voyage. Poker is far more than chance; it rewards keen observation and intuition. Fortunately, my business dealings have taught me a deft read."

"Can you read my thoughts dear lady?" Sam winks.

"Yes of course, my lovely girls cannot distract you. You focus on the game and must know the tell that emptied your pockets. Very well, the giveaway is your cigar."

"Beg pardon?" Sam spins the Cuban traitor twix his thumb and forefinger. "How can rolled tobacco betray me?"

"Pay attention Sam. A bluff sends the Belvedere to the ashtray and a sure grip is your tell of a good hand."

Fritz slaps Clemens on the back. "Aha! I varned you about Lou Graham. Smart men do business with her, not against her. A fool and his money are soon parted."

Sam leans towards Lou and whispers, "The man can't muster an original thought and quotes Tusser to harass me."

"Our dear Fritz is a simple fellow. Nevertheless, he speaks the truth. Fritz wins and loses his wallet at this table. I believe Thomas Tusser also said nothing ventured, nothing gained."

"Miss Lou you are a learn-ed beauty! Your talents do tempt me, and I see your point about Fritz. He made money by the bushel while I fed mine down a rabbit hole. The ferryman humbles the likes of me."

Lou pats Sam's arm. "No worries darling, there's more prince in you than pauper and your fortunes must rebound." Lou's smile melts candles and hearts at thirty paces.

"You are most kind and this pauper offers his humble thanks for a lovely evening. It was worth getting my pocket picked."

"How about I return your losses for a favor? My girl is a fan with no ticket to your talk. Might you arrange a seat?"

Clemens turns toward me. "Young lady which of my writings interests you?"

I cannot believe my ears; Mark Twain spoke to me! "Oh sir, your travelogues are wonderful! I hope to someday write a column just like you."

"Really? Sweet Lou your girl needs higher aspirations. Perhaps my boring lecture will dissuade her. I'm happy to secure tickets for you both."

True to his word Sam leaves two front row passes at will call and he's no bore. Au contraire! Sam captivates as his stories come alive on stage. Thinking about his scary recitation of 'The Man with the Golden Arm' still gives me goosebumps! Mr. Twain says a well-timed pause sucks us in and reading aloud engages the imagination. I believe it and I love a story read aloud.

Lou was right about Sam's tour. He remade his fortune wowing crowds from the Americas to Down Under.

Ellie comes back from her story. "Jack I'm desperate to be the next Mark Twain. Lou says I've got the talent, but I lack the tenacity. Tis a backhanded compliment, don't you think?" Ellie spots two women walking by her cell window; the women glance at us and bustle away. Ellie gives them a transfixed stare and frowns.

I bring her back asking, "Dearest are you alright?"

"Just dandy, you see those women out there. No doubt they came from your office. Mr. Chin postponed the will reading and it irks the snoots to no end. They claim it's undignified to have a houseboy dictate the proceedings. Lou wouldn't like that one-bit and my uncle set them straight. Sam told them to enjoy the sights and they still pester him."

"They speak a familiar tongue. Who are they?"

"Lou's half-sisters. You're a good Lutheran boy. Have you not sung a German hymn before? The twin tornadoes blew in the night of our séance. They put a real damper on the festivities." Ellie takes a moment to gather her thoughts. "Mike took me aside at the funeral to say I needn't worry about the will. I'm betting a filched inheritance won't sit well with those two biddies."

I reckon Ellie wishes she were Lou's birth daughter. The facts make me nervous as well. "Do you think the sisters will settle for a share of the estate?"

"Blood relatives are entitled to it all, but Mike and Lou worked long hours on that will. Contesting Lou's wishes gets them a fight from the grave!" Ellie's mood goes from feisty to pensive. "Mr. Fortune Cookie says we must outwit our attachments; let em go and they can't own us. The younger me obsessed over coins and sweets, but I'm wiser now. Lou's gift lives in my heart and her memory's worth more than any bobble." Ellie's breath softens and her soulful eyes stare at me. "You're a lucky bloke to have a caring family. Tis a comfort, yes?"

"Yes indeed." However, I've ignored Anne, and my amends are long overdue. Dad always said to buck up and take my lickin. He'd say, "Fetch a switch boy. Dawdling makes the sting worse so let's gitter over with."

Ellie reads my thoughts and nods her agreement as she spins an imagined wedding ring. "I'm not much on marriage, though a younger Uncle Hannibal might do."

"Or perhaps a Michael Quinn?" Could he manage our Ellie? She'd be a handful for any man.

Ellie offers a raised eyebrow. "Mind your manners Jack Hamby. I'm not certain if Mike nor I can weather a nuptial. Shall we return to my tale?"

CHAPTER 34

Pinched by the R.C.M.P.

Mr. Chin's my only kin now that Lou's gone, and his mama was like a granny to me. 'Twas sad to lose the ole girl. She passed at ninety-eight years old though her birthday's a mystery. Granny said her mama called her Hua cause she was born in the spring. Hua means Blossom.

The Chin family lived in Chinatown and granny ruled the roost. I grew up playing with Mr. Chin's nephews; the youngest, Professor Huang Chin, teaches Far East studies at Malaspina College in Victoria. Li Po's the oldest, but folks call him Little Po cause he's Mr. Chin's namesake. I call him Poo cause the boy's full of it. Poo married my friend Ling, and they sell antiques. Huang was their best man. I was the maid of honor, and we share a godchild named Ellie Hua.

Little Po worked Lou's houses with me though work's too strong a word. We were mischief and the steam behind a hornswaggle that's a legend. I'll tell you that one another time. Poo's been my best friend through it all and this is the tale of our Canadian holiday.

I was twelve years old when Mr. Chin brought Little Po with us to Vancouver B.C. Poo was there to keep me company while Miz Lou did business. The two of us had a grand time...once we bailed out of jail. It's all Poo's fault cause he's such a putz!

Here's what happened: Young Vancouver town was rowdy; its folks were as skittish as a herd of unbroke horses. The ruffians ignored a ramrod Mountie, and nothing irritates the Law more than a snubbing. Two visiting sprouts wandering about might show caution, yet we were too full of ourselves to notice a trouble brewing.

Lou made the trip to check on her tonic investments. Fermented berry elixirs are profitable and Vancouver's but a day's sail across the Strait of Juan de Fuca.

Lou says, "Our Canadian friends are continental souls except for the French trappers. They hate the Brits and hire the tribes to harass them. It's an unwinnable war; there are boatloads of immigrants sailing from Britain. The Froggie trappers remind me of our own so-called patriots. A Yank crimps his liberties to spite a rival and an irritable bowel is his just reward. There's profit in a fusspot's agony and my tonic offers relief."

Our first night in Vancouver mixes business with pleasure as Lou hosts a marathon bridge game in her suite. She and her vigneron join forces against a local magistrate and Uncle Fritz and the match plays into the wee hours.

C'mon! It's past noon! Our vacation's wasting away and my guardian rests whilst Poo and I fret with boredom. I say to Mr. Chin, "Might we roam the lobby or take in the boardwalk shops? We saved our tips for this trip on account of Miss Lou's birthday." Liar, liar, pants on fire! Shopping is an excuse to escape. Poo and I cannot sit a minute longer.

"You are disturbing Miss Lou's quiet. Leave us but do not let the hotel out of your sight."

"Yes sir, I promise."

We bolt for freedom as soon as Mr. Chin opens the door. I hit the boardwalk asking, "Where are we headed?" Deferring to Little Po's sense of direction is my first mistake. I've put myself in the hands of a bent compass.

Poo says, "There's a trolley stop. Let's see the sights."

We forsake my vow to stay put and hop on the streetcar. Its last stop is the gate to Chinatown. We feel safe walking in this homely district though a horde of bustling shoppers blocks our way.

"Poo I'm starving! There's a food cart on the right." With yummy satays in hand, we canvass the shops for Lou's gift. Poo's looking for a gawdy cameo.

"Hey Ellie, there's a pawn shop. I bet it has the perfect ivory brooch."

"You ninny! We can't get through the crowd."

Poo grabs my hand and pulls me into the alley. "No problem, we'll go this way and find a back entrance."

"I'm not so sure bucko. You best take the lead." Strike two for me; I ignore my inner caution and follow the eejit through a path of smelly trash and hissing rats.

Poo stops halfway down the alley. "Here it is."

"Really? All the doors look the same."

"I'm sure. Don't be such a scaredy cat."

"Am not! I don't see a sign for a pawn shop."

Hinges creak as Poo leans against the door. Yew! The eerie sound makes me shudder. I resist my intuition and follow Poo inside. That's strike three for me!

Poo grabs my hand. "C'mon girl keep moving towards the light up front."

Empty rice sacks cover the windows darkening an already dank room and my eyes struggle to adjust against a fog of incense. There's no furniture, just a few bales of straw littering the floor. "Poo I've got a bad feeling..." It's then I spot the foursome; a pair of Chinamen and two well-dressed white women lay sprawled on the bales to my right.

It's bad news for sure. There's but one reason for their supine pose. Drug addicts! This is an opium den. I poke Poo who yelps, "Yeezus, run for it!" We spin about and race for the alley exit. The doorway's full of daylight until a giant shadow blocks us. Unable to stop we slam into the muscled arms of the Vancouver Guard. "Whoa easy kiddies, what's the hurry? Makín a rush delivery is ya?"

Jesus, Mother Mary and Joseph, the gendarme thinks we're drug runners! The Mountie grabs our collars and yanks us off our feet. Our toes skip across the dirt as he drags us towards his paddy wagon. Great! Poo's search for a darn cameo got us pinched! The copper growls, "You two snipes best take notice; there's a new law against your dens and we're gonna wipe out the opium plague."

Ha! The pufferfish's so friggin proud of hisself, he doesn't know he's spoutín gibberish. Miss Lou thinks these hidey-hole raids are a waste of time and I agree. "Officer your raid's stupid and you need glasses. No bagman can afford these fine duds."

"You're a smarty pants ain't ya. Get in the feckín wagon." The blowfish tosses me to the back of the lorry and Poo lands beside me with a thud.

"Jeez Ellie watch your mouth. This guy ain't playing."

The boy has a point; I was a wee bit sarcastic, but I can't back down. Poo's retelling is destined to haunt me.

"Don't blame me, Cuz! It's the spoiled rich kids beggín a doctor for a laudanum script. Once they're hooked, he panics and cuts them off. Their dads lose their minds, and the police get busy. Opium's a curse, but a copper chasín addicts is no cure and your bargain search got us pinched, ya little arse!"

The guard isn't listening to my rant. He shackles our feet to the wagon and heads back inside. Those poor souls are o-so stoned. The copper tosses them at us like rag dolls and shuts the lorry door. Thanks be for a short ride to the station! They reek of piss and impending death.

The cops separate us, toss the Chinamen into jail, put the society dames in a private ambulance and I'm left alone in the sergeant's office. If the police expect a scared snitch, they got the wrong lass. I don't rat on a friend or foe and these blokes never tangled with a Flannery before.

A half-hour passes before a potbellied fella saunters into the room; his girth obliterates all but the bottom of his belt buckle. The man sits down in a swivel chair and scoots towards me. We are, as they say, nose to nose and the stench of stale tobacco chew settles on me like a malodorous fog. This holiday is becoming a real stinker.

"Hello girly, I am Constabulary watch sergeant Karl Higgins and who might you be?"

"Howdy Sarge. I be Ellis Flannery, but you can call me Ellie. What seems to be the problem?"

Ole Higgins huffs and dumps the contents of my purse onto the bench. A sizable mound of coin rolls every which way.

"Careful not to lose a penny Karl. May I call you Karl? I expect to get it all back once we resolve the mix up."

"You're a spirited one ain't ya. Tell me princess what's with the purse? You gotta bag of cash yet claim you're no runner. Maybe you robbed a till."

"Well, I never! I'm no thief Karl. I got principles and your man messed up. Li Po Chin and I are on holiday. We were scouting for souvenirs and got lost. You know Karl, your town lacks proper signage and a refined hospitality."

The sarge gives me a blank look and I fear there's a starless void twix those piggy ears. What tale will this copper believe? I opt for the truth. "C'mon Karl, we were on an innocent errand and got lost. There's no crime in that."

The sarge smirks and leans into his creaky chair.

"Jeez Louise! My mistress is Lou Graham and I'm not fetching drugs! We were after a dumb cameo and lost our way. Send a note to the Royal suite at the Regency Inn. Miz Graham has influential friends in this town."

Is Karl impressed? Will he spring us without talking to Miss Lou? She'll have my hide for disobeying Mr. Chin. Karl bites his lower lip and squints at me. "That's a whale of a tale half-pint. Know what I think?

"No Karl, I haven't a clue." Ya dumb flatfoot.

"Ellie girl, I think you're a little liar. Does your mistress work for the cartel or is she another rich junkie?" Higgins doesn't want my reply. He turns and shouts towards the hallway, "Corporal take a patrolman over to the Regency and grab the Graham woman. I can't wait to hear her yarn."

Unbelievable! Nobody grabs Lou Graham and ole Karl is barking crazy. I'm screwed, but not by the R.C.M.P. I don't know whether to laugh or barf, so I curl up on the bench, close my eyes and wait for the storm to blow in. Karl's stare and smelly breath are pissin me off! That's it! Vancouver's finest can go to hell. I smile a wide toothy grin and cross my eyes.

"This ain't funny missy. If I was you, I'd wise up."

"If I was you Karl, I'd hightail it for the Yukon. You have no idea what's comin your way."

It's not long before Miss Lou waltzes into the room. She grants me a cool look before twirling to face Karl. Lou leans on her pearl-handled bumpershoot and locks eyes with the potbellied peacekeeper. The piggy's face turns the shade of a ripe tomato, he snorts and refuses to blink. Tis obvious Karl's no fan of uppity women. I feel kinda sorry for him until his chubby fingers curl into a fist.

Whoa Sarge! Threatening Miz Lou is crazy stupid cause there's a spring blade on the tip of her umbrella. One step closer and you're gonna be a bloody pork filet!

Saints be praised! The stare down ends with a familiar voice. Sarge's face drains of color as our card playing judge orders Karl into the hallway. Lou stands her ground forcing the Fatbelly to sidestep her. His honor winks at me, closes the door and I'm left to face Miz Lou.

"Ellie dear, the police think me an addict and assume I send children to fetch my fix. Pray tell me, how did they get such a ridiculous notion?"

Her tone cuts me to the quick. Fibbing to Miz Lou never ends well and crocodile tears flow from me as I spill the beans. My blubbering ends in a frantic plea. "I haven't seen Poo for hours. The cops probably beat a confession outta him and he's on a work train bound for Hades!"

Lou sits down beside me and puts an arm around my shoulders. "Don't fret Ellie, everything's sorted out and you're both free to go." Lou shifts her tone. "However, you lied to Mr. Chin. He feels bad for not going with you."

Lou's sense of fairness confused me at first. My pops was old school; the number of lashes tolled his rage and stopped when he ran out of steam. Miss Lou abhors physical violence. She says, "There's no justice in rote retaliation. The very act condones what it condemns, and its lack of ingenuity pacifies with no cure. History says cruelty begets cruelty. Surely mankind will not evolve until we learn to captain our egos and control our primal urges."

Lou knows what tweaks this young offender. "You will apologize to Mr. Chin and serve his every whim. When we get home, you'll empty the spittoons for two weeks. Do enjoy what's left of your holiday."

"No, not slimey tobacco spit! I'll take the lash please."

"The proper ask is may I have a lashing. No, I will not sanction corporal abuse. Shall I add to your sentence?"

"Please no! Two weeks is penance enough."

There's no shaking Mr. Chin after the police incident. He insists on escorting us everywhere except the toilet. Poo gets his two-bit cameo and Lou stores the piece with her most precious gems. She says it sparks a fond memory and wears it on her birthday. Fond memory my sweet patoot!

CHAPTER 35

Lou Wrangles a Troll

We left Vancouver on the ferry that delivered us. I'm eating breakfast while Fritz regales us with boat trivia.

"She's the only ferry on the Seattle to Vancouver run. I named her for Elsa because za engine farts remind me of my vife's explosive temper. Today's fog slows our departure, but a high tide helps us exit the harbor."

I'm thinking Uncle please stop talking; I feel awful. The waves slapping against the boat make me seasick and it's all Poo's fault! We sampled the honor bar after everyone went to bed and Poo swore the mint schnapps was a fancy soda pop. Stupid Cuz! My tummy's churning and Lou insists I eat all my breakfast. Does she know about the midnight raid? Ugh! I can't take my potent burps of eggs, bangers, and mint.

The rolling rise and fall of the boat makes me queasy; I race for fresh air, grab the forward rail, and spew my breakfast into the bay. Good riddance, the fishes can have it! I swear on mama's Bible I'll not taste anything minty ever again, not even a peppermint puff!

A dense fog hangs on the bay; all around me is a heavy gray mist with the hint of minty sea foam below. Blah! Mint! Our foghorn sends a searing pain from one ear out the other and rips another agonizing blast before my ringing stops. Seconds later the lighthouse returns fire. I assume it's the lighthouse cause I can't see a darn thing.

We suddenly lurch a port and I grab the rail to keep from going overboard! What's that huge shadow looming to my left? I squint to see a red and black wedge breaking through the mist. Is it a freighter? Bloody hell! The goliath's on a collision course aimed right at me.

Both ships blare their horns in a frantic contest to outdo the other. The freighter's catchín us and I'm close enough to see its sailors frantically waving. Do they think their mime makes a ferryboat disappear? My life's been short but fanciful. I hope mama gets me to heaven before the devil knows I'm dead!

Tis a bleeping miracle! The giant tin-can passes us with inches to spare. Our ferry rocks in its wake and I let go a rant that would make a salty sailor blush.

There's a second miracle aboard the freighter as a young girl stands at its rail staring back at me. We don't know it yet, but she'll someday make me a godmother. Our sweet Ellie Hua Chin is lucky her mum and auntie survived. My story's a ways to go, so I'll not jump ahead.

Mr. Chin says life schools us if we're clever enough to allow it. A good emerges even from the pit of despair and what came after our return is the proof of it.

I'm fetching a spittoon from a guest suite; a kerchief over me mouth hinders a disease but not the raunchy smell. It's then I hear a piercing scream! I poke my head out the doorway as Earl races by with Lou and Marie in his tow.

The next thing I see is Earl yanking a half-naked man out of a room. The girls rush in, and Earl slams a pants-less foe against the wall forcing a resounding oomph from his prey. Our man bares his teeth like an angry wolf and his fist hangs at the ready. Earl is about to anoint the bastard when Lou reappears.

"Mr. Hazard you mustn't! Put him down right now."

"But Lou our girl's darn near unrecognizable!"

"I, I know. I feel your angst but hear me out. This man is a wealthy influencer, and we must take care."

Earl keeps an eerie stare on the man, releases his grip, and the creep lands on his bare arse with a thud. Lou rolls her eyes at our grinning bouncer and hands the duffer his britches. "Marcus I do not tolerate brutality. Please leave and return another day with your manners in tow."

The pudgy rogue struggles to stuff himself into his pants and stands to adjust his suspenders. I recognize him now. It's Marcus Pikar Meriwether III, but his workers call him the Troll. The nickname fits a huge head and arms too long for his frame. The Troll's a dock owner and he's Uncle Hannibal's chief competitor. What's this? Marcus takes a step towards our man. Is he nuts? Earl's hankering to whoop his arse. Phooey! Lou just stepped in between them.

"Marcus, I helped you once. Do not try my patience."

"Your boy's lucky you saved him. Give me my money back for the room and the Froggie bitch."

Lou doesn't protest. She reaches into a silk sash tied round her waist and hands Marcus his money. The Troll snatches it with a snarl and lumbers down the hall. I swear his knuckles touch the rug. Marcus utters a foul profanity against our house that even I can't repeat. It occurs to me to extend my foot and watch him tumble down the stairs, but Lou shakes a finger at me. The bastard bumps shoulders with Mr. Chin whose rushing up the stairs with his medicine bag.

Lou tells Earl to wait in the hall while she escorts our house doctor into the room.

She leaves Mr. Chin to do his best and returns to Earl. "All right dear, let me explain why I let the devil go. Marcus is held in high regard." Earl starts to protest so Lou puts up a hand. "Assaulting Marcus is a moment's satisfaction and bad for business. He'll press charges and the newspapers will feast on the sordid details. Our protection has its limits. No court convicts gentry for beating a working girl and what will become of Emma and your kiddies? I fear a midnight raid will burn your house down. Please let me protect your family and my business."

Tis the truth, our liberties come with a whitewashed qualifier. A family dog gets more respect than a whore or a negro. Earl outta count his blessings for Lou's cool head. Killing a troll ain't worth the trouble.

Lou adds, "I will take care of this. Marcus's reckoning awaits and my House will have its day."

Earl grumbles all the way down the stairs as Lou calls out, "Ellie fetch a pitcher of warm water for Mr. Chin."

Sweet Mother Mary! Earl's appraisal is spot on. I am not naïve, yet the grisly scene shocks even me. The stench of cruelty still lingers, Cherié's eyes are swollen shut and her nose is smashed. Spattering's of red stains the walls and the bedding. How can a petite girl spew so much blood? Marie cuddles Cherié and tries to comfort her with a French lullaby. Our poor Creole whimpers as Mr. Chin touches her ribs. Dear girl!

There are other damages besides the expensive linens and wallpaper. A new imported Indian rug lays bloodied, and Earl nearly yanked the door off its hinges.

Lou knows how my dad beat on me. I've no stomach for cruelty and won't inherit her business. Frankly, I don't want it.

Our mistress stays present and is already plotting the troll's atonement. Prominent men congregate at our house for leisure and business. Their status strokes a pathetic ego, but it won't grant a lick of common sense. Marcus will return and Lou's knitting a perfect redemption.

Tis but a fortnight before Meriwether struts into our bar. Earl's muscles ripple and he stiffens. I admire our man's restraint. If I had Earl's strength, I'd kill the cocky troll!

Miss Lou's quintessential demeanor oozes charm. "Marcus how nice to see you. No hard feelings: we business owners must protect our assets, yes? Have a seat at the bar. Your tab's on me today and it is my pleasure to serve you."

The smug cock puffs up and crows, "Glad you see it my way. Bartender, take your hands off the cheap stuff. I only drink from the top shelf."

Now a man with any brains might prickle at Lou's charismata. However, this arse is so full of hisself he can't read Lou's tell. Our cordial mistress slips behind the bar and nudges the bartender aside. "Only the finest for our Mr. Meriwether. I've the perfect import for a discerning palate." Lou reaches up top for a crystal decanter with a discreet X on the label. We've nothing to do with the opium trade so Lou asked a friend to get her a pinch as a mighty chaser. Our gracious hostess pours Marcus a glass and places the tainted bottle in front of him.

"Here you go dear, the best for the best! Do enjoy."

The Troll downs the shot, pours himself another and another and another until he's silly drunk. What comes next is Lou's justice served. She sends me for a photographer, and I return to find her in the parlor with a quartet of girls. I say four girls, but that's not right.

Lou and our beauties fuss over an odd looker. Oh Lordy, it's the stone-faced Troll all dolled up in makeup, wig, and a bright red dress! Granny Chin sewed the satin gown and stitched Miss Marcus inside the collar. She added an overstuffed brassiere for good measure. Lou employs a sweet lad, but this faker looks ridiculous. His stubbly chest and chin insults any meticulous Twila.

The photographer takes three shots of the hairy harlot. Our madame will frame one for the parlor mantel with the inscription: Gentlemen Mind Your Manners. The second photo is a gift for Cherié. Perhaps a laughable troll will heal her trauma. And what of the last photo? It's for Earl to show around at the docks. Mr. Chin donates the Troll's expensive waistcoat and trousers to charity and Lou splits the contents of his wallet as reparations for Cherié and house repairs.

Ready for her debut, Earl gently helps Miss Marcus down the back steps. Mr. Hazard isn't being nice; Lou wants the dress to make a perfect showing. Marcus soon loses a heel and stumbles down the alley. Disbelievers gawk as the imposter bobs up and down Dock Street. The crowd gasps when the ugly doll gets too close to a horse trough, but she avoids a dunking. The girly troll limps on with a gaggle of rowdy followers in her tow and the parade ambles on until a mounted copper stops Marcus.

It turns bad when the Troll yells, "Nobody calls me a hairy tomato" and punches the police horse in the snout! Of course, a mare doesn't talk, and her rider was just having a bit of fun. The cop stops laughing, takes out his baton, double thumps the hairy trollop and she slumps to the ground. Now the troll's got two knobby horns popping through his wig. A piece of advice should suffice. Never swing at a beloved filly, no matter what she calls you!

Two officers bring a cart and haul Miss Marcus to the Dock Street station. Each man grabs an arm, and they walk the Troll inside. The watch sergeant greets his men. "What we got here boys? That is one ugly fem fatale!"

"Tis a mystery Sarge, its collar says Miss Marcus."

"Does it now. That's nice stitching and my girl wants a new dress. Where'd you get this one sweetie? Housaboot you tell me who you be?"

Marcus blinks one eye into focus. "Where am I? What dress? My name, ahh, I can't recall. Don't ya know me? I must be somebody! What the bloody hell! I'm in a friggin dress. Where's my pants? Help police! I've been robbed!"

"Right here darlín. What can I do ya for?"

"Keep your manners flatfoot! You must know me."

"Apologies missy, I am stumped. Perhaps a little less face paint and I might recognize ya."

Just then a constable arrives with a frequent guest on his arm and helps the inebriated fella to a chair. "Lookie here Sarge. It's ole Frenchy with a snoot full."

The sergeant frowns. "Pierre tis midday, why ain't ya out trapp'n critters? You promised the missus no more booze. You're supposed to be on the wagon."

"Mais oui, Sargente, I no can stop! I climbs on ze wagon and falls off ageen. Mon Dieu! What a catch you got!"

"You know this fella? Enlighten us, si'l vous plait."

"You trapped a beeg boogger! He is the Troll, Monsieur Marcus Meriwether! Please Sargente, I cannot share a cell with heem! The wife no like."

The sergeant books Marcus for hitting a police horse and public lewdness. A quick-thinking newsman reads the police blotter and jumps on the story. His editor says the horse angle's a plus but the story lacks depth. "Did you ask about the pantaloons? Do the panties match the dress? It's irrelevant yet sparks a reader's imagination. Go back and get a look-see, or at least a quote from the bugger."

The intrepid reporter returns to the station and the cops toss him to the street. Sarge says, "Ya slimy hack! No one's lookín up a fella's skirt on my watch! The prisoner ain't talkín so go tell your editor to pound sand!"

The story's a hit despite the lack of intimate details and a society columnist fuels the public outrage saying, "The gown was a bold showing, but wearing red before sundown? Oh my, never!" Proper Seattle enlists in the torment as disgusted pulpits shame the sinner and clients avoid him like a leper at a beauty contest. Salty dockhands won't touch a crate except to paint it with lewd graffiti. Missus Meriwether drains her husband's accounts and skips town with their kiddies. Laughter follows Marcus everywhere. The final blow is bankruptcy and the Troll watches as the bank auctions his dock to his rival, Hannibal Conover. A defeated Marcus runs off for parts unknown and gossipers swear he's mining silver in Idaho. Yes, a troll might go underground and change his name, but he can't change his ways. Gorilla looks and a foul temper do betray his ugly secret.

Miz Lou finagled her hornswaggle into justice served. Our patrons are forewarned, Cherié has her reparations and, as Hannibal's partner, Lou profits. She parlayed her payback into a dandy trifecta. Sweet Lou insists, "Marcus paid his debt. It was a humble ploy; my businesses profit and Cherié can heal in peace. Let's move on and pray for a troll's spirited atonement."

Move on? Mr. Fortune Cookie says to let go of sorrow lest it binds you. Well buster, forgiveness ain't that easy! A bloody room still haunts my dreams and I struggle with an unfettered pardon. I am a work in progress.

However, Cherié and Marie do move on. Those two are oddly devoted. Employees have their own rooms, but this pair shares one. Tis a conundrum so I consult Miss Lou.

"Ellie, we honor love for love's sake. God's garden is full of unique flowers and sweet devotion is priceless. So what if I prefer roses and Cherié fancies tulips. I say do no harm and let His garden bloom as planted. I for one prefer the smelly rose, prickers and all."

Our tulips dreamt of more than parlor work. As soon as Cherié could travel they moved back to her home in New Orleans and opened a store called Mademoiselle's Dress & Accoutrement. Lou received a post from Marie soon after. 'Sales are good, but the cost of silk dampens my joy.' Lou writes back, 'Marie, did you forget about Miss Marcus? Count your blessings dear and forgive your woes. Mr. Chin says a worry slays while gratitude upholds us. Bless your profits and rejoice in Cherié's full recovery!'

The events of late weigh heavily on me as well and Lou suggests I stay with Granny Chin. She says, "A change of scenery eases a troubled mind. I'll send a tutor on Mondays, and you can help our granny."

A big yawn grabs Ellie. "Sorry Jack, I'm all tuckered out." I am done in as well. Ellie and I exchange pecks on the cheek, and I head for home.

CHAPTER 36

It All Makes Sense Now

The pungent wetlands signal an exceptional ebb tide as a shimmer of light clings to the horizon. Small netter boats, with their dim lanterns, dot the dark waters while fishermen troll for king salmon and squid. I love a grand salmon, but the odd squid's too exotic for me. Ah Jack, what's with the fishy thoughts? Why must my mind always wander? It's a nuisance especially when I've bigger fish to fry. Ha! Miss Lou would love the pun. Sweet Jesus, focus man!

Lou's cunning is an inspiration, and her true grit has awakened my sense of duty. I must help Mike Quinn free Ellie.

I remove my boots and hang my coat on the antler rack. Sweet Belle tugs on my pant leg begging to be held but my wife refuses to look up from her crochet. She motions to the pot on the stove. It was nice of Anne to keep my supper warm. Lord knows I deserve the cold shoulder.

"Annie I am so sorry. May I have a word please?"

"It's Belle's bedtime. Eat your dinner while you wait."

"Gimme a hug Bellybutton and go say your prayers." I put Belle down but not before my tickles force a giggle; then hand in hand my two loves disappear down the hallway.

My wife relishes this time with Belle. She says it makes for a fond memory. Does Anne have a fond memory of me? I hope she does.

Miss Lou says to count our blessings; sweet love found me, and I married the better for it.

I reckon my apology over a bowl of scalded stew. This must be how Floyd Snypes fairs; it is a fitting penalty for a fool. Anne deserves my best effort, so I wash my bowl. With no wife in sight, I make a pot of tea and set a plate of zucchini bread on the end table.

My girl finally appears, sits down next to me and I begin. I can see her jaw tighten with worry. "Good heavens Jackson! You should've spoken up before now. I need more facts; what exactly will you do for this Quinn fellow? Where will Belle and I be safe and what becomes of us if we lose you? Will your lawyer friend take us back to Indiana?"

It's obvious I haven't thought this through. Anne's concerns are valid. She never met her Grandpa Campbell. Doc was about Belle's age when his dad went off to war to die a hero at the battle of Gettysburg. Neither sanctity nor valor saved him from a rebel bullet, or was it friendly fire? The War Department wasn't sure. Doc's only memory of his dad is a wedding photo with the Medal of Honor hanging from its frame. I fear my quest is as much a gamble. Miss Lou left little to chance and I must protect my loved ones, no matter what the outcome for me.

My reunion with Anne is the calm I crave, but what's to come? Anne has a quiver of questions for Michael Quinn.

It is a glorious day! The sun's bright and my trek to the office is no obstacle at all. I embrace my newfound purpose with a message to Mike. My words are direct: 'A moment of your time. Please advise. Jackson Hamby, assistant Auditor.' The embellished title sounds official to a snooping courier. Quinn's response is brief: 'Certainly, see you this afternoon. Quinn, Esquire.'

It is a Déjà vu moment as my workmates depart and Mr. Barr waves me into his office. He moans, "Off I go to celebrate, ah heck, I can't recall what for! It doesn't matter. I'm there to kick the mayor under the table. The braggart drones on all the while taking credit for another man's work. No wonder the press preys on his boasting. I hope neither the food nor his honor gives me indigestion." Barr grabs his hat and opens the back door.

Mike says, "Why not give the ole boy a kick before his speech begins? A tender bruise will quiet the blather."

"Fat chance! The nincompoop loves to hear his own voice." Barr shuts the door and Mike motions for me to sit.

I can't. A case of jitters keeps my knees from bending. "I'll do it Mike, but Anne has concerns. If I don't survive this charade, I must provide for my girls."

"No worries lad, I am prepared. Your wife will publicly accuse you of an affair and set off for Indiana. My brother Aidan will meet her train in North Bend and your girls will stay with his family at his ranch. I respect your wife's worry and if it comes to it, I'll see to her. Lou's estate bequests $10,000 for my use. Anne gets it all and I'll accompany her back to Indiana. That said, I won't dwell on a bad outcome and beg your trust. Just stick to my plan and you'll be fine."

"Wow! Ten grand's a generous sum and I've been a challenge of late. I wouldn't blame Anne if she took the cash and ran. Your offer is very generous and I'm eager for those acting lessons." I hear my brave tenor, though my mind's in a panic.

"Good! Ellie's right about you; those thick spectacles hide a decent bloke. Jack you're more of a partner than hired hand, so don't take offense. No matter the outcome, I'd like you to have the stipend. Starting anew in a strange place is a hefty challenge and I'm sure Lou would've helped your plan. She once told my dad that a brave heart and kind eyes were all the collateral she needed."

"Thanks for the compliment but I can't take money to help a friend and Anne needs the contingency. So, what's our next move?"

"As you wish, the stipend's there all the same. My plan is simple and foolproof. You'll give Jimmy a note asking for a meeting..."

Mike lays out a forthright ruse. My part's less a bother than the worry I gave it. Frankly, it seems farfetched. "Who believes Ellie and I are lovers? It's a preposterous notion."

"I imagine most folks do. Tis plausible for an outsider to conjure you two together."

"Ha! I'm more four-eyed simpleton than a Don Juan."

"Go on with ya! I hear your wife's a charmer and you managed to snare her. Your jailhouse visits do make a tattler's tongue wag."

"Sorry Mike, I swear there's nothing going on."

"Relax lad, I trust you and Ellie. The point is Jimmy's brain is soaked in booze. He's desperate for cash and a bit of a mug. The dope believes anything that fits his purpose."

Mike's portrayal fits the man I met. We spend a couple of hours practicing my lines before I head down the steep hill. A chill forces me to quicken my gait and I respond with the exuberance of Mike's convictions. Whoa! Slow down Jack. I mustn't tumble in the darkness.

CHAPTER 37

Brava Missus Hamby!

---

*A*nne and I have a couple of days to practice before Ambary's reckoning. I'm gaining confidence, but even more amazing is my wife.

"Jackson there are days I'd trade you for ten dollars let alone thousands. Lucky for you, this isn't one of them. Mr. Quinn's ruse seems plausible, and I relish a part in it."

"Thank you dear, I'm humbled by your confidence."

Silly me! I forgot how I came to love Anne Campbell. The sweet girl once acted out stories that helped a scared little boy forget his illness. Annie knows all my faults yet she's still with me.

Practicing with Anne is fun. After the hornswoggle she wants to audition for a local theater group. Jeez Jack, focus!

Two days later, Anne climbs the marble staircase to start Act One. Belltown is a world away from First Hill. It's unusual for a wife to visit the office and my mates take notice. I stand to greet her with a well-rehearsed baffled look, Anne takes aim and wallops me! My surprise is genuine; this is not the slap we rehearsed.

Anne raises her voice for all to hear, "You adulterous scoundrel! Did you think me dense?"

"Darling this is a private matter. Let's take a walk."

I reach for her arm, and she yanks it away. Her nostrils flare as she steals the scene. Anne stomps on my foot and finishes me with a punch to the nose. It is a jab worthy of Earl the bouncer. Tears form as I stumble backward, trip over my own two feet and land on my butt.

Anne glowers down at me. "Traitor! Belle and I are going back to Indiana. Don't bother following us, daddy's lawyer will find you." My wife further embellishes her role with a huff and exits stage left.

What a performance! I am truly stunned; my nose is throbbing, and I feel a bit of blood trickle down my chin. Anne's wedding ring must've cut me. Wide-eyed Andy and Nesbitt duck behind their folders as Floyd Snypes sprints to my rescue. The expert panderer extends his hand and pulls me to my feet.

Floyd offers his kerchief for my scratch and whispers, "Be quick Jackie, go after her and fix your mess. Take my advice and keep it simple. Hang your head and blame the harlot. Say you was duped by a she-devil. Tell Anne the wicked wench meant nothing and promise it'll never happen again. That's what I do."

"It's good advice Floyd. I'll give it a go."

I sprint down the hill and wait behind our pumphouse for Anne's signal. Miss Carrie babysat Belle and I must wait for her to go. When it's all clear I enter through the back door. "Darling you were brilliant though the punch was unexpected!"

"Oh dear! I'll fetch a poultice for the swelling. Was I good enough? Did my nerves show?"

"Anne Hamby are you taking a bow? I've no flowers to toss at your feet, but my sore face says brava!"

We talk about the local theater group while we pack, and our silly giggles hide the worry until it's time for them to go. It's a tender moment filled with uncertainty. A tear stings my wound and Anne dabs the scratch with her hankie.

"Take care of yourself Jackson. Oh sorry I forgot it's Jack now, isn't it?"

I press her hand against my cheek. "I shall answer my wife no matter what she calls me. I adore you."

A hired hansom stops out front, and the driver shakes his bell. The curtain hides me while Anne pays the man his fee plus a hefty tip. He earns it by carrying two heavy bags from our porch to the wagon. Mike said to make a convincing exit for an Ambary spy. The driver helps my girls to their seats and off they go. Pangs of loneliness stab at me as I watch their exit. I'm already missing my girls so why stay here? This two-timing bastard has a role to play. I'll leave my empty nest, buy a bottle of hooch and head up the hill.

Ellie knew about the ruckus before I made it halfway home. Damn the tattlers! "I'm so sorry Jack, you're no flirt and this mess is mine. Go fetch Anne and I'll put her mind at ease."

"Thanks for the offer, but you're too late. My girls left by train an hour ago. I'm on my own now."

Ellie gives me a shove. "What are you doing here? Go after them you dolt!"

"And catch a moving train! No thank you, it's best I stay behind and let the dust settle."

"Jack Hamby you're not that stubborn or stupid."

Mike's words clatter inside my head. "No one can know." I do feel stupid and in no mood to match wits with Ellie. "For pity's sake!

I need time to clear my head. It's between Anne and I, so please butt out. If you truly want to help, open my bottle, and tell me a story."

Ellie's face softens from fiery to maternal. "Young man, I'll say this and let it be. All sorts of men waltz into our palace. Like Fritz and Hannibal, you're the loyal kind. I fear you'll lose Anne if you wait too long. Tis like Lou always says, we best honor love when it finds us."

The advice is sound if only our split were real, and my acquiescent nod brings my storyteller back to me. Ellie taps her lips and raises an eyebrow, "Well now, where did I leave off? Oh yes, the story of Granny Chin."

I grab my jug and Ellie recoils. "Yuck, laddy put down the pigswill! Your cheap mash is kerosene compared to my stash. We'll fill the lamps with it."

I trade my swill for a Macallan scotch, take a cookie and stand before the haunted chair. Hmm, its aura seems inviting. The wily ghost must like Mike's plan, but what does she think of me? I sink my behind into the soft cushion. "Miss Lou thank you for not jabbing me. I do admire your spirit despite its muddled reputation." Sweet Lord in heaven! I sound just like my mother.

CHAPTER 38

Look at All the Angles

Never mind a baffling specter. Ellie's begun her tale.

As I was saying: I needed a getaway after the Marcus incident. Damn that ugly Troll! Sensing my weariness Lou sends me to Granny Chin. Granny doesn't need my help, tis a convenience to give my growing pains a rest.

Our granny smokes Three Castle tobacco from a pipe bowl made of an antler tine. A Salish man carved the bowl to look like a sleeping bear and traded it for one of granny's woks. It's scandalous for a woman to smoke in public, but granny doesn't care. The ole girl puffs at a passersby from her porch rocker. "Nosey person what you staring at? If my bisness botter you, den look away! I don't let my babies smoke. I'm too old to botter wit, so let me be." Jack Hamby don't give me that look. My granny voice is spot on and I'm not being mean.

Another of granny's quirks is a sipper called Tullamore Dew. Lou imports the Irish brand just for granny. You'd think this Eire lass might want a whiskey on a winter's day. Truth is, I've no use for it lest I'm dunkín a cookie. Shoot! I've wandered off topic again.

Our granny speaks a Pidgeon English. It's my keen observation with no slight intended cause granny's English is far better than my Mandarin. The ole girl rambles on so fast her choppers jump right into her lap. Tis why she keeps them in a pickle jar on the kitchen table. With her quick tongue and no teeth, you best listen up.

Granny has another peculiarity; she reads tea leaves with an amazing accuracy. Granny predicted I'd travel to faraway places and be rich beyond all fancy. I hope to see half the places she foretold.

As fate would have it, granny was my saving grace. I dreamt poorly after mama died and granny's advice helped me find my way. She told me, "Little one do not insult the Dà àomi. The Dà lives in our dreams. If you have no dreams, den only darkness lives in you. My tea leaves say big dreams filled your fatter's sails. Your mutter was his rudder, but she die. Berry sad for dem, but Ellie it was der boat, not yours. Leave der doldrums girl and set your own sails."

Granny was right of course. I let go of dad's anchor and set us both free. Now every morn I bless the new day. Tis my way of keeping granny in my dreams.

Granny Chin has two sons and two grandsons. She says having girls in the house balances the masculine energy. There's me, her daughter-in-law Mei, and Ling Lu Han. Ling's my age so we get along just fine. Our laundryman owns Ling and it's unseemly for a single man to live with his underaged servant, so granny keeps Ling with her.

Ellie breaks from her narrative. "Pay attention Jack! 'Twas Ling Lu who came out of the fog in Vancouver Bay on the freighter that almost sunk me. That moment ties us together like sisters."

"Yes dear, I remember the tale."

Ellie nods and slips back in time: As I said, the tong brought Ling to North America. Those racketeers plague our Chinatowns and it's dangerous for decent folks. The China emperor's spies and our cops pursue them, but the ruthless bastards hide behind bribes and unkept promises. I swear the tong have no soul! They steal from their homeland and sell their booty at auction. Tis evil to pillage antiquities but slave trafficking is way worse. The tong cracks a head, chains the bloke, and sails him overseas. He's sold as an indentured and if he escapes, he's got no way home. And what of the girl trade? Lings' father bartered her to pay his debts and was promised an arranged marriage. Of course, the tong stiffed him. A snatched girl has but two fates: be a brothel hag or a house servant.

Ling dodged a seedy brothel life, but she was far from free. One race enslaving another is awful but it's worse when your own kind shackles you. Our laundryman's a decent bloke but an invisible yoke is still a yoke. Tis a man's world with no laws protecting us girls.

Little Po's smitten with Ling. He can't sprout a whisker yet acts manly around her. Tis laughable to watch Poo puff up his chest and lower his voice. The boy sounds like a croaking toad. Ling's oblivious and calls him 'Cuz' just like me. The only one taking him seriously is Poo himself. His brother Huang's a tease and begs a thrashing, if only Poo could catch him. Lucky for Lil' Huang, Poo's slow afoot.

Tis yours truly who suffers most from the one-sided love. Pining takes all the fun out of Poo, and I turn to Miss Lou for help. "Ma'am the nimenog's gone soft in the head. He languishes about the shop just to be near Ling. I like the girl and all, but Poo's driving me crazy. I miss my Cuz."

"Ellie, it's normal for Little Po to act this way. Your childhood is ending and you must accept growing up. Stop wasting your time in denial."

"I do want to grow up, but I despise having no say in the matter. Why must Poo be so lovey-dovey? I want my old boy back."

"Liebchen listen to yourself; this cannot go your way. Friends grow up with or without you. You best understand this and lend your support."

"Yeah sure, I know. Please may I have my allowance. I have an urge for a bite of licorice."

The inevitable sun does rise, Poo gets a chin whisker and all's predictable until it isn't. One morning a frenzied Poo shows up at our door. He must talk to our mistress and neither Mr. Chin nor I will do. Poo wants Miz Lou, and he wants her now!

I sit Mr. Hysterics at the table and fetch Lou who's in her office with Mr. Chin. The pair follows me back to a most miserable sight. Poo is fighting back tears and I'd laugh at the bugger if he wasn't so pitiful.

Mr. Chin speaks first. "What is the problem boy?"

"Oh uncle, my Ling Lu is gone! I went to the shop with a bag of Ling's favorite candy. Granny says the tailor sold my girl to pay his mahjong debt and a coalman named Keswitch has her contract!"

Lou corrects Poo. "You mean Mr. Keswick from the Black Diamond mine. Dame Keswitch is his wife." Miz Lou never forgets a debt. Muriel Keswick tried to axe Pearl's school just to spite us and Lou says Keswitch so often we assume it's the hag's surname.

"Miss Lou please, this is important! The miner bought Ling's contract. My pops saw Keswick and Harry Turner lock Ling in a boxcar at the railyard. Bàba overheard them talking about my girl."

Keswick says, "I forgot Muriel's anniversary and she booted me out of her bed. I paid a pretty penny for the servant girl, so my wife best relent."

Turner winks, "Ha! Mr. Keswick sir, no worries. If ya can't bed your wife just doodle the Ching Chong."

Keswick snickers. "Sounds fair to me. I'm gonna get something for my money one way or another."

"Miss Lou these are awful men! Bàba says they leave tomorrow with Ling locked in the boxcar like a bag of flour. She is a royal consort! This cannot be!"

A royal consort? What in Sam hill is a royal consort? I try to ask but Mr. Chin cuts me off. "Boy we don't intervene in legal matters."

"But I must! I'll buy her contract from Mr. Keswick. Miss Lou, please loan me the money. I promise to pay back every cent with interest!"

Mr. Chin shakes his head. "I forbid it. Your ask makes you a slave for life. I cannot allow this."

Lou intervenes. "There'll be no loan, but Little Po is right about Keswick. He cannot keep the girl. I believe those men have rooms with us. Ellie bring me the register."

"No need Miss Lou, I was the one who checked them in yesterday noon."

Mr. Chin looks into Lou's sparkling eyes and knows a mischief's brewing. "I appreciate your concern, but..."

"No worries, I've waited long enough to take down the wicked witch! Artemis fancies himself a poker expert so his ego makes it easy to free Ling Lu. But first let's hear the story of the royal consort."

Hurrah for Lou! I am dying to know the tale, but Poo crosses his arms. His eyes are as big as a Jumeau baby doll's peepers. "Ma'am I misspoke before; Ling told me her secret in trust, and I swore an oath."

"You are an honorable young man, good for you! However, you can't suck your words back in. I will help and my price is the tale of a consort. Do you want to save your girl or not?"

Lou's bluffing yet her look say she's all in. A calm boy sees through the ploy, but a frazzled Poo couldn't catch her tell with a drift net. He'll talk and I'm on the edge of my seat.

CHAPTER 39

Ling Lu Who?

L ing Lu says it happened like this: My birth name is Yu Yan Liu.
The tong did not cheat my father and I lied about my abduction. Desperate men make ugly choices to save their family. My father gave me up to the province Lord Xizang to pay his taxes.

Xizang's girls were dressing me in fine robes when three men burst into the harem chamber. They took me to the Shanghai harbor and manifested me as a slave bound for a Portland Oregon brothel.

I was saved by a royal spy who saw my captors leave the ship. The spy told me he needed time to summon help, he dressed me in peasant garb and burned my fancy clothes. To further confuse the tong, the spy took me to a ship bound for Canada. He manifested me as a house servant called Ling Lu Han. "Girl remember this your life depends on it. You answer only as Ling Lu Han a servant bound for auction. This ship sails in a few hours but fear not. I shall return with my army. Remember you are Ling Lu Han."

The Royal Guard received his note, but the spy never returned. An informant saw the spy and surrendered him to the tong.

My hero kept mum until his torturer relented. "Spy, I admire loyalty, but I am out of patience. I will find the harem girl without you."

The tong searched in vain for a silk-adorned Yu Yan until the Royal Guardsmen came to kill everyone including the boorish torturer. The soldiers found the spy's severed head hanging from a yardarm, but the harem girl was gone.

My ship sailed minutes before the mêlée began and I watched from its stern as the battle shrank from view. I realized that Yu Yan Liu was dead and whispered to the wind, "My sister now pays Bàba's debt. Yu Yan must be buried at sea to be celebrated each Remembrance Day. I am Ling Lu Han, a slave to be auctioned in a land called Canada.

Six weeks later my ship docks in Vancouver British Columbia where I'm sold to a kind man. He says we'll travel to his cousin's house in Seattle where I'll live out my days. Yu Yan is Ling Lu's secret for as long as the tong exists. This humble servant is grateful to live with your granny. It could be so much worse.

A teary-eyed Poo returns to the present and puts his face on the table. His head in his arms he whimpers, "My beloved confessed only to me and now I've betrayed her. I've lost her trust forever and cannot be redeemed."

The boy has a flair for the dramatic, but he needn't worry. Lou will save them both. "Little Po do not give up. This is a time for certainty. Ling's secret is safe with us, and we will get her back. Look up boy! You shall be Ling's new champion!"

Lou's call-to-arms delights Poo and he stands with a ready salute shouting, "What must we do?"

I too jump into the fray. The wee children shall follow our lady general hither and yon! And yes, I can be a bit dramatic when swept up in the reverie.

Alas a contrary Mr. Chin sits glued to his chair shaking his head and grunting. The constipated look says he needs a swig of berry elixir. Lou smiles and places a hand on his shoulder. Our defeated man sighs as he stands and exits for a breath of fresh air. Lou says,

"Ellie fetch my dermatoid garnet necklace from the safe. Do you remember it?"

"Of course, you got it for the lamppost trial. The clasp snaps into its snakehead mouth. So amazing!"

"Yes, put it on my bed with my emerald satin dress. You know the one with the revealing bodice. Stay with the necklace and I'll be up soon to change for dinner. First Little Po and I must write a note to his consort."

Lou rummages through Mr. Chin's desk for pen and paper. She dictates to Poo who writes her message in hánzi script. Lou says to sign the note with his affections and has Little Po seal the envelope with Mr. Chin's dragon stamp. Poo gets his final marching orders and heads for the railyard while Lou leaves a note for Artemis Keswick.

It reads: 'My dear Artemis, thank you for staying with us. Please dine at my table tonight. I hope 6:45 is satisfactory. I look forward to hearing the news from your quaint little village. Hannibal Conover and Fritz Heigl are coming for drinks and poker after supper so please join us. A man of your skill keeps us dabblers on our toes! Warmest regards, Lou Graham.' A summons to Miss Lou's private table is a coveted prize. No one dares refuse her invitation.

Lou comes up the stairs where I've prepared a basin of honeysuckle water. Lou freshens up and asks for the corset she calls her lucky battle armor. It pushes her bosoms up revealing most all her goods. Lou complains of the pinch, but the bodice serves its purpose. A dark green dress with a black lattice lace hugs her voluptuous frame. We do up her hair securing a peacock-feather comb in back and emeralds dangle from her ears. However, the piéce de résistance is the dermatoid snake around Lou's neck. Its head sits blissfully atop her uplifted breasts while its slithering body of green garnets and diamonds blink in the sunlight. The downstairs lamps will make our madame a shimmering vision. Yes siree bub, like the garden of Eden, no Adam can refuse them apples!

Lou walks over to a plain leather-bound jewelry box reserved for her costume pieces. She withdraws a snake replica of her fancy necklace and places the forgery in the real necklace's box. Lou says, "This box has embroidered gold-leaf stitching worth twice the fake it holds. Do you recall where I got the knockoff?"

"Yes ma'am I do. It was a gift from a lumber baron up north of Edmonds. As I recall you sent him packing."

"The man courted me with a counterfeit. Shame on him for thinking me a dupe. What a der Gauner!"

Lou tosses the box onto the bed. "Do I have all I need?" She no longer speaks to me; her eyes gaze upwards to the heavens. This is Miss Lou conversing with her spirit guides. She trusts her guides more than us mortals. "Ah yes, the old double-switch will do. I shan't surrender my priceless jewels to the likes of an Artemis Keswick!"

Lou points to the box of worthless jewels on the bed. "Ellie take the box to the safe and keep mum about it. You must stay alert tonight and follow my lead. Remember, this is our secret. No one must know of our plan."

"Yes ma'am, it's our secret." Questioning Lou's intent is pointless. Truth is, I never fully grasp her plans. Her tactics are a puzzle with a crucial piece always missing. Screw the details! Her strategy is outright conviction and double-down gutsy. Lou's focus is absolute. She'll go all in to save Ling.

"Good girl, now go fetch Uncles Fritz and Hannibal. Say I need them to come to the kitchen door without being seen by Artemis or his man."

"Got it. Miss Lou needs you. Come to our back door and don't be seen by Keswick or Harry Turner."

"Excellent! Now be quick and don't dally. Come right home once you've delivered my message."

Uncle Fritz is at his dock office. He'll come as soon as he sends an excuse to Miz Elsa. Uncle Hannibal is a bigger challenge; his private office door is half-open revealing the backside of Artemis Keswick. I take cover, put a finger to my lips and motion for my uncle to join me. Hannibal obeys whispering, "Thank you Ellie, tell Miss Lou I'll be there as soon as I can."

Lou sits knitting at the kitchen table while Mr. Chin and Little Po prepare supper. Poo returned from the railyard to watch the show and Mr. Chin put him to work. "Nephew your favor requires many chores; be prepared to pay the price." Mr. Chin is not a fan of Lou's hornswoggles. Poo could use a friend, so I grab my knife to help cut vegetables and we pass the time hearing about Poo's visit with Harry Turner.

Poo says it went like this: I saw Keswick's man barking at a laborer three boxcars down from me. Harry's supposed to notice me, so I shout for Ling Lu. She answers from the car next to me, but I can't slide her note under the door just yet. Miss Lou said Harry's supposed to catch me.

Turner runs up yelling. "Hey ya little yellow bandit, git away from Mr. Keswick's freight!"

"I'm no thief sir, I have an urgent note for Ling Lu!"

Harry grabs it and rips open the envelope. "Tarnation! What do these chicken scratches say?"

Poo stops his story and turns to Miss Lou. "Writing in hánzi script was a brilliant ploy. Smelly ole Turner couldn't decipher it. I bet he can't read at all, but good on you not to risk it. The creep riles me. I wanted to kick the ignorant zounderkite in the..."

Lou interrupts. "Ignorant zounderkite is a redundant phrase and the overuse of slang and cussing is a wasteful habit. The articulate choose more powerful words."

"Yes ma'am. I'll watch my words."

I say to Turner, "Ling Lu left the shop without my grandma's recipe. It's Nâinai's remedy for..." I lower my voice to a whisper, "Mr. Turner, the girl's got an awful itch down there." I cringe and point 'tween his legs.

Harry wrings his hands and frets something awful. "Ah Jeez the little witch scratched me before I could tie her up." Harry rubs his injured paw, "Is the snatch-rash catching?"

Poo breaks from his tale. "Miss Lou the creep laid his grimy hands on my girl! It got to me, so I took a breath and kept my temper. I didn't want to sack your plans."

I swear Mr. Chin almost smiled. He thinks wrangling anger shows maturity and Poo struggles to keep his temper.

Poo says to Turner, "Oh yes Mr. Harry, it's awful catching. Maybe Ling will share her ointment."

"She will or else. Now git the hell outta here!"

Turner shoves the note under the boxcar door, and I call out in Mandarin, "Read the note Ling. Your rescue is at hand."

The fathead son of a...ah, sorry ma'am. The scoundrel deserves a comeuppance, and I can't wait!

We're applauding Poo's performance when the back-door swings open and in walks a pair of uncles. Lou stands to give her friends a hug and a kiss. "Hello my darlings! Thank you for coming."

Hannibal growls with a mock impatience. "Lou what's up? My wife has a pan of apple betty's cooling in the kitchen window. Gracie says a hand-pie's yours if she can join in the fun. What exactly are you up to?"

"My apologies to our dear Grace; she can play another time. I need you after supper and I promise a good story for your bedtime!"

"Is this costing me money?" Herr Fritz always protects his wallet.

"We're playing poker so lose if you must. I'll make it simple; we're going to play cards with Artemis Keswick. You must play along with whatever I say and do. It's imperative that Artemis goes all in."

Fritz purses his lips. "Hmm. We'll hornswoggle the coalminer then?"

"Yes dear. We'll play a few rounds and on Hannibal's deal I'll tell Ellie to go to bed. That's when she'll ask to stay up a bit longer." Lou gives me a look.

"I'm listening ma'am. You say go to bed and I beg to keep my seat."

"No begging missy. Do not over-dramatize your part. Keep it simple."

She gives me the obey or pay look and I bob my head with a dutiful yes. Lou turns back to Fritz and Hannibal. "I'll give in to Ellie and that gentlemen is your cue to fold. I don't care what Hannibal deals; you fold and leave Artemis to me." This time Lou's fixed on Uncle Fritz.

"I am not an idiot woman; you want to play Keswick alone. I get it, I fold."

Lou smiles. "I know you Fritz Heigl, if dealt a good hand you'll wager the farm. Do not cross me up!"

Fritz gets the obey look as well and neither man gives her any grief after that. "Thank you so much boys, the game starts at seven-thirty sharp."

Hannibal kisses Lou's cheek and turns to Fritz. "Mr. Heigl, may I offer you a plate of fried chicken?"

"Why thank you young man, only a fool turns down your wife's cooking. Are there biscuits and gravy?"

"Does a one-legged duck swim in circles?"

"Ya sure it does, lead the way bub!" Fritz opens the door for Hannibal who calls his goodbyes as he descends the stairs.

I turn to Lou. "Why not take Miss Grace's apple betty? Hannibal ships the fruit all the way from the Wenatchee Valley. Those apples are the best ever and her pies win at the county fair every year!"

"Let's feed your sweet tooth another time, shall we? We must keep our intention on the hornswoggle." Lou picks up her knitting and starts to hum.

Meanwhile Artemis Keswick waltzes in our front door to check his messages. The coalman smiles and waves Lou's note at his foreman. "By cracky Harry, I'm having supper with Lou Graham!" Artemis raises his voice so all can hear. "Barkeep, you tell your boss I accept her gracious invite. I'm delighted to dine with Sweet Lou and to play a little poker after. It's my pleasure to take her money!"

Tis like Poo says, Keswick and Turner are a pair of ignorant zounderkites. It can't be redundant if they're both double-down stupid!

CHAPTER 40

A Deal for the Ages

The clock strikes 7:30 on the dot. Lou motions for me to clear the dishes as Uncle Hannibal walks in the door. He pauses to shake Earl's hand who whispers something to his former boss causing both men to chuckle. Hannibal glances at Lou before heading to the bar. Lou said not to enter together so Fritz walks in a minute later.

I remove the tablecloth and my mistress gestures to the boys. At last the game's afoot! Lou greets Fritz with a warm embrace and a peck on the cheek. "Hello darling, how have you been? Thank you so much for coming."

Her demeanor changes when she turns to Hannibal. Lou extends her hand and offers a businesslike handshake. "Mr. Conover thank you for joining our little game." Lou's voice is friendly yet kinda formal. Curious, yes?

Hannibal doesn't miss a beat. "The pleasure's all mine ma'am. It's after business hours, do call me Hannibal."

Lou gives a polite smile and continues her pleasantries, "Artemis, I believe you know Mr. Conover."

Artemis grabs Hannibal's hand with a vigorous shake. "Yes indeedy, the Conover's are wonderful companions. Muriel and myself we love, ah, Mrs. Conover's cooking." Keswick holds onto Hannibal's hand, but he manages to wrangle free.

Well, that was awkward. Favorite companions my patootie! The man can't recall Gracie's given name. Ole Keswick's spewing balderdash like an overflowing crapper at high tide. And what of the grammar faux pas? Jeez Louise! The 'Muriel and myself' gaffe must tweak Lou's sensibilities.

Lou cringes at Arty's faulty syntax but recovers with a smile. "Yes good company is a must. May I introduce Fritz Heigl? Herr Heigl and I are Bavarian born and our family ties go back many generations."

Keswick extends his hand. "Splendid, I'm of Anglican decent as is my wife. Our family coat of arms helped settle these colonies. Did you know the British crown has royal Prussian ties? Purebloods must keep the intended natural order. Herr Heigl, I hear you run a top-notch shipping line. Perhaps we can do business sometime."

Fritz cringes at the mention of the Prussian royals. "Putz Blitz! Sullied tyrants, the Hohenzollern crown be damned! We Bavarians are Austrian cousins, not rutting Prussian pigs and I do not ferry filthy coal. Keep your freight and the Peifke to yourself." Fritz ignores the handshake and sits down leaving a stunned Artemis to steam.

Wow! Tis good that Earl's about or these two might go at it. Mr. Chin distracts Artemis with the cards basket and Lou changes the subject. "Artemis, please choose a deck and break the seal; high card gets first deal. Bartender do freshen our drinks before we begin."

Lou motions for everyone to sit and Hannibal says, "Miss Lou, you look stunning! Your outfit's fetching and that necklace is utterly spectacular!"

Did he say utterly? What's a cow's utter gots to do with a sparkling trinket? Lou said not to overdo it yet Hannibal's blubbering nonsense.

"Why thank you Mr. Conover. It's kind of you to notice. This designer jewel is a rare find."

Fritz gets a subtle kick under the table and growls, "The snake thing's pretty all right. Cost a penny, did it?" Sam Clemens did peg ole Fritz; small talk is not his strong suit.

"Oh darling! This necklace has a dozen green garnets and diamond studs. The Queen of Denmark owns one and it's all the rage in Europe!"

Hannibal chimes in, "Well good thing my Gracie isn't here. I'd be at the jewelers tomorrow for sure." Our retired gambler plays his part with no effort at all.

"Yes indeedy! My Muriel loves a shiny trinket. Lucky for me I already bought her a gift. I hope it gets me back in, ahh, her good graces."

Lou seizes the moment. "Oh Artemis, did you miss a birthday?"

"No, but it's just as bad; I forgot the girl's anniversary. You'd think twenty years married was no big deal, but I'm in hot water all the same. The silly woman knows nothing about business. She thinks I'm supervising a shipment. My engineer oversees these trips for me. You remember Jacob Daley; he stole one of your girls awhile back. Anyway, I snuck away for a gift to restore the peace."

"A special find and no doubt expensive?"

"Indeedy, I got Muriel an indentured girl for the house, and I'll get my money's worth one way or another."

Artemis gives the men a wink. Ha! Keswick thinks his slimy twitch is clever. Clueless must run in his pureblood veins. Lou's kettle should be bustín a whistle, but her expression is as still as a portrait. A vulgar man cannot break her focus.

Lou leans in. "Might your gift be misconstrued dear?"

Fritz surprises us with a useful add. "Ya, my Elsa would explode if I bought her a slave girl!"

Artemis's cheeks turn an ugly blotched pink. "Sir, I do not own slaves! The China girl has a legal contract. What say you Hannibal, was it a good transaction?"

"Well Arty I'd pass on the deal. My lawyer rebukes contract servancy and a jealous Gracie might divorce me."

Lou jumps back in. "You see your friend agrees. This gift sullies your reputation and you risk infuriating the wife. Phooey! I fold. Mr. Conover, this hand's a stinker and your deals are my bad luck."

"Sorry Miss Lou; fate deals a hand, not me. I fear this isn't your night." Hannibal is a seamless second fiddle.

Artemis lays down three kings. "Well Lou's bad luck is my good turn!"

"Verdammt!" Fritz tosses his cards at Lou; it's her turn to deal. The foursome socializes for a few more rounds. Whenever Hannibal deals Artemis wins, and Lou loses. At nine o'clock the deck circles back to Hannibal and Lou looks to me. "Missy, I believe it's your bedtime."

"Is it? Please can I stay up a bit longer?" Oops, my grammar's slipped and, of course, Lou's gonna catch it.

She raises an eyebrow. "Ellie say again."

"May I stay up?"

"Perhaps a bit longer; you have lessons tomorrow." Hannibal shuffles and deals a round of five card stud. Lou eyes her hand and opens with a dollar.

Fritz sighs, "I fold." Did our ferryman keep to the plan or did Hannibal help him decide?

Artemis smiles. "I'm in and raise two dollars." I swear the goof's molars are showing.

Says Hannibal, "Dealer folds. Miss Lou back to you."

"I call and take three cards." Lou puts her hand on the deck before Hannibal can deal. Here we go! "Artemis, shall we sweeten the pot? I'll wager a real anniversary gift against whatever's in your hand."

"I'm in if it's worth my time. What's your offer?"

Keswick's reticence fools no one. The man's caressing his cards like a letch. Lou asked for three cards, so Arty must know she has, at best, a pair.

"Harry's been at the bar all night and could use a walk. Have him fetch the maid and if worth my time, I'll wager my necklace. Win these jewels and Muriel will forgive all your faults." Miss Lou fingers the glittering snake atop her bosom and waits on her prey.

Fritz looks as if Lou sneezed in his drink. The duffer clears his throat once, and again for emphasis.

Hannibal says, "Ma'am, I doubt the price of a maid matches your necklace. Am I right Artemis?"

Lou gives Hannibal a perturbed glance. "No worries sir, a gentleman doesn't cheat and the wager's negotiable. What say you Artemis?"

Keswick's coveting his cards, but he manages to tear himself away. "Harry go get her and be quick about it!"

The lackey slides off his stool muttering, "Ah Jesus crackers why me."

Lou lays her cards on the table and calls to the kitchen. "Mr. Chin, please serve us your delicious chocolate cake and a pot of coffee." She adds, "Bartender bring us a topple of my top shelf whiskey to sweeten the brew. Only the best for my good friends."

We're finishing our cake when Harry walks in with a distant Ling in his tow. Poo's itchy fib is keeping Harry at bay. He yanks the leash and Ling lands in front of Miss Lou.

Neither Lou nor Ling act as if they've met. Lou says, "Thank you Harry, please drop the rope." She studies Ling while making a twirling motion with her finger. Ling spins around until she again faces Lou. "Do you speak English?"

"Yes ma'am, a little."

"Excellent. Now give us your best smile."

"Why do I smile? I am not happy."

Whoa! Artemis jumps up with a hand poised to strike. "You little wisenheimer! How dare you talk back!"

Earl leaves his post but Lou waves him off. "Artemis, the girl's a foreigner who doesn't understand our ways. Please take your chair."

Artemis glares at Ling and snarls, "Later." 'Tis a tense moment before he sits his butt down.

Lou says, "I like her. She's a rough-cut gem, smart and spunky. However, her age is a concern. I fear she's too young for the parlor. Anyone disagree?"

Lou waits on a gentleman's perspective but Harry Turner chimes in. "I reckon I'd take a poke." You might guess Harry's sullied reputation and you'd be right. Even a wagtail crosses the street to avoid the weasel. He's a menace to girls and livestock alike.

Keswick grimaces. "You're breathing on me dimwit. Go back to your bottle."

"I said what the boys was thinkin, eh fellas?"

"Leave me be Harry!" Keswick elbows Turner in the nethers and he limps away. Artemis smiles at Lou. "Let the little twat work the kitchen until she fills out. That one over there isn't getting any younger. She can work the parlor."

Rawmaish! Is he pointing his fat finger at me? I'm a head taller than Ling, but we're the same age. Assuming arse! I'll show you ya puffy punching bag! Ah crap, Lou gives me the look before she turns back to the game.

Lou read Arty's tell. She knows he's got a barnburner hand but keeps a tranquil pose. "Artemis, this is a unique wager. Shall we raise the ante to say three hundred dollars?"

"No can do. I've got my winnings and a hundred in my pocket." Artemis takes a hundred-dollar bill from his wallet and lays it a top the ante.

Lou says, "I see another hundred tucked inside. How about I forgive your stay and you bet the wallet? Or you can fold and it's game over."

Empty his wallet? I think Lou pushed too far but she doesn't look worried. Keswick eyes his cards, shows a sly smile and goes all in.

Lou motions for Ling to sit next to me. I offer a knowing wink and the girl grabs my hand in a death grip. Ouch! She won't let go.

Artemis taps his cards. "I'll play these bad boys."

Why is Keswick so crazy confident?

Lou nods and Hannibal deals three cards face down. She leaves them on the table and drums her fingers. Artemis cannot contain himself. "Sweet Lou you've overreached!"

Keswick tosses down three aces and two jacks. Have mercy! It's an ace-high full house. The gas lamps flicker as onlookers suck in air. Keswick offers a Cheshire grin and Lou nods her appreciation. She seems content to let Artemis have his moment.

Finally, my mistress makes her move. Lou flips one card at a time revealing a six of hearts, a six of diamonds, a six of clubs and a queen of hearts. Lou gives Hannibal a discreet glance and flips…the six of spades. It's an improbable quad known as four of a kind!

A bug-eyed Artemis stares at Lou's cards. Hannibal bites his lower lip and Fritz slowly claps his hands. From the kitchen comes a resounding Wahoo! Lou glances at Mr. Chin who's already headed that way. Poo better run for it before his uncle catches him.

Ling Lu gives me a puzzled look and I say, "It's good for you. Miss Lou won the hand." Ling sighs and lets go my pinched fingers.

That's when Artemis Keswick erupts. "Oh lordy, I am a dead man! Can't go home now, no sir, never ever. How do I explain this? I've lost Muriel's gift and my wallet playing the devil's poker. I'm busted and for what? Diddly squat, that's what! Muriel's gonna lock me out for good!"

I check his arithmetic and, minus the ante, Arty paid seventy-five dollars for Ling Lu. Damnation! Lou's necklace is worth way more. This coalman's a fancy pants grifter. Go on Earl, toss the bugger and his clown to the street!

Sweaty ole Keswick stares at his cards. "I'll be doing housework and eating with the pitmen until Christmas."

Our mistress gives Arty a sympathetic look. "Oh dear, is there anything I can do? Anything at all?"

Keswick looks up into Lou's sympathetic eyes. "For real Lou? Housabout you give me your jewelry!"

Fritz chuckles, "Good one dummkopf! No amount of groveling can save you now."

Lou gives Uncle Fritz the bad child look. "Actually old friend, Artemis has an interesting notion." Lou undoes her necklace and lets the serpent slither down her breasts.

The googly-eyed gallery captivates on the madame's expert diversion. No man thinks when his reason drains from noggin to nethers. Lou winks at me and hands me her necklace. "Ellie put this trinket in its box for Mr. Keswick."

I head for the safe as Fritz's booming voice breaks Lou's spell on the room. "Woman what in blazes are you doing!"

Hannibal chimes in, "Miss Lou you mustn't. It's a kind gesture but..."

"Have a heart Mr. Conover, your friend's marriage is at stake." Besides, it's time I had a fresh look; perhaps in rubies."

I return and hand the velveteen box to Keswick who wastes no time popping the latch. He's none the wiser when the fake twinkles back at him. Arty blubbers, "I don't know what to say. Lou you are a lifesaver and much too kind. I am in your debt."

Is it the lamplight or are those tears in Keswick's eyes?

"The pleasure's all mine dear. However, I fear my cast-off will insult your wife. Perhaps you'll say it came from a reputable jeweler. I'm sure Mr. Chin has a pretty ribbon to wrap a gift."

"Yes of course, clever indeed. Oh goodness, look at the time! I have a long trip tomorrow; you really must excuse me." Keswick grips the gift and scoots back his chair.

Such a bogus act! A luxury coach awaits and the bugger acts like he's hiking it. He'll no doubt nap all the way home. And look at those white knuckles, no way is Keswick letting go of the fake. He'll sleep on it and his pistol tonight.

Artemis walks to the bar and grabs Harry's arm. The foreman reaches for his bottle as Keswick snatches him off the stool and nudges Turner up the stairs. The bartender watches the men ascend the steps and gives Lou a thumbs up when they're out a sight.

A wide-eyed Fritz lights into Lou. "That is the craziest thing you have ever done. You blew him up and let him rise from the ashes! Woman what is wrong with you?"

"Was conceding the necklace too generous? A change of luck must've swayed me. Drawing four sixes is a rarity. Do you know the odds, dear sweet Hannibal?"

"Luck my keister! Lou you played me. I couldn't let that slime-ball win from family and you knew it."

"I am shocked! Did the respectable Hannibal Conover fix a hand?"

Now I'm confused. Is Uncle Hannibal a target as well? What was the hornswoggle again?

Lou continues, "Dealing Artemis aces full was a nice touch darling. You played your part with such panache. I knew you'd come through for me."

"You bet the farm on my chivalry? Why didn't you let me in on the fix?" Hannibal's frown turns into a boyish grin. "Did you see the look on Keswick's face? The dupe thought he'd won, and he lost it all! I admit I'm as confused as Fritz. Why sacrifice your prize piece?"

"Liebchen the necklace was the ruse. I wanted Artemis to beg for it and, of course, he did. A good plan always finds its own way. I apologize for the deception, but I needed your believable indignation. You mustn't worry. Artemis is the proud owner of a knockoff.

Ellie stashed a replica in my safe before the game and switched real for fake. Gents, this was never about Arty; I'm after Lady Keswitch. She'll wear the necklace at functions all over the region. If it weren't a snake, she'd wear it to church! A trained eye will soon spot the fake, Muriel will combusts in spontaneous humiliation, and she'll grill Artemis until he admits it was mine! What a pity to miss the fireworks; I do hope our Pearl has a front row seat."

Lou glows as she splits the pot between Hannibal and Fritz. Her reward is freeing Ling and cooking Muriel's goose! Miss Lou can let go the wicked witch, but Uncle Fritz isn't celebrating. "Shouldn't you be worried about the sheriff?"

"No dear, a deputy's been at the bar all night and Artemis chose from a basketful of sealed decks. His dear friend Hannibal dealt the hand, and everyone here saw him ask me for the necklace. How could I possibly fix the game? I have papers of authenticity and I paid a ransom for the necklace. I'll be crushed to learn of its bogus nature."

Hannibal chuckles, "You're a clever one Lou Graham. Gracie's gonna love this."

"Thank you darling, it was fun wasn't it? The Lady Witch and her dope have their just desserts."

Hannibal receives a belated kiss from Lou while Mr. Chin helps a grumbling Fritz with his overcoat. Fritz says, "I see now, it was always the wife. You resented her snubbing, and the husband was just a pawn."

"Muriel's a pesky bird deserving of justice served. It's an apostasy to prey on the weak and the Keswick's deserve their reckoning. Let them devour each other in blame and contempt. Some say I'm a fallen woman, yet I'll stand with the Archangel Michael against a Muriel or Arty Keswick!"

An exhausted Ling endured a cold boxcar with no food or water and so her adoring schmuck helps her to our kitchen table. Poo pours her a cup of tea and Ling reaches out to touch his hand.

An invisible me enters the room unnoticed to see the first signs of mutual affection. There's no snub intended so I must hold my tongue. Lou insists I yield to what is and not trespass upon their path. I say Ling deserves a medal for taking on our putzy Poo!

Tis sad to see my childhood wither on the vine. An observant Mr. Chin reads my sorrow and offers another bite of cake. Bless his kindness. I retreat up the back stairs with my slice of heaven. The nibble of sweet distraction lessens the sting, but it is no miracle cure. Mr. Fortune Cookie says a truer fix comes with an open-heart and the passage of time.

My serenity awaits amongst the stars, and I will search for it as soon as I lick every crumb from my plate.

CHAPTER 41

Showtime!

Daybreak creeps through the cell window putting an end to Ellie's tale. I am exhausted.

"Look Jack. The sunrise announces another grand new day. You must eat before we get some shuteye. I'll summon the help for breakfast."

I watch through the window as shadows morph into distinct shapes. Granny Chin reminded us that nighttime yields to light, with or without our consent. Why do I always cling to yesterday as if I can remake or change the past? Thank you granny, I am content with this dawn come what may.

Ellie's tale trumpeted the end of her childhood. What was the Bible verse my dad always quoted? Oh yes, Corinthians 13:11: "When I was a child, I understood as a child, I thought as a child: but when I became a man, I put away childish things."

I am now Belle's caregiver; I see with my dad's eyes and feel his angst. No farmer lets his seed go unattended. I cannot fault my dad for tending the farm and me with equal onus. My hiding in the loft helped no one. Truth is, my ego and not my dad hindered my dreams. I pray I inherited dad's grit. It will all be revealed sooner than later.

"Thank you Ellie, your story helped me reconcile past and present. You and Lou always provide what I need. Wow! Your granny was right; the sunrise is spectacular. A hopeful vision really does fire up the new day."

Ellie nods, pulls back the curtains, puts two fingers to her lips and whistles. Her piercing shrill reverberates the air, the sergeant's door clanks open and sprinting boots echo down the hall. The cell door opens revealing a small fellow in an oversized police coat.

Before us stands a clumsy goof tugging at his gun belt. He is far too young to be a copper. The boy spots me and his eagerness fades; does he assume we shared more than a night of storytelling? Is the little man jealous?

Ellie sees the sprite's ire and draws his attention back to her. "Sorry Max, did I wake you?"

"Huh? Certainly not! I'm a sworn officer of the law at your service. What can I do you for, Miss Ellie?"

"Well officer, we're hungry and in need of a courier. Please fetch two Chin breakfasts and walk a message up to Sam Barr's office."

The boy commits her words to a notebook hauled from his back pocket. "Got it. Anything else ma'am?"

"Yes, three pieces of chocolate cake. One's yours if you're quick about it and officer you mustn't call me ma'am. I'm no matron yet."

Ellie tosses the half-pint's hair making his freckled face turn a scarlet red. He's not the first nor the last man-child smitten by this Irish lass. The frazzled boy turns and races off to please his prisoner. Officer Max forgot to shut the cell door, so Ellie pulls on it until the lock clicks.

"Ellie, the boy's far too young for a badge. What's his story?"

"Oh, heavens no! The little guy's sort of an intern. His pops works the night shift and Max runs a few harmless errands for the boys. He wants to be a constable and it gives him a taste of the boredom without the peril. Max wears his dad's old holster and sports a cherry-wood nightstick he widdled himself."

"Well, he needs suspenders. The weight of that belt's gonna drop his trousers!"

My eyelids begin to droop, and I crawl atop her bed to nap until the aroma of food awakens me.

Ellie sits at her desk writing my alibi to Sam Barr. 'Dearest Uncle: Jack's sleeping it off in an adjacent cell. He'll be a bit late today. Loving regards, your Ellie.'

"I'm just a hired hand and Mr. Barr won't spare me."

Ellie pours my tea. "No worries, Sam heard your wife's snit and surely sympathizes." Ellie takes a bite of her cake. Dessert is her first course now that Lou's gone. "Don't give me that look mister. I'll not apologize for eating my cake first. A sweet piece loses its magic when dumped on a full stomach."

I smile and get back to my boss. "I doubt Mr. Barr pities his underlings. I fear my fate is a lecture on the unblemished reputation. If not for you, I'd be quite invisible. Nevertheless, I'll not waste a delectable meal on fretting!"

"Don't underestimate yourself Jack Hamby. You're not as unseen as you might think or hope. No one is."

Max opens my cell after breakfast. It's the first lockup just inside the metal door. Pounding a lumpy mattress seems a waste of energy, so I collapse on the torture provided.

Sweet dreams of Anne and Belle come easy. The three of us enjoy a pleasant day at the beach with Annie and I on a blanket watching Belle collect seashells. All of a sudden the sweet scene goes dark!

A giant hand appears and grabs my shoulder in a torturous vice grip. I shouldn't feel pain in a dream, so why the hurt?

Of course! The pain is real, and the hand belongs to a disgruntled Michael Quinn. Mike whispers, "Jack wake up! What the hell are you doing?"

"What? Where am I? What time is it?" I sound like a drunkard roused from a bender.

"It's time to get your arse upstairs!"

A fog rushes out my ears leaving behind clear panic. It's time and I'm sleeping through it. "Shoot! I'm so sorry."

"Yeah, well, Sam's tired of stalling. Don't go blowin our chance at Jimmy."

A sleepy Ellie calls out, "Mike darlín is that you?"

Quinn frowns and puts an index finger to his lips. We leave Ellie wondering and sprint for the exit. I run up the indoor staircase while Mike dashes outside to Sam Barr's private stairs.

An office of critical stares greets me and why not? I am a wrinkled unshaven mess. On the bench outside of Barr's office sits a fidgeting James Ambary. Moments later Mr. Barr opens his door. "Sorry to keep you waiting James, such a busy morning. Come on in and we'll get this matter settled." He ushers Ambary inside, gives me a disgusted look and closes his door. I'll get no sympathy from my boss.

Mike left a note for me to copy in my hand. I'm finishing it when shouts erupt from behind Mr. Barr's door. James Ambary yells, "I don't give a damn! I want my map. I get it or Ellie hangs!"

Mike Quinn barks back, "Oh Christ, be reasonable for once. Heed my warning buster, you dare harm Ellie and I'll send you to bloody hell!"

Sam Barr intercedes. "Settle down boys, James there's no map in the will. It was a sailor's blustering and Lou conned you to protect Ellie. Face facts boy and let go this nonsense."

The conversation simmers until the door bursts open. James Ambary faces Sam and Mike with his back to the rest of us. Jimmy growls, "Make Ellie cooperate. I get my map or your precious whore swings!" So much for gentil reason. Ambary executes an about face and stomps into the hallway.

Pay attention Jack! Jimmy's exit is my cue. I race after Ambary and catch him at the top of the stairs. "Mr. Ambary, a word please."

"What do *you* want? I don't answer to Barr's flunkies." Ambary steps back. "Jeez man you smell like a beached whale."

"I apologize for my appearance; it's been a trying time. My wife left me and…"

"Like I give a tinker's cuss. Hamblin what do you want?"

I want to clobber the imbecile! However, the gambit's in play and I must temper my response.

"The name's Hamby, not Hamblin. Please make note of it for future dealings. Neither Ellie, Mr. Barr nor Mike Quinn knows of this. You must deal with me to get your prize, but not here. It's too public a place and the walls have ears." I look over my shoulder for effect, tap Ambary's hand and slip him the envelope.

"What's this? Passing notes out of school? Are you saying you have my map? How did you get it?"

"Pipe down man. Read the note and let me know your answer by day's end." I offer an insidious wink and turn towards my office without looking back.

Jimmy rips into the envelope. The note reads, 'I have what you seek, and my cut is fifty percent. Period. Keep this a secret as it serves us both. You mustn't tell anyone, especially Ellie. Your reputation precedes you, so said item is in a foolproof hiding place. Any attempt to cheat me and you lose the cache forever. Meet me at Oyster Rock tomorrow's eve at eight o'clock. Come alone and mind you, no tricks. You dare swindle me and all is lost.'

I sit at my desk reading petition after petition of hitherto this or beget that. Sleeping on a rock-hard mattress hurt my neck causing my fingers to twitch and my three office mates caucus in the corner not caring if I hear.

Andy says, "Is Hamby tumbling into melancholy? His wife ran off you know."

"He looks awful," says Floyd. "I've a bottle of Daffy's elixir in my desk. That'll improve his mood."

Snippy ole Nesbitt concludes, "All I know is he smells like rotting garbage. Let's buy him a bath."

Mike told me to stay at work until day's end and to watch my backside. Floyd, an enigma of fault and kindness, offers to walk me home. "Thanks Floyd, I appreciate the company. Let's take a well-traveled path, shall we?"

Floyd lingers in front of my house. He's worried about my unkept look and paranoia. "Jackie you mustn't be alone. Go clean up and come over to my place for supper. Carrie won't mind."

I beg to differ. Carrie Snypes just might snap. How can she resist poisoning not one, but two idiot adulterers? "Thanks Floyd but all I need is a good night's sleep."

I ascend my stairs waving to Floyd as he ambles on home. A weird aura hangs at the top of the steps. Is someone watching me? What's this? My door's ajar though I swear I closed it. Against all caution, I step inside.

Oh God! The landlord's gonna have a cow. There's furniture stuffing and picture glass on the floor. Someone punched a hole in the wall and pulled up floorboards. No, no, no! Annie's precious China lay smashed to pieces. Such horrific destruction! What can I say to my grieving wife?

It's then I hear footsteps coming from my bedroom. Out of my hallway steps a burly duffer with a pistol in his hand; all he need do is aim and fire. The ogre grins showing teeth kiltered every which way. My intruder says, "Lawdy! Ambary's boys outdid themselves. Relax Jack, ain't nobody here but you and me. Go ahead and look around."

I glance from his face to the gun and back to his grin. "Who the hell are you?"

The stranger blushes and holsters his firearm. "Sorry boy, forgot my manners did I? I be Thomas Hart but most folks call me Tommy. Mike Quinn hired me to look after ya for a spell. I'm your side-kick day and night, like a guardian angel with a six-shooter." Tommy Hart snickers and slaps his holster.

"Jesus man you scared the piss out of me!"

"Apologies again boy, I followed you home in the shadows and snuck round back. Don't want to tip off the goony brothers. You know they be out front."

Was that the twinge I felt on the stairs? I sidestep the mess and stand next to my bodyguard. "The bastards did all this. Why do they linger outside?"

"Relax boy. They're across the road behind that wagon. It's obvious they didn't find what they was after. Those two cain't pour piss outta boot without readin the heel for directions. I reckon their waitin on Jimmy. The dunderheads won't pounce without his say so. Tis a shame about your stuff. Ain't nothin left unturned."

Annie put food in the ice box for me to warm up. I see it's tossed onto the floor.

"Sorry lad, they dumped every last bite."

"Well, the courthouse is safer than staying here. Are you coming?"

"Wherever you go Jackie. Mike says if you git hurt he'll dock my pay."

"Please stand guard while I change and pack a bag for the morning."

"Sure thing but don't ya dally none. The goons must a sent a runner for Jimmy. We cain't be here when he comes."

I do not dally. Tommy scouts the backyard, and we descend into the twilight. Behind us is a sad sticky mess, an empty China hutch and generations of ceramic memories shattered on the floor. I can't let this be Anne's last memory of her treasure; I'll clean up before the girls get home.

Tommy Hart and I maneuver through backyards until we've cleared the Ambary goons. We have a safe lead for now, but Tom's sure they'll figure us out.

My mind wanders and I say to myself: I despise this hill. Why do the wealthy insist on living above the rest of us? They're no closer to heaven and it's a miserable trek for me. Oh Lord, forgive my whining. I'm blessed as any rich man could hope to be. What's that? Tommy is still talking.

"I live in Ballard town just north of here. Known Ellie girl most all her life cause I worked the docks with her dad. Wasn't long after he passed that I cracked my hip and had to retire from longshoring. I did fix-it jobs for Miz Lou but now I keeps busy tracking deadbeats for the union. Tis best I stay clear of my missus, the woman slogs me harder than a dock foreman ever did."

Twenty minutes more and we're at Ellie's door. She eyes my knapsack. "Well hello Jack, back so soon?"

"There isn't much going on at my place. I hoped you might share your supper. I'm guessing you have extra."

"Ha! Folks will think you're moving in." Ellie turns to my guard. "Tommy Hart long time no see, why are you hanging about with this miserable bloke?"

Tom and I rehearsed our story while climbing the hill. "Ellie girl, it's nice to see you. Your boy and I met on the trail. The union's got me lookín for a slacker what missed his shift. I'm out checking cat houses and jails for the lazy bugger."

"Okay then, hello back at ya and my regards to the missus. You no doubt saw the buffet out front. Long as you're here, you might as well eat. There's plenty and Mr. Chin left a kegger for the boys." Ellie has a queer look on her face. She must be playing along to guess our secret. Tom gives me a wink and leaves us be.

Is his twitch a nod to the rumors about Ellie and me? The gossip flatters, bewilders, and shames me all at the same time. Life in Seattle is a head scratcher. Ellie pokes at a tray of dim sum treats and I whimper in hopes she'll share.

"So what's with the satchel Jack, you movín in?"

I am a terrible liar, and her slippery question makes me watch my words. "My place is a mess; I can't find a usable dish or linen and I'd like to spend the night on the hill."

"Go on with ya! You're no helpless hubby. What aren't you sayín and what was the ruckus this mornín? You and Mike are up to somethín."

Checkmate! Ellie's got me in her sights. I can't muster a believable fib, so I grab my bag. "Maybe I'll join the boys. I already have a nagging wife."

"Ha! No you don't lad. Annie left ya, remember? Sit down and spill yer guts. Why be so skittish? You've got me wondering and I do hate a secret."

"Duly noted dear, but please let's skip the inquisition. Housabout we do supper and a story instead. Pretty please?"

Ellie looks to Lou's portrait. "The boy doth protest too much, but he is pitiful." She hands me her chopsticks. "Okay chancer try these pick-up sticks. It'll humor me while I spin my tale. I reckon it's time you heard about Caleb. The newspaper stories are far from the truth of it."

Yes finally, I'll hear Ellie's side of the story!

CHAPTER 42

'Twas a Good Plan Until

"Where was I in my tale of tales? Let's see. Yesterday was about Poo's coming of age but the numbskull wasn't alone. Puberty struck me as well; I was busting out of every blouse I owned. Men took notice and I liked it. That's when a lanky, confident fella came a courtin. So handsome was the sweet-talking lad with his dimpled smile. James Ambary was an uptown gent who treated me like a princess. He lit up my world."

Ellie slips into her tale: Jimmy puts Lou and me at odds for the very first time. Lou doesn't trust an Ambary and I agree with her about Caleb and the mother; most everyone keeps a wary eye on those two. A young Caleb boobytrapped outhouses and tortured a poor crab for sport and his older self-graduated to stealing from neighbors and blaming their servants. Their mum dismisses Caleb's antics as youthful pranks, but gossip says Miz Gretchen has an unfit bent for Caleb. The boy's a dead ringer for his pops.

I stay clear of that widow's wicked web; tis a dislike for her politics as much as her parenting. Miz Ambary claims to be a suffragist but a closer angle reveals why she wants the right to vote. She'll stop all work on the Lord's Day cause her religion says so. Of course her servants are exempt from the rule. How does Dame Selfish defend her privilege to those who work every day to survive? Ha! She'll not talk to the low life lest it's to order something.

My Jimmy is different. Yes, he hangs with Caleb but not out of brotherly love. Jimmy needs his mother's praise and I can save him from her spell. A good woman leads her man down a better path.

Ellie stops her tale and frowns. "I see the smirk Jack Hamby. Did my goodness or womanhood amuse you?"

"Perhaps a little of both. C'mon Ellie, it's natural for a youngling to be a know-it-all."

"Yes, 'twas foolish of me to think I was a woman fully grown. My intuition did twang, but I ignored it."

Ellie continues her tale. My friends think me naïve. I won't hear their slander and they don't know Jimmy like I do. "Y'all can save your breath cause my man's freckles won't turn to warts. Our love is special. You just wait and see. We'll sail north and I'll get Jimmy away from his mum!"

How could it go so wrong? Jimmy pinched more than my virginity that summer; his curse wilted my trusting nature and put a discerning wrinkle on my brow. He ignored my feelings, and I lost all focus. Eejit me traded sweet intuition for a perilous revenge. Uncle Fritz says vengeance is the bitter end of an unleashed anchor rope. The rope unravels and yanks a slipshod avenger into the abyss. Yes, an unraveled revenge almost got me killed.

Ellie takes hold of my hand. "I own but one secret and it's a doozy. Not even Michael knows all about that night. I can talk with you like no one since Miss Lou. Tell me Jack, are you truly loyal? Can I trust you with my life?"

"Of course, I am honored to be your confidant."

"Well then, this is my side of the awful tale."

Caleb's demise starts with a visit from a Philadelphia influencer. A man named Hamadan comes looking for relics for his East coast museum tour and our proper uptowners are agog. Hamadan says he needs upstanding young men to assist him, but he speaks with a grifter's tongue. He knows a poor lad expects to be paid for his labor and the dizzy gentry will do it as a lark. Hamadan's right, all the fancy lemmings vie for their boy to make the special voyage.

Uncle Fritz outfits his biggest ship for the north coast expedition and invites us along. Lou loves traveling with Fritz, but she hears Jimmy's aboard and vows to leave me behind. Ha! I can be a persistent pest and talk my way back onboard within the week. Tis the only time I wish Lou hadn't spoiled me.

The captain designates most all the ship for antiquity storage. Decent sleepers are scarce, and rank has its privilege. Uncle Fritz takes the captain's quarters for the three of us and Mr. Chin is next door with Earl. Our chef runs the officer's mess feeding us, the officers, Hamadan's men, and a lucky invite. The rest of the crew eats galley viddles in the forecastle below deck.

Mr. Hamadan's group has first-class passage, and the skipper assigns the remaining racks by rank. He ousts his chief mate who bumps the engineer, who bounces his assistant and so on. A tiny steerage cabin holds four gentry each. Can ya imagine the brats sharing quarters like servants. Poor babies! Their hoity mamas will faint dead away.

Caleb is up to his old tricks stealing a cabin for himself and his brother. I dare not ask how the two bunkmates were ousted. Jimmy says it's best not to question Caleb's ways.

Lowly sign-on mates grab a nook in the hold amidst the engine noise and stifled air. Mike Quinn signed-on but he can't take the claustrophobic echo chamber and opts to sleep up top. Mike grabs a lifeboat suspended from the starboard launch rigging and uses its canvas tarp and an extra wool blanket to keep out the chill. The bobbing of the waves make him seasick but it passes after a couple of days.

Tis the second night at sea when Jimmy knocks at our cabin door. I rush to open it ahead of Mr. Chin. My love says, "Wow! You're a lucky girl, nice cabin. Shall we take a stroll on the deck?"

Mr. Chin stands right behind me. "You must wait on Mr. Earl."

"Balderdash! We're never alone with folks stacked everywhere. We don't need a chaperone." I nudge Jimmy aside, step into the hall and close the door. Hand-in-hand, we run off to explore the ship.

The vessel is a four-masted sailing Barque with a coal-fired engine added to tackle the strong currents. It's outfitted for stops along the shoreline where the tribal villages stand. Mr. Hamadan wants to fill the ship with all sorts of relics and intends to collect everything from baby rattles to giant totems. Tis a tall order but the fatcat swears his suckers will pay to see an Indian's belongings. Go figure.

Sparce storage creates more problems for the captain. He takes pride in keeping his crew well fed but the hold's full of Hamadan's boxes. With no space for perishables, our Indian guides must hunt and forage at every stop. Darn it, I digress.

Anyways, tis a calm night. A colossal full moon reflects off the sea's white foam and the scene mimics vast fields of shimmering snowdrifts. It is a dazzling wintry illusion!

Seasoned sailors stow rum and reefer in their duffels and it's a flogging for those caught with the contraband. We stumble upon a few sailors huddled behind a stack of empty crates away from the watchman's view. One bloke offers us a toke and a warm blast of his rum. Jimmy helps himself to both and jumps into the conversation.

"Howdy fellas. Nice weather, eh?"

All eyes narrow and stare daggers at my man. One sailor snarls while another spits on Jimmy's boots. The spatterer says, "Bite your tongue laddy! Jealous waters can hear yar blasphemy. Don't go praisín the good winds. The spiteful sea seizes on a disrespect and scuttles a ship against the reef. Them ghost stories are true ya know. Us Limeys respect the legends and the curses."

Legends and curses? Oh yes, tell me more! Besides, tis best I get their minds off a Jimmy's blunder. "I'm an expat from the Isle of Eire and I'd love to hear a story!"

The spatterer smiles. "Lassy I know yer accent! I be a Paddy boy me self. Here's a ghostly tale for ya dearie. Tis no blarney in telling the fate of a lost ship called the Jade Princess. The wretched tong sailed her under a pirate flag and a Brit disowned by the Queen herself stood at the helm. They sailed from Shanghai to Victoria on Vancouver Isle, but the Princess ne'er made it. A powerful typhoon scuttled her on the windward side of Port Harbor. There she sat on a precarious reef not far from shore. A band of tribesmen spots her, an ebbing tide grants them access and they wade into the shallows bent on pillaging.

One of them is Jesuit raised and can read the manifest. It lists eight crew and twenty slaves yet neigh a soul's aboard, not even a corpse. Tis a mystery where they be but my bet's on Davey Jones locker. The cargo's what catches a savage eye. A fortune in antiquities and jewels lay below deck for the takin. All of a sudden, a vicious rip tide grips the ship heaving one Injun into the surf! There be little choice for the rest; drown with their brother or leave the treasure behind. The brave takes the logbook and swims for it.

He and his band are safe ashore when another wave carries the Princess out to sea. The doomed ship drifts off the reef, takes on water and comes to rest several fathoms below the shelf. The learnt Indian is tortured by the hidden riches. He tears out a logbook page and draws a crude sketch of the locale. The savage plans a return at the next double-minus tide, but he vanishes just like the ship's crew. Rumor says his friends oft-ed him for the map, yet every man denies it. They say the Jade's wraiths got him. Maybe so, but a living man's greed is just as wretched.

The next double-minus tide shows the Jade's mast above the waterline and six Indians wade out to the wreck. Twice they dive but the undertow's too strong. On the third try, a rogue wave breaks the mast into pieces and drowns the tribesmen. 'Twas the ship's curse what put an end to their curiosity! Now the only path to the riches is the lost map." The sailor lowers his voice to a whisper, and we all lean in to hear. "No one knows for sure. Any of our guides might have the map and partner," he points a finger at Jimmy and roars, "With the Likes of You!"

A startled Jimmy falls backwards onto his arse and the circle explodes with laughter, save me. Tis my duty to stifle my smirk. Jimmy hung on the sailor's every word and the jokester reeled him in. My lad gets up, growls, and clinches his fist. I see his folly and drag Jimmy away before he gets whipped or worse.

We walk in silence, but I know Jimmy's plotting his revenge. I let him be until his grumbling stops. Finally Jimmy takes my hand. "Ellie girl."

"Yes dearest?"

"I wonder which of the ship's savages has the map?"

"Oh babe our scouts aren't savages. They're guiding Mr. Hamadan up the coast. The wreck is just a tale and not worth a second thought. We best let it be."

"Silly girl, all legends rise from a spit of truth. I'll be the richest man in the territory; richer than father ever was and mother will finally give me my due!"

"How lovely to be free of your mum and Caleb."

We walk arm in arm to the Ambary cabin. The room's empty and Jimmy ties a kerchief on the outside doorknob. Tis a sign for Caleb to get lost.

Aided by spirits and inclination, we let primal nature take us. Romance novels describe a rapturous bliss, but I beg to differ. There's no passion in our swift and painful bump. Euphoric bodies entwined? Ya right. Jimmy's a snoring lump passed out on top of me. I want to talk and jab at his ribs but the wasted pig snorts and rolls away.

A sudden panic overtakes me. What if a nasty Caleb ignores the kerchief and helps himself? I dress in haste and sprint for the safety of my suite.

Lou and Fritz are enjoying a late-night biscuit and offer me a bite, but I wave them off in favor of my bed. I can't deal with family right now. Not even a tasty treat can save me from my misery.

The wall clock strikes midnight and I say through my tears, "Whatever have I done? Up is down and can never be put right again."

CHAPTER 43

Ellie's Hornswoggle

The morning's light reveals a different Jimmy; he's all hands and acts like he owns me. I slap him away demanding to clear the air, but the bloke pushes me up against a crate and clenches his fist. A witness rounds the corner and Jimmy uncurls his paw. He nods to the sailor and waits. Once we're alone he presses hard against me.

"You're a disappointment girl, a prissy wag not worth my time. Sure I fell asleep; you bored the stiffy outta me." Jimmy smirks, punches my arm, and walks away.

I can feel a bruise rising, so much for star-crossed love. For the first time ever I am speechless. What of our undying affection? Am I really a terrible lover? I want to run to Lou and blather away, but I fear an 'I told you so.'

Dammit! I can't bear the hurt alone and must swallow my pride. I interrupt their morning tea shooing everyone out the door except Lou. She senses my fragile state and opts not to correct my manners.

Lou pours me a cup and listens to my rant without a scolding; her quiet way helps me let go my pent-up stink. So this is how a church confessional works, my unbosoming allows for a deep cleansing sigh.

"Lou why didn't I listen to you? Why was I so stupid?"

"Ellie you mustn't demean yourself. You didn't listen because my advice was contrary to your wants. Fixing blame and ignoring the lesson won't help. Let me ask you this: why so very distraught? Perhaps the ego's bruised more than the body? You must face facts. Take an honest look at the affair in its entirety."

"Well then it's all on Jimmy."

"Oh Ellie, listen to yourself. Yours was a mutual tryst of self-import and lust. Your prince was always a toad but what of the princess? You saw how Jimmy treated others, yet you absolved the boy and blamed his family. Did you really think a voyage would alter a lifetime of petty wants? Jimmy wooed your naive ego, and you ignored intuition. The boy is not your toy to fix. His fate belongs to him and him alone. Learn the lesson and let Jimmy go."

"Well then how do I fix my part?"

"Dear girl there's no fixing lang syne. Be thankful you survived and start anew. Do you want a healing task? Mr. Chin says every sunrise turns a page. Let the sun and sea breeze soothe you, drop the loathing and enjoy your true friends."

"Are you going to send Earl after Jimmy?"

"Did you hear a word I said? I cannot avenge an act of mutual consent and retaliation is never a do-over. Trust me, Jimmy is his own reckoning. Life is akin to a roulette table; blame, fear, and vengeance are sucker bets. The wise bet on grace, hope, and charity. You made one bad bet, but it needn't ruin you unless you let it."

Our chats are maturing. Lou acts the same so it must be me. Lawdy, am I a grownup? Well not quite, I pull Earl aside after supper. "Mr. Hazard a favor please. You must pummel Jimmy for me. Don't kill the boney bastard, maybe just break an arm, or bust a jaw so he can't bedazzle another poor sap."

"Sorry Sweet Pea, you're too late. I'd enjoy it but Miz Lou says no." It isn't easy to outfox my mistress.

The nuns say the forgiven must first forgive but they never said how saintly hard it is to let go a misery. Jimmy's insults scraped me raw, so how do I avoid the smug bastard on a ship? I can't hide in my room and my anger festers as I watch Jimmy pretend to work. Honest lads load heavy totems while the slimy rat tallies a small relic. Sorry Jack, there's no sweat in pushing a pencil. I hate the slacker!

Our captain twice catches the boys pocketing pieces meant for the museums. An Ambary doesn't hear authority, so why warn them instead of the whip? The skipper might as well piss into a forward wind.

Yes! A third time's the charm! Mr. Hamadan, Uncle Fritz, and the captain sit at our table with a bottle of scotch whisky between them as I eavesdrop at the kitchen door.

The skipper says, "Mr. Hamadan I warned you about those two. I didn't want the scalawags aboard; it was you who insisted and now I must act. My crew expects discipline, and I can't disappoint. I'm gonna banish the pair and put them ashore. Given their age, I might grant a compass and a week's hardtack. That's all the mercy I can muster."

Mercy sir? The hell you say! Why coddle the bumbles? Let the tenderfoots forage their way home! Wait, what's Mr. Hamadan saying?

"Captain, I see my mistake and honor your position, but what happens if the boys go missing? I'll be sued for all I'm worth. Perhaps a lesser penalty will suffice."

C'mon! Ole Stuffypants is afraid of Miss Gretchen. Don't relent captain, give the bastards their due. At least tie the pair to the mast and flog em!

The skipper says, "You needn't be keel-hauled by that old bat. My crew will accept another penalty. I'll shave their heads and brand the letters BC above an ear."

Hamadan gasps, "Oh dear me! A hot-iron branding sounds gruesome. What does the BC mean?"

"It foretells a bad character; I'll tattoo the scallywags, so another captain knows they're trouble."

Fritz shakes his head. "The boys aren't real sailors. It's fair to shave a head but I can't allow a branding. Make them work the galley and let the crew taunt them. That protects Mr. Hamadan's artifacts and satisfies the crew."

Uncle Fritz is kissing Hamadan's arse. Since when is serving food a dishonor? It's what I do for a living! No, a slice of humble pie won't do. Jimmy must suffer more than a blush. Why not dip his privates in a bait bucket and let the seagulls have at him!

Alas, the captain scalps the bastards and makes them work the galley. To mollify his crew he tattoos BC above each boy's ear but it's only a pine tar stain. I'm not impressed cause the stinky sap will fade away in a month. I mope about and Lou invites Mike Quinn to supper.

The summer sunset clings to the tree line as Mike and I stand on the deck. "Ellie would you like to go ashore?"

"Sure, why not? I need shells for a necklace."

Mike fights the currents and manages to get the dinghy ashore. We walk the beach near the dunes until we spot an old native sitting aside his shanty. Mike's a generous sort so he offers the man a chew. Yuk! Tobacco chew reminds me of spittoons. Thanks be, Mike is no spitter. He keeps a tin out of manly obligation.

The Indian shakes off Mike's offer with a chilly growl and Mike says, "Perhaps a warm blanket then?"

"No boy, your fathers left a pile of the scratchy wool. They'll wrap a sweat lodge but not a body."

The Taku elder seems sane. Why did he make a poor trade with Mr. Hamadan and why is he abandoned here?

"Hello, my name is Ellie and I'm wondering why your people left you?"

"Those left behind are too old to fish the ocean. My people return when the hunt is done."

Mike asks, "Why did you let us take your belongings?"

The Indian gives him a look. "Let you? This body no longer fights a thieving pirate. Your fathers prey on a band of nothings with no regard for our ways."

Did the old man not understand our intent? "Sir, I'm so sorry for the mix-up. What can we do for you?"

"Mix-up? Silly girl! Your fathers are scoundrels. Go away and leave me be." The old tribesman turns and crawls inside his shelter.

"Oh Ellie, is the elder daft or do we rob the feeble? We're supposed to be the civilized ones. Where are our manners?"

"I don't know; maybe he's right. This whole trip's a revelation, for sure. I always thought carved in stone meant forever, but that's a convenient fib. Only the spirit endures. Mr. Chin's altar haiku says it all: 'A stone wears away as does a weary body. Be free endless soul.' I wish I understood its meaning before this sail."

I lean against Mike's broad shoulder. He looks at me with such sad eyes. "We were happy kids and I don't get why growing up is so friggin hard. I'm overcome of late and don't like the feelins one bit. Tis a shame what Jimmy did to you. Your first time deserved better than an Ambary. Please know it changes nothing between us."

I've no use for his pity. What embarrassing secrets did Lou share with Mike? How do I respond? I decide to go with bewildered. "Michael Quinn, what are you blathering on about?"

Mike gives me a look and says matter of fact, like all the world knows, "You know how Jimmy bet Caleb five bucks he could nail you. What a bollocks!"

"That is not true. Take it back!" I stand up with fists clenched. We wrestled as kids and I won the matches until Mike outgrew me. He'd win now for sure.

Mike stands and raises his hands in mock surrender. "Sorry girl. Gosh, you didn't know about the bet? Honey, everyone knows. I was with the boys when Jimmy took a bow. So full of hisself for besting Caleb at your expense, I shoulda belted him then and there! I'm so sorry I didn't defend you."

"Thanks for the sentiment muttonhead, but it's not your fight. Everyone knows Jimmy banged me for a fiver! How pathetic am I? The gall of that boney bastard! Now he's gonna pay." An unwanted tear trickles down my cheek. Mike puts his arm around my shoulder but his kindness only makes me hotter and I push him away. "Don't you worry about me Michael Quinn! I'll give Jimmy his fin's worth!"

Fueled by rage, I race towards the dinghy and push off from shore all the while screaming back at Mike, "You mark my words friend. This girl's neither ancient nor feeble and a thieving Jimmy's gonna pay!"

A baffled Mike stands where I left him. "Come on Ellie wait for me!"

"Wait on the likes of you? Hell no Mikie! Your mates can fetch ya!"

Yes, tis mean-spirited to strand him; like I give a tinker's cuss! I keep on ranting as I row the dinghy into the crashing surf. A soaked

me shouts back at Mike, "Some friend you are! You shoulda bloodied Jimmy but instead you rat him out. Sit on the beach and stew, ya
gobshite! There's no man aboard this boat worth his salt. You're all a
bunch of useless gullyfluffs!

I know my speech is redundant, like the number of dongers in this
world! It's the maddest I've ever been and I bless the surf for muffling
my tirade. However, having left my oarsman ashore is a serious blunder. Rowing against the relentless tide begs Mike's muscle and skill. I
struggle to stay on course for the better part of an hour and using fury
as my rudder, I ponder a vengeful plot. So many questions: like how
do I dispose of Jimmy's body and how can I keep my plan a secret
from Miss Lou? How will my rage overcome the searing pain in my
shoulders? "Keep on rowing girl, if you drown then Jimmy goes free!"

I make it back aboard and collapse onto my bed. Only then does
my exhausted ego allow a saner thought. Killing an Ambary satisfies
the moment but it lacks imagination. I am Lou Graham's girl with
the wits to get justice served. All I need is a foolproof plan!

I start with reconnaissance. Tis a curse to be near an Ambary yet I
must put aside the smell. With his endless talk of treasure it's Caleb
who sparks my genius plot. "If only we had the map Jimbo, we'd be
the richest men alive."

Poof! I'll grant your wish a-hole! I lift a blank page from our
captain's log and study the Port Harbor chart for a believable watery
grave. My rendering of the storied map is good but it looks too new
so I dampen it, torch the edges, and rub it on a dirty canvas sail.

The weathering works: now all I need is an Indian in search of
treasure. Mike's friendly with a scout who wants the part. I offer to

pay but the guide refuses. The Ambary clan makes enemies wherever they go. Tis an inbred talent.

I'm mostly ready and feel awful soliciting Mike's help again, yet his shame is useful. I need him to set up the boys and Mike cannot refuse me. I coach him to say, "Hey Caleb want to hear a good one? Tis the luck of the Irish I tell ya. Ellie stumbled on a guide looking for the Jade Princess. He has a map and plans to dive for it. All he needs is help with equipment and supplies."

Caleb's lizard eyes widen into saucers. "Tell me more! Which savage is it? An Indian can't salvage a sunken ship. I'll take it on and give him a cut for the map."

Mike thinks to himself, 'Give him a cut? I reckon Caleb ain't talkín money. He probably means a cut of his blade. I hope Ellie knows what she's doing. This bastard deserves a comeuppance.'

Mike says to Caleb, "Jeez Ambary I don't know. Ellie and the guide are meeting tonight. Go pester her."

The artic sun refuses to set below the horizon as the scout and I walk the deck. Fearing an ambush, we stay in plain sight while the evil boys mount a feeble attempt to track us. The hide and seek game is fun but it's getting late. The guide and I lean against a stack of to-tems with a watchman on the bridge above us. The wicked duo hide in the shadows close enough to hear what's said.

"You got the map scout?"

"Yes miss, what is your plan?"

As if on cue, the brothers break from the shadows and I feign a surprised gasp. "What the heck!" I point at Jim's bald head glistening in the late-night sun. "Wowzer! The captain scalped you good; the glare off your noggin's blinding me. You should wear a hat."

"Ah Ellie shut it; you be civil after all we've shared."

"We shared nothing maggot, and you're not the boss of me." Proud words spoken with a true poker face.

Caleb makes his move. "Listen up Ellie. You and your boy can't do this alone. We've got the brains and backing you need. Housabout a truce to make us all rich. Come on baby girl, show me the map."

My pops and the nuns called me baby girl. I hate it; how dare the arrogant bastard remind me. I stare down Caleb thinking to myself, 'you say you got a brain, but can't prove it. Go on with ya, so I can dance on your grave!' I snap out of it as the guide takes the map from his shirt. Caleb and I go for it and I win.

"You two gumnuts best behave. This map's goin into Lou's safe. You steal from us and my giant's gonna toss you to the crabbies!"

Tis a convenient fib. I've defied Lou's wishes and she mustn't find out. I'll put the map under my mattress. It's a twofer to keep Lou in the dark and these boys at bay.

The scout and I aren't alone for the rest of the sail. I do relish the brother's surveillance. It must be exhausting for them to work the galley and keep tabs on us. Mama always said there's no rest for the wicked.

I arrange a topside meet for our last night at sea. Caleb wants to plan a trip to the wreck. Who cares what he wants! I'm gonna sucker-punch the boys with my reveal. It's a perfect scheme until it all goes to hell.

Tis a dark and dreary night. No, I'm not spouting poetry. The fog is as thick as, well, pea soup. The four of us meet under the watchman's bridge with Jimmy leaning his drunken self against a cargo barrel. Caleb has the bottle, but he's not as squiffy as his brother.

I'm eager to start the chinwag so I say, "A bit early to celebrate, don't you think?"

Caleb sneers, even his grin is menacing. "My brother's right about you. Loosen up girl. Take a swig."

"No thank you, I'll keep my wits."

"Suit yourself. How about your fella?" Caleb waves the bottle at the scout and quickly snatches it back. "Oops! What was I thinking? Can't hold your liquor, huh boy?"

The scout ignores the taunt and pulls my map from under his shirt. He waves the map at Caleb who grabs for it but the guide's too quick. Caleb makes another grab with the same result. The scene's kind of comical, yet it won't end well. Too much taunting and an Ambary snaps.

I say, "Caleb stop yer clownín. I got bad news, so you best listen up. The scout isn't after the Jade Princess. Fact is, he never heard of it. This lowly snipe played you two uptown snots. I fashioned a fake map with my own hand as payback for your lousy bet. Run you rag-ged I did and it's my turn to gloat. I got the last laugh on you two limp wicks!"

The boys freeze like deer caught in a buggy's lamplight. The fog can't hide Caleb's red-hot cheeks. Yes, he's stunned but it doesn't last. The brut starts huffín and puffín like a rutting buck. "The hell you say you little pecker-chaser. You can't welch on us! Gimme the map."

Tis then Caleb lunges for my guide. The next thing I know I'm jumping between them. I've no idea what came over me but Mr. Earl says my insanity wore a brave mask.

I scream in Caleb's face, "Ambary shut up and listen! You scumbags bet at my expense and your cruelty deserves an avenge. Got you good I did!"

Jimmy howls but he's too sloshed to move his feet. Caleb scrunches both eyebrows into one mean brow and shouts, "Liar, you're not that clever! You're out to shame us and keep the riches for yourself. Give me the map!"

Caleb grabs for it and misses. The sober scout taunts, "Poor pickle brain can't hold his liquor, hey T'kope?"

His insult isn't helping. The Ambary's are pickle brains but it's their temper what worries me. Caleb's snarl exposes his yellow fangs. His nostrils flare again as he pulls a tiny gun from his pocket. Sweet Mother Mary! I've lost control!

Tis then I hear my mum say, 'Grab me knife darlín and save yourself.' Her calm voice is my Saving Grace. I slip the blade from its sheath and steady my hand.

Jimmy stumbles, the lantern crashes onto the deck and I'm in the dark amidst a choir of cussing shadows. I can't tell friend from foe. What if I stab the scout?

All of a sudden, a fierce hand reaches out of the abyss and grabs my throat; its vice-like grip crushes my airway. I beg for a breath but the chokehold silences me. Oh no, my neck's gonna snap!

CHAPTER 44

The Plot Thickens

Bam! Bam! Bam! A resounding beat on the cell door stops Ellie's story. It's way late; what's going on at this hour? Another loud bang bounces Ellie from her bed.

"What in tarnation!"

"Missy, we need young Jack up front right away."

"What do you want me for? It's late and we just got to the good part. Go away and come back in the morning."

"This can't wait boy, you best button your britches and get out here."

Ha! The sarge thinks we're in bed together. It's silly but he seems upset. I give Ellie a bewildered look. "Okay Sarge don't get all wheezy. Ellie keep your story and I'll be right back."

I step out the door with Ellie on my heels. The guard puts up a hand. "You wait here young lady." He leaves Ellie to stew, locks the cell door, and shoves me forward. Why is he so protective? The man hasn't shown a worry until now.

Sarge holds me back when we reach the iron gate. He draws his pistol, lowers it to his side and opens the door. Three men and my bodyguard sit frozen at the poker table. Each man has a cocked revolver in his lap with all eyes fixed on a figure standing in the doorway.

Oh crap! It's James Ambary motioning for me to join him. Tommy narrows his gaze waiting on the slightest foul twitch. I walk towards Ambary mindful to keep away from friendly fire.

"You've got some nerve coming here after you trashed my place." My reproachful voice has an air of confidence. Like Mr. Hazard says, a brave mask hides a fool.

Ambary stares at me and smirks, "It was a regrettable miscue and my boys outdid themselves. Look at you all fired up; you're more a man than I gave you credit for."

I double down on my distain. "Regrettable miscue! Is that your apology? Do you ever own your wrongdoings?"

The poker boys shift on their buttocks and one of them whispers to Tommy, "An Ambary ain't nothin to play with. What's your boy doin? He's gonna get us all killed!"

The man's voice carries allowing Ambary to hear his alarm. Jimmy flashes a smile towards the players. "No worries boys, Jack didn't like my housewarming gift. Go on back to your cards, you hear."

Jimmy turns to me and lowers his voice, "Be careful Jack. You mustn't blow a fortune over a few broken plates. I'm coming to you mano-a-mano, so play nice. We'll meet just as you asked, Oyster Rock, tomorrow at eight."

A few broken plates! I take in a calming breath. "Let's be clear, the meeting is private so no goons."

"Sure enough Jack, you're driving the buggy now."

Ambary pats my shoulder and tips his hat to the boys. Just like that the snake slithers into the darkness. The click of gun-hammers signals a return to normal and I look to Tommy who gives me a low whistle. The Ambary ancestral wheel has a deceptive spin and its one remaining spoke is bent on betrayal. I get a case of the willies making me flick his touch from my shoulder. Tommy reads my disgust and spats towards the doorway.

"Sergeant please retrieve my bag from Ellie's cell and don't mention Jimmy's visit. Mr. Quinn doesn't want her to worry."

"No need telling me boy. I know the score. Ellie ain't gonna like it but I'll say you was called away without a why or where."

What score? Does the sarge know of Mike's plan? I've lost track of all the secrets. And what about Caleb? Did Ellie kill him? My gut fears what my heart cannot believe. Focus Jack and save your own hide! Ellie's perfect trick fell apart and I won't let her fate befall me. I'll rehearse until I can recite my part at will.

"Tom please fetch Mike Quinn for me."

"Now? Jeez Jack, this hand's the best I've seen."

"I'll cover your pennies win or lose. Please get Mike." "He ain't gonna like me rousing him at this hour. I'll go but don't you mess with my luck! Boys the kid's got my cards so keep it on the up and up."

Tommy walks into the night air. His cards win the pot no thanks to me. My beginner's luck wins two more rounds with Tom a dime ahead when he returns. A disgruntled Mike Quinn is not far behind.

"Jack I consider myself a prepared man but you'd pack a trunk for a midday stroll."

"Sorry Mike, I can't end up like my battered house. Anne deserves better."

"Tommy told me about Ambary trashing your place. It was low even for that jackass. I'll see what I can do to ease your wife's loss. Let's rehearse upstairs to calm your nerves."

Mike pulls Tommy aside for a chat and my disgruntled bodyguard again wanders out the door. Quinn gestures for me to follow him to Barr's office.

Our practice whittles away the remaining darkness. I can't say if I'm calmer or exhausted. However Mike seems energized by the run-through.

"Are you hungry Jack? I'm starving and can't sleep without a bite."

Mike sends a runner to fetch breakfast and Mr. Chin delivers. I move the tasty morsels around my plate while my partner shovels it in. Mike rambles with a mouth full of food. "Tossing your place is twistical even for Jimmy and the dumbass came back here after I warned him to stay away. That was brass-balled stupid! Tis a shame there'll be no trial. Oh to get that braggart on the stand!"

"Yeah well, his touch made my skin crawl. The devil in him scares this farm boy to death."

"Jack me boy, you keep to the script and it'll go as planned."

I want Mike's confidence but what about my battered house? Will Jimmy trash our perfect plan? Mike lays a banger onto a flapjack, rolls it up like a cigar and inhales the whole thing. Nerves ruin my appetite and my first bite requires a cup of coffee to get it down.

Ahh, but the coffee! Mike ordered a steaming pot with cream and a flask of whiskey. "Drink up laddy, it'll calm the jitters!"

"Hmm, tasty yet there's no kick to the brew."

"Keep sippín and give it time. Can I finish your food?"

I drink coffee while Mike cleans my plate and exalts in Jimmy's evisceration. He swears our plan wins the day, so what can I do? I down more coffee. Mama always says it's bad manners to insult a host. I gulp away as Mike's voice flows in one ear and out the other.

I have no idea how I got to bed. My last memory is of Mike bemoaning the empty flask. Drifting from one dream to the next, I land in dad's cornfield. I'm chewing on a piece of straw and raise my hand to block the sun's glare. A blink of the eye and the cornfield disappears.

I'm back in my cell, my hand shielding me from the morning rays. Oh gag me! A piece of gnawed mattress straw hangs from my lip. I spit the musty twig to the floor and sit up ever so slowly. Interesting, except for a mouth as dry as dust, I've no hangover at all. I am clearheaded.

The hornswoggle ends soon and I could use a normal day. Ha! Normal, that's a good one. Ellie says normal is a convenient fib. A younger me scorned normalcy. My dad's right about me; I'm a smart ass with no common sense. All the hollow agrees with him. They say, "Bless Ben Hamby's heart, his youngest ain't right in the head!" And, what of today's unfolding? Can this knucklehead play his part?

Pew! There's a stench permeating my cell and a sniff of my armpit reveals the smelly culprit. When was the last time I bathed? I have no idea. Mama's consternation rattles in my head, 'Jackson honey, a clean body and a virtuous mouth herald a tidy mind.'

"Yes ma'am, be it triumph or tragedy, I shall meet my fate well-ordered."

Ellie snorts and rolls over. Did the sleeping girl read my thoughts? Why can't she divine Mike's plan? Focus Jack! I've things to do and best be on my way. I grab my bag and smile, "Sweet dreams princess, your rescue is at hand. Sir Jack the Fool shall free you!"

My bodyguard sits at the poker table with head and arms resting on his winnings. His trusty pistol is in a hand next to his ear. Sarge motions me out of the line of fire and I call out to Tom. On the third try my guard growls, "Why ya fellas hidin in the corner?"

Sarge grunts, "We're stayin alive dummy. Git your fat finger off the trigger fore you hurt somebody."

Ole Tom mutters an unkind cuss and closes his eyes so I say, "Come on man wake up, I need a bath and a shave. You know a place?"

The codger holsters his gun, grabs his coins, and heads for the door. "Well ya comín or not?"

CHAPTER 45

A Fitting Last Meal

Tommy leads me down the hill to the docks where a pier juts out above the tidewaters. Atop the pier is a building with a smokehouse, a bait shop, and the barber. The sign over the barber's door reads Mutt's Bath and Trim. This rowdy district has a slew of unkept mutts and my scrubby looks do fit the bill.

Nope. You're wrong again Jack Hamby. Why do I bother assuming? Turns out Mutt is short for Muttenheimer. A stout Mr. Mutt greets us at the door. Tommy's quick to drag a chair outside where he settles into his post. I pay two bits for the deluxe cleanup and sit down in the barber chair. Who is the stranger in the mirror? The disheveled bohemian must be me.

"I am a challenge Mr. Mutt, please do your best."

"Relax sasquatch, I fixed worse. Let's see what's under all that fuzz."

The haircut and shave take no time at all with just one nick. Mr. Mutt says, "Sorry boy the leather straps gone brittle. Damn saltwater!"

Next is a soak in a backroom tub. The hot water is bliss to the touch and I plunge the rest of me into the relaxing heat. With time to myself I reflect on life's odd unfoldment: a new Jack Hamby doesn't much resemble my former self. Why do I risk it all for strangers? I can't say. And what about my lifelong pals? My past life seems a distant memory yet not in miles traveled. I'm a changed man and can't say how. I followed my dreams with an ending not yet revealed.

Burr, I am shriveling! The water's gone cold and the kettle on the Franklin stove is empty. I crawl out of the tub and wrap myself in a fluffy towel. Mr. Mutt says a strong vinegar wash kills critters and softens the thread. That's okay by me.

Beside me is a tray with anise soda water, an alum jar, and a talc shaker. I plaster my pits with the spiced alum, powder the rest of me and shake the rest of the talc into my boots for luck. Did I say luck? Yes, in trying times even a modern man clings to an irrational belief. I brush a finger over my teeth and rinse with soda water. One pass doesn't seem enough so I rinse again and spit into the tub. A pull of its plug sends the dingy soak through the floor drain and into the bay. I put on my clean duds and check myself in the cracked mirror. Not bad at all and I am ready to meet my fate. Well almost ready, a hero knight rates a first-class meal!

Tommy's where I left him snoozing in a chair with his feet propped up on a stool, a tattered Montgomery Ward catalog lays open across his chest. I kick the stool sending the catalog crashing to the deck.

"Ha, some guard you are!"

Tom's trusty pistol is under the leaflet, his grip tightens and the gun stays put. "Boy don't startle a man with a loaded firearm! I warnt sleepín. I had ya covered but ya took so long I thought you might a drowned. I was restín and thinkín up an excuse for Michael. If you die, he'll surely cut my fee."

"Thanks for the sentiment. It's curious how you think and snore at the same time. Never mind, I'm too hungry to bicker. Housabout I buy us a steak at the Rainier."

"You rich all of a sudden? I ain't never been inside that palace. Lead the way moneybags but be warned I'm hungrier than a legion of men."

"No worries, you just save room for dessert and stay awake. Ambary's goons can't be far away."

The Rainier Hotel has a well-intended restaurant. I'm told Mr. Chin's food taste better, but this is a proper place for a family to dine. We've arrived before the afternoon tea crowd but are refused service. Seems the hotel has a dress code and a pigheaded Tommy won't comply.

The maître d pleads, "Sir I must insist, I cannot seat you without a coat and tie. Our Lost and Found surely has something apropos."

"I don't need no aye-poo-poo duds. I eat with a fork, not a damn silk noose!"

"C'mon Tommy be reasonable and take the clothes, for me?"

"Okay Jack but it's an asinine rule for sure!"

I stifle a laugh. The waistcoat sleeves are too short and a Winsor knot looks clownish against Tommy's flannel shirt. Our host reaches for the tie. "You look much better sir; might I straighten this for you?"

"Git your mitts off me ya pompous snit! I can dress myself. Go on with ya and find us a friggin table."

"One moment please while I seat a reservation."

"Say what? If those don't beat all. You insults my garb and sits a Bigbug down before me. Where I eats it's first come, first serve. My pub don't care what you wear. Well, maybe they'd toss a man with no pants!" Tommy snickers and elbows my ribs. I smile and nod, it's best I play along.

The maître d' escorts us to a table worth the wait and our server's quick with drinks and food. The starter plate has German rye crisps, assorted shaved cheese, duck liver pâté swirls, vermouth-pickled pearl onions and sweet gherkins.

Ole Tom snaps, "Confound it what's with the table scraps. I ordered a steak!" Our server gives me a pleading look and I wade into the impasse.

"Relax ole man. He knows our order but the meal's served in courses. The menu says we get an appetizer salát and soup before the steak arrives.

"Well that's kinda showy. I say just bring it all on! Hey, what's with the suds in kiddy glasses? Don't ya got no manly pints?"

The Bigbugs begin to stare and our server whispers, "Sir, the chilled pitcher on the table has refills. May I pour you a glass?"

That's a hoot! The waiter thinks a softer tone quiets my guard. Tommy roars back, "No kiddín! My saloon serves from a keg atop the bar. The ale's cold in the winter and warm in summer. Ain't no fancy tin pitchers and a pint's all ya git, lest you buy another round. Stand down sonny, I can pour for myself. Housabout you fetch our grub."

An encounter with James Ambary requires sobriety so I limit myself to one beer. My bodyguard's mumbling about the wait and I try to calm him by reading the menu. "Hey Tommy, the house specialty is a Marseille bouillabaisse broth. Its chardonnay wine & clam broth has bits of garlic, mullet, and Penn Cove mussels steamed to perfection. A side of fresh soda bread and a dollop of mayonnaise rouille adorn the dish. Pretty fancy huh?"

The broth appears and Tommy digs in with wanton abandon. He takes several slurps and comes up for air. "This here's a decent soup. The bread's okay, but dipp'n it in the funny mayo tastes peculiar. They must a run outta butter."

My guard's a humble man with simple tastes. We finish our starters and the waiter brings us two medium-rare T-bones with herbed butter. Tommy smiles his approval. "Good thing it ain't got the funny mayo on it." Our waiter returns with bowls of roasted potatoes and walnut-glazed carrots. The walnuts stick between Tommy's teeth and he cleans up with a fork and linen napkin. A basket of flaky croissants arrives to mop up every bit of steak juice and Tom says, "Yum, these little twists melt in your mouth. Sadie's Place has a hard-tack biscuit that cracks a crab shell. If ya ain't careful her rusks might chip a tooth!"

That explains Tommy's wayward bite. "Sadie's place sounds interesting. You can buy me lunch there sometime."

Our dessert arrives on cue. It's a cinnamon roll baked in its own ramekin with a crème center and a caramel-bourbon drizzle. I'm stuffed to the gills and the tab's a wallet buster but it's all worth it. "What say you Tommy, you like this place?"

"They can keep the tie, but the food's good. The waiter needn't serve us one plate at a time; he shoulda saved his corns and brung it out all at once."

I cannot argue with Tom's empathy. He reminds me of my dad's homespun ways. I never thought I'd miss my father, wrong again Jack Hamby. "You have a point ole man. If I don't survive the night, at least I had a decent sendoff." My bravado is a lame attempt to calm my nerves.

It's all good laddy; the Lord protects Irishmen and bumpkins."

"Tommy I'm not an Irish man."

"Hell no you ain't! You be the other." Tommy shows all his walnut-glazed teeth and slaps me on the back.

We've time to kill and wander into the hotel pub. Tom thinks the place dull compared to Lou's house. Probably so, but it's closer to Oyster Cove and we're already here. I win a beer playing pitch-a-penny with the bartender. Tommy loses his coin and I give him my beer. Mama says generosity clears the way to heaven and it can't hurt to pad my chances.

It's time to go so we stop by the post office enroute to the cove. My box has a perfumed letter from Anne and the folder Mike promised. I pocket the letter and take a peek at my weathered map. Mike replicated it just as Ellie described. I'm ready to meet my fate so Tommy walks me along the shoreline into the wooded dunes where a towering rock sits at the end of the trail. Sure enough, its shaped like a giant mummified oyster. Hence the obvious name: Oyster Cove.

My guard puts his hand on my shoulder. "Jackie boy you be safe now. I gotta fondest for ya that's more than the pay." Tommy crosses himself, points to the sky and heads back down the trail. Without looking back my protector walks into the brilliant gold and purple sunset. I watch his every step until he's out of sight.

CHAPTER 46

Get Out of the Way Jack!

The only sounds I hear are waves washing ashore and an amorous frog croaking from somewhere in the dunes. My pocket watch says I'm ten minutes early and I lean against the massive rock to read Annie's letter.

'My dearest husband: One day has passed, yet it seems like forever and the wait's unbearable. I pray this note finds you well. Are you as miserable without us? Your baby girl asks for you and takes our wedding picture to bed. Was agreeing to this a mistake? Is Mr. Quinn still confident? Are you prepared? What were we thinking!

Sorry dear, I should be upbeat yet my misery begs your company. I shall change the subject for both our sakes. Aidan Quinn's a lumberman who breeds rodeo horses for sport. His stable enchants our girl who wants a pony for Christmas. Adele Quinn is a wonderful host with a lovely home. This must be the luxury you promised me. I cannot wait to be the lady of your manor. Are you smiling dearest? In truth my fears are mighty. There I go again. Why can't I stop the worry? We miss you so. Belle's come in to pester me; she and Aidan are riding into town to post my letter so I must sign off. I love you dearest, your Anne."

I swipe away a tear and return to my surroundings. There's rustling in the fir limbs high above me. Relax Jack, the twilight gives any noise an eerie feel; it's probably just the sunset breeze. Oops, my opulent meal triggers a colossal belch and a cackle sounds from high up in the cedar tree to my left. Perhaps a spying raccoon or woodland pixie finds me amusing.

Dammit focus Jack! There's a spark of light coming up the trail. Yes, a lantern dances ahead of a dark silhouette. My pocket watch says James Ambary's spot-on time. The lamp glare obscures his menacing shadow as he calls out, "Jack Hamby you alone?"

"No doubt you waited on my man to leave. And you Jimmy, are you alone?"

"Humph." That must mean his gang's nearby. Ambary ambles closer with a strong odor of alcohol preceding him. Of course he fortified himself with liquid courage. Does he think a drink ensures his invincibility?

Jimmy stops in front of me and raises his lamp. What did Mike say? An Ambary is bonkers and desperate. Yes indeed, this is the face of a crazed man.

Can Ambary sense my quaking knees? I mustn't foster a ballad of a fleeing coward shot in the back. Anne deserves better. I'll make a go of it, come what may.

"We're in luck Jimmy. The Farmer's Almanac says there's a double-minus tide in three days' time. The wreck of the Jade Princess will soon be ours."

"Yes, the soggy dame awaits her rightful owner. Hand over my map."

"Steady man, tell me about the night Caleb died."

"What? Why?" Ambary stiffens like a watchdog on alert, circles behind Oyster Rock and returns to his relaxed stance. "Just checking for a shadow ready to pounce. You're a brave little mouse coming here all alone. Why do you care about my brother?"

"I don't really. I need to know something before I escape this backwater spit with Ellie. Is she a gold digger who stabs men for treasure?" I sound convincing.

"The gossipers say the wag sent your wife packing."

"Careful Jimmy, I'm fond of the girl."

"So why believe me? She must've warned you."

"Yes, and I'll decide for myself."

"You won't like it but here goes. There was a scuffle and I tried to join in but I bumped the lantern instead. It all went dark and a pistol fired. I was sure Caleb shot Ellie until I saw the knife stuck in my brother's gut."

"Anyone could've stab your brother. Perhaps it was the guide or maybe you did it for the inheritance."

"I was too drunk or I might a thought of it. Truth is, I was about to puke. The Indian didn't do it cause he was closer to me and Ellie held the knife."

"You didn't have a corroborating witness back then and now you've resurrected the drowned scout?"

"Yup. Lou's boy tossed the injun overboard so I hired a scummy Wop to play the part. He'll do fine all dressed up in buckskins. A stupid juror won't know the difference."

Jimmy mutters that he's spilled the beans. Will he clam up? Mike swears an Ambary can't help but take a bow. Do I wait for the braggart to crack or give a little nudge. "Caleb and your mother underestimated you. Did you pay the watchman to change his story as well?"

Jimmy backs up and wrinkles his nose. "What do you know about the smelly brat and my mother?"

"I've heard the stories."

"Ya well, good for me! I started those rumors to get even. Their moaning kept me up at night and her filthy bed was the first to go when my money dried up. Felt good to be rid of it but the solicitors kept coming. My whole house's empty now. It goes to auction next week. Bastard bankers!"

"Bad luck Jimmy, you mentioned the watchman?"

"I did? Well, the man's wife has consumption and begs a drier climate. I gave him traveling money to say how Ellie murdered Caleb."

"And the knife how did you get hold of it?"

"Lou took the map; I needed leverage and the knife was in the medic's locker. He's a boozer, so I shared a bottle and waited for him to pass out."

"So where's the knife?"

Ambary narrows his eyes and pulls the blade from his boot. I regret my question and back up against Oyster Rock. "Whoa! We agreed to no weapons and what about the treasure hunt?"

"Stupid greenhorn, we said no goons. I'm done with you; we aren't partners and you'll call me Mr. Ambary. No more questions and no stealing half my treasure. Hand over my map or die where you stand."

I reach into my coat pocket, grab the map, and let the envelope drop to the ground. A shiver runs through me as two shadows fall in behind James Ambary. I didn't hear their footsteps but the lantern lights the duo who trashed my house. "These gents are my real partners. Fellas say hello to Mr. Jackass Hamby." Their laughter harmonizes into one ominous guffaw.

I steady myself to keep the course. "No goons aye Mr. Ambary? Sorry to waste your time fellas. The map's a fake; nothing more than a fantasy born of reefer and rum. If I were you I'd cut my losses and skedaddle."

The two goonies stare at me without a blink between them. Ambary shakes his head. "A feeble attempt bucko, my men won't budge. You've got no backup and I owe you a beatdown. You might live if you cry and beg for mercy."

I inhale and say with conviction, "Jimmy the only one getting whipped is you. I got a posse good and loyal."

Ambary's cheeks flush. "That's it! The buzzards can have ya!"

It's then the tree branches creak and a baritone chuckle wafts down. "Oh-ho! Off the mark as usual. Look up Jimmy! You're done harassing my friend."

It's about time! My mettle was fading. Earl and Mike jump from the high branches and land to the left and right of me. I hear the distinct pumping of two shotguns as Tom and the Sarge emerge from the dunes behind the thugs.

Jimmy spits at Mike, but his spittle lacks the distance. "Mike Quinn I shoulda known. You're still Lou's lackey."

"And darn proud of it. We've been tracking you boys for a while now. I swear you couldn't spot a tail stuck to your butts. The Sarge has warrants for trashing Jack's home. I appreciate the forthright confession Jimbo, and you mustn't worry about a debtor's prison. I'd stifle the ornery cause you're goín to a real jail."

"Go bugger yourself, ya mick bastard!"

"You repeat that in prison and see what happens."

The sergeant pulls out two cuffs and says, "Boys sit down and put your mitts on your heads. Don't go spookín my deputy cause he's got a twitchy trigger finger."

The two crooks spin to the ground like ballerinas. Ambary stands with eyes narrowed as his tongue rolls across his lips. What is the loon thinking?

Oh God! He lunges at me stabbing Ellie's knife deep into my left arm. I let go the map and grab my pulsing limb. Bright red blood oozes between my fingers as I look up into the face of a madman.

Jimmy's frantic eyes dart to the woods. He sees a clearing, grabs the map and steps toward Earl. The giant smiles, Jimmy stops in his tracks and pivots left to face Michael Quinn. Jimmy clutches his knife and charges, "Be damned paddy, you're a dead man!"

Ambary closes in but Mike doesn't budge. At the very last instant, Quinn cocks his pistol and fires a single shot. Jimmy stumbles to his knees, drops the map and swats at it as he falls. It's Mike who catches the map and looks down at a crumpled Jimmy. Quinn exaggerates his Irish drawl. "Ya still want the map maggot. I made it special fer ya." Mike stuffs the map into Ambary's bloodied vest. "Stupid scut, you chased a curse-ed tale. 'Twas never a treasure dummy; I'm done with ya so sod off and leave me be."

"Curse you Quinn. I'll see you in hell!"

"Nah laddy, me mum swears I'm an angel. Off with ya now. Go give my regards to Caleb and yer mum."

Ambary gasps for air but there's no exhalation. The fool's gone home. Mike makes the sign of the Cross and steps over Jimmy to get to me. An uncanny amount of blood spurts from my carved-up arm. I don't feel so good. Earl catches my limp body as I slide down Oyster Rock.

"Fellas do you hear a choir? So angelic, I think it's Paradise calling me."

"Jack Hamby don't you dare leave! Jeez eejit, ya stood there like a friggin fence post."

"I told you so Michael. All your silly rehearsing and not one fist lesson. You're in big trouble cause Sweet Pea's gonna lose it if the boy dies."

"Ya hear that lad. Earl's right, you mustn't leave me alone with Ellie! And what of Anne and Belle?"

"It's so peaceful fellas, I can hear angels singing."

An array of soft lights stands on the far side of a misty bridge. It must be heaven's gate. So this is it, I'm dead and a familiar voice beckons. Grammy Clara is that you? I was a tiny fellow when you passed. It's nice to see you again.

Wait; there's another shadow forming on my side of the bridge. She sits in a rocker smiling down at a bundle in her arms. I move closer to see Anne cuddling a newborn with Belle at her side tickling the baby.

"Honey can you hear me? Is that a son or another precious baby girl."

Anne doesn't acknowledge me and the vision fades. Oh no! My wife's pregnant and I sense this isn't my time to leave her. I look at the choir across the bridge. "Dear ones thank you for helping me. I understand and am humbled by your concern. I won't forget you or your foretelling."

CHAPTER 47

Home Sweet Home

Whoosh! I'm back in my body gasping for air. Did I miss my chance at heaven? No, an honorable life and granny Clara hold my seat. My eyes open to the darkness save a flickering sconce on the wall. Am I in a hospital? Is that Tom's voice?

"You awake boy? Gave us a scare you did! Jimmy cut you bad and you was bleeding out 'til Mike tied up your arm. He prayed over you like a priest whilst Earl and I ran you to the lorry. You're a damn sight heavier than you look, it must a been that big meal. I whipped them horses like crazy to save ya! Took off so fast Sarge got left with the bad guys. Mike sent Earl back to git them once you was in surgery. I told Earl to sprinkle a pinch of sugar on Jimmy and leave him for the critters. Damn sour cuss! Earl was on board but Mike said no way. He insisted the coroner get the ornery corpse."

"Huh? Tommy I can't follow you. Am I gonna live? Did I lose my arm? I can't feel a thing."

"Oh you'll hurt plenty once the drugs wear off and you'll have a dandy scar but Doc swears the arm's a keeper." Tom pats my numb limb and keeps on talking. I can't hold my eyelids open and his voice fades.

I'm soaring above the surf supported by my bandaged wing. I fly about void of worry or sorrow. Adrift on the breeze, I spot my girls and a little boy on the beach below me. Do they see me or am I a phantom eagle floating above them? I tip my wing and glide upward.

Daylight streams through the curtains. I open my eyes to a stranger undoing my bandages. "Good morning Mr. Hamby. I'm Doc Bennett. How are you feeling?"

"The arm hurts and my noggin's as dense as a rock."

"Ether tends to leave a hangover but it'll ease up once you get moving. I ordered a nux vomica from the apothecary to help with any nausea. There's no sign of infection or fever and you'll heal with time. How about a bite and a walkabout? Stand up straight and I'll sign your release but you'll return tomorrow and the day-after for bandage changes. There's a pain elixir in your personal affects. The syrup's addictive, so stop taking it when the hurt's tolerable. You'll not get more from me. Do you have someone to take you home?"

"That would be me." Tommy pulls back the privacy curtain. "Hey boy you gonna sleep all day? We've got places to be!"

The doctor gives his seat to Tom. My guard is like a persistent wart and that's a good thing. I wonder if Tommy might pass for a surrogate grandpa. Will Anne tolerate his wonky ways? The nurse comes in with a plate of eggs and bacon. Tommy grabs a fork and helps himself. "Not bad pretty lady, you got any fer da boy?" The nurse gives Tommy an icy stare and walks away. His antics are harmless though he'll try Anne's patience.

My nurse returns with a signed release and an orderly. The escort is for Grandpa Tom. Both men are mindful of my arm as they load me into Mike's buggy.

Tommy tries to avoid the ruts, but it's a lost cause. Twenty minutes later we're in front of my tiny rental. "Got a surprise for ya Jack. Close your eyes and I'll git you up the steps."

I've had enough surprises. All I want is a nap before my afternoon appointment. However, there's no stopping Tommy; the giggling fool leads me up the stairs and into my living room.

"Welcome home! What'd ya think? Nice huh."

Whoa! I walkabout surveying all the repairs. The room smells of salty wallpaper paste not quite dry, the furniture's new, the pantry's stocked, and the hall closet has new linens. Best of all is the beautiful set of dishes! A note addressed to me hangs on the hutch door.

The lovely handwriting reads: Jack, thank heavens you survived the ordeal. James was a terrible man and his villains left an awful mess. Your landlord wanted to evict you so Michael bought the house with Lou's bequest money. I'm sure my dear friend would approve. Hannibal did the repairs and I took care of the design. It was a pity to lose your wife's precious heirlooms so young Li Po provided an antique set; the lotus blossom design was his granny's favorite. We are all grateful for your bravery. You must come to dinner when Anne returns. I look forward to meeting you both. Warmest regards, Grace Fletcher Conover.

"Tommy it'll take a lifetime to repay this!"

"No boy, it's all a gift. Ellie's people are thankin ya. Yer a hero, so you be gracious and enjoy their good works. I'll be back in a while to fetch ya." Tommy pats me on the shoulder and takes his leave.

I actually own a home and I wander room to room to take it in. Anne will be amazed at our good fortune. There's even an apple crate full of new toys for Belle. God bless Mike Quinn and the Conover's.

A sudden tiredness overwhelms me. I find our bed, remove my bloodied clothes, and slip under its new down comforter. The cozy feel makes it easy to drift off but not before I say a thanks for the kindness of strangers. It will surely help ease Annie's loss.

The nap was glorious and my clean clothes are a welcome fit. There's no need for a hot water cleanup; pumping cold water over my head invigorates the senses. I stoke the fire and put on the kettle. It is a simple celebration of being amongst the living.

This afternoon is the will-reading demanded by Lou's half-sisters. No one'll miss those two biddies and Mike's eager to be rid of them. It's time Miss Lou had her say and I can't skip the spectacle. I kick back a double shot of bitter elixir and hope for the best.

Mrs. Conover added two rockers to the front porch and I swear they match the one in my dream. Mama says to pay attention; a dream is just a dream unless it's a foretelling. She always says to trust my knowing nature. Yes mama, I trust it was more than a dream. I feel dizzy and sit down to wait on my driver. Walking up Profanity hill is definitely out of the question.

Tommy arrives in a shiny, swank carriage. Elegant is the only way to describe this buggy. It feels pretentious to sit alone in the cab, so Tom helps me onto the driver's bench with him. "You like the fancy ride? This was Sweet Lou's chariot. Ellie insists you deserve the royal treatment and she's wait'n on ya at Lou's mansion."

"I never thanked you for saving my life. I am forever grateful."

"It warnt nothin; a good friend goes the distance. Maybe you'll buy me a pint sometime."

My chauffeur pulls up to Graham manor and hands me over to a smiling doorman. Gone is the butler's curtness. "Please come in Mr. Hamby. We've been expecting you. So glad to see you up and about. May I take your coat? Perhaps a glass of brandy?"

"No thank you, I can't mix liquor with my pain elixir."

"Of course, please call if you need anything, anything at all."

The man leaves me alone in my Déjà vu moment. I'm again very early and feel compelled to greet Lou's enchanted portrait. Damn! My arm seizes up causing me to shift the sling. Tom's assessment is spot-on; twenty stitches mended the deep gash and a grisly scar will tell the tale of Oyster Cove. If it weren't for Mike's quick thinking, Ellie's knife might've killed again.

"Is it terribly painful? I'm so sorry you're hurt. Mike's no horn-swoggler and you both should've known better! My dimwitted heroes, how can I repay your bravery?"

I know that voice! I turn and kiss Ellie on the cheek. "Hello jailbird, it's grand to see you home again! Don't fret about the arm. Your freedom's worth a little discomfort and Anne will surely pamper me. Oh Ellie, it was so magical! My angels paid me a visit and sent me back to the living. It felt so real to see Annie with our baby boy. No, it was as real as you are standing here. I can't wait for the girls to come home. Hey guess what! A Post-Intelligencer reporter left his calling card on my porch. He's writing a serial piece about my journey and settling in Seattle. I'm downright infamous just like you and Lou!"

"Jackson Filmore Hamby don't go exalting over a news story. Tis blarney with a spit of truth. You are a chatty fellow; how much elixir did you swallow?"

Using my full name is a jab at my farm boy gullibility and I do deserve it. Ellie takes my good hand and guides me towards the sofa. "Sit with me macushla, for one last tale. After what's happened, it may seem a letdown but I swear tis the final piece to the puzzle."

CHAPTER 48

No Regrets

Ellie begins with a sigh: Terrible as it was, the Ambary fiasco wasn't the worst of it. A winter's day brings word of Lou's terminal illness and it's a devastating diagnosis all too common in these times.

Well-meaning bosses tell Lou, "Those filthy street girls spread their disease amongst us. It is a travesty!"

No, it's pure poppycock! How dare they curse the girls and conveniently forget their part. A fatcat infected Lou and scapegoating the chippies changes nothing. I say shut up and pay for a cure, ya rich weasels! Mr. Chin says my sorrow speaks as anger. He suggests we raise money with a tip jar so I put it on the bar. I know it's too late for Miss Lou and my sorrow hurts like the dickens.

Mr. Chin's herbal creams ease Lou's itch until one day the rashes cease. Two months of bless-ed normalcy raises our hopes but the doctor says, "Sorry every typhoon has its lull. The calm deceives while the worst awaits on the back end. Like a two-part storm, this illness has a sad second act."

The symptoms are a nuisance until the aching starts. Lou says it's like needles piercing her bones and unbearable migraines cause her to sometimes lose her sight. Daylight pains her and she goes to her bed with curtains drawn. I'm there in the dim lamplight reading whatever Lou wants to hear. Sometimes it's a favorite author or a news article. Lou lays still with a cool cloth over her eyes. If the pain permits she comments on the reading.

We celebrate the good days in her beloved garden where our most meaningful talks unfold. Lou calls them my coming-of-age lessons and no topic is off limits with honest dialog being her only rule. I take no credit for my part as Lou gives value to my lame observations. One day I ask if she regrets a life most folks call sinful.

"Ellie only fools waste their time on regret; the wise let it go. This life is not random but a path of many choices. Finding our way is both smooth and twisted, so be leery of turns marked must and should. Remember we came here with a soulful compass. Don't let false notions of sin, power, hurt, or fear interpret your stay. No, not all my choices were stellar and when I ignored intuition, hindsight rarely offered a second chance. I lived as best I could with no regret." Lou pauses for a breath. Her energy isn't what it was. "Ellie do not confuse regret with an honest grieving. We must grieve in earnest and let it be. However, a regret is not grief. It is a crapperful of self-pity. It moans we're stuck without offering a solution.

A practiced intuition is the true compass because it points towards kindness. Why must we choose kindness? We see from the inside out so what does it say of us if we see only cruelty and blame? And what good comes from blame? It's bitter anchor rope ruins a good intent.

And where is the sweetness? It's in forgiveness and I begin with me. Silly me gambled with fate when I let primal urge override reason. I tested my mortal limits and must now pay the toll. It is forgiveness that lets go this body to catch the Infinite winds. Mostly, I forgive myself for leaving you and I beg your forgiveness as well. I've no choice now but to turn my sails into the Wind."

"Those are pretty words Miss Lou, though I'm not convinced. Was your folly worth the agony?" Oh dear me! That was blunt and insensitive! My excuse is the sorrow. It hurts to see Lou suffer and to be left behind.

Lou touches my cheek. "Liebling you mustn't curse inevitability. From the day we're born a sheer Veil separates us from hither and yon. You ask if sin condemns me? Is this disease a Righteous wrath? And what if a saintly woman lays beneath her septic husband tonight? Is she also a sinner? Of course not. Disease never faults and shame can't quicken a cure. The one shouting gibberish is the selfish shamer.

As for me, I've lived a life of wonder with risks great and small. I accept its entirety with no regrets."

"Okay ma'am, what about poor Kettie?" Kettie's the tribal girl I met in Lou's kitchen. Her Makah name was a tongue-twister so we settled on Kettie.

"What about dear Kettie?" Lou repeats my questions so I might hear my silliness.

"Ma'am is your mind confused. Did you forget how Kettie died? She left no note but I know Kettie felt trapped in this life. She waded into treacherous waters and let an obliging sea snatch her home." Lou's frown says I'm off the mark. "Why the look dearest? Is my notion so far adrift?"

"Ellie you saw Kettie's end but not how she came to be. Please consider all the angles."

Kettie started out much like us: Her father was a white fur trapper working amongst the tribes. One day he forgot his upbringing and traded his pelts for a pretty girl. Logic says to stay with her people but the trapper opted for home. Kettie said her dad was obliged to keep his widowed mother.

The trapper knew full well his mother's bias, yet he often left his girls to suffer the old hag. The granny's vile nature knew no bounds. When an 1880 census taker asked, the widow named her own kin as servant with child.

Kettie's mama died of the influenza on the girl's sixth birthday and Kettie spent every birthday thereafter in mourning. The spiteful granny shunned her and told the negro housekeeper, "Keep the papoose away from me. If it wants my food, hand it a broom." The teenage servant was kind but she was no mutti.

Kettie first pondered suicide on her eighth birthday and it became an annual longing. The poor child lacked a way to let go her grief. Kettie's daddy was out trapping for a long while and was unaware of his squaw's death. He returned to find his child sleeping in the pelt shed. It was obvious that Kettie couldn't stay in Seattle, so the trapper took Kettie back to her mother's people. He vowed to visit when he could but the man never did. Don't weep for Kettie; desertion is often a blessing disguised as cruelty.

Her native auntie and uncle took Kettie as their own. The uncle's a whaler who risks his life on the ocean. He knows chance is often the price of freedom. Kettie loves her Makah family and longs to fit in but a fierce loyalty isn't enough. Teenage Kettie runs back to the city and becomes a misfit in this whitewashed locale. This choice fed her regret so let's look at every angle, shall we?

This is Kettie before you came to us: One night our house entertained a Russian braggart who relished telling gruesome tales of his whale hunting. The burly captain says, "It was a great pod of Grays. Mind you, the oil of a Sperm whale pays more but we was out a long time looking when a dozen Grays breeched in front of us. We haul in the big ones first and then the babies until the deck is slick with innards and our hold overflows. It was a good take, so I rewarded my men. I said fire away and the men lit off our cannons like fireworks. The harpoons sailed every which way and the bloody fishes went fin up!"

Kettie gags at the mention of killing babies and leaving the wounded beauties to drown was the last straw. She assails the whaler like a suffragist lambasting a brewery owner. "You murderer! Hunters don't kill for sport! Hunting is a prayerful sacrifice of survival. Only a tiny peckered yellow-belly uses a cannon on the unarmed!"

The whaler laughs until Kettie insults his manhood. It's then he charges Kettie and I summon Earl. However, Kettie doesn't need our help. The captain throws the first punch and Kettie dodges it. She dives in, bites off the tip of his enormous nose, and ends it with a driving kick to his nethers.

The show's over so I forgive the blowhole's tab and Earl tosses him to the curb. My payment is a fond memory of a spirited girl.

Of course, the sailor limps away after a copper. Locals don't like poachers fishing their waters so the patrolman dismisses the dodel saying, "Go back to yer boat Bohunk. A word of advice to ya; don't go confessin a twattle bested ya. Lucky fer you she chomped a nose and nothin else!" The Russkie set sail and we never saw him again.

"Our dear Kettie was feisty but she couldn't forgive her sadness."

"Lou, your story's a puzzle with a piece missing. Why did Kettie leave her coastal people? She found true love and it makes no sense to go."

"Life is a puzzle with a piece missing and seeking it makes us wander. The coastal bloom is beautiful, but it makes Kettie sick and not everyone welcomes her. Purebloods claim a half-blood weakens the tribe and they blame every bad hunt or fierce storm on her wickedness."

Their shaman disagrees. "Do not insult our ancestors. Not blood but a purity of heart upholds our ways. You seek an enemy? Look within and see what weakens us all." The holy man swears Kettie's frailness is curable and prepares a rigorous cleansing ceremony.

The ceremony frightens Kettie and she runs back to Seattle only to find a house in desperate need of repair. Kettie knocks on the door and calls to the negro girl but the granny opens an upstairs window. "I have no servant. An avalanche took my boy and left me penniless. Get off my porch bastard seed. You're no kin of mine!"

The spiteful hag sees life from one angle. A grandchild might help but her closed mind forbids it. People say love is blind. Not so, a lack of love takes our good sight.

The only choice for Kettie is the streets. A mutual client mentions her and I feed Kettie a lunch. She's content with us but I see the sadness in her eyes. Neither shame nor ridicule forced Kettie into the sea. The girl held tight to her regret and drowned in its sorrow."

I change course in favor of my Catholic upbringing. "The nuns say suicide keeps us out of heaven. It's a snub to the Lord and a deal-breaker sin."

"Oh Ellie, not the nuns again. Kettie didn't worry about Judgement Day because living was her purgatory. The blamers called Kettie a half-blood and a sinner. Yes, the taunts hurt but it was her regret that pulled Kettie under."

I get stuck at the Pearly Gates. "It makes no sense at all. Why would a loving Creator keep a bouncer at the gate? I reckon a caring Maker sends our departed mamas to greet us. Tis a better welcome for sure."

"Liebling did you hear a word I said?" Lou's irritation fades and her voice softens. "I will accept the arms of Grace when my time comes. I can think of nothing sweeter than to see my smiling mutti again."

Ellie slips into silence and I sit in the quiet to respect my friend. After a while Ellie takes my hand. "We had a good cry that day, it was a bittersweet time and I miss her so."

It is my turn to flip the script. "Ellie, did you mean to kill Caleb Ambary?"

"Honey are you worried for my soul? To be sure it was Caleb's undoing. He let the devil in and it aimed a gun at my heart. If I did nothing, the scout and I were goners."

It all happened so fast! Caleb's pistol went off just as I slapped it away. His free hand crushed my windpipe and I had but one choice though it was never my intention.

Turns out my prank was a bust. So naïve was I to misjudge the Ambary nature. I called forth a hellfire and it burned me. Mind you I'm not passing the blame. A puffy ego was my undoing. Lou said to find the lesson and I admit my scheme was bogus. I endangered a good scout with a family to feed and I had to save him. No, it wasn't a vengeful blade that stuck Caleb, it was survival. I learned a hard lesson that day, did my humble reckoning and let it be."

"But your lawyer pleaded self-defense and the captain agreed. Why didn't the verdict set the record straight?"

"Do you remember the tale of the pious pigeonhole? Righteous superiority is a truth twister and Miz Ambary was a damnable tornado. She wouldn't rest until she avenged her son and Lou knew it.

Miz Lou feared for the scout and hid him in our cabin until we docked in Seattle. The next day Uncle Fritz sailed him home to the San Juan isles. I laid low and Lou silenced Jimmy. Tis a pity she wasn't a fortune teller though none of us knew he'd circle back.

Michael ended the curse and I hope it gives him peace. He felt he owed me something and this eases his conscience. As for you bub, you needn't worry about my salvation. Up amongst the stars Miz Lou, mum, and granny Chin are playín a game of cribbage. It's a sure bet there's room for me. Ahh, what a reunion that'll be!"

CHAPTER 49

Lou's Last Hurrah

I get a case of the shivers. Does Lou Graham's ghost agree with Ellie? No, a cool breeze came in when the butler opened the front door for a smiling Michael Quinn. I think back to Oyster Rock where Mike hid in the tree limbs above me. He inherited his agility from his grandpa Angus. Angus was a high climber back when timber was gold but it was Mike's dad who dreamt of their independence. Donovan Quinn's gumption made them rich and the startup cash came from Miss Lou. She believed in the Quinn's and they returned her loyalty. Young Mike worked the storefront and dreamt of being a lawyer. That is how Michael Angus Quinn became Lou's attorney.

Mike gives Ellie a warm hug, shakes my good hand and wastes no time in hustling everyone into the library. "Let's get this party started, shall we? I'm sure you're all anxious to hear from Miss Lou!"

Mike and I lead the way into Lou's library and I take my place behind a presiding chair. Ellie meets Mr. Chin at the door, takes his arm and they walk to their seats on the left side of the aisle. How sweet it is to see the tender moment. A younger likeness sits down next to Mr. Chin. I reckon this is the mischievous Poo.

The other invitees are a mix of humanity. Hannibal and Grace Conover help a feeble Fritz Heigl to a seat on the right side next to an eminent entourage including Sam Barr. Gentry men ogle the parade of Lou's girls who enter and sit behind Ellie and Mr. Chin.

Four well-heeled women with buttons pinned to their dresses take a seat next to the proper folk. Their buttons promote alcohol prohibition and a woman's right to vote. The society dames refuse eye contact with anyone seated across the aisle. Their snub seems rude considering this is Lou's house.

The Oben sisters strut in and take front row seats with their Seattle lawyer. One sister says so all can hear, "Finally Greta, we claim what is ours and go back to civilization."

Ellie whispers to Mr. Chin, "Hoity words coming from the womb of an upstairs maid. Tis convenient to forget how their mama bedded the Oben fortune." Mr. Chin gives Ellie a resolute look and squeezes her hand.

Earl appears at the door and closes it behind him. Is he an invited guest or keeping order for Mike. I nod to Earl and take my seat next to Michael Quinn. The room buzzes with gossip about last night's mischief but Mike ignores the chatter. He sits behind Lou's antique desk and spreads the will out in front of him. It doesn't quiet the whispers, so Mike taps a letter opener.

"Well finally we hear Lou Graham's last wishes. Let's see what the ole girl has to say, shall we?"

§ I, Lou Graham, being of sound mind and betrayed health, do swear this to be my last will and testament. In death, as in life, my part's done with a wink and a smile.

Those who truly knew Lou murmur their agreement. Michael tries not to smile but his Irish eyes betray him. The lawyer clears his throat and continues.

§ I, Lou Graham put considerable thought into this will and will not regard duty or penitence as criteria. It seems contrary in death to kowtow to those I ignored in life.

Michael stops again until the amused quiet down.

§ I hereby bestow my earthly goods as I see fit. For those gathered today, let it be known: your joy or discontent is of your own making.

That settled the room. The women's guild and Lou's sisters glower with impatience; no doubt they regard Lou's words as ooze from a diseased mind and they're wrong. I choose to side with those who knew and loved Lou.

Mike continues the bequests in a timely fashion. Lou releases all the uncles from their promissory notes and Gracie receives Lou's dermatoid snake necklace. The Graham House staff all receive a whopping three-thousand-dollars severance and generous stock portfolios. Mike hands an envelope to each of them with a warm handshake and the rewarded seem pleased.

The next offerings go to the women's league of causes. Mr. Chin shakes his head as I imagine he did before each of Lou's hornswoggles.

§ To the Ladies Guild I bestow my favorite pillow from my parlor. It's the one I embroidered with a quote from Shakespeare's Hamlet: To Thine Own Self Be True.

The proper women stare darts to the left side of the room and Mr. Chin offers a polite nod. Lou sewn the pillow herself and it's fitting she gets the last stitch. Mike smiles and keeps on reading.

§ To the ladies temperance league, I leave my cheap whiskey and a 10-penny sledge. Have a smashing good time girls! PS: I'd leave you the good liquor but Mr. Chin needs it for my wake.

There's laughter from all save the red-faced teetotalers. Mike taps his letter opener and resumes the reading.

§ To my so-called blood sisters absent from me all this time, I leave my personal residence and the furniture therein. The only exceptions being my antique parlor chair and the contents of Miss Ellie Flannery and Mr. Li Po Chin's rooms.

Lou's Bavarian relatives stiffen and one sister whispers to their lawyer, "We didn't come all this way for furniture. You said the woman was rich; where is our fortune?"
Where is it indeed? Mike keeps things moving.

§ To young Mr. Li Po Chin I leave the aforementioned chair. Keep it if you must Little Po but a smart man sells it.

The young man smiles. No doubt Lou's chair will sit in Poo's parlor next to granny Chin's rocker and pipe.

§ To the elder Mr. Li Po Chin, my longtime manager and friend, I leave four thousand dollars, a stock portfolio, and a gold pocket watch.

§ To Miss Ellis Flannery, my sweet girl, I leave four thousand dollars, a stock portfolio, and my ivory cameo.

What! That's it? Four thousand dollars is a hefty annual wage, but it's no fortune. What is Ellie's reaction?

The girl whispers across Mr. Chin. "Poo, Lou left me your silly cameo from Vancouver. I don't understand."

Lou Graham kept a wealth of stocks, money, and gems in her underground safe. The woman was richer than rich so why leave her ward a pittance and a two-bit pendant? Mike Quinn's reaction is just as bizarre; he aims a mad grin at Ellie and Mr. Chin but the room's growing tenor distracts him. Mike moves onto a finale the likes of which stuns everyone!

§ I, Lou Graham, do hereby liquidate the rest of my estate to include my business, real estate, and remaining stocks in favor of charity. Education is the great equalizer and the foundation of our miraculous freedom. To wit, my estate goes to benefit schools granting a girl's education. I hope the young women understand the real prize here. May they use their ordained gifts to make the world a better place.

A gasp from the German twins nearly sucks the air out of the room and I can feel the heat of their fury. Mike feels it too and uses the lull to end the proceeding. "Good folks we're done here. That's all Lou had to say. Our girl is free to roam and so are we. Invited guests can now head down the hill for Lou's wake."

Mike gathers his papers and the crowd doesn't dally. First away is the gaggle of gilded ladies. Did the biddies really expect Lou to leave them an expensive penance? Next to go are Lou's red-faced sisters who march upstairs with their sad-faced attorney in tow. They shall no doubt refute the will as Ellie predicted.

It is Lou's friends who excitedly depart for the overdue party. Lou planned a lavish wake telling Mr. Chin, "Make it a grand fête, my friend. Let days come and go before the revelry ends."

I stay to notarize papers. Mr. Chin and Ellie stayed as well; I assume stunned by their gifts. It's a paltry reward for two loyal friends.

Mike reaches for his valise and waves the pair forward. There are two envelopes left: one marked Chin and the other Flannery. Michael stands to greet them. "Mr. Chin this is for you and Ellie this one's yours."

Neither one opens an envelope but instead stare at Mike who's chuckling like an idiot. What cruel joke is this? I thought better of Michael Quinn.

Mike notices Ellie's quiet gaze and stops laughing. She is as lovely and reticent as ever. Mr. Chin says what's freely let go can't be taken from us. Unlike her younger self, Ellie will let go. I understand her resolve but something's amiss. What is unaccounted for?

Mike breaks the spell, "C'mon open the envelopes."

A normally sedate Mr. Chin laughs as if he gets Mike's twisted joke. Quinn eyes me and waves a dismissive hand. "Jack please give us a moment."

I am crestfallen yet must obey Mike's wishes. I turn to leave and Ellie says, "Michael Quinn don't be rude. Jack's been loyal and has endured so much for us." Mike shrugs his shoulders and Ellie winks at me.

Mr. Chin is not amused. "Michael no more secrets. What did Lou do that's left unsaid?"

"Not the least bit fooled were you. I bet against you and owe the school fund twenty-five bucks. Did my hint at the funeral give it away? I should've let you two squirm." Ellie gives Quinn a look likely learned from Lou. "Mike stop messin with us."

Quinn gives Ellie his familiar smitten grin. "Okay, so here it is. Lou knew about her siblings. She said they'd refute the will and she didn't want your shares held in escrow. Your sums today are meant to throw the snits off the trail. Open the envelopes and I'll explain."

Ellie and Mr. Chin rip at the seals. They ignore the money and stock notes in favor of the trinkets. We three give Mike a perplexed look, so Quinn points to the watch and cameo. "Open your gifts and look inside. Careful not to lose anything."

Mr. Chin opens his watch and Ellie opens the broach. Each piece hides an identical key.

"Did you not wonder why a deathly ill woman goes on holiday? I offered to be her proxy but Lou refused. She said it was hers to do and the darn trip killed the stubborn girl."

Mike isn't exaggerating; Miss Lou died on the train's return trip. Ellie reaches out for Mike's hand. "Lou wanted to say goodbye to old friends."

"Maybe so, but this was business. One of Lou's friends is a vice president at the Bank of California where Lou setup accounts in your names. Those keys unlock boxes holding account papers and a note for each of you. Your benefactor adored you both and she gave it her all."

"Oh honey she loved you like a son."

Quinn drops Ellie's hand to grab his kerchief. He takes a moment before assuming his appointed task. "Yes I know. Anyway, Lou laid her estate to rest before her death. The schools fared well enough but you two split the bulk of it. Tis all accounted for in your papers. No doubt Jack and I stand before two very wealthy heirs."

The threesome go lost in the memory of their beloved benefactor while I ponder Miss Lou's genius. The contented mistress kept her wits and never let a disease define her. Lou knew her time was up so she played her final hornswoggle. Her gist of fairness won the hand or as Lou always said, it was justice served. What a feat to leave on her terms cradled in the arms of her chosen kin.

CHAPTER 50

A Pact Done and Done

My mind wanders back to the start of Ellie's tale. She began it with a riddle: Was Lou Graham an infamous sinner or a patron saint? How might Miss Lou answer the question?

Whoosh! The air turns a wintry cold giving me goosebumps. A shade takes shape beside me and I recognize her immediately. Her likeness hangs above the fireplace in Lou's parlor. The madame's ghost smiles and winks at me. My friends don't seem to notice. Why am I the only one who sees the apparition?

"I'm not here for the others dear."

"You can hear my thoughts?"

"Yes of course, my mortal bind is gone."

"Are you real or an effect of the elixir?"

"My old pedantic friend, living this life hasn't changed you much. Pity you can't remember our unfinished business but we mustn't dally. Let's get to it, shall we?"

"Old friends? I don't recall meeting you."

"Time is a silly mortal convenience; the eternal realm has no use for it and the sacred veil kept our pact from us. The shroud has a purpose but it is a nuisance! Anyway, you've done your part ole chum and I must finish mine."

Lou's playfulness eases my anxiety. I smile, "Well old chum what's owed me?"

Lou touches her index finger to my forehead causing me to blink. I open my eyes as a smiling Lou fades away.

"Wait! Don't leave! You promised me a gift." The floor begins to shake under my feet. This region's known for its tremors; perhaps a dormant volcano awakens. No that's not it. The room stands as is and my companions are unfazed.

What is happening to me? A fiery tingle shoots from where Lou touched me. My ears ring like church bells, my eyes burn, my jaw clamps shut and my ego treads into fearful waters. How can I stay afloat? What does a drowning man do? He holds his breath of course! How long can I hold on? Ah jeez, I can't think straight!

I hear a calm voice whisper, "Let go the panic, be still and breathe." I inhale and exhale as best I can, an eerie quiet takes over and I inhale deeper, exhale, and wait.

The burning sensation, lock jaw and ringing fades. A peace beats my heart and I hear Lou's songbirds tootling outside the window. I feel somehow cleansed.

"Lou where are you? What did you do? Did heaven's speak do this or was it the elixir?" No, not the elixir. It was a heavenly calm from within. What did Lou say? Mortals invent time as a convenience. Well then, it's my intention to let go my past with all its worry. A giggle bubbles up from deep inside me and I feel a quietude beyond all explanation. "Thank you ole chum."

Why is the room out of focus? I remove my spectacles and behold a newfound lucidity. Colors brighten before me with perfect clarity. Without the need for my glasses a miracle unfolds in the eyes of this beholder!

And what of Ellie's riddle? Is Lou Graham a sinner or a patron saint? She is neither of course. Like timekeeping, the need to define everything is just mortal dribble.

I glance out the window at a bee feeding on a flower. Lucky buzzer! He minds his own business and his reward is sanity and contentment. I now understand that the lazy dog chases a convenient tale. Not me! I shan't be leashed to my assumptions any longer. No shallow blatherskite can distract or mislead me. My sight is perfect so I toss my spectacles into the trash. "Yes Lou, release is glorious. I can't restrain my bliss and why would a sane man try?"

Ellie clears her throat; what lunacy did she witness? Did I speak it all aloud? Lou says sharing a revelation dulls its miracle. She came for me, not the congregation and our tête-à-tête was private. Done and done, aye ole chum?

I give Ellie an impish grin and she grabs my good hand. "C'mon silly, you must come to Miss Lou's wake."

Yes indeed! As I said first we met: "Miss Ellie, I am delighted to have your company."

Keeping the Dream Alive

The three musketeers descend the hill toward Washington Street planning their trip to San Francisco. I am beside them with an irrepressible grin plastered to my face.

Lost in thought I ponder: why travel thousands of miles to discover what was always inside me? Dad is at home in his cornfield, so why did I roam far away from my birthplace? Perhaps the distance helped realize a promise made beyond this lifetime. Lou said Bavaria was the start of her earthly travels. Thereafter this life was hers. Are there other seekers bound by an ethereal pact? I have more questions than answers and that's okay. The unknown keeps my journey fresh.

There's a blustery breeze from an approaching storm swirling the leaves about. The wind pushes billowing clouds and wreaks havoc on the gray-blue-green chop of the bay. A perfect sensation cleanses my body and soul. Jack Hamby you are home at last.

I wonder how Lou's wake will unfold. Will it last for days? Of course, no one refuses a Lou Graham invitation. Odd thoughts pop into my head. One bubble is of my Sicilian friend from the train. Nuncio's address is still in my vest pocket and I wonder what he's up to. Writing seems a clever idea now. Who knows what might unfold? Visiting an Oregon farm, tasting fresh cheese and helping muck out a barn seems worthwhile again. Belle loves cows and goats. Ahh, Bellie and her mommy come home tomorrow. Was it a dream or is

Anne really pregnant? I cannot wait to see her; we have so much to discuss. My head spins like a carousel. That's it! Wisdom calls: 'Pay attention Jack, the ego's run amuck and must be bridled.' Yes of course, how iniquitous of me to ramble on about events yet to be.

Step-by-step our little band marches towards Lou's den of iniquity. So exciting! I hope Lou's apparition lingers still. Please dear spirit stay on a bit longer. I imagine you'll say, "Hello ole chum, come on in. Loosen your collar and leave your worries at the door. My business is pleasure with no proper ma'am or mister needed here."

When it's time to go Lou will raise her glass. "Do keep a fond memory of me. I've no regrets. The Champagne Express whistles and it's time to bid you adieu. This life was a fanciful layover but destiny beckons. Goodbye friends, please take loving care of my Ellie."

In the blink of an eye Miss Lou is but a memory and her party is in full swing. The band fills the air with lighthearted music and Ellie's at the piano playing one of Lou's favorites.

I'm leaning against the bar to steady myself. Yes, I'm drinking despite the doc's orders. The elixir wore off hours ago and Lou's finest now eases my throbbing arm.

"Bartender please ring your bell. I need the rooms' attention. Thanks so much. Hear ye ladies and gents, join me in toasting the Queen of Seattle. Cheers to the grand dame who rescued so many including me. Lou freed this blurry-eyed crow so I might see every angle clear as day. God bless and keep you ole chum! Prost!"

The room roars 'Prost!' back at me and an inebriated man stumbles onto a nearby barstool. "Jackson Hamby I presume. My name is Henry Sullivan. I write for the Post and wonder if you'll answer a question."

"Well Hank that depends on the question. May I call you Hank? Henry's a bit formal, don't you think? A given name's but a start and I prefer Jack over Jackson. Sweet Lou tossed little Emilé overboard as did Ling Lu with her Yu Yan. And me? I left ole Jackson to haunt the North Coast Limited. I am Jack Hamby, at your service."

"Okay? Whatever you say. Tell me Jack how did an Indiana farm boy end up in a notorious madame's saloon with a Chinaman, an Irish murderess and her lawyer lover?"

"Aww Hank, we're more than your cryptic headline. You ask me what all transpired? Well for starters, I learned a secret's mere gully-fluff that always comes out in the wash. And a saint or a sinner is in the eye of the beholder. To find the Truth, we remove our blinders and see every angle cause this life's a puzzler with many a lost clue.

I let ego drag me into a fog of convenient tales but I've learned my lesson. Now Intuition guides me home. How's that possible you ask? I no longer assume and I've pardoned my regrets. I've let go my worry once I saw behind the sacred Veil. Oops! My intuition's telling me to stop. You best find your own miracles.

Where was I? Oh yes, Ellie plays a wonderful piano. She gives Lou all the credit but listen to the girl play.

My inner melody sounds much like her song. Mind you it's more by design than coincidence. Ancient wisdom says we are all related. Mr. Chin calls it our chee-day. For your notes, he spells it Qi-De. I don't claim to know much about his ways. The gist of it seems to be Life's more than earning a sawbuck or sucking on a peppermint puff. Yes, there's stinkweed along the way and the wise let intuition find a sweeter path. Simple yet elusive, ain't it?

Later on in the starry stillness I'll let go yesterday and await the dawn untethered. It's a precious gift to sit under the stars or meet the dawn. They herald miracles for anyone to see. What miracles you ask? The ones all-around us, of course. I dare you to take off your limiting blinders and see for yourself. If a fella as thick as me can figure it out, I reckon anyone can."

About the Author

Nina Curttright, a decorated retired Air Force MSgt and former City of Seattle Environmental Remedial Analyst, makes her literary debut with Infamous Madame's Will. With a BA in English focused on fiction writing, she spent her career in technical writing and personal creative endeavors. Living in Edmonds, WA with her family and pets, Curttright's interests in cultural exploration, history, nature, and spiritual philosophy deeply influence her writing. Her commitment to exploring the human condition and our relationship with the universe shines through in her storytelling, blending entertainment, lyricism, and profound insights into the human spirit.

9 798822 935402